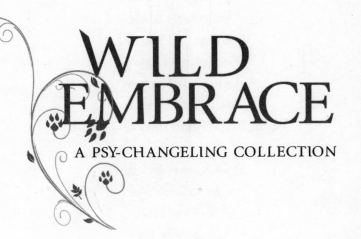

WILD EMBRACE

A PSY-CHANGELING COLLECTION

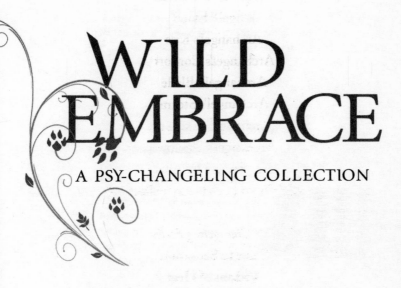

WILD EMBRACE

A PSY-CHANGELING COLLECTION

NALINI SINGH

GOLLANCZ

LONDON

First published in Great Britain in 2016 by Gollancz
an imprint of The Orion Publishing Group Ltd
Carmelite House, 50 Victoria Embankment
London EC4Y 0DZ

An Hachette UK Company

1 3 5 7 9 10 8 6 4 2

A CIP catalogue record for this book is
available from the British Library.

ISBN 978 1 473 22159 8

Printed in Great Britain by Clays Ltd, St Ives plc

www.nalinisingh.com
www.orionbooks.co.uk
www.gollancz.co.uk

CONTENTS

AUTHOR'S NOTE

Welcome to *Wild Embrace*, a collection of Psy-Changeling stories. If this is your introduction to the Psy-Changeling world, I hope you enjoy the journey! You don't need to have read the prior books in the series to dive into the stories within.

If, however, you're a long-term reader of the series, the stories in *Wild Embrace* provide more depth and nuance to facets of the Psy-Changeling world. I wrote each one because I felt that even though these stories take place away from the main story line, they're important to the world—the characters all contribute to the richness of the Psy-Changeling tapestry, even if we only glimpse them in passing in the full-length books.

It's the same reason I write the free "slice of life" vignettes for my newsletter. I want to know about every tiny corner of this world, want to see what the characters are up to even when they're not in the spotlight. (If you aren't yet a subscriber to my newsletter, you can subscribe quickly and easily at nalinisingh.com.)

In terms of the series timeline, each story in this collection falls at a different point. "Echo of Silence" occurs after *Visions of Heat*, while "Dorian" spans a number of years, with the final part of the story set in the months after *Hostage to Pleasure*. The novella "Partners in Persuasion" begins toward the end of *Tangle of Need*. Last but not least is the mystery in "Flirtation of Fate," which takes place near the end of *Heart of Obsidian*.

AUTHOR'S NOTE

Whichever order you choose to read the stories, I hope you love traveling through different areas of the Psy-Changeling world and into the smaller, more intimate worlds inhabited by each of these characters.

Take care and happy reading,
Nalini

ECHO OF SILENCE

Disruption

THE YEAR 2079 has been a year of change, of disruption. The Psy, long considered the most powerful race on the planet, their telepaths and telekinetics, foreseers and psychometrics gifted and feared, are starting to fracture.

The Silence Protocol has begun to be questioned—one hundred years after that protocol was put into place in an effort to fight the madness and insanity that is the flip side to the Psy race's powerful gifts. Now the Psy, conditioned to be as cold and emotionless as the changelings are untamed and passionate, have begun to question . . . to *feel*.

Two cardinal Psy have defected, shaking the status quo. But despite the changes, the fractures, the two are outliers. Millions of Psy remain locked in Silence, for to break Silence is to sentence yourself to a horror worse than death, the total psychic brainwipe of rehabilitation leaving behind only a shambling shell that is little more than a walking vegetable.

For these millions, life continues as it has done for the past hundred years.

A life without love, without laughter, without pain, without sadness, without misery, without heartbreak, without . . . just without.

Chapter 1

THOUSANDS OF METERS below the surface of the ocean, in the depths of the Pacific and not too distant from the Mariana Trench, Tazia Nerif looked out the window in the control room of the deep-sea station Alaris, and wondered if there really were changeling sharks.

Andres, the junior geological oceanographer, had just spent ten minutes trying to convince her of that fact. "The next time you're prancing around naked in your quarters, have a look outside the windows and see what's looking back."

Since Tazia was an engineer who lived in grease-stained blue coveralls and had never pranced in her life, that wasn't going to be a problem. But still, the idea of changeling sharks intrigued her. *If* Andres wasn't trying to pull one over on her. Fiddling with her electronic wrench to calibrate it for her next task, she decided to do some research on the subject so she could beat him at his own game.

"Ms. Nerif, is the life-support system back to full strength?"

Her heart slammed into her throat.

As usual, she hadn't heard Stefan approach. Tall, with dark hair, and highly intelligent, he walked with the tread not of a sailor, but of a Psy. He was a Tk, a telekinetic, and fully enmeshed in the emotionless existence that was the Psy way.

From the fleeting but telling references in the dusty old history book Tazia had found in an antique shop on her last trip upside, she'd worked out that the Psy race had once felt the same emotions as humans and changelings. But something had changed long enough ago that in the present, it seemed as if they had always been formed of ice.

Brilliant at business and at science, the Psy race knew nothing of sorrow or love, joy or hate; they created no art, wrote no music, felt no passion.

Not that Tazia knew much about that last, either.

"I'm finished." Sliding the wrench into her tool belt, she picked up and slotted in the cover of the panel she'd been working on, safely concealing the complex computronic systems beyond. "You can boot it up and switch off the backup system." It had been a routine inspection, something she was fanatical about. Her type-A, check-every-nut-and-bolt-twice personality was why she'd won the coveted position on Alaris. This far below the surface, no one wanted an engineer who wasn't obsessively precise.

Stefan, of course, took precise to the next level. If Alaris had been peopled solely by Psy, nothing technical would have ever gone wrong. But of course, most Psy didn't see the point in exploring the deep when there was only a slim chance of discovering anything that could lead to financial gain. Which was why Alaris had humans like Tazia holding it together, along with the odd changeling who could stand being shut up inside the station—or who had the capacity to survive in the mysterious dark water beyond the windows.

There were several sea-based changelings on station courtesy of the fact that Alaris was funded in large part by a worldwide water changeling organization named BlackSea. Tazia didn't know too much about BlackSea, but she knew a number of the sea changeling station personnel very well.

Andres was a sea snake in his animal form. He'd shifted for her once in a sparkling shower of color and light. *Beautiful.* His snake form was big, shiny, and capable of sneaking around parts of the station she'd never be able to access without using the miniature maintenance bots she'd built after realizing the need. When he was in a good mood, he sometimes checked the ducts for her.

"Everything looks operational." Stefan entered the final command on the razor-thin computer screen mounted on the wall, then put his eye to the biometric reader to confirm the authorization.

The systems switched over with no appreciable delay.

Stepping back from the computer, Stefan scanned her face. Sometimes, she wanted to tell him nothing had changed since the last time he'd subjected her to an inspection. She still had black hair, worn in a rough ponytail to keep it out of the way, and streaky brown eyes set in a face covered in light brown skin. The end.

"You have grease on your cheek."

She fought her blush and the urge to wipe at her face with the sleeve of her coveralls. "What else is new?"

"The mail."

"The mail?"

"It just arrived."

Her smile was instant. "Oh!" Grabbing her tool kit, she went to walk past him.

He stopped her, his hand on her arm.

Startled at the strange behavior—Stefan didn't touch anyone unless absolutely necessary—she froze. "What?" she asked, tilting back her head to look up at him, his scent in her every inhale.

Stefan always smelled crisp, clean, distant. No grease on his cheek and certainly no dirty work coveralls. On duty or off, he always wore the uniform of the station commander, the collar of his military-style fitted jacket rising partway up his neck and fastened to the side by a simple silver stud that denoted his rank. Everything else was stark black, from his boots to his pants to, she assumed, the shirt he wore under his jacket. She didn't know, had never seen him with the jacket open.

Now his dark gray eyes focused on her. "It is not there."

Disappointment uncurled in a leaden wave in her stomach, wiping away her surprise at his touch. "Are you sure?"

"I checked all the return addresses on the letters and packages." She swallowed, nodded. "Why?"

"Because every time the mail comes and your package doesn't arrive, you give in to the human failing of disappointment, which leads to at least two days of depression during which you don't function at optimum levels."

Her eyes narrowed. "Ah, so it was concern for my well-being, then?" She snorted and tried to shrug off his hand. "I function perfectly fine—everything gets done, doesn't it?"

"Yes." He didn't release her. "But you have a tendency to snap at anyone who comes near you."

"What do you care?" she asked, feeling cornered and sad and angry at him for being the bearer of news she didn't want to hear. "Emotion makes no difference to you."

"The humans and changelings care."

That made her face heat up. Stefan ran the show, contracted to manage Alaris at what had to be an exorbitant fee. If he said people were complaining because she got a little down a couple of days a month, then people were complaining. "It won't happen again."

"Of course it will. Unless you stop waiting for a package that will never arrive."

It was a stab to her soul, a blade made of ice that broke inside her as she bled. "Let me go." Wrenching herself out of his hold, she walked quietly out of the control room and headed down into the true guts of Alaris, where no one else ever ventured. Only when she was sure he hadn't followed her did she curl up in a corner and put her head on her knees.

No tears.

Tazia had stopped crying a long time ago. But the sadness was a crushing weight, a brick on her heart. She'd truly believed that the passage of time would soften her parents' anger, bring forgiveness. But it had been five years since she'd walked out on her arranged marriage, and still her family shunned her.

A year ago, when she'd won a place on Alaris's first mission team, she'd written to them. It was an honor to be on the deep-sea station. *Surely* they would forgive her now that she'd brought such acclaim to the Nerif name, now that she'd become more than the daughter who had not followed the wishes of her elders.

The first month on board, she hadn't been too disappointed at the lack of a response. Her parents lived in a remote region of desert and wind, a region their people had chosen to keep deliberately untouched by technology except that which was needed to assure the safety of the settlement. They also didn't believe in wasting money on costly transportation when other, more economical methods were readily available. Their reply would come slowly, via camelback until it reached the nearest major city.

The second month, she'd told herself there must've been a storm to delay things. That happened at times, the wind howling across the desert to create sand devils that could strip the skin right off anyone unlucky enough to be caught in the center of one.

The third month, she'd blamed it on her name. People were always getting her mixed up with Nazia, who worked on Alaris's surface base. No doubt Nazia would forward the letter with the next mail drop.

The fourth month, a knot grew in her stomach.

And kept growing.

A year and still no reply, no message. She would've worried about their well-being, but she knew they were safe. She still had one friend in the village. Busy with two young children, a demanding husband, and elderly in-laws—and utterly delighted to be in the center of that cheerful chaos—Mina wrote to Tazia when she could, gave her the news.

Tazia's brother had found a "pretty and shy" bride, his marriage celebrations followed nine months later by a healthy son.

Tazia's mother was no longer coughing; Tazia's father had taken her to be seen by the city doctor who'd settled permanently in the village and who was happy to barter his services for a good, home-cooked meal and a little company, his wife having passed on.

Tazia's father was enamored of his grandson and spoiling the boy terribly ("as a grandparent should," Mina had added).

Tazia's parents had given the money Tazia had sent them to the holy man.

She knew. Of course she knew. In her heart she knew she would never again drink her mother's sweet milk-tea or hear her father's gravelly voice. She would never again laugh with her brother, never meet his bride or her nephew. And she would never again feel her beloved *teta*'s kisses and hugs, her grandmother who had so patiently brushed her hair the many times Tazia had returned with tangles after a day of scrambling up trees and rolling down sand dunes.

She knew.

She knew.

NEXT mail drop, she ensured she was fixing a hydraulic lift on the lowest floor of the station, where no one would come looking for her and where she didn't have to hear the excited cries and see the beaming smiles of her colleagues as they received care packages or unexpected gifts, or letters that made them shed tears of joy.

"Great," she muttered when the relay tube turned out to have a hole in it.

"A problem?"

Her back stiffening where she crouched in front of the exposed inner machinery of the lift, she glanced up at Stefan. "Can't you wear a bell or something?"

"No."

Of course he didn't have a sense of humor. Psy never did. She still couldn't get her mind around the fact that two powerful cardinal Psy, including a gifted foreseer, had recently defected into a changeling pack. How could that possibly work? Changelings were as primal as Psy were cerebral. Like Stefan with his remote gaze and cool words.

"The tube is busted," she told him. "I missed the last equipment request, so we'll have to wait till next month."

"Is it urgent?"

She considered it, aware Stefan was a teleport-capable Tk. He could bring in emergency equipment in the space of mere minutes if not seconds, his mind reaching across vast distances in a way she could barely comprehend, but the unspoken rule was that the rest of the station personnel didn't ask him for anything that wasn't critical. Everyone knew that if Alaris sprang a fatal pressure leak, they'd need every last ounce of Stefan's abilities to get them to the surface.

"The other lift is still functional," she said, hooking her spanner into her tool belt and tapping in the code that meant the computer would bypass this lift until she recorded it as being back online. "We can survive a month."

He nodded, his dark brown hair military short. Since he wasn't part of the Psy race's armed forces, she thought it was because he had curls; Psy hated anything that was out of control. When he continued to loom over her, she rubbed her hands on her thighs and stood up. That didn't exactly even things out since he was so much taller, but it made her feel better.

He reached out and gripped a lock of hair that had escaped her ponytail. "Grease."

Rolling her eyes, she pulled it out of his grasp. "Was there anything else you wanted?"

"It appears I made a mistake last month in telling you no letter or package would come."

Pain in her heart, her throat. "No, I needed to hear that."

"However, instead of having you snap at everyone for two days a month, you're now so quiet that people are becoming concerned."

Tazia remembered how Andres had been poking at her this morning, trying to make her smile with those silly jokes of his. But he was her friend. Stefan was nothing. "I'm not Psy," she said point-blank. "I can't ignore hurt or forget that my family hates me."

He didn't flinch. "You knew that before. What changed?"

"You took away my hope."

There was a small silence that seemed to reverberate with a thousand unspoken things. For a single instant captured in time, she thought she saw a fracture in his icy composure, a hint of something unexpected in those eyes she'd always thought were beautiful despite their coldness.

Then a tool fell off Tazia's belt and she bent to grab it off the floor. By the time she rose, Stefan was gone. Just as well, she thought, though there was a strange hollowness in her stomach. She wasn't some bug under a microscope for him to study. She was a flesh-and-blood human being with hopes and dreams and emotions. Maybe those emotions made her heart heavy with sorrow and her soul hurt, but she would never choose to erase them in the way of Stefan's people.

What use was it to have such power if you saw no beauty in a child's smile or in the sea's turbulent moods? If you didn't understand friendship or laughter? No, she'd rather feel, even if it hurt so much she could hardly breathe through it at times.

Chapter 2

TAZIA WAS ON her way back to her room three days later, her shift complete, when she decided to take a different corridor. Andres's room was that way and he'd told her to go in and grab a reader on which he'd loaded the latest chapter in a continuing thriller from a shared favorite author. Having finished it already, he wanted her to read it so they could dissect the mystery from start to finish.

He was convinced he'd figured out the murderer.

Using his code to get in, she found the reader where he'd said it would be and shook her head at the state of his room. Clothes thrown on the bed and the floor, a T-shirt hanging off a wall lamp, a single shoe lying in solitary splendor on a bunched-up rug, while a used plate and cup sat precariously balanced on a nightstand crammed with candy, cookies, and a mess of data cubes.

It was a good thing this wasn't a military station or he'd be in constant trouble, she thought with a smile as she stepped back out into the corridor and shut the door behind herself. The funny thing was, Andres was an excellent and organized oceanographer, not a paper clip out of place in his office.

The dissonance between Andres's public and private selves made her wonder what Stefan's living space was like. She tried to imagine him in a room full of chaotic debris: clothes strewn about, tangled here and there, hard copies of station reports piled up on random flat surfaces, and ran up against a mental roadblock. Stefan's room, her brain informed her, would be as neat and as tidy and as flawless as Stefan—so perfect it had no personality.

Still angry at him, though she knew he hadn't meant to hurt her, she had to bite back a gasp when she suddenly found herself looking at the object of her thoughts. He was in his quarters, but the door was open and it gave her an uninterrupted view of a shirtless Stefan doing chin-ups using a bar that had been bolted in at one end of his room; his muscles bunched and flexed in a smooth, effortless rhythm that was a silent statement of his strength.

Skin heating, she knew she should look away, but the temptation was too great. Men had always been something of an exotic animal to her—she'd never been the girl who knew how to flirt, or who had a secret boyfriend in the village. That hadn't changed after she left her homeland. Always more comfortable with tools and machines, she'd never learned the "feminine arts," as Teta Aya used to describe them.

Neither had she been "awakened." Another one of her grandmother's scandalous euphemisms, the elderly woman having outlived three husbands, and who knew how many lovers. Tazia had begun to think she simply didn't have that gene, the one that made the other girls sparkle with anticipation at the sight of a boy. All Tazia had wanted to do was learn, build, explore—and none of the boys in the village had ever found that the least bit interesting.

Now, as she watched Stefan's body move, her stomach fluttered, her blood grew thick and languid under her skin, and her breath turned jagged. He was beautiful. Never had she thought that about a man, but no other word did him justice. His shoulders were broad, his hips slim, the muscle on him sleek and fluid. Those muscles moved like liquid silk under the pale gold of his skin, the color having held even after months under the sea, which told her it was genetic, his ancestry not as obvious as it might appear.

A single bead of sweat trickled down his spine as she watched. Her throat went dry. At that instant, she wanted nothing more than to run her fingertip along the path taken by that droplet.

Buzz. Buzz.

Jerking down her head, she turned off the specialized comm they used inside the station, and moved quickly away before Stefan could turn, see that she'd been spying on him. Her cheeks burned as she hurried out of sight. Only once she was in her own section did she check the comm—to find a message from a friend asking if she'd like to have dinner together.

About to refuse, she decided she needed a distraction and said yes. Because if she was fantasizing about Stefan, then she'd clearly been working too hard. Should he ever discover her unusual response to the sight of his body, he'd be faintly quizzical but otherwise unaffected. A few Psy around the world might be starting to question Silence, as their way of life was apparently called according to recent rumors, but Alaris's station commander wasn't part of that group—he was the most emotionless person she'd ever met.

TAZIA didn't run into Stefan again until five days later—possibly because she'd done everything in her power to avoid contact. When she did end up in the same space as him, it was at the senior staff meeting where they went over the health of the station piece by piece, including the health of the crew and anything else that might affect the smooth running of Alaris.

Not up for discussion were any current research projects.

Because while it was Stefan's task to make sure Alaris ran

smoothly, all staff and crew safe, it was water changeling Dr. Night who headed the research team and through whom all related data was funneled. Tazia figured the split had something to do with BlackSea not wanting the Psy to co-opt research they'd funded. She wondered if Stefan was troubled by the implied lack of trust, then realized he wasn't troubled by anything.

"I think we should have another station event midmonth." That came from Allie Livingstone, the station's chief counselor. "A single monthly get-together isn't enough, not when some people inevitably miss it because of their shifts. As a result, it might be two months before they have a chance to blow off steam in a group setting."

"I'm willing to take your lead on this, Ms. Livingstone." Stefan's tone was even, his form motionless where he stood at the front of the room. Around him, some of the crew slouched in sofas, a few held up the wall, while Tazia leaned against a sofa arm.

"However," Stefan added, "you must ensure these social events do not leave the crew unable to function. The researchers set their own hours, but I need my crew alert if the station is to run at maximum efficiency."

Allie shoved a hand through her strawberry blonde hair. "Yeah, sorry about that. No more hangovers, I promise. I was thinking about a quiz night." She held up her hands when several people groaned. "You mock me now but I bet you all get into it. Competitive lot that you are."

"Are there any other nonstandard matters that require discussion?" Stefan looked straight at Tazia.

And she wondered if he could see her thoughts, see how her mind kept replaying the sight of his strong, beautiful body doing those chin-ups.

He was telepathic after all.

No, she reminded herself, uninvited telepathic contact was against the rules of the Psy race, and Stefan would never break the rules.

"The lift situation remains stable?"

She nodded in response to his question. "We'll be fine until the next delivery." Breaking the piercing intensity of the eye contact, she glanced around the room. "If any of you have noticed anything else buggy, let me know. I've got some leeway this week with the routine maintenance completed."

She kept her head down the rest of the meeting, but swore she could feel Stefan's eyes on her throughout. Impossible, of course. He'd never pay extra attention to a particular crew member when he already had the information he needed from that crew member. Slipping out as soon as he dismissed the meeting, she headed down into the bowels of Alaris to tinker with a nonessential system.

He found her there fifteen minutes later. "Is there a problem with that component?"

"No," she said shortly, frustrated that he'd followed her into *her* territory.

When he simply waited, she blew out a breath and wiped away a tendril of hair using the back of her hand. "I have an idea about streamlining this system for better efficiency and I have the time to work on it today."

"I see." His eyes lingered on her cheek.

Flushing as she realized she'd no doubt streaked her skin with grease yet again, she turned back to her work, determined to ignore both him and her stupidly thudding heart. When she turned around a few minutes later, Stefan was gone.

"I think you two would make a cute couple!" Allie nudged Andres as they sat at one of the tables in the dining room a few days later, the station's complement small enough that a larger space wasn't needed, especially given that only a third of them were on shift at any given time.

"Very funny." Andres scowled, black eyebrows drawn ominously together over the rich hazel of his eyes. "Courtney would rip my nuts off—in fact, I think that's what she tried to do today." He rubbed at his face, his deep brown skin holding that too-long-without-actual-sunlight pallor. "All I said was that maybe she should double-check her results since they didn't line up with current data, and boom! It was like I'd impugned her honor or something."

"She has had a hair-trigger temper of late," Allie murmured. "I'll have a talk with her." The counselor's perceptive eyes shifted to Tazia, the vivid blue color of her irises something Tazia had never seen while living in the village.

It still took her by surprise at times, that brightness.

"Talking of talking," Allie said, "you've been very quiet the past few weeks."

Tazia took what Teta Aya would've told her was a rudely big bite of her pasta in order to give herself an excuse to delay replying. "Just tired, I guess," she said after chewing and swallowing.

Allie let her get away with that, though it was obvious the counselor didn't buy her answer. "You haven't rotated upside for the maximum period—good thing it's only going to be a couple more weeks."

Tazia made a noncommittal noise, which Allie took as agreement. It wasn't. Tazia's stomach dropped at the idea of leaving the cocoon of Alaris and emerging back out into a world where no one wanted her, no one claimed her. Her closest friends were station folk, and those who were rotating out with her would go home to their families for the duration, leaving her to rock about alone until the month of mandatory shore leave had passed.

Still, there was no way to avoid it; two weeks after that conversation with Allie, she grabbed her duffel and walked over to the docked transport that would ferry her upside. The psych team had a firm rule about rotating people out every three to four months, no excuses accepted once you were at the end of the fourth month. Something to do with psychological stress and close quarters.

No one had ever asked Tazia's opinion on that or she'd have told them that she was fine with close quarters and staying underwater with people she knew, the station's comforting bulk around her. She had no need for the horrible nothingness that was the hell of shore leave.

"What do they expect us to do?" she muttered as she and Andres boarded the advanced submersible that would take them up to the surface along a specially designed "rail" that had been built with the help of Tks like Stefan. "Go loco and shoot up the place?"

Andres snorted, his scrubbed-clean skin gleaming in the lights inside the submersible and his shirt neatly pressed for once. "The first time I met you, you didn't even know what 'loco' meant."

Tazia laughed because he was right. The two of them had met three years earlier, when she came on board the Alaris construction and development team. She *had* been green, still was in so many ways, but she'd learned enough to fit into this world that was now the only one that would accept her.

"One thing you can say for close quarters," she said, gut clenching against the fresh wave of pain, "you get to know your station mates very well."

"Tell me about it." Andres groaned. "Goddamn Trev snores loud enough to make the walls rattle."

A step on the entryway before she could respond, a tall, rangy body with close-cut dark brown hair getting into the submersible. *Stefan*. She hadn't realized he had an upside trip scheduled. As usual, he made no effort to engage in casual conversation; he was so remote and self-contained that she could barely connect this man to the flesh-and-blood one she'd seen that day in his room . . . and later in her dreams.

Even as her shoulders tensed at the memory, she had the strangest urge to poke at him, to needle him into reacting—except, of course, he wouldn't. He was Psy.

On the entryway, the maligned Trev gave them a grinning salute, then shut the door, spinning the lock. The submersible was now sealed for the duration. It would take them some time to reach the surface—they didn't have to worry about decompression sickness, since both Alaris and the sub were at a regulated pressure, but there was no getting around the fact that they were on the ocean floor, far, far beneath the surface.

Andres, of course, could have gone up on his own. Sea changelings were built to transition from ocean to land without issue.

"One day," he said, as if he'd read her thoughts, "I'm going to swim up and surprise everyone."

Tazia raised an eyebrow. "You're too lazy to swim that far." His self-professed favorite thing to do in his snake form was to curl up and nap; even when he went out of the station through the special exits built for sea changeling staff, he'd told her he mostly just lazed about in the water while the others "got all acrobatic."

"True," he admitted. "That's why it would be a surprise." Putting on his headphones with an unrepentant wink, he started making final corrections on a piece of work he needed to complete.

Tazia had intended to read a book, as Stefan was now doing. Had she been in this same situation even two months ago, she'd have given him the space and quiet he so plainly wanted, but since he'd continually invaded her own space in the preceding weeks, she decided he'd lost all right to her forbearance.

"You could've teleported upside," she said. By some quirk of telekinetic power, a 'port caused no issues with pressure, regardless of the to and from locations.

"My assistance has been requested at the site of a major earthquake and teleporting to the surface takes energy." Dark gray eyes looking into her, seeing too much. "I decided it would be better to arrive a few hours later but at full strength than otherwise."

Tazia saw his point: he'd make up for the delay by shifting twice as much twice as fast. "I wouldn't have thought the medics would permit you to take on the work." Tazia herself was under strict instructions to relax and recuperate, and she was only the engineer.

Stefan, in contrast, was undoubtedly the most financially valuable member of the Alaris team. Given the scarcity of Tks as powerful as Stefan, the short-term replacements Alaris brought in to cover for him during his absences had to cost them double what he did on his permanent contract. No way would they want him out of commission for any longer than strictly necessary.

Stefan took so much time to reply that she thought he was simply going to ignore her implied question, but then the stone gray of his eyes met her own and he said, "I'm listed as a volunteer Tk with International Search and Rescue."

She blinked, having assumed that he was being called in to assist a commercial enterprise of some kind. Beside her, Andres—who'd taken off his headphones because he couldn't bear to miss out on any discussions in his vicinity—was more vocal in his surprise. "Say what?"

Tazia could understand her friend's befuddled response. There was no money in search and rescue. As such, the Psy Council would never authorize the "waste" of resources. Not unless there was a political angle. "Is it a Psy enclave?" she asked, wondering if the Council was trying to curry favor with its populace due to the recent unrest.

"No. Human."

Andres shook his head. "No offense, Stefan, but Psy don't step in to help humans, and they definitely don't send in high-powered telekinetics."

"Incorrect, since I am both Psy and a Tk."

"You know what I mean."

"No." His tone made it clear the discussion was over.

Chapter 3

DISEMBARKING UPSIDE AT last, the trip having passed both too slowly and too fast, Tazia blinked at the tropical sunlight, had to admit it felt good on her skin. Part of her would always miss the desert sands of home, though it had never been *her* place, the place where she could put down her roots. "See you in a month," she said to Andres as he grinned and waved at the gaggle of relatives who'd come to claim him.

Standing impatiently behind the glass wall of the waiting area, they were so proud of him it was a joyous brightness. Small, excited children pressed their hands to the glass, an older woman cried happy tears while others just beamed at Andres, and two teenagers held up a banner that said, *We missed you, bro!*

Tiny hands had drawn colorful marine animals all over the banner.

This was what it should be like. Family was the bedrock of life; that was what Tazia had always been taught, still what she believed. A person could weather anything so long as she had the strength of her family at her back. To be without family was to be a ghost, lost in the wilderness.

Andres turned toward her. "Will you—"

"I'll check in for you at the office." She smiled and took his ID card. "Go on, I think your mom's going to burst if you don't hug her soon." It was his mother who was crying; Tazia recognized her from many earlier meetings.

Andres's mother had invited Tazia home for dinner on countless occasions during Tazia's time working on the construction and development team.

"Thanks, Tazi." Andres hesitated. "You know you're always welcome to come home with me. One more body won't be any trouble. Ma loves to feed people and she adores you."

She cherished him for his friendship, but she also knew that this time should be his . . . and much as Tazia loved his family, it made her so sad inside to witness their love, their togetherness. It was a terrible thing to admit, but their joy reminded her too much of all that she had lost. Better for such a guest to stay away; never would she risk putting a damper on Andres's visit by inadvertently betraying her own painful homesickness.

"I'll be fine," she said, her heart a dull ache in her chest but her smile and wave for his family very much real. "I've got a few dates set up."

A gleam in his eye. "Secretive. I like it." He kissed her on the cheek before heading off, turning to walk backward long enough to call out, "I'll expect a full report!"

Then he was gone, excitedly swallowed up by his boisterous family.

"You lied."

She didn't startle, having felt Stefan's cool presence at her back.

Taking a step forward in an effort to fight the temptation to turn around and push at him until he cracked, until he acted *human*, she said, "It's a lie that'll ensure he doesn't worry about me during his break." With that, she hefted her small duffel and strode toward the office building to check in; she'd leave both her own and

Andres's ID badges there. It was easy enough to verify ID with a DNA scan when it was time to return to Alaris, and this way there was no risk of losing the IDs.

Stefan fell into step beside her, shortening his long strides to match hers. "What will you do?"

Concerned? Stefan? No, she thought. He probably just wanted to make sure his engineer would return to Alaris without problematic psychological issues. The smooth running of the station, after all, was his mandate. "I'll rent a room for the month I'm upside."

The office staff had shown her how to arrange such temporary accommodation her first trip upside. Now she had a list of places she could call to see if they had vacancies—advance bookings were difficult, as no one could guarantee exactly when conditions would be right for the submersible to come up.

If everything was booked, there were always the bunks at the back of the office building. No one would mind if she used one of those, though Tazia intended to do her best to avoid that scenario. She'd spent a week there her first rotation upside, and the quiet pity she'd seen in the eyes of those who went home every day to their families was nothing she ever wanted to repeat.

"What will you do in your room?"

Fingers tightening on the handles of her duffel at Stefan's question, she fought the burning in her throat, the flame of anger in her stomach. He had no idea what he was doing to her, how his questions were forcing her to face her cold, lonely existence headlong. No playing with Mina's children for her, no cuddling her nephew or helping her father fix the machines the desert sand was constantly clogging.

That was what a daughter who was wanted and loved would do. Not one who'd been forsaken. "I'll hang out," she said, keeping her pain to herself. "Read a few books, maybe go to the theater, have fun."

"Do you wish to do that?"

"No." Temper snapping, she spun around to face him, her jaw tight and her fury caustic acid in her veins. "But it's the best I can do. Satisfied?"

"You could come with me."

The world froze and when it started moving again, nothing was as it had been. "What?"

Eyes unreadable, face expressionless, his body held in straight lines that spoke once again of a military background, Stefan said, "They're in desperate need of volunteers at the location of the quake. It's an isolated settlement. An engineer would be more than welcome."

"I can't." Frustration churned in her gut. "If the company finds out I'm moonlighting, even on a volunteer basis, they might ground me for another month." And she needed to return to Alaris, to the place where she could almost forget how very lonely it was out here in the world.

Stefan's eyes held hers, the dark gray intense. "I may be able to get you clearance."

"If you can," she said, "I'm yours."

For an instant, her words lingered in the air, a strange tension between them. Then Stefan nodded and the taut thread broke in two. It had probably just been her imagination anyway. She'd never seen any indication that Stefan wasn't completely Silent, his emotions contained behind a chilly wall of reserve.

Tazia wondered what he would've been like in a world without Silence, tried to imagine him with a smile, and felt her breath catch in her throat, her stomach flipping. He was handsome now in a stark, hard, military way . . . but she thought he might be heartbreakingly so if he smiled.

"I'll return soon," he said to her and disappeared beyond the front office.

Needing to keep herself busy in the interim, she handed Andres's

ID as well as her own to the unfamiliar older man manning the desk. "My friend's family was waiting for him," she said when the clerk held up Andres's pass. "He scanned out at the submersible."

The clerk ran the pass through his scanner. "Yep, all set. Was he the one with the entire clan that came out to get him? Mother wearing a yellow dress?"

"Yes, that was them."

"Proud as punch they were." His stern expression softened. "She came in here to check they had the right time for the submersible and spent ten minutes talking about how her boy was the smartest, most handsome creature on the planet."

Tazia smiled with him. "He always comes back on board with the most enormous care packages and we all eat very well for a week."

Laughing, the clerk finished the paperwork, then said, "You want to withdraw some cash from your account?"

Tazia thought about it. Almost everything in this port city ran on plastic, but if she went with Stefan to a more remote area, she'd probably need cash. "Yes," she said and hoped the decision sent a loud signal to the universe about her intentions and desires.

She'd just completed the transaction when she was called into the back office and asked for her reasons for wanting to volunteer at the quake site. Stefan stood silently by the window as she looked the Living Resources director in the eye and told the blunt truth. "I've got no one upside. The month passes at a snail's pace and I return to Alaris no more relaxed than when I got out. I'd prefer to spend that time helping people rather than feeling sorry for myself."

The director tucked a wing of blonde hair behind her ear and said, "Well, that's certainly honest enough." She tapped something into the datapad in front of her. "I'm clearing you for volunteer duty with Stefan, but remember, you'll have a physical before returning to Alaris. Make sure you're rested and well nourished by then or I *will* bench you for another month—and you'll lose that month's salary, too."

"Yes, ma'am." Joy burst to life in Tazia's bloodstream. *She wouldn't be alone and useless upside. Not this time.*

IT was on the high-speed jet out of the country that Tazia glanced at the man who sat next to her, their arms so close they almost touched, and said, "Thank you."

"There's no need. Your skills are necessary."

Eyes on the black of his shirt where his arm lay on the armrest, she said, "Andres was right, you know. Telekinetics like you are so valuable they aren't allowed to volunteer." She didn't know why she was pushing this; maybe because Stefan was an enigma, something she couldn't take apart to figure out how it worked.

He'd been that way from the start, had always fascinated her, but something had changed in the time since the mail incident. Now she wasn't only fascinated by the idea of him, but compelled by Stefan himself. *Foolish Tazi,* Teta Aya would've said, *trying to understand the stars when they are beyond mortal ken.*

Stefan was as unreachable as one of those cold, burning stars. And yet . . . "Why do they let you?"

"My entire town was buried by a landslide when I was a very young child," he said at last, his tone quiet enough that it wouldn't travel beyond their seats. "I survived by 'porting out instinctively. However, I was psychologically scarred by the resulting loss of family." A pause. "The incident reports state I tried for hours to teleport back to get my mother and brother, only for the 'port to abort because the place I needed to go no longer existed."

Tazia's heart hurt for him, but he continued on before she could say anything.

"The landslide crushed our home, trapping them both under tons of dirt and rock." No change in his tone, but she could imagine the small, scared boy he'd been, the boy trying so desperately to save those he loved.

"Psy-Med," he added, "believes such volunteer work helps keep me stable."

From a human, such a confession would've been the deepest of intimacies. From Stefan, it was an even deeper trust. Shaken, she said, "I won't betray the confidence."

"If I thought you would, I wouldn't have told you." Dark gray eyes held her own, the contact unbreakable. "You have more questions."

"I always have more questions," she said with an ache in her soul because that had been her father's lament: *Here comes my Tazi. What questions for me today, my daughter with her smart mind and curious spirit?*

Watching her with those penetrating eyes that made her feel hunted, Stefan said, "You may ask your questions, but not here. When we are alone."

"You might regret saying that." This conversation, it wasn't one she'd ever thought she'd have, not with Stefan. "You'll be answering questions till you're old and gray."

"Perhaps I will prove in no way as interesting as your mechanical devices."

Somehow, Tazia didn't believe that.

Tapping out a request on the computer screen built into the arm of his seat when she didn't answer, Stefan ordered them meals. "Eat as much as you can. Our meals will be erratic once we land."

Chapter 4

THEY CHANGED IN the private cubicles on board the jet, getting into clothing suitable for the quake-hit region. She wore her own work boots, scuffed and comfortable, but Stefan had sourced a search and rescue uniform for her that was similar to his own. The color of sand, the thin, breathable, but tough material covered her arms and legs, providing protection from the rubble and the sun both. The lightweight jacket, worn over a T-shirt, sealed up the front, which meant she could tear it open should it get too hot.

What on her looked merely serviceable looked like a pressed military uniform on Stefan, his bearing was so erect. "Ready?" he said as soon as they'd landed and been processed through to the hot, desert land not so very far from her own.

Blowing out a breath, she nodded. "I haven't done this before."

"You might feel some disorientation." He stepped close, her heart slammed into her rib cage . . . and a second later, she was being teleported for the first time in her life, the world spinning before it settled.

In the space of three heartbeats, they'd gone from a modern, gleaming airport to a village deep in the interior, where a massive quake had buried ancient and lovingly handcrafted homes the color of sunbaked mud, cracking and buckling the land in every direction.

There were no screams, no cries. Only an eerie silence as people worked with frantic hands to unearth the buried. Many had nothing but those hands, fingers bloodied and nails broken. Stefan began to lift huge chunks of material within a minute of arriving. The relief on the townspeople's haggard faces was so visceral, it tore a hole inside of Tazia.

"Right," she said and, dumping her gear in the same spot where Stefan had dropped his duffel, headed out to talk to the person who seemed to be coordinating the rescue efforts. The grateful local woman soon had her out fixing everything from broken pipes to checking wiring for danger, to jerry-rigging communications equipment that kept breaking down.

Only a small rescue team had made it to the village so far, the rest still en route. As a result, the available able-bodied volunteers— trained and untrained—were stretched to the limit.

Tazia fell exhausted on her sleeping bag hours after full dark, some kind person having rolled it out after putting up a tent for her and Stefan. When Stefan came in bare minutes later, his face drawn, and, digging into his duffel, threw her a Psy nutrition bar, she gulped down the tasteless thing. It was only then that she realized she hadn't eaten since the plane. "Will you be okay?"

"I'll need at least six hours of sleep to recover to a level where I can continue to shift material." With that, he threw her another bar, ate four more himself, and went to sleep.

Or she thought he must have. Because she woke with the nutrition bar still in her hand. A glance at the clock showed only five hours had passed. Moving about quietly so as not to wake Stefan, she stuck her feet into her boots and ducked out to use the facilities. Afterward, she rinsed out her mouth with careful use of water, then took a long drink as she finished off the bar. Shower facilities were nonexistent, the well having been crushed in the quake, but the locals had repeatedly cautioned her to make sure she drank enough water to stay strong and hydrated.

Tazia had forgotten how easily the desert sun could sap a person's strength.

Tankers were on the way and those villagers not involved in attempting to rescue buried survivors were trying to resurrect the well, but until then, personal hygiene had to take a backseat to survival. It was better not to ask Stefan to 'port in more water—he was already being pushed to the edge of his endurance lifting the debris.

Stepping back inside the tent, she found the box of wet wipes she'd grabbed from the little shop next to the Alaris offices and glanced over at Stefan. He hadn't moved, his breathing steady. Six hours he'd said, and six hours it would be. Turning her back to him, she stripped off the clothing on her upper half, her skin burning at the idea of being near-naked with a man who wasn't her husband, then quickly wiped herself down as much as possible, before getting into a fresh bra and T-shirt.

Her clean clothing wasn't going to last, since she'd brought only three changes, but that was a nonissue given the devastation. Tazia had been dirty before, would be again. Putting the used wipes in a plastic bag for later disposal, she placed the box of wipes by Stefan's duffel so he'd see them when he woke. That done, she grabbed her jacket—dusty and grease streaked from the day before—and went to see what she could do about a damaged generator that was the backup power source for the village's small medical clinic should its primary generator malfunction.

STEFAN woke after exactly six hours of sleep. Like any trained soldier, he'd been aware of Tazia coming and going, but his mind knew she was no threat, and so he'd continued to sleep. Had it been otherwise, she'd have been immobilized before she realized he'd moved. He might've been deemed too psychologically flawed to be an Arrow, an elite black ops soldier, but the training had stuck.

And officially an Arrow or not, the men and women of the squad considered him one of theirs. He'd been given off-the-books training, and still sparred with active-duty Arrows whenever possible, considered them his brethren. No one could sneak up on him even when he slept—but with Tazia, the risk profile was nil.

Violence was simply not part of her nature.

Getting up, he did what needed to be done, then returned to the location of the worst collapse. If he could have, he'd have worked through the night; he knew there were people trapped under that rubble. He'd had to force himself to be logical, to remind himself that he'd be useless to everyone for far longer than six hours if he burned out his psychic abilities.

Now, recharged, he focused on the most unstable section and got to work. He was conscious of Tazia moving around the village, picked up her voice speaking a language that was close enough to the one spoken in this land that she was understood. When she said, "Stefan," he glanced down.

Her head only just reached his breastbone but he'd never thought of Tazia as small. She had too much inside her to be small—like a storm gathering up its power before it struck.

"Is there a problem?"

"You haven't had a drink of water in three hours." Frowning, she passed him a reusable bottle filled to the brim. "You know you can't do that, not in this heat, especially with the amount of rubble you're shifting."

As he took the water, he catalogued his body and realized he'd come perilously close to dehydration. "Thank you." No one had been concerned about his welfare, except as it impacted their own needs and wants, since he was a child.

"No thanks needed." Her eyes took in the area in front of him as he drank the water in slow, measured swallows so as not to overload his parched body. "This is bad enough, but I keep waiting for the aftershocks."

He nodded, lowering the bottle after emptying half of it. "They're apt to be severe, given the magnitude of the quake. That's why I have to get the trapped out now—the rubble is too unstable to hold in a major tremor."

Working without a break for the next four hours—not stopping even when Tazia passed him water and he gulped it down—he got half the trapped out before the world shook again. Screams pierced the air as things crashed and people bled, but his first thought was for Tazia. Reaching out with his mind as he crouched down to ride out the aftershock, he searched for the brilliance that was hers. He didn't invade her mind to find her—he didn't have to. Tazia's mental signature was as unique as a fingerprint to him . . . and there she was.

Safe.

When the shaking finally stopped, he could no longer sense living minds below the closest section of rubble. As, long ago, he'd no longer been able to find his mother or brother, though he'd searched for hours. Until rescue services had arrived and found him wandering barefoot over the debris, his skin cut and bleeding and blood pouring from his nose and ears as he continued to try to shift the entire landslide on his own.

"They're dead," a Psy-Med specialist had told him, cold and no-nonsense, the words like stones smashing into his face. "You aren't strong enough to assist. Sit here and don't be a nuisance."

No longer was he a child, but he couldn't help the dead here, either.

Leaving them, he moved to a section that still held the living, and when Tazia came by again with water, he saw the tear tracks in the dust on her face. His instincts zeroed in on her. "You're hurt?" He scanned her body to check for injuries.

She shook her head. "There was this little girl—she followed me around all day yesterday, said she wanted to learn what I did. The aftershock . . . She was . . ." Sobs shook her small frame, her face crumpling.

When she would've turned away, he stepped close, protecting her from the gaze of others. He knew she needed contact, needed touch, but he hadn't touched anyone except out of necessity since before the landslide that had ended his childhood, for the Silent did not touch. So he simply stood close, and when her tears ended, he made her drink some of the water she'd brought him.

"I'd better go," she said, her voice husky. "Don't forget to eat a nutrition bar."

The clock had just ticked past midnight when he was forced to stop. Mental muscles strained to the last degree, his uniform hanging on a frame that was burning energy faster than he could replenish it, he made himself walk away from the rubble. Tazia was inside the tent, working on a small component by the light of the solar-powered emergency lantern she'd bought in the same little shop where she'd bought the box of cleansing wipes she'd shared with him.

"There's not enough electricity to do computronic work after dark," she murmured absently, then looked up. "Stefan, sit before you fall down." The words were sharp.

"I'm fine, just low on energy." But he sat, his body feeling as if it was held together by strings that could snap at any moment.

Digging into his duffel, Tazia pulled out a pack of the high-density nutrition bars he'd brought. She peeled one open and pushed it at him. "Eat." Watching him to make sure he obeyed the order, she found some water and gave that to him after dosing it with a vitamin and mineral powder. "There's enough drinking water that we don't have to ration it. Tankers will be here tomorrow."

He drank the water, ate another bar when she gave it to him. "Have you eaten?"

A nod. "Some of the villagers managed to put together an outdoor oven, made flatbread. I had that. I think you need these bars more than I do."

"Did you have the vitamins?" She could easily fall victim to malnutrition.

"Yes." Putting aside the component she'd been working on, she thrust her hands through her hair, then dropped both her hands and her gaze. "Sorry about breaking down like that."

"There's no need to be sorry. You are human. You feel."

Her eyes met his, so open and heavy with sorrow. "Do you remember feeling? As a child?"

"Yes." He remembered screaming and clawing at the mountains of muddy rocks that covered his family, but the memories were distant, numbed by time and his conditioning under Silence. "You should sleep."

"So should you." She lay down in her sleeping bag but didn't switch off the lantern until he'd finished his meal. "Good night."

"Good night," he said, and it was the first time he'd said that to anyone as an adult. In the barracks where he'd been trained before it was decided he was too psychologically fractured to make a good soldier, they hadn't spoken beyond that which was needed for training.

And after that, he'd always been alone.

· · ·

TAZIA woke suddenly. A glance at the face of her watch, the softly glowing numerals visible in the dark, told her only two hours had passed since she went to sleep. About to close her eyes, she heard it again, the sound that had wakened her . . . No, it was a *lack* of sound. Stefan wasn't breathing.

Scrambling up, she fumbled for the lantern, flicked it on. When she turned the beam toward Stefan, she saw he was rigid, his hands fisted by his sides and his neck stiff. Not needing to see anything further, she dropped the lantern, causing it to blink out, and put her hands on his shoulders in an attempt to shake him free from the nightmare. "Stefan!"

It should've been impossible, how fast he moved. One instant, she was crouching worried over him, and the next, she was flat on her back with him over her, one of his hands at her throat. Heart thudding, she kept her hands where they'd fallen when he flipped her. "Stefan, it's me, Tazia."

His face was shadowed, but she saw him shake his head. "Tazia?"

"Yes." Moving very carefully, she lifted a hand to his wrist, tugged, deliberately using his name again as she said, "Let go of my throat, Stefan."

A jerk and he was gone, back on his side of the tent. "I hurt you?"

"No." Sitting up, she tried to catch her breath. "You just surprised me."

"I apologize. I should've warned you not to touch me in sleep."

"You weren't breathing."

"It's temporary. My brain wakes me up when my CO_2 levels get too high."

Such scientific words to describe the raw pain she'd seen in him—as if he were caught in the throes of a horror so terrible, it pierced his Silence. "What did you dream?"

"Psy don't dream."

"That's not what I asked."

The pause was long and heavy. "This situation awakens memories of the disaster when I was a boy. It's having an impact on my sleeping patterns."

She was so used to seeing him as remote, untouched by the pain and chaos of life, that his admission shook her, made her question everything she thought she knew. Not sure what to do, she'd opened her mouth to say something—she didn't know what—when he lay back down.

"You should return to sleep," he said. "The work is by no means complete."

Hearing the finality of his tone, she did lie down, but then thought again of the way he'd pushed into her space, saw in that permission to push into his. "How old were you?" she asked quietly. "When it happened."

A long silence, his breathing even enough that she might've believed him asleep if she hadn't been able to sense the conscious life of him, the force of it a pulse against her skin. Rather than asking again, she gave him the time to think, to decide what to share. After all, they both had their secrets.

"Four," he said at last. "My conditioning was fragile."

Conditioning. Tazia turned that word around in her head, considered its meaning.

For the longest time, she'd believed that Psy came out of the womb emotionless, that this was who they were as a people—as a tiger was fierce and a snake sinuous. A simple fact of nature. Only after leaving her village had she begun to hear different whispers, begun to hear that the Psy did this to themselves. Then she'd found that old history book and her suspicions had been confirmed.

"It must've been a terrifying experience," she said, her voice soft in the total darkness. "You lost your whole family?"

"My mother was my custodial parent. I lost her, and a sibling. An elder brother."

Having turned to face his back, Tazia thought about reaching out and touching him as she might a fellow human in pain, but Stefan was Psy. He rarely initiated any physical contact. She didn't know much about the process of conditioning a person to be Silent, but logic told her it would fail in the face of constant physical contact.

And she didn't want him to feel any more pain, this extraordinary man who helped others even when providing that help pushed him back into memories of the most heartbreaking loss. Her eyes burned. *Four years old.* His grief and confusion would've been incalculable.

So she kept her distance, said, "I'm sorry for your hurt."

He didn't answer, and she didn't force herself any deeper into him. But that night, she slept with an ear open for Stefan's breathing, and when he stopped again, she said, "Stefan," until he snapped out of it.

They didn't speak otherwise.

Chapter 5

IT WAS TWO days later, all known survivors rescued, that the villagers began the cleanup operation. Tazia continued to fix anything and everything she could. Stefan, meanwhile, was needed as much as he'd ever been, the large structures that had collapsed impossible to shift otherwise. Heavy equipment was coming, but the roads to the village were treacherous, and several trucks had already broken down.

The good news was that the water tankers had arrived on schedule. "There's more than enough drinking water, especially since it looks like the well will be fully operational soon," she told Stefan late that afternoon, after he stopped working before nightfall for once.

The only reason he'd stopped was because a piece of debris had fallen on him, causing significant bruising to his torso. He'd have been out there minutes afterward regardless, but thankfully one of the volunteer medics had told him to rest and keep his muscles from stiffening up, or he'd be useless the next day.

"Good," he said, doing a stretch as they stood outside their tent; his wince broke through the normal lack of expression on his face.

"Stop it," she muttered, glaring at him. "It's a bruise, needs a cold pack on it." Except, with power at a premium, no one was using it to make ice, much less chill cold packs.

"Heat may do as well." Stefan glanced at the sun-warmed sand that surrounded them. "I could bury myself for a short period."

Shaking her head, she said, "Scorpions."

"You have a point." He stilled as an elderly man from the village began to walk in their direction.

She could tell the elder's respectful nod made Stefan uncomfortable. His face had settled back into its usual expressionless lines, but she'd begun to learn to read his moods . . . or at least she'd fooled herself in believing she could. Now she glanced away from him to find the elder waving her over.

When she went to him, he gave her a painstakingly hand-drawn map and said a single beautiful thing in the language that mirrored that of her homeland closely enough that she could understand him. "Hot spring."

Her eyes widened. "I thank you," she said, then glanced at Stefan before turning back to the elder. "He will not be comfortable with others around."

"There will be no others. It is my family's secret, the spring." He passed her a faded photograph with wrinkled hands that held an age tremor. "Go there." Then he pointed out the location on his map.

"I thank you," Tazia began, but the white-bearded man waved it off.

"The gratitude," he said, "is ours."

Walking over to Stefan after the elder left, Tazia told him of the hot spring, showed him the photograph of the distinctive rock formation not far from that spring. "Have you enough energy to 'port there?"

Stefan considered the image. "I won't know until I try."

"You should try," Tazia said. "The hot spring will soothe the ache, help you be in shape for further work." She added the last because that was the only thing about which Stefan seemed to care—his own health was important only when it threatened to become an impediment to his task.

"You hate being dirty," he said, to her surprise. "You can come and bathe in the spring."

Tazia sucked in a breath. To be naked with Stefan . . . But no, he'd never expect that. So they'd take turns. She could handle that, knew he'd never peek . . . though she might. Skin flushing, she rubbed her hands over her face. "I should stay, do some more work on the power station. Sooner I get that up and running at full capacity, the better."

"You said yourself the fading light is dangerous. You could make an error with the finer components."

Tazia nodded. She'd stopped work fifteen minutes prior for that very reason. "All right," she said, but glanced around the area, guilt still gnawing at her. "Do you think it's okay?" She felt filthy, but that was nothing, not in comparison to the destruction around them. "I don't want to waste time."

"We won't be gone long." Stefan glanced at the rubble. "And there are only the dead waiting below now."

Her hand rose toward his arm; she had to consciously wrench it back before she made contact. "You're sure?" she whispered.

"Yes." No expression on his face, no change in his tone . . . but his eyes, they were fixed on the crushed ruin of the village. "At night," he added, "when the humans fall into exhausted sleep, the area is clear and I can search with my telepathic senses. There are no longer any living minds under the rubble."

Heart a lump of pain in her chest and mind filling with the name of the little girl who'd wanted to be an engineer, Tazia closed her eyes in a moment of remembrance. When she opened them, it was on a swell of quiet determination. Nothing could turn back the clock, bring the dead back to life. What she could do was ensure Stefan's health.

The death toll would've been far higher without his dogged efforts.

"Come on, we should get to the spring before it gets dark." Ducking into the tent, she grabbed a towel from her gear, and two sets of dirty clothing. She could at least rinse them out; they should dry quickly in this heat.

Stefan did the same before stepping close to her.

"Ready?" he said, as he had the first time he 'ported her.

"Yes."

They arrived at the rock formation an eyeblink later, which spoke to the relative proximity of the area—and yet it was far enough away that she couldn't see or hear anything from the village. Taking out the map, she pinpointed their current position, then traced the line that should lead them to the spring itself.

"I have it," Stefan said and set off without another glimpse at the map.

A ten-minute walk later, they ducked into the mouth of a cave and followed the sense of damp heat until they found themselves in a chamber lit by the fading evening light that poured in through a hole in the roof, the air hazy with curls of steam.

"In," she ordered Stefan, putting down her stuff and taking his. "Now, Stefan."

"You should—"

"Don't be chivalrous," she ordered. "You're moving more stiffly already. Get in before I push you in."

A small pause before he lifted his fingers to the seal of his jacket, their eyes locked. It felt shockingly intimate to watch him do that simple act, butterflies taking mad flight in her stomach. Turning her back to give him privacy, she tried to focus on the wall in front of her, but was breath-stealingly aware of every tiny sound Stefan made as he stripped out of his clothes.

"You never speak so authoritatively to me on Alaris," he murmured, his voice stroking over her skin.

She fought a shiver. "You're my boss on Alaris."

The sound of water lapping, a slight hiss. "It is extremely hot."

"Good." Keeping her back to him, she frowned and stepped closer to another area of misty vapor. "I think there's a tiny spring here, too." Smiling when she discovered she was right, she took all their clothes and began to dump them piece by piece into the water, pulling out each in turn to scrub it against a large wet stone in an effort to get some of the dirt out at least. Once she had an armful, she walked outside and placed the clothes on sun-warmed rocks to dry.

"I can do mine, Tazia," Stefan said when she came back in and returned to her task.

Rolling her eyes, she looked over her shoulder. "Can you ever just accept a favor and say thank you?"

Wide shoulders exposed by the way he sat in the spring, his strong arms braced along the stone edge, he held her gaze. "Thank you."

The words felt like a caress. "You need to sink lower into the water. That falling beam hit your shoulder, too." She'd felt her heart stop beating when she'd seen him go down, had dropped everything to run to his side, check he was alive. The memory of fear made her voice sharp as she said, "Or do you want me to push you down?"

TAZIA was in a very bad temper today, Stefan thought, as she turned back to her chore. "Have I done something to offend you?" he asked when she came back inside the cave after taking care of the last of their clothing.

She sat down on the cave floor with her back to him. "No."

He didn't understand emotion, but he knew she wasn't telling him the truth. "The spring is large. You can share the space," he offered, though it was difficult for him to be in such close proximity to another being, and particularly to Tazia.

"Tazia," he said when she didn't reply.

"I can't." Keeping her back to him, she leaned forward as if she'd drawn up her knees and wrapped her arms around them. "I know it may seem irrational and old-fashioned to you, but I was brought up to be . . . chaste." The words were taut. "To be naked only with the man I took as my husband. I don't live in that world anymore"— harsh strain in those words—"but I can't discard who I am like it's an old coat."

"I understand," Stefan said, having already guessed at Tazia's value system after so carefully noting every single thing about her in the year they'd worked together. "Your cultural mores are no more or less irrational than the protocol under which my people are conditioned."

He saw her shoulders relax. Rising, she walked over to sit on a rock nearer the spring, her eyes on the entrance and her body in profile to him. "Have you ever thought of breaking Silence?" she asked. "I . . . broke some of the rules when I left home."

"Important rules?" he asked quietly.

"Yes. The most important." Her hand fisted on her thigh, small and so fine boned that he sometimes wondered how she handled the tools necessary to her profession. Even with all the advances in tech, wrenches were still heavy; torque still required muscle.

"I never did think about breaking the rules," Stefan said. "The rules are safe. It's why my race chose Silence over a hundred years ago." Of course, had his conditioning been without flaw, he would've had difficulty even talking about the protocol.

Tazia turned a little on the rock, enough that she could look at his face. "I've heard rumors about why, but never knew if they were true."

"Our psychic abilities are powerful, but they predispose us to insanity and violence."

"Doesn't that scare you?" Then she half smiled. "Of course not. You're Silent."

Stefan thought about how to respond to that. It was something he'd never have considered before Tazia, but her honesty deserved his own. "My Silence is problematic because of the trauma I suffered in childhood."

What even most Psy didn't know about Silence was that the conditioning for those like Stefan, people with dangerously strong abilities, was reinforced by pain controls termed dissonance. If Stefan broke Silence on any level, he'd be punished with pain. The worse the breach, the more debilitating the pain, until it was possible it could kill him . . . Or that was how it was *meant* to work.

Part of the reason Stefan had been shifted from Arrow training to the commercial arm of the Council's telekinetic arsenal was that his brain was deeply resistant to certain aspects of the conditioning process, including the dissonance controls. His psychic trainers had finally declared it to be a fundamental flaw, one that could not be fixed.

No one had wanted to release such a strong telekinetic into the commercial team, but a soldier without foolproof conditioning couldn't be trusted in the field. He might fracture and, with his dissonance controls erratic at best, no one could be certain he wouldn't take his partner or team with him when he lost control of his telekinetic powers.

Tazia's eyes widened. "So do you feel?"

"I don't know." What he did know was that things had begun

to change in him the first time he'd spoken to Tazia Nerif, parts of the conditioning just falling away. "I'm not as perfect a Psy as I should be."

"No, you're not." Tazia's dark eyes held his. "You care too much about these people."

Even if Stefan didn't know if he felt, Tazia knew. He'd almost burned himself down to the bone already.

When he straightened in the water, his shoulders and upper body came fully into view. She sucked in a breath, her gaze taking in the muscle and tendon that was all that was holding him together at the moment. "You're too thin, Stefan." She hadn't understood until this week just how much energy psychic power burned.

"I can run until it's no longer necessary," he said, as if he were a machine.

"*Stefan.*"

He met her furious gaze. "I am keeping track of my physical health, Tazia . . . I promise."

She nodded jerkily, his words feeling as if they meant far more than he'd said. When he rose farther, she blushed and looked away. "Are you feeling better?"

"Yes. You should bathe—your muscles are as tired."

"I didn't have half a house fall on me." Waiting until he was dressed in a slightly damp pair of pants that she'd fetched for him, she said, "It's still hot out. Go check on the clothes I left on the rocks. Your pants will dry quicker outside, too."

Stefan accepted the command without argument and left. Stripping quickly, she got into the water—*oh, it was hot!*—and used handfuls of the sand she could feel around the bottom of the pool to scrub her body. Might as well exfoliate if she couldn't wash properly. It would get all the dirt off.

She even used the sand on her face, albeit a little more gently. As for her hair, she dunked it under the water and hoped the minerals in the spring would help cleanse it.

Though she tried to be quick, she couldn't fight the need to linger for just a few minutes, let the heat soak into her aching flesh. Groaning as she got out, she dried off then, skin hot, wrapped the towel around herself before gathering up the clothes she'd stripped off and walking through the gloom to the entrance. "Stefan?"

"I'm here." He stirred in the shadows to the left.

Placing the dirty items next to her, she said, "I need some clean clothes."

A whisper of movement and then he was handing them to her. "They're a little damp still, but nothing that your body heat won't dry."

She took the small bundle and shifted back inside far enough that the shadows gave her cover. After quickly shimmying into the clothing—while trying not to think about the fact that Stefan had handled it all, including her panties and bra—she walked out, towel and dirty clothes in hand. "Thanks."

"You're welcome. Thank you for rinsing out the clothing; I believe the minerals in the spring did a good job of cleaning them."

Still embarrassed at their inadvertent intimacy, she kept her head down as they collected up the other clothing. It didn't take long, and soon enough, she was standing next to Stefan again, ready to be 'ported back to the village. "Wait," she said, urging him to turn toward her. "Let me see that bruise."

"It's too dark," Stefan murmured, but stepped close enough that she could push up his T-shirt and check the damage.

With so little distance between them, she could see him clearly, even in the dim early evening light. "It doesn't look as raw and swollen at least." Lowering the T-shirt lest she give in to the urge to touch him, feel his heart beating safe and strong under her palm, she said, "Okay, let's go. The villagers feel better just knowing you're nearby, especially with the aftershocks."

"I think they feel the same about you."

He 'ported before she could reply.

Chapter 6

THE NEXT DAY passed as the others had done—in hours of hard work. Sometime just after dark, Tazia blew out a breath and glanced at the villager who'd been her assistant throughout the continuing repair operation of the village's small power plant. The teenager had just begun an electronics course but was the most qualified person after the station manager—who was currently in an emergency medical tent with two broken arms and a bruised skull.

"Here we go," she said to her teen assistant and flicked a switch.

Nothing sparked, a low hum filled the air . . . and lights flickered on all around them. Cries of joy from outside told her the effect wasn't localized. High-fiving the boy when he raised his hand, she used the light to give the entire plant a thorough going-over.

Of course Stefan was still working when she finished; the lights had given him a longer work window. Shaking her head, she was walking toward him with the intention of giving him the nutrition bar in her pocket when the aftershock hit. It was violent, throwing her to the ground and making the already weakened structures around them collapse. She saw Stefan turn, yell out her name, and—

She was in the desert just outside the village, away from all the buildings, Stefan beside her. "Wait! Stefan!" Except it was too late. He was already gone.

He returned a second later with a small child, then another and another.

The shaking finally stopped.

Hugging the crying, distressed children, she calmed them down enough that they could walk back into the village. It was a mess. Leaving the children in the care of two previously injured women who were nonetheless stable and strong enough to take charge, she ran to what appeared to be the worst-affected part of the village.

Stefan was already lifting debris. Shoving up her sleeves, she joined in.

Hours passed.

Taking him water, she put her hand on his arm when he swayed. "You're about to flame out." He'd mentioned that term to her one night in their tent, told her it was worse than taking a rest. If he flamed out, his body and mind would just shut down, possibly for an entire twenty-four hours.

"I can feel a life, Tazia." His eyes were turbulent when he looked at her. "A small, flickering life beneath all the rubble."

"Oh, God." She looked at the sheer amount of debris that had to be shifted. "Okay, okay." Turning, she ran as hard as she could toward their tent. She grabbed a spare water bottle, filled it with fresh water and dumped in two vitamin packets, then shook it as she dug out several nutrition bars.

Stefan was shifting more of the wreckage when she returned. "Stop." She stood in front of him, touched her hand to his face when he didn't seem to see her.

"I can't."

"You'll be useless if you fall down. Drink." Ripping the wrappers off the nutrition bars one by one, she made him eat all of them.

His eyes didn't move off the rubble the entire time, the villagers focusing their efforts on the area he'd indicated. Looking at them, Tazia had an idea. "Look, you can't shift all that. It's too much."

"There's someone—"

She touched his face again, well aware she was breaking all kinds of taboos. His and her own. "Be smart, Stefan. I'm an engineer—I can see a way through that rubble. Shift only what's necessary to create a stable tunnel to the victim."

That got his attention. "How?"

"Step by step."

They worked together for the next two hours to create that tunnel, Tazia making judicious and careful use of Stefan's depleted abilities as well as the hands of the villagers. When the little girl who'd been trapped actually scrambled out of the tunnel on her own power, Tazia wanted to collapse to her knees in tears. Instead, she looked at Stefan and said, "Enough."

This time, he listened, going back to the tent to fall into an exhausted sleep so deep, she knew it'd be longer than six hours. That didn't matter. The important work had been done this night.

STEFAN woke to the scent of some kind of liniment. Glancing down, he realized immediately that someone had put it on his chest as well as on the shoulder he'd injured.

Tazia.

Regardless of his exhaustion, he'd have woken at any other touch. He didn't trust anyone else that much, wasn't physically comfortable so close to anyone but her; their time together here had erased any barriers he might've had. And when it came to Tazia, those barriers had always been thin at best.

Rising on that thought, he glanced at his timepiece and saw he'd been out for ten hours. Better than he'd expected, especially since he'd come to within a hairbreadth of a true flameout. When he stepped out into the sunshine, he saw nothing to say that there'd been a second aftershock.

Ten minutes later, he returned to work—after first consuming the fortified water and nutrition bars Tazia had left out for him. It was strange to know that someone who gained no current benefit from his abilities cared if he lived or died. He thought his mother must've truly cared because Stefan was her child, but after that, people had only cared because he was a Tk.

As the people on Alaris cared—if something happened to him, there went their emergency escape hatch.

However, out here, Tazia had no reason to care for him. He was doing nothing for her, and it wasn't as if she was trapped. Emergency transports were going in and out now on a relatively regular basis, so she didn't even need him to get her out of here. Her ticket back to the Alaris offices was also prepaid and in her possession.

There was no reason for her to care for him enough to find the liniment and smooth it on his chest; no reason to care enough to make sure he ate. It was as if she cared . . . for him. For Stefan, the man aside from his gift. He hadn't known that was possible.

"Sir." One of the villagers came to stand near him.

"Yes?" he said, having stopped telling them to use his name. They were in awe of his ability and refused to treat him any other way.

"Thank you." The man's eyes burned with wetness before he blinked the tears away, his throat moving as he swallowed. "My daughter," he said in what was clearly an unfamiliar language. "You save." He waved at the rubble where the tunnel had been. "Thank you."

Stefan went to say it had been a group effort, then recalled Tazia's words about being gracious. "Is she well?"

"Yes." The man beamed. "Happy."

Stefan nodded, and that seemed to be enough.

Later that night, as they lay in their tent, he told Tazia what had happened.

She said, "They see you as a god. If you moved here, you could have your own fiefdom, complete with the requisite nubile virgins to attend to your every need."

Having witnessed such interaction between other members of the Alaris crew, including between Tazia and her friend Andres, he thought perhaps he was being teased. It was . . . welcome. No longer was he standing outside looking into Tazia's complex, mul-tihued world; she had invited him in.

"I wouldn't wish to rule," he said seriously. "There is no privacy for those who rule."

"And you like yours." Rustling sounds, as if she was shifting in her sleeping bag to face him. "How's your chest, your shoulder?"

"Fine."

A sigh before she got up and flicked on a flashlight. "Let me see."

A week ago, he wouldn't have cooperated, but tonight, he made no protest as she pointed the light at his bare skin. He'd peeled off his T-shirt before lying down on his sleeping bag to rest; he'd first asked Tazia if it was all right. She'd blushed under the warm dark honey of her skin but nodded. Now, however, there was no blush, just clear-eyed concern as she touched him gently after glancing at him to check if he objected.

He didn't.

He watched her as she examined him, and his hand rose as if of its own volition to tuck a tendril of her hair behind her ear. Fingers stilling, she glanced at him for an endless heartbeat, then continued her examination. "It looks all right, but let me put on some more of the liniment. It helped earlier, didn't it?"

"Yes." He could've easily put the liniment on himself, but he didn't offer to do so. And as she ministered to him, he bore the psychic stabs of pain generated by his mind, without flinching.

The dissonance was nothing, less painful than when the debris had fallen on him. It *should've* been much sharper and brighter—had been a year ago, when he'd first seen Tazia's eyes light up as she smiled, and felt something strange happen inside him. He'd thought his inexorable compulsion toward the station engineer would fade once he knew her, but it had grown with each word they'd spoken to one another, each time he'd seen her or heard her laugh or even read a report she'd turned in.

At this rate, his already erratic dissonance would degrade into nothing soon. If he wanted to keep his mind free of psychic coercion and not attract any unwanted Psy-Med attention, he'd have to be very, very careful not to give any indication of the disintegration in public.

In private, however . . .

He lay quietly as Tazia spread the liniment gently over his bruises, her delicate touch rippling sensation over every inch of his skin. "There," she murmured, not mentioning the fact that one of his hands was brushing her knee. "Sleep now."

Stefan didn't want her to move away, but he remembered what she'd said about her cultural mores and kept his silence. He would not do anything to cause her distress. Listening to her settling in, he waited for the rhythm of sleep, and when he heard only wakefulness, said, "Our next trip upside, would you like to see the northern lights?"

"What?"

"The timing will be right. I can 'port us to a suitable location without problems." Pausing, he said, "No visas, no airfares required."

Her laughter was startled and bright. "I've always wanted to see them."

"You'll find them beautiful." Her spirit would see more than color and sky and movement. She'd see something deeper, and she'd teach him to see it, too. As she'd taught him how to interact with the people here. "Good night, Tazia."

"Tazi," she whispered softly. "You can call me Tazi."

IT was just over a week later that they left. Additional rescue forces had arrived in bulk, bringing with them machinery capable of shifting the remaining rubble. With the aftershocks having died down, the village was now in good shape.

"Our assistance is no longer required here," Stefan said that morning. "I suggest we decamp and start getting back in shape. They'll never let us back on Alaris like this."

"Agreed." When she reached out to touch the jut of his collarbone, he didn't flinch. Somehow, they'd become accustomed to each other after so many days sleeping next to one another. For her, a girl who'd been brought up to share her intimate space with only her husband, it had been as much a discovery as for him. "You've lost considerable weight." His telekinesis burned massive amounts of energy.

"So have you." He didn't touch her, but his eyes, those *eyes*, they ran over her from head to foot.

The two of them left quietly minutes later, though she knew full well Stefan would've been feted like a hero should he have given anyone the slightest indication that he was leaving. But that wasn't who he was. 'Porting them to the closest large city for which he had a visual location lock, he checked them into a two-bedroom suite in a small, family-run hotel that had once been the residence of a famous artist.

She didn't object to the intimacy, no matter if it was breaking another taboo to cohabit with him in such private quarters. Being with Stefan made her happier than she'd been for a long time.

"What do you want to do?" he asked, after they'd dropped their bags in their rooms.

"Shower properly, eat, then sleep."

"You can have the bathroom first." He sat down to take off his dusty boots. "I'll research where we can find a good meal."

Laughing, she said, "There are market stalls everywhere. We'll get some street food."

"Is that wise? Our bodies aren't used to the bacteria in this region."

"We've both had our inoculations." It was ridiculous how many things they had to get inoculated against in order to work on Alaris.

"We also have to be healthy to get back on board."

"Hmph." Giving in, she went and showered, scrubbing and scrubbing until she finally felt clean.

Afterward, she dressed in the local clothes she'd bought from the hotel boutique downstairs. She'd wanted something new and fresh, but she wasn't prepared for how the long, colorful skirt and pretty white blouse would remind her of home, the memories knives stabbing into her soul.

"Are you all right?" Stefan asked when she emerged.

"I will be." Her heart's ache would never disappear, but at times she could forget. "Go, shower."

He looked at her for long moments before disappearing into the bathroom. In the meantime, she separated out their dirty clothes from the duffels, no longer shy about going through his things after the many times she'd grabbed nutrition bars for him. Gathering it all, she sent it down to the hotel laundry.

Stefan, too, had bought new clothes and emerged wearing plain black pants in a material suitable for the desert climate, along with a long-sleeved white tunic that had white embroidery along the bottom edges and the neckline.

She smiled. "You look like one of the men from my village." Her fingers itched. "And your hair doesn't curl." She wanted to touch the silken strands, to run her fingers through them. "It has a wave." If he let it grow out, it'd be beautiful.

"I'll need to get it cut soon."

"Wait," she whispered. "Wait until you absolutely have to."

His look was quiet. "There is no requirement that I cut it, but it gives the correct impression. You understand?"

Because his Silence, she remembered, wasn't without flaw. "Yes." She would give up his beautiful hair if she could have this quiet, strong, courageous man who spoke to her, who looked at her in a way that made her feel as if she was a beauty. "Did you find somewhere for us to eat?"

"No," he said. "I investigated if the inoculations we received will protect us from the microorganisms in this region."

A smile in her heart. "And?"

"We should be safe."

Laughing, feeling giddy and young and happy, she walked downstairs with him and out onto the busy street.

Chapter 7

VOICES ROSE AND fell around them, a hundred conversations in progress.

Their hotel was located in the old quarter, where the streets were narrow and homes backed onto shops, the market stalls snug against one another. Cobblestones lay beneath their feet, the walls around them set with mosaics and the food cooked over flaming open-air stoves.

"Let's try this," she said, stopping at a stall serving up grilled vegetables on skewers.

She didn't say anything when Stefan paid, because in this part of the city, she could sense it was expected that he would pay. It would draw attention to them should she insist otherwise. Taking two skewers, she gave him one, then said, "Wait," and bit into hers.

Spices burst to life on her tongue, along with a hint of honey.

"Mmm. Delicious, but I think it may be too intense for you." Nutrition bars were tasteless, as was most Psy food from what she knew. "Have a little bite first."

He did, chewed carefully. "Do you want the rest?"

Nodding, she took it. "That stall there." She pointed to one doing flatbreads. "It looks like it has a simple potato filling. I think you'll like that."

He took her advice and bought one for himself after she shook her head, enjoying the vegetable shish kebabs. Biting into the stuffed flatbread, he nodded to tell her that she'd been right, and they continued to walk and look at things. Once they'd finished the first things they'd bought, the two of them tried more, succeeded with some, not with others, but they were full soon enough.

Sipping at a cup of sweet, spiced milk tea as they walked, the taste making her remember home, miss home, she tried to focus on the color and beauty all around them. "I *desperately* want to buy that," she said to Stefan, pointing out a vivid aqua and silver two-piece garment; the skirt glittered with hundreds of tiny mirrors, the simpler top long sleeved and cuffed at the wrists, thin silvery threads woven into the fabric. There was a silver scarf, too, she suddenly saw, made of the finest, most expensive hand-woven lace.

"Why don't you?"

Her shoulders shook. "Where would I wear it? Something like that is meant to be worn at a wedding or some other big function." She grinned at him. "Maybe I should work on the engines wearing it. Tazia, Queen of the Engine Room."

"The grease would ruin it."

Clapping a hand over her mouth to stifle her laughter, she looked at his expressionless face. Despite that, she was certain he'd made a joke. "How about one of those for you?" She pointed to a fez, the traditional round hat with a tassel attached to the top that hung down the side.

"I'm not sure it would inspire confidence in my abilities."

This time, she gave in to her laughter, leaning up against a wall opposite a stall selling nuts of every conceivable kind. Stefan stood to her left and slightly in front of her, blocking her from the view of a passing group of young males. Again, it was exactly what he should've done—most people would assume that she was in his care, and as such, he was responsible for her safety.

"Have you studied this region?" she asked, curious how he knew what he should do, when the Psy culture was so very different from this place where time moved at a slower pace.

"Yes." Pushing off the wall when she indicated she was happy to continue walking, he walked silently beside her.

"Why? Were you stationed here?"

"No." A pause. "Because of you. I wanted to know where you came from."

Tazia felt her cheeks color, the tips of her ears growing hot. "You never spoke to me much except about station business."

He didn't answer her until they were almost to the end of the street, heading toward a garden that had an old fountain as its centerpiece. "I didn't know how."

Taking a seat on the stone bench around the fountain, Tazia put the half-empty cup of tea beside her and rubbed her hands on her skirt, her nerves taut. Stefan stood in front of her, his bearing as military-straight as always. Protected from the sun by the shadow thrown by his body, she looked up into his eyes and said, "Sit with me."

He took a seat, his gaze watchful though the garden was relatively empty.

"My father always called me a spark," she began, and it was the first time she'd spoken to anyone about the life she'd once had. "My brother was the steady, calm one of the two of us. He was well suited to life in our village, to working in the huge fig and date groves that bring the village its income."

"You weren't born to be a farmer."

"No." She smiled a bittersweet smile, her hands gripping the edge of the bench on which they sat. "My father said that, too. That was why he supported my studies—he made me do my homework, got me what I needed in terms of study aids, paid for advanced classes I could take through the computer."

"It sounds like he was proud of you."

"Yes." She swallowed. "But you see, he thought I'd end up running the power station in the village—it's the biggest, most prestigious job there. And really, really important."

"So far out, power can save lives."

"Yes." As they'd both seen in the quake zone. "But I'd learned how to run the power station by age sixteen, and I knew there was so much more out there in the world. So I applied for a scholarship on my own, one that meant I could study engineering." She could still remember how her pulse had fluttered, how her palms had sweated as she filled in the online application form.

"Did the rift happen then?"

"No." Her heart ached again, a throb of sorrow. "I was so scared he'd be angry at what I'd done, but my father was *so* proud that his daughter was one of only five students in the entire country chosen for a scholarship based on academic merit. He told everyone, held a celebration." Tazia swallowed her tears as her mind filled with memories of the way her father had danced her across the square, her skirt swirling around her legs.

"When the time came, I was afraid to go to the big city to study." All at once, she'd realized she'd be far from home, from family. "But my father spoke to a friend he had in the city, and I boarded with them." Jedim Nerif had made sure his spark of a daughter had a family away from family. "They had a girl at university, too, and she helped me, but I went home every holiday I could. I missed everyone so much."

Stefan no doubt knew how this story would end, but he stayed silent, let her speak.

"I was happy to be done with my studies, to return home. But I knew even then that I'd have to leave again if I was to practice as an engineer." She blew out a breath. "I thought I could send money back, help the village, but my father, he hadn't given up on his dream that I'd run the power station . . . or that I'd marry the son of the man who was a good friend."

Stefan, forearms braced on his thighs, sun on his hair, seemed to go motionless. "He wished to force you into marriage?"

"No, Stefan, it wasn't like that. He knew Kabir and I were friends, that Kabir was a good man who would care for me and who would support me in my important job." She tried to make Stefan understand. "In my culture, the father is responsible for his daughter's happiness. If I'd said I didn't like Kabir, or even that I'd met another suitable man, he might've been angry, but he wouldn't have forced the match.

"But what I said was that I didn't want to marry at all." She could still see the shock on her father's face at her declaration. "I knew if I did, I'd never be able to do what I wanted to with my life, which was to work on the Alaris team. If not that, then another location that'd test my skills." She'd been so hungry for knowledge. "All the men my father would've accepted as suitable came from the village, and they would've all wanted me to stay there. Even Kabir wouldn't have been so accepting as to allow his wife to work on an island far from the village, then in an undersea station, and only return home one month out of four or five."

Stefan's eyes were dark when they met hers. "Your father could not forgive you for stepping so far outside the lines?"

"He'd gone as far as he was able, and you have to understand," she said softly, "it was *far* for a man of his age and time and culture. He was a very good father." Shuddering, she surreptitiously wiped away the tears she hadn't been able to keep from falling. "But when I walked away from the marriage and from his dream of me holding the most important job in the village, it was too far."

. . .

STEFAN didn't know how a normal man, one whose emotions hadn't been Silenced as a child, would react in such a situation, but he knew what Tazia needed. Except he had to wait until they were alone, where there was no risk he'd be reported. This area wasn't heavily populated by Psy, but there were enough around that he might be recognized.

He held his instincts in check the entire way back to the hotel, the control grinding at him. Tazia's shoulders were bowed, her face wan. Closing and locking the hotel door behind them, he put his hands on her shoulders and turned her around. When she didn't resist, he enclosed her in his arms, keeping his hold gentle.

Until she burrowed into him, her hands fisted against his chest. He tightened his hold, held her as she cried. Right then he was helpless in a way he hadn't been since he was that bleeding, desperate child trying to shift half a mountain off his family. There was nothing he could move or shift for her, nowhere he could take her at this instant.

All he could do was hold her.

When he felt her stop crying after a long, long time, he lifted her into his arms and carried her to her bedroom. Placing her on the bed, he lay down beside her curled-up body . . . and sensed the pain controls snap one by one, the fragile foundations on which they'd been laid no longer in any way hospitable.

It should've been excruciating, but he felt only a sense of freedom, as if he could finally *breathe*. The medics who'd evaluated him couldn't have known the extent of the weakness in his conditioning or they'd never have let him out into the world. But then, he hadn't realized the magnitude of the fault lines inside him until Tazia had walked into the station.

Something in him had broken that day.

Today, the already fractured ice splintered into countless shards.

Curving his body around her smaller one, one arm under her neck, the hand of his other on her hair, he just stayed with her. She didn't reject his touch, her body melting into his as they lay there beneath the afternoon sunlight that slanted into the room through the blue-painted wooden blinds. Used to the rhythms of her sleep, he sensed when she gave in to exhaustion.

He knew he should rise. Tazia wouldn't want a man who wasn't her husband to sleep with her in her bed. But when he tried to retrieve his arm, she made a complaining sound and wriggled closer. He could've easily reached into her mind, her human shields thin, and woken her, but he would never breach that trust. The only time he would ever enter Tazia's mind was if she invited him in.

"Stefan." A sleepy murmur.

"Shh. I'll go."

"No." She curled her fingers over his arm. "Stay."

It was the only word he needed to hear. Settling, he let the sun warm his skin as Tazia's presence warmed parts of him he hadn't known existed, and he slept.

THEY didn't wake again until sometime in the night hours, the world hushed around them. Having forgotten to bring in food for later, they ate all the tiny boxes of crackers and cheese in the hotel suite, as well as the packets of nuts, drank enough water to counter the salt, then fell asleep again. And this time when they ended up in the same bed, it wasn't by happenstance.

Tazia turned in the doorway to her room, looked at him over her shoulder, and in her eyes was a quiet invitation. He went because he couldn't say no to Tazia, and they slept again, this time even more closely intertwined, his legs tangled with hers, her arm around his waist and his hand fisted in her hair.

He woke in the morning to the feel of her slipping away, but there was no awkwardness when they met again afterward. This day followed the same pattern as the last, their bodies yet needing rest and fuel. They ate more, rested more, spoke of things Stefan had never spoken about with anyone.

"Telekinetics are a very useful designation," he told her where she sat beside him on the small sofa in their hotel suite, the two of them involved in demolishing a room service meal set out on the coffee table in front of them.

"Try this." She fed him a small bite of a pastry of some kind. "Yes?"

Nodding, he took it to eat the rest. She'd easily understood what tastes he could and couldn't tolerate, was skilled at finding things he could eat. "Is there more of this?"

"Yes." A smile. "I put the rest on the counter, so we'd have more space here." Sipping at a glass of water, she said, "So because telekinetics are so useful, you're of more interest to the powers that be?"

He nodded. "We're almost always taken for very early training, and inducted into the Council's superstructure on some level."

"Don't the families get a say?"

"Of course. A child is a family's genetic legacy and a Tk is a financial one as well. Most families are agreeable to child Tks being trained under the Council's aegis because it can be expensive as well as difficult to train us—we can be volatile and inadvertently danger-ous." He telekinetically lifted and "threw" the serrated bread knife in a silent demonstration of the chaos a child might cause.

Chapter 8

STOPPING THE KNIFE'S trajectory before it hit the wall, he brought it back to the coffee table. "Once trained, we earn excellent incomes; if the family didn't agree to a lump sum when they signed the child over to the Council, they later receive a percentage of the adult child's income."

Lines on her forehead. "Is that usual?"

"Yes. In many ways, Psy families are as linked as changeling packs and human family groups."

Tazia was silent for a long time. "But to give up a child . . ."

"Yes." He'd thought about the duality of loyalty among his people more than once. "Yet consider it from my mother's point of view. She cared for me, of that I have no doubt." Even a Psy child could tell when his mother's hand was gentle on his head, when his hurts were tended to with more than cold distance. "But she was an M-Psy, a medic. She didn't have any idea how to protect a telekinetic child from his own power."

Seeing he had Tazia's full attention, he continued. "According to my records, one day when I was just over a year old, I apparently broke every glass in the kitchen while playing. My mother found me sitting on the floor surrounded by shards of glass. It was a miracle I hadn't been sliced or cut."

"My God," Tazia gasped. "If you'd crawled over the shards . . ."

"Yes. So you see, when my mother arranged training for me, she did so out of a need to protect me from myself." Stefan had never felt anything but grateful to his mother for that. "She also never gave me up totally as some families do. I came home after school, and I knew I had a choice about where I would go with my life."

"Didn't the Council object?" she asked. "Since telekinetics are so rare?"

"I'm sure they must've pressured her, but even the Council can't steal children, though I'm sure some children *are* simply taken, if their parents are too weak or too low-profile for anyone to notice if they have an 'accident.'" Stefan had no illusions about the leadership of his race. "But my mother was a respected medic, well published in her field."

"You don't think the landslide was caused by a Council Tk, do you?"

"No. There was too much damage—the Council lost an adult telekinetic in the same event, as well as a cardinal telepath. It was a natural disaster." A disaster that had forever altered the course of his existence. "My mother was the last of her line, and after her death, my care fell to the state."

"What about your father?"

"He had no rights per the conception and fertilization agreement that resulted in my birth—and, given the Council's interest in me, he made no move to void the agreement and gain custody." Even now, though Stefan knew his father's identity, he felt no sense of kinship—the other man was a stranger to him. "As a result, I ended up where my mother had never wanted me to end up: alone in the hands of the Council."

Tazia curled her fingers gently around his. "I think she would've been proud of the man you became."

Looking into her face, Stefan could almost believe that. "I'm fractured inside, Tazi. The scars of childhood should've long healed, and yet they mark me still."

Her eyes intent, she broke their handclasp to push up the sleeve of the soft blue blouse she'd bought from the market. "See this?" She pointed to a scar just below her elbow. "I got this when I fell onto a rock while playing with my brother."

Rubbing his finger over the faded line, he said, "A physical scar is permitted. A mental one, never."

"According to who?" Her fingers delicate against his jaw, the touch a fleeting one. "We're all marked by life, Stefan. The only difference is that your people like to pretend they aren't, that the Psy go through it coated in protective armor." Breath soft against him as their faces drew closer. "You're not fractured. You're just like the rest of us, living life and getting a few knocks and bumps along the way."

Her lips were so close, he could've bent his head, ended that distance, initiated a physical intimacy unlike any he'd ever experienced in his life. Even had the pain controls still been functioning, he wouldn't have cared, would've done it. The thing that stopped him was the thought of harming Tazia.

"Tazi," he said softly, and it was a question.

Skin flushing with color, a sparkle in her eye. "My friends in the village," she whispered, her lips brushing his, "they stole kisses during the festivals." Her fingers curved around his nape. "I was always too shy and too awkward to do so, but the elders looked the other way if things didn't go further."

His hand cupping her neck and the side of her jaw, he angled his head to deepen the contact. Her pulse stuttered under his hand, her skin hot as he closed his lips over her bottom one. Making a delicate sound in her throat, she held on tighter to his nape.

"Tazi."

"Yes?" Her pupils were huge when she met his gaze.

"I've never done this before."

A startled pause before her lips curved and she wrapped both arms around his neck. "Neither have I. Do you think we can figure it out?"

"You're the engineer," he murmured, enthralled by the vibrant life of her. "You're very good at figuring things out."

Eyes lit from within, she said, "Let me see." A heartbeat later, she did the same thing to his lip that he'd done to hers, the caress a sweet courtship.

It was natural to respond to her touch by tasting her upper lip, and then . . . then there was no more thought, simply the furious thudding of their hearts and the damp heat of their kisses as they explored and learned together. Neither of them tutored in the skill, they simply did what felt good and everything felt good.

So good that his shields on the PsyNet would've come under critical strain had he not been bolstering them since the day Tazia walked onto the station and into his life. Layers and layers and layers, those shields kept these forbidden sensations from leaking out into the vast psychic network that connected all Psy on the planet but for the renegades. His telekinetic power was more difficult to control; it strained at the leash until the bed in the next room thumped up then down.

Tazia jerked, glanced over. "Did you do that?"

"Yes. I can't control the Tk." Not when she was cradled in his arms, her body almost on his lap. "My focus is too fractured." That could prove catastrophic.

Tazia ran her finger over his lips. "As an engineer, I think you should focus your telekinesis into something that requires large amounts of energy but that is nondestructive."

Thinking about it, he kissed her again. When they broke apart this time, the water in the jug was boiling so hard, steam puffed in the air, and Tazia was laughing. "Can you train yourself to do that automatically?"

"I should be able to." It would work for a kiss, but anything deeper and he'd have to come up with other ways to safely discharge his telekinetic energy. On Alaris, it could be dangerous to . . . but he was thinking too far ahead, wanting too much. This was a moment out of time. Nothing Tazia had said gave him a reason to believe their relationship would continue on Alaris.

"Now I understand," she said, stroking her fingers along his jaw, "why my friends stole those kisses."

And though Tazia had no other such experience with which to compare it, she knew Stefan's kiss was the only one she wanted. A woman knows, her mother had said to her once.

"When my father said for me to meet your father, I knew he was hoping for a match, for I'd already turned down three offers. But I was determined not to say yes until I knew—and the instant your father took my hand as we walked in the family gardens, I knew."

It had taken Tazia longer because she hadn't *seen* Stefan for a long time, hadn't known the flesh-and-blood man beneath the Psy armor, a man of honor and courage and incredible heart. "I'm sorry," she whispered, "for not knowing you."

"How could you?" he said, one of his hands heavy and warm on her lower back. "I didn't let you see me. I haven't let anyone see me since childhood. Not even my Arrow brethren know me as you do." He'd told her about the squad, about how he was a shadow member of it.

Swallowing, Tazia laid her head against his shoulder. "I'm the same. I haven't let anyone truly see me either, not since I left the village. Only you know the real Tazi."

He stroked her hair. "It is a gift you give me, Tazi. One I will always honor."

As she lay in his arms, Tazia thought about what would happen when this break was over and they were back on Alaris. Would they return to their shells until the next time? The thought was unbearable. Yet, what was the alternative? That she become his clandestine lover? No, she couldn't do that; it would be a step too far from the rules of her people. Slowly but surely, such a thing would break her heart into irreparable pieces.

And it wasn't only her needs and desires at stake.

"What happens if someone finds out you've breached Silence?" she whispered.

Stefan's embrace tightened. "Normally, for such a critical breach, the individual would be rehabilitated, his or her mind erased by a psychic brainwipe that would leave the rehabilitated near to a vegetable." Speaking past her cry of horror, he said, "That's unlikely to happen to me—I'm too valuable. But they would do their best to erase the Stefan you know, erase the part of me that says you are mine."

Such a beautiful declaration hidden in the horror, such an impossible situation.

THEY slept and rested further for the two days that followed, and by unspoken agreement, they always slept together. Tazia well understood that she was breaking the rules in this, too, but knowing their time here would end all too soon, she couldn't not steal the joy of sleeping in Stefan's arms. Who would know if she broke faith with the teachings of her people? Her people, after all, had disowned her.

And yet, it mattered.

"I wish I could be like the new scientist on Dr. Night's team," she whispered to Stefan as they lay together on the bed, the moonlight coming through the blinds to create elusive patterns on their clothed bodies.

"Avril Lee?"

"Yes." Avril had bright pink hair and a mouth that knew no boundaries. "I would like to not care what the world thought of me, not care about the rules."

"If you were like Avril, you would not be Tazi."

Her lips curved. "So simple?"

"Yes." Playing with her hair as he so often did now, he said, "You told me we are shaped by life. Your life has shaped you into a woman who honors the ways of her people even as she walks her own path. There is nothing to be sorry about in that."

Heart falling ever deeper for him, she thought of an eternity where all they could have were broken pieces of time, hidden from the world. Her soul keened. But to never have him at all? No, that was the worse sentence.

Could she become his secret lover after all?

Could she live with herself if she made that choice, or would her feelings of guilt poison the heartbreaking tenderness of the luminous thing between them?

She wished she could ask Teta Aya, or ask her mother, but there was no elder here to offer her guidance.

So she slept, her dreams a torment.

The next day, while they sat on the bed, playing a board game for no reason but that it was fun, Stefan said, "Your village is not far from here."

"Yes." She placed a hand over her heart as the bruise pulsed.

"I've recovered fully." Quiet words. "I can 'port you there."

Hope was a hot burn . . . followed by cold ashes. "No. It'll only distress my family." She wouldn't hurt her parents for all that she needed to see them. "And I can't bear to have them turn away from me again." The image of her parents turning their backs the first time haunted her.

Stefan said nothing, not for long moments. "Do you have an image of a public place in your town?"

"Yes, I have digital images." The wind from the open window brought with it the scents and sounds of the thriving city beyond. "But that would be worse than teleporting into the family home."

"Not if we do it in the heart of night."

Game forgotten, she stared at him. "There's never anyone in the small square behind the markets after dark. I took pictures of it because it's beautifully tiled." Getting off the bed, she found her phone and got back on beside him, quickly scrolling through the photos. "There, see?"

Stefan went through all her images of the square. "I can 'port there," he said at last. "The pattern of tiling combined with the cracked section on the left is highly distinctive."

That afternoon, they went out and bought scarves to hide their faces, as well as black local dress for Stefan so that he'd attract as little attention as possible, despite his height. As for her, she wore one of the skirts and tops she'd already purchased. Getting him to sit on the bed long after night had fallen, the world so very quiet, she wrapped the black scarf around him desert-style, covering his hair, then bringing it around to cover his mouth and nose.

"You look like a warrior out of the old movies," she teased him, her stomach flipping at the intensity of the eyes that watched her.

Stefan could say more with his eyes than most men could with a thousand words.

As she wrapped a more feminine scarf around her head in a gentler style, leaving her mouth and nose visible for now, he told her he found her beautiful. And looking into his eyes, she felt that way. "No grease streaks for once," she said, nervous.

"I have a confession." He rose from the bed. "I only used to say that to have an excuse to speak to you. Sometimes you didn't have grease on your face. I lied."

Startled into laughter, she walked into his arms. "Like a boy pulling at a girl's pigtails to get her attention?"

"Yes. I've never lied to you about any other thing."

"I know." She stepped back with that, looked into his face and touched her fingertips to his. "I'm ready."

Chapter 9

WITHOUT A WORD, he 'ported her to the place that had been her home and her heartbreak. Tears burned in her eyes as she looked around the square currently swathed in shadows, dawn about four hours away, but she didn't let them fall. The fountain was quiet this night, likely because the rains hadn't yet come and no one wanted to waste water, even for such a pretty sight. Instead, painted flowerpots ringed the fountain, no doubt put there by those in the neighborhood, the villagers taking pride in their public spaces.

She saw a child's toy set neatly atop one of the tables to the side of the square, to be picked up by a parent or the child the next day. No one worried about their belongings being stolen or lost, the community large enough for a relatively big power station but too small and tightly knit for people to be strangers. Any would-be miscreant was quickly brought to heel.

"Are we in the right place?" Stefan's voice was dark velvet against her senses.

She gave a jerky nod. "This way." Taking his hand, she led him through night-dark streets to a home with a simple door that she knew led to a spacious, graceful courtyard within. It wasn't locked when she tested the latch, and, heart thudding, she dared walk into the paved front entranceway before sneaking around to the side gate to enter the main courtyard.

A tiny red light flared in the dark just as her foot touched the courtyard. Tazia froze. *"Teta."* Her voice shook, her eyes wet.

Dropping her sneaky rolled cigarette, her grandmother rose and almost ran to her. "Tazi, it's you," she said joyously in a language Tazia hadn't heard for years. "My sweet Tazi come home at last."

Letting her grandmother's wrinkled arms wrap around her, Tazia allowed the tears to fall. Beside her, Stefan remained a quiet, dark statue. When her grandmother drew back, her own eyes were red, her cheeks wet. "So long you have been gone, Tazia."

"I wasn't wanted," Tazia said. "You know I wasn't wanted."

"Pfft!" Her grandmother waved her hand, but there was sadness in her eyes for the years lost. "Come, sit with your *teta*."

They sat, her grandmother tiptoeing inside to make them cups of sweet milk tea, over Tazia's protests, and bring out tiny cakes flavored with almonds and figs. "Your young man is very quiet."

"Yes," she said, her gaze meeting Stefan's.

He'd pulled away the scarf from his mouth and nose to bare his face, a face that was so precious to her now.

"So." Her grandmother narrowed her eyes at him, switching languages at the same instant. "What are your intentions toward my Tazi?"

Coloring, Tazia went to speak, but Stefan beat her to it. "I would marry her if she will have me," he said, and her heart thundered. "Yet I cannot, not in a way that could get back to the Council."

"You're Psy then." Her grandmother nodded. "If it's marriage you want, then there are ways."

"Teta Aya, as soon as we file the paperwork," Tazia said, all the while wanting to run into Stefan's arms, "the Council will—"

"Pfft!" Her grandmother waved her hand again. "Paperwork is

a creation of the modern world. Do you think they had paperwork four hundred years ago—no, all they had was love and witnesses. That is how my great-grandmother many times removed was married, and no one said she was unmarried."

Tazia's nails dug into her palms. "Will you give us your blessing?" At least one of her family would bless her marriage.

"Always." Her grandmother put down her tea and cupped Tazia's face in her soft, warm hands. "You are my grandchild, Tazia. Always you will be my grandchild, should you decide to marry a goat." A twinkling laugh. "Though your young man is no goat. He is handsome and will help you make beautiful babies."

Said in English, the words had Tazia blushing and refusing to look at Stefan. For an instant, she almost felt like a bride, shy with her would-be husband, and then the moment passed. Still, the cold within her was not so bad anymore, not with her grandmother's hands warm on her face. "I love you, Teta." It was a balm on her soul, the knowledge that at least one person in her family still accepted her.

Her grandmother shook her head, her lips suddenly set in a thin line. "Wait." Heading inside, she was gone for so long that Tazia began to worry. When she did walk out, it was to tug Tazia inside.

"I can't," she whispered, heart in her throat.

"Shh." Her grandmother glanced at Stefan. "You will wait here."

Stefan inclined his head in a respectful nod, as if understanding that while Teta Aya was old, she was a power.

Quiet as a whisper, they tiptoed through the house until her grandmother brought her to a standstill in front of the open door to her parents' bedroom. Given that that door was never open at night, Tazia knew what her grandmother had been up to when she first came in. Leaning into the doorway, Tazia looked at the sleeping faces of her parents and cried silent tears.

I'm sorry I wasn't the daughter you wanted me to be.

Knowing she couldn't chance staying too long, she was about to leave when her grandmother pointed to something on the bed stand. Frowning, she squinted . . . and felt her whole world tilt sideways. Half a year ago, Alaris had allowed a photographer to come on board, do a photo essay. To her extreme embarrassment, a wrench-carrying Tazia had ended up on the cover of the magazine—in blue coveralls and complete with a streak of grease on her cheek as she stood laughing beside the guts of the facility.

That image sat lovingly framed in pride of place on the bed stand, beside photos of her brother's family. Shaking, she stepped back and out of the house. "Thank you, Teta." For giving her a gift of love that could never be stolen from her.

Her grandmother's hug was fierce. "You make us all proud, though some are too stubborn to show it." She kissed Tazia's cheeks. "Your father, he misses his small spark so fiercely. If only you weren't as stubborn as one another."

Tazia frowned. "I've tried so many times."

"Letters? Money?" Scowling, her grandmother shook her head. "You are the child, Tazi, a *beloved* child. If you wish for forgiveness, you must ask for it in person, as is respectful."

"She doesn't need forgiveness for she has committed no crime," Stefan said into the quiet, her grandmother having spoken in English.

Rolling her eyes, Teta Aya looked from one to the other. "Foolish children. It may be truth that you committed no crime, Tazi, but you broke your father's heart." The words hurt Tazia's own heart. "Whether he was right to feel thus is irrelevant; whether he is being a stubborn goat who is wrong in his thinking is irrelevant. Do you understand?"

Tazia stared at her grandmother's wise and elegant face, nodded slowly. "He can't set aside his pride, so I must set aside mine." When

Stefan stirred, she knew he didn't understand. "My father is a won-derful man," she told him, "but if he has a flaw, it is that he can't bear to be wrong." She touched her fingers to Stefan's jaw. "I don't mind bowing my head to him, Stefan. He is my father and I can forgive him this flaw."

Stefan nodded. "I understand now, Tazi. We are none of us per-fect." He stroked her hair. "And you are strong enough to be the one who bends."

"Ah, he understands you." Her grandmother smiled in beaming pride. "Yes, my Tazi bends, she does not break."

Turning, Tazia went to ask her grandmother how she could do this, how she could meet her father and apologize in a way that would let him save face with the village, when there was a noise in the doorway to the house. "Tazia?"

Her blood a deafening rush in her ears, she turned to find her father there; her mother stood behind him, her eyes sheened wet and a trem-bling hand raised to her mouth. There was no time to think, no time to come up with a plan, to work it all out. Wanting to wrap her hand tight around Stefan's but knowing that wouldn't be acceptable, not yet, she instead clasped her hands in front of her and bowed her head.

"I've come to ask forgiveness, Father," she said softly, barely able to hear her own words through the pained hope that was the hard beat of her pulse. "And your blessing on my marriage."

A gasp from her mother, silence from her father for so long that she began to worry . . . but then she saw his slippered feet in front of her, felt his hand on her hair. "So now you think to marry a man I do not know."

Tears in her throat, she swallowed. "That's why I've come home, Father. So you could meet him."

"Why should I listen to a daughter who takes so long to come home?"

That was when Tazia knew she'd been forgiven, because that was how her conversations with her father had always gone when she'd done something wrong. And her answer was the same as it had ever been. "Because I am your spark who does not always do what she should."

Enclosing her in his arms, her father squeezed her so tight that she couldn't breathe. She didn't care, and when her mother tugged her away to clasp her close, both of them crying, she forgot the world . . . but never Stefan. Wiping away her tears, she went to introduce him to her father but her mother squeezed her hand in a silent warning, a reminder that the man who came to ask for her hand would be judged on his own strengths and merits.

"So," her father said to Stefan, "you wish to marry my daughter."

"Yes. I am Stefan Berg." Stefan bowed his head enough for respect, but not enough that it would be seen as obsequious. "I would walk proudly with her, but to do so would put her at risk, so I ask you to give her to me in secret—I promise you I will guard her honor with my life, for I have no life without Tazia."

Her father's eyes were unreadable. "Come, Stefan Berg."

Watching after them as they walked off into the darkness, Tazia looked desperately to her grandmother. Who shook her head and said, "Sit, talk with your mother. If the man is worthy of you, he will prove his worth."

"He's never prepared for—"

"Who prepares?" her mother interrupted, eyes still teary. "Your father, he almost sweated off half his body weight when he came to ask my father for my hand after seeing me at a festival."

Nerves fluttering, Tazia nonetheless allowed her mother to lead her inside the house and to the kitchen. There, Kaya Nerif bustled around, making more tea and setting out snacks. "Mother," Tazia said, "this is a lot of food."

"Of course it is." Her mother tapped her on the cheek, then leaned down to press her lips to Tazia's forehead. "We'll have much talking to do if you are to be married before you leave—and others will come."

"No." Panic and fear bloomed in Tazia's heart. "We have to be careful. Stefan—"

"Is Psy." Her mother smiled. "I know, baby. Your brother, his wife and child, your friend Mina, who, you will be glad to know, has been cross with us this whole time." Her voice shook and she came to take Tazia into her arms again. "I am so sorry, my baby, but I had to stand with him in public. You two always made up before—I expected you would again in a heartbeat."

Tazia hugged her mother, the two of them rocking one another gently. "It's all right," she whispered, knowing her mother had been caught in a hard place. "I expected the same. I just . . . I didn't know I could simply come home."

"That is our fault," her mother said and her grandmother nodded. "We didn't love you enough that you ever doubted that."

Tazia started crying again. "No, you loved me so much."

They cried many more times through the hours, and in between the tears, Tazia learned that while her parents *had* given the money she'd sent to the holy man, they had done so as an offering, asking the holy man to pray for a cherished daughter who was alone so very far from home. More tears fell then, and all their eyes were red rimmed by the time her father and Stefan returned home.

Tazia was at the table rolling out sweet dough for tiny pastries, while her grandmother drank strong coffee in a small cup, and her mother put together fresh fruits and breads for breakfast. None of the food, Tazia was happy to see, would challenge Stefan.

Neither man said anything as they took their seats at the table with Teta Aya, the huge wooden sprawl of it big enough that Tazia could continue rolling out the dough as dawn colored the sky out-side and the men ate. She was bursting to ask what had happened, but she knew she had to be patient, wait for her father.

He laughed suddenly, eyes on her. "Still my spark, so impatient!" Kissing his wife's hand as she came to put tea in front of him and Stefan, he said, "We will hold your wedding in the courtyard at dawn tomorrow, while the village sleeps.

"Today, you will rest, then you and your man will spend time with your family, and the villagers will know only that my Tazi has come home to ask her family's blessing on her marriage, for she is a cherished daughter who knows that family is everything."

TAZIA had no private time with Stefan in the hours that followed, the two of them surrounded by family at every instant. Despite her mother's urgings, she didn't sleep, not even for an hour or two—she didn't want to waste a moment. Joy filled her veins at being with those she loved, and she kept looking over to check that Stefan was all right, especially when her brother insisted that he hold the baby.

Taking the fat, happy babe gingerly into his arms, Stefan looked very carefully into the child's face. "Your son's eyes are Tazia's," he said at last.

Tazia's brother grinned and looked to his wife. "Did I not say the same when he was but two days old?"

Tazia's sister-in-law, a sweet woman, smiled affectionately. "You did." Turning to Tazia, she said, "He insisted our son's second name be Tazir."

Tears burned Tazia's eyes again, and then she was being hugged by her brother, who whispered, "Why did you never sneak in to see me?" A question that held hurt and anger both. "I waited for you."

Tazia sobbed. "I thought you were angry with me."

"I was—but you are my sister." A crushing squeeze. "I will always protect you."

And that was how it continued for all the hours of the day, family and only the most trusted friends allowed in. Mina and her family, her father's dearest, oldest friend and his wife. That friend also happened to be the village official authorized to marry people.

"I will make the legal papers," the white-haired elder told them solemnly when he met with her and Stefan. "But I will not file them. Instead, I will give them into your keeping. When and if you can, you will file them."

"Thank you," Stefan said. "We'll do so the instant it becomes safe."

The older man nodded. "It is a thing for the world. You will be married in the eyes of the family and the village as soon as the dawn ceremony is complete."

Stefan disappeared for an hour after that, and Tazia worried until she saw his tall form beside her father and brother in the courtyard, where he was helping to put up the wedding pavilion of hanging silks. Not strictly according to tradition, for the groom wasn't meant to be at the bride's home until the time of the wedding, but the family was being flexible.

It was hard to sleep that night, and she twisted and turned. Part of her hoped Stefan would teleport to her, but she knew he was too respectful of her family to do so. The hours passed torturously . . . and heatedly, as she imagined the intimacies they would share once they were man and wife. She wanted to touch him, wanted to kiss him again and again, wanted his hands on her, wanted . . .

Sheets tangled around her legs, she came awake to her mother's soft, "Tazi, my Tazi. It is time to bathe and dress for your wedding." A gentle hand brushing back her hair, a kiss on the forehead, a smile in Kaya Nerif's dark gaze. "He loves you very much, your Stefan."

"I know," Tazia whispered. She didn't need words, saw the truth in those eyes that said so much.

It wasn't until a half hour later, after she'd bathed in rose-scented water that left her skin soft and silky, and her mother came in to help her dry her hair, that Tazia realized how her mother knew the truth of Stefan's love. "Oh." Her lower lip quivered.

In her mother's arms lay the beautiful aqua and silver outfit she'd admired, complete with the stunning scarf of fine silver lace.

Smiling, her mother laid out the clothing and cupped Tazia's cheeks. "You did well, daughter. A quiet man who does such things is worth far more than a man who says much and forgets to care for his treasures." Another kiss on her forehead. "Now sit and let me dry your hair. Today, my daughter gets married and I would have her look a princess."

Chapter 10

TAZIA FELT EXACTLY like a princess when she entered the wedding pavilion in her finery. Stefan, dressed in formal black but for a black and silver man's scarf she recognized as her father's, waited for her.

Oh, but she could not wait to call him her husband.

The ceremony was simple and poignant, the embraces afterward warm and loving.

"I wish we could stay," she said to Stefan when they had a moment together in a quiet corner as the delicate hues of dawn became true daylight.

"We can stay another day or two," he replied. "That'll give us enough time to get back to the Alaris offices on the jet and get in some exercise to further strengthen our bodies before we go back under."

"No." Tazia ducked her head, cheeks heating. "Much as I want to stay, I want more for us to have time as husband and wife."

Stefan cupped the side of her face. "As do I."

Turning her cheek into his touch, she blushed as Mina came over and waggled a finger. "Not yet, Tazi." Laughter filled her friend's expression. "You are yet in your father's house."

They stayed for another two hours and the leave-taking was filled not with tears but with joy, as they were ordered to return on their next trip upside. Many kisses and hugs later, Tazia walked into Stefan's arms, and with a last look at her family until the next time, they 'ported directly to their hotel suite.

It was warm with sunlight, the windows opened by the staff.

"I don't know how far we'll be able to go," Stefan said. "If there's a risk my ability will totally slip the leash, hurt you—"

She pressed her fingers to his lips. "I know. We go as far as we can go."

They kissed in the light, but the heat between them had nothing to do with the sun. His hands on either side of her face, Stefan glanced at the windows.

They all shut with a quiet snick, the shutters just open enough to color the room with a soft light that allowed them to see one another but kept the world out. When he lifted his hand to the pins that held her veil to her hair, she curled her hands against his chest and waited quietly. He took it off with care, and she saw it float to a gentle rest on the table.

"For our daughter," he said quietly, and owned her heart all over again. "She will not have to marry in secret."

She kissed him this time, this man who loved her and who she loved until it hurt, her fingers fisting in the silken, wavy hair that was just long enough to grip and that he'd get cut before they left. Mouth hot and wet, he thrust his own hands into her hair. Pins fell to the floor, her curls escaping her mother's loving creation for Tazia's wedding day.

Straining on tiptoe, she met him kiss for kiss, and when he swept her up into his arms, she sipped and sucked and licked at his lips until they tumbled into bed. The weight of his body on her own was unfamiliar, the scent of him in her every breath. And his smile, it was the most wonderful thing she'd ever seen. "I don't know how to do this either," he murmured against her mouth.

Nerves snapping into laughter, she touched fingers to his lips. "Neither do I. What will we do?"

"There's probably a manual," he said seriously.

"Probably." She reached for the collar of his tunic, her fingers trembling. "How hard can it be?"

Stefan's own hand slid up her stomach to lie on her breast. "Let's see," he murmured as her heart kicked.

Feeling scandalous, she tugged at his tunic and he pulled it over his head to throw it aside. When his eyes dipped to her own fitted top, she lifted her hands and undid the two hidden zips, then raised her arms. Reaching down, he stripped it off her in a single smooth motion. She brushed her hair off her face afterward to find his eyes on her breasts.

Those breasts were cupped in insubstantial black lace, the pretty underthings a gift from Mina. Her best friend had bought the set for Tazia on her own wedding trip and kept it until now, cheerfully optimistic that Tazia would one day find her own perfect mate and marry.

And she had.

That perfect mate bent to press a kiss to the creamy, never-exposed-to-sunlight curve of her breast, and she shivered . . . and realized he was trembling. His big body was held in fierce check, his hands gentle. Utterly undone, she clasped his face in her hands and kissed him with all the passion in her heart.

Warm muscle and strength, he gave her control, but then his hand closed over her lace-covered breast and neither one of them had any control. She didn't remember how they got the rest of their clothing off, but oh, it felt wonderful to have his skin against her own all over, to have his mouth taste her secret places, to taste him in turn.

They probably rushed everything, but they'd been waiting so long that patience was a futile hope. Locked together, their bodies connected on the most intimate level and their breaths one, they completed the final bond that made them husband and wife.

"Perhaps not a technically assured performance," Stefan murmured afterward, "but I have no complaints. What does my wife say?"

Feeling loose and soft and pleasured and his, she said, "That we should do it again."

They took it slower this time and it was just as good as the first fury. And this time, they remembered to fill the bath with water so that Stefan could redirect his energy, hoping it would work. As for the broken furniture, splintered kitchen counter and crushed ceiling fan, he would 'port it all away and they'd pay for the mysteriously missing items.

Luckily, no one had reported the noise of the destruction, the neighboring rooms apparently empty at this time of day.

The most important thing was that even in the throes of passion, Stefan had directed his Tk outward, not at her. "Silence did that at least," he said. "It gave me the skill to make sure I never inadvertently hurt you."

She sighed and shuddered as he stroked his hand over her body from breast to thigh, his eyes intent—as if he was drinking in the sight of her. She did the same in turn, his body beautiful in its strength and grace.

Dipping his head, he kissed her breasts with an open mouth, licking at the sensitive skin, and when she gasped, suckled wetly at one taut nipple. She bit her lip to keep from crying out, but then Stefan ran his hand over her ribs and lifted his mouth to repeat the caress on her neglected breast. Tugging at his hair, she brought him to her for a kiss as she wrapped her legs around his hips in shameless seduction.

One of his hands cupped the back of her thigh; he stroked as they kissed, said, "I love the way you feel. So silky and soft."

Breasts crushed up against his muscled chest, the surface abrasive with a light layer of chest hair, she shivered. "You feel better." All hard and rough and beautiful.

She petted his shoulders, shaped the muscle of him. "How are you so patient?" she asked, still a little shy with him. She might not be experienced, but she'd overheard the married women in the village talking, knew enough of biology to know a man often lost all control when he had a naked woman underneath him—especially a man who was violently aroused.

Like Stefan was right now.

His hand clenched on her thigh. "I wasn't the first time."

"Neither was I." She kissed his shoulder, a silly, happy smile on her face. "I'm not patient now, either." He was the one who was keeping them from rushing—left to her own devices, Tazia would've driven them over again by now, forgetting all about the slight, intimate soreness of her body.

"There are certain advantages to the kind of training I underwent as a Tk." Another lush kiss as he shifted his hand inward, touched the plump, wet folds between her thighs with a single caressing finger. "Does that feel good?"

Nodding at the low murmur, she kissed his throat, asked the same question. And they learned. For two days and two nights, they learned each other until there was no shyness and his skin against her own was something she needed to feel whole.

And they didn't speak about what would happen when the interlude ended.

Epilogue

THE TWO OF them passed their physicals with flying colors. Sitting in the small green park behind the offices the day before their departure for Alaris, Stefan said, "Tazi."

Her stomach tight, she turned. "Yes?"

"Do you have hope again?"

He'd remembered. It shouldn't have startled her, but it did. "Yes," she said, though her heart ached at having to go back to what they'd been before this, to waiting at least three more months until they could touch again. "Did you know, Stefan?"

"What?"

"That my home wasn't far from the site of the quake."

"Yes."

Of course he had. Stefan never did anything by chance. "Thank you."

"There's no need. You've given me yourself, a gift beyond price."

Love burned in her, a hot flame. "What will we do?" She couldn't not touch him, couldn't not be with him.

Deep gray eyes looked at her with a thousand hidden secrets . . . hidden from everyone but her. "I cannot break the rules on the surface. I must be perfect."

"I know."

Concealed between their bodies, his hand, strong and warm, closed over her own where it lay pressed against the grass.

"I'm a teleporter, Tazi."

Oh.

She covered her hand with her mouth, her smile so huge it cracked her face. "Will I sleep with my husband every night?"

"Of course. Going from one part of Alaris to another takes no effort."

"I suppose I can bear the distance during the day then."

It would be hard, but she'd think of it simply as if they were going to work like other husbands and wives. Knowing they'd meet again at the end of their shifts would be enough to carry her through, a secret joy inside her heart.

"No one but you," Stefan said, "ever goes into the engine room at Alaris."

Her pulse turned to thunder. "And," she added, turning her hand palm-side up so their fingers could entwine, "there is no surveillance." They could touch there at times when the need was deep, love there, safe in the darkness until they could come up into the light again.

"I can redirect my telekinetic energy into the sea when we love. It's so vast, the effect won't even raise the temperature a minute degree."

Her fingers locking with his. The tightness in her chest blooming out in rays of fire. And a laugh bubbling into her throat. "Do you think changeling sharks exist?"

"Nothing is impossible."

DORIAN

1

DORIAN CLIMBED UP the tree at the far end of the play area. Even though he knew he shouldn't, he kept climbing past the branch where his mom had told him he had to stop until he got bigger. He kept climbing and climbing and climbing until the branches got too far apart and he couldn't go any farther. Curling up against the trunk, he folded his arms and stared at the dark green leaves all around him.

Stupid, they were all stupid, he thought, his eyes burning.

When he heard his mom calling out for him, he didn't move.

"Dorian! Sweetheart, I know you're up there!" she called up.

Then the tree shook slightly and he knew she was climbing up to him. "Hey," she said when she reached his branch. "That's quite a scowl."

Folding his arms even tighter, he tucked his knees into himself.

"I see." Her smile was deep, her blue eyes sparkling like they always did. "No talking, huh?" Hitching herself up beside him, she kicked her legs gently outward, her sunshiny hair in a braid down her back. "You climbed far today."

Now he was in trouble, he thought, feeling mutinous and not the least bit sorry.

Except instead of being angry with him, his mother winked. "You did well, baby."

"I'm *not* a baby!"

She held up her hands, palms out. "Sorry, kitten, but you'll always be a baby to me. You know Emmett's mom still calls him her baby and he's bigger than you."

Dorian had to think about that. His mom was right. Emmett was a juvenile and really nice, and yesterday, his mom had said, "Baby, come help me with this," and Emmett had rolled his eyes and sighed but he'd gone over with a grin.

"Okay," he said, deciding if it was okay with a big boy, it was okay with him.

Reaching over, his mom brushed his hair off his face. "What's wrong?"

Dorian scowled and huddled deeper into himself. "Nothing." He wasn't going to cry. No one would make him cry.

Face softening, his mom cupped his face and rubbed her nose against his. "I love you, my beautiful, strong, perfect boy."

He blinked really hard so he wouldn't cry. When she drew back, he could still smell her. It was the smell of his mom and it made him feel like he was being hugged all over. But today, it wasn't enough. "I don't wanna come down," he said, his claws pricking the inside of his skin.

His mother looked at him for a long minute before nodding. "All right, baby." Leaning over, she kissed him on the cheek. "I'm going to go home and start dinner. Your favorite meat loaf."

Dorian thought about going with his mom when she left, but he wasn't sure he wouldn't cry. And he *wasn't* going to cry. Not because of the stupids. Swallowing the thick thing in his throat, he breathed in and out and tried to get his leopard to stop clawing him inside. It hurt, but the leopard was really angry and sad, and it was hard.

Until another scent filtered into the air.

Dorian stared wide-eyed as Lachlan stopped on the branch

below him. "Come down, Dorian," his alpha said, the dominance in his brown eyes making Dorian's leopard come to attention. "We're going for a walk."

Dorian really didn't want to come down, but his leopard pushed him to obey his alpha. "Yes, sir."

It was harder to climb down than it had been to climb up, but Lachlan didn't help him, simply waited for him at the bottom. Even when Dorian slipped and skinned his palms, his alpha didn't offer to help. Getting down, Dorian looked up with a small grin. "I did it."

Lachlan ruffled his hair, his hand big and warm. "I knew you would."

Dorian slipped his hand into Lachlan's and they started to walk. His heart thudded inside his chest when his alpha led him past the edge of the safe area where the cubs were meant to play—he'd tried to go past it a few times, been scolded. He still tried sometimes, with his best friend, Mercy. They both wanted to know what was outside. Now he was going to see.

Excited enough that he was a little less angry and sad, he looked around at everything as they walked. The trees were much bigger the farther out they went, the spaces between them less. "Is it fun running here?"

"Yeah." Lachlan grinned and when he met Dorian's gaze, Dorian saw his alpha's eyes now glinted yellow-green. "Sometimes, we play a game where we aren't allowed to touch the ground."

Dorian looked up at the thick canopy above. "All the way?" he asked, awed.

"Yes. You'll be able to do that, too, one day. You're already the best climber in your age group."

"No, I'm not." Head down, he kicked at the pine needles below him. "I can't do things like everyone else."

"That's true," Lachlan said and, dropping Dorian's hand, lifted him up with a grip under his arms; the alpha put him on a standing position on a huge boulder.

Dorian could now look straight into Lachlan's eyes. It was hard because Lachlan was alpha and Dorian was just a kid, but Dorian didn't look away. "I'm not a leopard."

"Did someone say that to you?" Lachlan's voice held a growl.

Shaking his head, Dorian swallowed and folded his arms again. He wasn't going to be a tattletale crybaby. Especially since the cubs who'd been so mean weren't even his real friends or pack. They were just visiting from another pack. He'd only been playing with them because Mercy and Barker were grounded.

"I'm not dumb," he said instead. "I *try* really hard to shift, Lachlan! I don't know why I can't do it!" It made him so angry and hot inside and it hurt.

"I know you try hard." Lachlan put his hands on his hips, the leopard in his voice as he spoke. "The fact that you can't shift doesn't have anything to do with that."

"I know! I'm latent!" Dorian didn't really understand what that was; he just knew he hated it. "Why can't Shayla fix me?" The pack's healer could fix everything else, even Mercy's broken leg when she'd slipped and fallen on the rocks by a waterfall.

"Dorian, you're a smart boy. I'm not going to patronize you by telling you things will be easy for you," Lachlan said, speaking to him in a way no grown-up had ever done. "It's going to be harder than it is for your friends."

Dorian stared at his alpha, his leopard at attention. "What do I do?"

"You're not only smart but strong," Lachlan said. "One of the strongest, most dominant young cubs in DarkRiver. I think you could be a sentinel one day."

"But I can't shift."

"Neither can Zeph and he's my sentinel."

Dorian frowned, having never really considered that. Zeph was human, but he was still DarkRiver, even if he couldn't change into a leopard. "He's really good at stuff."

"Yeah, he is." Lachlan held his gaze. "You can become good at stuff, too. You just have to work hard and never, ever forget that you're a member of DarkRiver. What keeps us strong as a pack are our members. I can't have you giving up."

Dorian growled. "I don't give up!"

"Yeah, that's what I figured." Lachlan looked at him without blinking, his eyes leopard again. "So, what will you do the next time someone makes you feel bad because you can't shift?"

Dorian thought about his angry-sad feelings, and he thought about Zeph who was so good at stuff, and he thought about how his mom and dad said he was a wonderful son, and he thought about what Lachlan had said. Then he nodded. "I won't let them," he said, his leopard standing straight inside him. "Just 'cause I can't shift doesn't mean I can't do everything. I just gotta try harder."

"Good." Lachlan nodded up toward the canopy. "You want me to start teaching you how to climb from tree to tree?"

"Really?" Dorian jumped down to the ground, landing easily because his cat told him what to do. "Let's go!"

11

DORIAN LAY HIGH on the branch above the battle zone, his body as still as stone. The leaves rustled around him, but he didn't move, barely breathed. Inside him, his leopard was contained, held back with sheer willpower. It had taken him time to learn to do that, to contain the animal so it didn't claw him bloody on the inside.

For a long time, he'd woken curled up in agony as the leopard fought him for a freedom he couldn't give it. At first, he'd cried out and his parents had run in to pet him and cuddle him. It was kind of embarrassing to think about now, but, like his mom said, he was their baby so he just had to suck it up. Because she still petted and cuddled him even though he was fourteen.

His little sister Kylie always giggled when Mom did that. And then he had to growl and chase the real baby of the family around the house and tickle her until she shifted into her cub form and tried to tickle him back using her paws.

He grinned within, while remaining unmoving on the outside.

At least Mercy's mom did the same hugging-cuddling thing to her. And both his mom *and* Mercy's mom did it to Lucas and Vaughn—who were older—so none of them could hassle one another. But these days, his parents didn't need to come to him at night anymore. His leopard did still get out of control at times, but he didn't scream, just woke up breathing hard and fast. Then he used the techniques Emmett's mom had taught him to calm himself.

Keelie called it meditating.

Dorian would get ribbed so hard if he admitted to meditating, so he called it mental discipline. Just like the discipline his friends had to learn to deal with their own leopards. Only they were learning how to balance their wild instincts with the human part of their nature, and he was learning to keep his trapped and angry leopard from driving him insane.

There.

Zeroing in on the tiny movement, he used the same mental discipline to hold utterly still, so that his scent wouldn't shift along the air currents. He'd already messed up his scent trail using a few other tricks, so if he stayed motionless . . . He took the shot.

"Fuck!" Lucas glared up at the tree as if he could see Dorian, the splatter of green on his T-shirt marking him as a "kill."

Dorian grinned but didn't shift position as, growling, Lucas came up his tree to lie down on the branch beside him. "How the fuck did you make that shot?" he said on a subvocal level. "From here you can't even see where I came out."

"I knew you were there." Dorian had practiced and practiced until he could make these shots blindfolded. He didn't need to see his target to hit it. "Just like you always know where we are, even if we hide our scent and stay out of sight." The only reason he'd got Luc today was because his seventeen-year-old friend hadn't expected him to make the shot.

"Yeah, well," Lucas said in that same subvocal tone. "That doesn't give me much of an advantage with you guys. I don't even know how Mercy does that thing where she disappears from sight."

Dorian hadn't figured that out, either, and it was one hell of a trick. What he had figured out was that Lucas would one day be his alpha, and that these exercises were meant to hone them all. Because DarkRiver wasn't the happy place it had been when Dorian had been a cub. The ShadowWalkers had hurt them—Lucas's parents were gone, and he'd been wounded badly before the pack found him.

Dorian and Mercy would probably be too young to join the hunt for the ShadowWalkers when it took place, but they could help protect their packmates while the hunters were gone.

Now Tamsyn was the healer even though everyone said she was too young. Dorian thought she was amazing, so calm and gentle. She reminded him of Shayla. Lucas's mom had trained Tammy, and Dorian was sure she'd be real proud of her student. "You think Nate and Tammy are gonna have cubs?" Dorian didn't usually think about stuff like that, but his mom and Mercy's mom had been talking about it that morning.

Lucas made a sound low in his throat. "I dunno. I heard Emmett's dad say Nate was being stubborn because he thinks Tammy's too young."

"Yeah, but she's a healer. They're, like, cub magnets."

"Adults."

"Yeah."

They fell silent for long minutes, and then Dorian felt it. A faint whisper along the air currents, a bare hint of a familiar scent. He couldn't see Mercy but he knew she was in the trees to his left. Shifting with extreme care so as not to give away his position, he closed his eyes and listened. And then he took the shot.

The curses that sounded from the canopy were so colorful that had Mercy's parents heard her, she'd have been grounded into the next century. "I'll get you for this, Dorian!" Jumping down to the ground, she glared in his general direction and he realized exactly why she was so pissed.

He'd gotten her in the face, the green bright against the pale gold of her skin.

"Shit," he muttered. "That'll leave a bruise." Because his job was to be a sniper, he was using relatively small paintball pellets rather than the larger ones the others had been issued, but at that velocity it would've hurt regardless. "Her mom's going to smack me. I don't even want to think about her dad."

"Yeah. Sucks to be you."

Watching Mercy wipe off the green paint using her forearm, he tracked her as she strode over, sniffed around to confirm their location, then climbed up the tree to join them. "Sorry, Merce," he said. "I wasn't aiming for your face."

A scowl but no real anger from Mercy, his friend as quick to forgive as her temper was hot. "Don't worry about it." She finished cleaning off the paint. "Tell me what gave me away."

"Caught your scent, but it was your gun that gave me your exact position," he said. "You should've primed it earlier." The faint click had been all he needed.

"Damn." She looked at Lucas. "What gave you away?"

"I was overconfident, knew Blondie was here but didn't think he'd make the shot before I got him."

The three of them fell silent as a unit as something changed in the air. *Vaughn.* The jaguar changeling moved differently from the leopards, was quieter, a shadow. That made him near impossible to hit at night, but it was late afternoon now, which meant Dorian had a slightly better chance if he didn't screw up.

Falling into the quiet space where he could hear his pulse as a soft echo in his ears, slow and easy, he didn't look. No, he just was. And when his body wanted to turn in a hard motion and his finger wanted to squeeze the trigger, he did it before his conscious mind realized Vaughn had doubled back on him.

Vaughn didn't swear like the others. He just snarled. "Next night hunt, Blondie," he said. "Your ass is toast."

Dorian allowed his body to relax now that the exercise was complete. Jumping down after Mercy and Lucas, he grinned at the jaguar. "Bet you ten bucks I can hit you at night." He enjoyed giving himself a challenge, enjoyed pushing himself.

"Like taking money from a cub." Shoving a hand through the thick amber of his hair, Vaughn looked at Lucas and Mercy. "Who do you put your money on?"

"Lucas." Mercy placed her hands on her hips, her tone snarky. "He's a black panther, you idiots. You think you're going to see him?"

That, Dorian admitted, was an excellent point. So far, he'd never managed to take Lucas down on a night hunt, but neither had he managed to hit Vaughn. The two of them were really good at night. Just like Mercy was really, really good at dawn. She was a ghost. He was still considering that when Nate appeared out of the trees with an unfamiliar male by his side. The guy looked like he was around Luc's or Vaughn's age; his green eyes were a little wild in his dark-skinned face, as if his leopard was just waiting to explode out of his skin.

Taking in the scene, Nate gave Dorian an approving nod. "We'll talk through the exercise tonight at dinner," he said. "For now, I want you to meet Clay. Lachlan's just accepted him into DarkRiver."

The older boy didn't smile, didn't look particularly as if he wanted to be in a pack, but he nodded at their greetings.

"Clay's been on his own for a while," Nate said. "I want the four of you to store your paint guns and take him for a run, show him around."

On his own? Dorian didn't know any cats that young who'd been on their own. Wild cats might be okay with a solitary life, but changeling cats were human, too, and they needed to be with pack. Even the loners didn't always roam alone. "You like paintball?" he asked Clay as they walked to store their guns in back of a truck Nate had parked some distance away.

"Never played."

"Here." Mercy passed him her gun. "Have a go at some trees. It's pretty fun." A scowl. "Except if Blondie here is shooting at your face."

"Hey! I said sorry!"

Clay looked from one to the other, a slight easing in his expression. "Jeez, you hit a girl in the face?"

Mercy punched Clay in the arm at the same time that Lucas choked and Vaughn hissed out a breath. "She's not a girl," Dorian told the confused guy. "She's a dominant and she can probably kick your ass in hand-to-hand combat."

"Huh." Clay stared at Mercy. "Really?"

Mercy raised an eyebrow, then looked her far bigger opponent up and down. "You want a demonstration?"

She put Clay on his ass three minutes later. Slapping her hands together as if dusting them off, she said, "And my work here is done."

Getting up, Clay settled his shoulders, and Dorian wondered if he realized they were all waiting to see how the big stranger with the green eyes would react. It was obvious to all of them that Clay was very, very dominant as far as the pack hierarchy was concerned, but working as an effective unit had to do with more than simple strength. If Clay was one of those dominants who couldn't handle a strong female, then they were going to have a serious problem. Because Mercy wasn't the only dominant female in DarkRiver.

"I want to learn how to do that," their new packmate said to Mercy. "Will you teach me?"

Mercy smiled as the rest of them blew out quietly relieved breaths. "Yeah, sure."

It was strange, but a half hour later, as they ran through the forest, Dorian realized he understood more about being a leopard than Clay did, even though the older boy could shift. It made him wonder what had happened to Clay to make him so close to his leopard—and yet so unaware of how to be a cat in a pack.

He didn't ask, though; he understood that sometimes, a guy just had to be who he was. Luc, Vaughn, Mercy, Nate—none of them treated Dorian as any different than them. He knew he *was* different, but his latency no longer made him angry-sad as it had when he'd been a cub. Lachlan had helped him a lot, as had his parents. Then, one freezing night, when he was only six, he'd run and run and run, and somewhere in there, he'd come to a kind of peace with himself.

It still hurt deep inside, and he knew it probably always would, his leopard horribly wounded, but he was a valued member of the pack and that was what mattered.

DORIAN LAY STUNNED next to the fire with Shaya. He had his head in his mate's lap and she was using a comb on his damp hair. He'd just have thrust his fingers through the white-blond strands and left it after he took a dip in the nearby stream, but Shaya had offered and he liked it when she petted him, so he was happy to lie here looking up at the brilliant stars above.

"I shifted," he said, not quite able to believe he'd run through the forest on four feet, the wind rippling through his fur.

"You were beautiful," Shaya told him again, her own joy a vibrant pulse along the mating bond that linked their hearts to one another. "And so cute."

"Hey." He growled, grabbing her hand to nip playfully at it. "I am a DarkRiver sentinel. We aren't cute."

Laughing, she bent down and kissed him, her tight curls electric with energy around them. "How about adorable?" she teased before going back to her combing of his hair, the rhythmic motion making him feel lazy and cherished both. "What was it like? When you first found yourself on four feet?"

"Disorienting," he said, thinking of that first shock after Shaya's gene therapy had taken sudden, unexpected effect. "You have no idea how difficult it is to coordinate four paws at one time."

Smile luminous, Shaya put aside the comb and placed one hand on his bare chest, playing with his hair with the other. "I've seen the cubs," she said. "No wonder they're always tumbling."

"Yeah." He felt like a cub himself, was conscious he had so much more to learn. But one thing he knew beyond doubt: "Your voice, telling me to trust the leopard to know what to do—that's what I needed to hear." All his life, he'd fought to control his leopard, to restrain it so it wouldn't claw him bloody in its frustration, wouldn't drive him insane.

That discipline had given him a life and a strong, trusted position in the pack, but in that moment after the shift, it had also left him alone and lost. "My leopard was waiting, ready," he said to Shaya, wonder bright in him. "As soon as I surrendered to it, I understood how I needed to balance, how my body was meant to move." He shuddered out a breath at the glorious memory of freedom. "I know I'm not anywhere near graceful yet, but I don't care. It feels incredible."

"I know." It was a whisper, Shaya's eyes shining wet in the firelight. "I could feel your joy through our bond."

Lifting her hand to his mouth again, he pressed his lips to her palm, drawing in the lush, sensual scent of her. Of his smart, sexy, beautiful mate. "I didn't spend my life feeling sorry for myself," he said, thinking of the years past. "I became the best I could be, and then I pushed myself even harder."

His packmates teased him affectionately about his overachieving tendencies, but that drive was all that had kept him together for a long time. Then, it had simply become part of him. "But it hurt," he said, admitting his vulnerability to the woman who held his heart— and who already understood his pain. "Deep inside me, so deep down that I almost forgot it at times, it always hurt.

"I want to say it felt like a piece of me was missing, but that isn't true. It was worse than that. It was feeling that piece trapped inside me, feeling as if I was betraying my leopard every day of our existence." He swallowed. "I wouldn't have blamed my cat if it never forgave me, but it does, Shaya. It *does*."

"Of course it does. You're not two separate beings, Dorian, you're one."

"Yeah." He smiled because it was true. After a lifetime of being separated from his cat, he didn't have to fight it anymore. They could just be. Now that leopard rubbed against the inside of his skin, as excited as he was, as happy. Its emotions were wilder than his own, its mind thinking in far simpler patterns. "The cat doesn't see the point in worrying about the past."

Shifting off Shaya's lap on those words, he said, "Come lie with me."

When she would've lain down on the picnic blanket beside him, he tugged her on top of his body. She was dressed in a plain white tank top and a pair of black boxers she'd stolen from him and that would've hung off her if she hadn't tightened the elastic. "Why aren't you naked?" he complained after slipping his hand into the back of the boxers to cup her gorgeous ass.

Nipping at his lower lip, she kicked up her legs after tucking her curls behind her ears in a futile effort to control them. "Because we have two tiny and very curious chaperones."

He grinned. "They get to sleep okay?"

"Yeah. Fell asleep waiting for you." Her blue-gray eyes danced. "Noor wants to brush you."

His chest rumbled with laughter. "I have a feeling she'll get her way." Their son's best friend was an adorable little cub who'd survived a terrible start to life with her sweetness and heart intact. "And Keenan?"

"He wants to go running with you." Shaya kissed him again. "If you'd rather have some privacy to explore the leopard, I can—"

"No." Stroking his hands up her back and under the tank top, he smiled. "The leopard wants to play with them, too." Cubs were to be looked after, said the leopard, even if that meant being brushed by a sparkly pink hairbrush. "It needs to care for them . . . it's never had the chance to exercise that instinct." And the instinct was a visceral one—Dorian had had it his entire life.

Shaya smiled. "You really should call Lucas back."

His alpha had called soon after Dorian shifted for the first time. "What did he say?" Dorian asked.

"Just that he'd felt the urge to check up on you. I didn't want to steal your news, so I told him you were fine and would call him back." She bit her lower lip. "That was a few hours ago."

Blowing out a breath, Dorian nodded. "Right, where's the phone?" His alpha was worried, no doubt having sensed something staggering through the blood bond that linked all the sentinels to their alpha. If Dorian didn't get in touch, Luc might decide to come and check things out in person and Dorian wasn't ready for that.

He needed to settle into his new skin first.

"Here." Shaya sat up and picked up the phone from another part of the blanket, the laz-fire turning her into a lush goddess above him, the rich brown of her skin glowing in the light.

Stroking her thighs, he just looked at her. "You're so pretty, Shaya."

A lopsided smile. "Let me go check the babies are still asleep. Then maybe we can play a little."

His body definitely liked that idea. Watching her walk away to duck into the tent, he sat up and blew out a breath before calling Lucas. "Hey, Luc, Shaya said you'd called."

"You okay?" Lucas asked straight off. "I've been fighting the urge to find you all day, check on you."

"Oh, jeez, Luc." Dorian groaned. "I just got Shaya to agree to—"

He bit off his words as his mate came out of the tent and scowled at him.

Grinning, he said, "To play chess."

Lucas snorted on the other end. "Yeah, I know that kind of chess," he said with a grin in his voice. "You sure there's nothing I need to know?"

Dorian had never lied to his alpha. "There is something," he said. "Nothing bad, but something I need to work out for myself first."

A pause, before Lucas said, "All right. You know where I am when you're ready."

Hanging up after a few more words, Dorian put aside the phone and watched Shaya come to him. "Hey," he whispered before a wild craving tore through him.

Sharp concern in his mate's eyes. "Dorian?" She dropped to her knees beside him. "What's wrong?"

"Nothing. Just . . . change of plans." Cupping her face as he held back the shift so he could speak to her, he said, "The leopard . . . it needs your touch." And then he surrendered to the painful beauty and sheer joy of the shift, allowing the human part of him to recede into the background as the leopard took center stage.

The leopard he was folded its legs and put its head in Shaya's lap, its eyes closing as her hands stroked through its fur.

Peace sank into the bones of man and leopard both.

IV

THREE HOURS AFTER returning home from their camping trip, Dorian loitered in the trees outside his alpha's aerie. He didn't know quite how to tell Lucas, how to share the joy of what had happened. Any words seemed inadequate.

"Dorian?" Lucas landed on the forest floor in a smooth crouch, having jumped down from the aerie. He was dressed in jeans and a faded blue T-shirt, his feet bare.

Dorian shifted out of the trees. "Yeah, it's me."

"Since when do you lurk?" His alpha walked over. "Come on up. Sascha's mak—" Lucas froze, his eyes turning panther in the space of a single heartbeat. Then he moved with alpha speed to capture Dorian's face between his hands.

Dorian felt his own leopard rise to the surface in response, knew his eyes were changing, his claws releasing. But the leopard stopped there, as if aware they both needed to be in this instant. The animal was as nervous as the man, though Dorian knew full well there was no cause for it—still, he felt like a cub for some reason . . . and then he knew why. This was the first time his leopard had come into direct contact with his alpha.

"*Something?*" Lucas said, his lips starting to curve. "You describe this as *something?*"

Dorian shrugged a little sheepishly. "I didn't know how to say it."

Laughing, Lucas wrapped his arms around his neck and hauled him close. Dorian went, returning the hug as fiercely as it was given. When he felt wet against his neck, he realized his alpha—his *friend*—was crying for joy for him. And damn, fuck, he was crying, too.

Drawing back, Lucas grabbed his face in his hands again, kissed him. It was hard, fleeting, and it held the power of the entire pack, Lucas's veins pulsing with the energy that was DarkRiver. And that energy spoke to his leopard, told it that it was home, that it was welcome, that there was no cause to fear.

"Damn it, Dorian," Lucas said, slapping him lightly as they both laughed through the tears. "You fucking made me cry."

"Better not let Hawke see you," Dorian managed to get out. "You know that wolf would never let you forget it."

"Like I care." Stepping back, Lucas gave a single nod.

Dorian didn't know how he understood, but he did. Ignoring the fact that he didn't have spare clothes with him, he allowed the shift to take him over, his jeans and sweatshirt disintegrating off him as he became the leopard that was his other half. When it was over, he found himself face-to-face with a black panther with night-glow eyes.

Lifting a paw, Lucas patted the side of his face as he'd done in human form, except this was harder. Cat to cat. Alpha to sentinel. A rough welcome that made his cat's entire body vibrate with decades of withheld joy. When Lucas opened his mouth and growled, Dorian growled back.

Light sparked in the air, and then a man with black shoulder-length hair and green eyes, his skin muted gold, was crouching in front of him. "Well," Lucas said with a grin, "thank God you're not a white-blond fucking leopard. We'd have had to dip you in mud before every operation."

Snarling, Dorian head-butted his alpha and they sprawled to the ground. Where Lucas held up his hands, eyes bright with untrammeled happiness. "Want to go surprise the others? Let's see if they recognize you."

Dorian snapped his teeth and nodded, his cat excited at the game.

In front of him, Lucas shifted, then ran over to climb up to his aerie. When he jumped back down, Dorian growled a greeting up at a wide-eyed Sascha. His alpha's mate waved at him, her lips curved in a dazzling smile. A second later, he was following his alpha carefully through the trees.

Lucas didn't go too fast, and when Dorian stumbled, he didn't baby him, just waited for him to get his feet back under him before they began to run again. They went first to his parents' house, and hell, there were a lot of tears there, too, a lot of hugs and petting. His mom called him "baby" again and, grabbing his leopard's face, smothered it in kisses.

The leopard, shameless creature, rubbed its cheek against her, a cub happy its parent was happy. It was the first time he'd seen such joy in his mother and father since they'd lost Kylie, and it meant everything. He'd already visited the pretty, sunny spot where he felt closest to his little sister, told her of the gift he'd been given.

I wish you were here, squirt. I'd finally be able to nip your butt when you got too sassy.

He'd heard his sister's cheeky laugh on the air, had almost felt her slender arms wrap around him as she laid her face against his chest. *I love you, Dori.* Only Kylie had ever dared to call him Dori, the habit formed as a toddler when she couldn't say his full name.

I love you, too, squirt.

Now, covered in the scent of family, he left his parents laughing and padded beside Lucas as they went hunting the other sentinels.

Mercy had come off a night shift and opened her door with a bad-tempered look on her face when they scratched on it. "Do you two know what ti—" Her bleary eyes focused and then she screamed in delight and jumped on Dorian, shifting midjump to roll with him onto the pine needles that carpeted the area outside her cabin.

Growling and nipping at him as they tumbled like pups, she kept patting his face as if to make certain he was really there. When she shifted back into human form, her red hair cascading down her back, tears streaked her face. "I'm leaking," she said in an accusatory tone. "Because of you."

Then she wrapped her arms around his neck and hugged him tight.

By the time he met the rest of the sentinels, he'd been pounced on multiple times, each and every one of his packmates recognizing him on sight, though they'd never before seen his leopard. "It's the eyes and the scent," Vaughn had said after knocking all the air out of Dorian with his enthusiastic welcome, the jaguar's heavier body having taken his inexperienced one to the earth a few minutes earlier. "You're still Dorian, just in a different skin."

Yes.

Finally, he had the ability to live in both his skins, to be cat and to be human. But whatever shape he took, he thought as he returned home, he would always be DarkRiver . . . and he would always love Shaya and the little boy who was now his own.

Both were waiting for him at home, their identical eyes lighting up when he stepped into the room. Of all the gifts he'd been given, that was the biggest and most precious. Leopard and man, man and leopard, his mate and his child were his reason for living.

V

DORIAN TOOK A deep breath and gave in to the shift. The agony and ecstasy of it was beyond anything he could've ever imagined. His body broke apart in a thousand sparks of light, and then re-formed, and it amazed him anew to find himself so much lower to the ground, his body on four paws instead of two human feet.

When he moved, it still took him a second to find his balance. At least he no longer fell on his face, he thought with a huffing growl. The sound made the black panther in front of him turn, give him a questioning look. Dorian shook his head at his alpha, but Lucas's eyes sparked with feline laughter.

If they'd been in human form, Dorian thought, Lucas would be ragging on him. Everyone thought it was hilarious that he was so clumsy in cat form when he was sniper-quiet in his human body. But there was a deep, deep joy mixed in with all the teasing, an almost crushing wave of love from the pack that had not only accepted him, but respected him exactly as he was—and who were now delighted with his happiness in being able to set his leopard free.

Thanks to Shaya.

His back arching at the thought of his mate, a low, pleased growl rumbling in his throat, he padded off after his alpha as Lucas led him on an easy run through the trees. He'd have stumbled over his feet at least five times by now only a few months back, but had no such trouble today, taking the small jumps over fallen logs with ease, even using flat stones to cross a tumbling stream.

Then Lucas disappeared in a streak of black lightning.

Dorian froze.

This was something he'd done to trainees all too often himself, though he'd been in human form at the time. The aim of the game was to track Lucas within a reasonable time frame—how long depended on the trainee in question. In Dorian's case, in human form, Lucas would give no quarter.

It annoyed him that he wasn't as attuned to his senses in leopard form, but he still had his brain. Standing very, very still, he let the leopard rise to the surface. He'd become so used to controlling it that for the first month, he'd had real trouble letting go—until his mate had taken his face into her hands, kissed the life out of him, and told him that she wanted to speak to his leopard.

Turned out his leopard wanted to play with her, too.

"So beautiful," she'd murmured as she ran those long, capable fingers through his fur as the leopard placed its head in her lap and closed its eyes. "And so lazy."

He'd growled then, heard her laugh, both man and leopard entranced by the sound. No matter what form he held, he loved her, *adored* her. That simply, she'd made him understand that he was still himself, even when the leopard took precedence.

Today, the cat plucked out Lucas's powerful scent from the air and began to run over the fallen autumn leaves, its steps light and silent. Deep within, the human part of Dorian watched in quiet pleasure—he wasn't as clumsy as he'd thought, not anymore. Because though it had been forced to live within a human skin all those years, the leopard hadn't ever given up. Instead, it had learned from the sniper.

Today it veered sharply away as it caught the barest whisper of movement from the right, rolling onto a heavy carpet of leaves just as a large leopard slammed out at him. The gold and black cat hit him on the side in a glancing blow, but Dorian had already danced out of reach. Snarling, he turned to bring down his opponent . . . to see Clay sitting there watching him with pure calm—as if he hadn't just tried to make Dorian eat dust.

When he snarled again, his fellow sentinel laid his head on his paws and pretended to go to sleep.

This wasn't only hide-and-seek. This was a hunt. And Dorian had just lost a point.

Exhilaration raced through him—because his fellow sentinels and his alpha *weren't* cutting him a break. They were treating him as exactly what he was: one of them.

With that in mind, he began to move with even more stealth. All the sentinels were powerful, and they all had their own personal strengths. Vaughn, for example, was one hell of a climber, while Mercy could hide in plain sight by standing utterly motionless.

A new scent in his nose, so faint the man might have ignored it. But the leopard froze . . . and changed direction, to circle back in on its prey.

The jaguar lying in wait on a tree branch didn't see him as he came around to stand below the tree, staring up.

Point to me.

He gave a pointed cough-growl.

Vaughn's head whipped back, and even from this far away, Dorian could tell the jaguar was pissed at having been shown up by "the newborn," as his friends liked to call him when they were trying to drive him nuts.

Snorting in disgruntlement, Vaughn padded down the branch

and jumped off to disappear into the trees. Dorian smiled inwardly and was just about to head back on the trail when he was hit again—this time from above. And it wasn't Vaughn.

Fuck! he thought as he rolled out of the way.

Except his attacker had his—*her*—teeth in the ruff of his neck and she wasn't letting go. Twisting his body, he managed to nip her side enough to make her release him, but she was on him again before he could get out of the way, and she was trying to go for his throat. Protecting the vulnerable area by ducking his head, he plowed into her chest.

She growled, but didn't back down, bringing up her clawed paw to rake him down the side.

Shit.

The marks were light, would heal within the next few hours, but the fight was done because she'd drawn first blood. Pulling away, he huffed as he caught his breath.

In front of him, the other leopard shifted in a shower of sparks to become a woman with flame red hair crouching on the forest floor. "Tut-tut," Mercy said, waving a finger. "Overconfidence be the endeth of the man."

When Dorian growled at her, she leaned down until they were nose to nose. "Listen to your leopard, Boy Genius. Stop thinking." She tapped the side of his head. "The cat has had to trust you its whole life, but you've never had to rely on it. If you can learn to do that, you'll be unstoppable—I would've never been able to get the jump on you in human form. But you can't think like a human in leopard form or you'll only hobble the animal."

Lifting her head, she shifted back into her leopard form—which happened to be slightly smaller than his own. As he watched her leave, her tail curling lazily, he considered her words. Sure he'd given in to the cat, but . . . while the cat's cunning had allowed him to sneak up on Vaughn, he'd relied mostly on his human mind, not trusting the leopard's instincts.

For a man who had built his life around the word "control," giving in was one hell of a hard ask.

"Stop fighting it! Dorian, please!"

His mate had said those words to him the first time he shifted. Stunned and in shock, and so in love with her it hurt, he'd done as she asked. And it had felt like . . . coming home.

Flexing his claws on the ground, he reached for the mating bond, for the love that had only become stronger with the passing days. Leopard and man, they both held on to it like a lifeline as he once more did as his Shaya had asked.

He gave in.

An explosion of scents and sounds, textures against his fur, so many noises to explore that it threatened to overwhelm. The man began to fight his way out, to take control.

"Dorian, please!"

Shaya's voice again from that fateful day, reminding him that he was leopard and man both and this was the leopard's playground.

The human part of Dorian fell back.

The leopard took a deep breath, separated out the important scents from the not-so-important—though it did pause to consider chasing a rabbit—and began to run after Lucas. Dorian felt his/their heart pump with exhilaration, their muscles flex, their fur rush back in the wind as the leopard, its mind sharp and cunning and furiously intelligent, caught Lucas's double-back and switched direction so that they might be able to sneak up on their alpha.

Pride bloomed within the heart of the leopard as it thought of telling its mate of its skill, imagined her stroking those long capable fingers through his fur and saying, "Beautiful." Later, after she'd all but put him into a coma with her petting, she'd laugh and murmur, "Lazy."

The leopard halted, sniffed. And backed away.

Trap, it thought to the man when Dorian surfaced, and that was all that needed to be said as they switched back, skirting around the danger. Six more traps later, both leopard and man were snarling at his packmates. He'd avoided the rope tie, the tripwire, and two others, but they *had* managed to dump him into a slimy mud pool and successfully snapped a branch painfully in his face. His fur matted and his nose smarting from the trick—one his leopard was *most* annoyed that it hadn't sensed—he almost walked right into a pit.

Pausing with one foot on the edge of the disguised hole in the forest floor, he didn't back away but instead went right and into the forest, after Lucas's scent. Instinct told him his alpha had created this trap while the others had been keeping him busy. Staring up at the trees, the leopard thought, *Hmm*, and then it jumped.

Dorian didn't know which one of them was more surprised when they ended up on the branch with a single lunge. For a moment, the leopard retreated, startled by its own skill, and the man took control. Looking around, he realized exactly what his alpha had done. A second later, the leopard was back, its breath caught, and they began to race along the skyway of the trees, tracking Lucas from above— because Luc had underestimated him.

And Dorian's nose was still smarting enough that he took great delight in jumping down on top of his alpha from his hiding place in the branches. Then he took even more delight in ensuring he got as much of the mud slime as possible on Lucas before letting go.

A sparkle of light and color and then a very dirty Lucas was sitting there scowling. "Damn it, Dorian. This stuff stinks."

The leopard satisfied, Dorian gave in to the shift again, his human body covered in mud when he re-formed, his hair sticking up in spikes. The shift made clothes disintegrate like clockwork, but it was a crapshoot as to whether a single shift would get rid of ordinary stains or dyes, or stuff that was stuck to the body itself. Sometimes one shift and it was all gone, and sometimes it took six shifts to get even partially clean.

Today was clearly not a lucky day for either Lucas or Dorian. "Serves you fucking right," Dorian told his alpha.

"Wasn't my idea," Lucas muttered. "Nate came up with that one. He wanted to join in even though we couldn't shift the out-of-state meeting today."

A feminine laugh from the right. "You have a stripe across your face, Blondie. Turning tiger on us?"

Dorian fixed Mercy with a narrow-eyed glare. "I *know* that was your trick."

She blew him a kiss before shifting into animal form and scrambling up to lie on a tree branch as Vaughn and Clay prowled out of the trees. Vaughn shifted, while Clay curled up at the foot of Mercy's tree. "I was hoping you'd fall into the pit," the amber-haired sentinel said with a grin. "I told Luc to line it with banana peels and mushy apples, even stashed the supplies for him."

Closing his eyes, Dorian wiped off a bit of mud that was stuck to his eyelid, giving Vaughn the finger with his other hand. It took him a second to realize the other sentinel hadn't replied. Looking up, he saw Vaughn and Lucas had shifted back into animal form. They gave him a bare instant to complete his own shift . . . and then all four swarmed him, tumbling into him like overgrown kittens.

Startled, he kept his own claws sheathed and mock-battled with them.

And then, as Vaughn pushed him aside and Mercy took his side so that they could bully the jaguar, while Clay and Lucas stood there with feline laughter in their eyes, he understood.

No special favors.

No expecting anything less from him.

No being considered anything but capable.

He was a sentinel. He was one of them. Always had been. Always would be.

A crash of love down the mating bond, as if his mate had felt his elation. Laughing as he and Mercy managed to pin Vaughn, only to be attacked by Clay, who'd decided to turn traitor, Dorian thought his mate would surely help him devise a worse "foul" than a stinking slime pit or a snapping branch.

And then he stopped thinking and let the leopard play.

PARTNERS
IN PERSUASION

Chapter 1

FELIX LOOKED UP from checking a row of baby trees planted by a juvenile and found himself the target of a stunning smile. Bright green eyes, her hair in a million fine braids, and her skin bronze brushed with gold, she was more beautiful than any woman he'd ever seen. She was also a senior DarkRiver soldier who'd likely make sentinel in the next year or two if the interpack scuttlebutt was to be believed.

She raised a hand, wiggled her fingers, her eyes sparkling.

Blushing, Felix looked down at the plant he was checking. The juvenile had done a good job, but the boy was new at this . . . and he could still feel her looking at him. Glancing up from below his lashes a minute later, he found her leather-clad legs angled away, so he looked up fully. She was talking to Hawke, Felix's alpha having run down to see how things were going with the planting of the area that had been decimated during the battle with Pure Psy.

The beautiful green-eyed soldier's name was Desiree and, unlike Felix, she was a leopard changeling. The cats were pitching in to help keep the area secure during the replanting—the part of the forest that had been destroyed during the fight against Pure Psy was so open right now that they'd be sitting ducks otherwise. Similarly to the other wolves in SnowDancer, it had taken Felix a while to become accustomed to the fact that their pack now had a blood bond with the leopards; the feline changelings were as welcome in their territory as the wolves were in DarkRiver's lower-elevation territory. Of course, it was still considered courteous to ask if you ran into a sentry, one predator to another.

Laughing at something Hawke had said, Desiree nodded and waved good-bye to the alpha. Hawke had already spoken to Felix, so the other man just shot him a salute before heading out. Which left only Felix and Desiree in this section. Felix had wanted to spend some extra time prepping the soil for the next day's planting after everyone else had left—everyone, that is, except for the evening security shift.

"Hey." Booted feet hunkering down on the other side of the seedlings he was checking. "I'm Desiree."

Felix knew he should be polite, reply with his own name, but Desiree's dominance was so overwhelming that his wolf quivered, ready to run. It didn't matter that she was leopard rather than wolf— she was a predator far stronger than him and his wolf knew it.

Angling her head a little to the side, her braids falling over her shoulder, she attempted to catch his eye. "I don't bite. Well, not until I'm asked, anyway."

He felt his skin heat again. Damn it. He'd worked in the world of high fashion modeling, dealt with plenty of strong personalities without problem. Of course, none of them had been an astonishingly beautiful leopard female who made him want to touch when he knew it would be a very, very bad idea. Dominants ate submissives like him alive for breakfast, then got hungry for lunch.

A pause before Desiree rose to her feet. "I'll let you get back to your work."

Felix watched her walk away, her body lithe with muscle, and had the strong urge to kick himself. He wanted to talk to her, wanted to know her . . . but he'd been down this road before. God, he'd been such a stupid kid, fallen so hard for the dominant who'd been visiting from another wolf pack, had been ready to give up everything for her, including his first big modeling gig.

But after his heartfelt profession of love, every part of him vulnerable and laid out in the open, she'd patted him on the cheek, kissed him, and said, "I'm sorry, sweetheart. You're gorgeous and a delight, but I need a dominant as a partner."

The thing was, she hadn't meant to hurt him. She'd really believed they were simply sharing intimate skin privileges as friends and that Felix understood the facts of life: that while dominants often mated with submissives, it was usually a male dominant with a female submissive. The opposite direction was far rarer, and when it came to dominant leopard females, he'd *never* heard of it. They were so wild and independent that it took a stubbornly strong male to haul them into a long-term relationship, much less a mating.

Riley's courtship of Mercy was the perfect example. The leopard sentinel had run the wolf lieutenant a merry chase. Fascinated and delighted for them, Felix had watched from the sidelines along with the rest of the pack, but that kind of a dance wasn't in his future. He'd make a wonderful mate, he knew that. He was loyal, good with his hands, and he adored children. However, that relationship wouldn't be with a dominant female.

No matter how beautiful.

He was through with being used.

DESIREE leaned up against a tree far enough into the shadows of the forest surrounding the denuded area that SnowDancer's horticultural expert couldn't see her, and watched him. Tall and muscled, with mink brown hair and thickly lashed brown eyes, he had strong hands that touched the seedlings with competent care, his expression intent.

He'd folded the sleeves of his checked work shirt to just below his elbows, exposing golden skin with a powerful tracery of veins beneath. His skin made her want to lick; his hands made her want to feel their strong, callused heat on her skin. His touch would be rough, thorough, unhurried. It made her shiver just thinking about it.

First, however, she had to get him to talk to her.

Her cat stretched inside her, fur rubbing up against the insides of her skin. It, too, was fascinated by the man who worked among the newly planted trees with such total and quiet concentration. It wasn't his looks that had first drawn her attention—though the man was certifiably hot—it was the way he worked with plants. She'd watched him without him noticing her for over an hour, seen him handle the fragile seedlings with a breathtaking gentleness.

Yet the very hands that had done that had also lifted up a fifty-pound bag of soil as if it weighed nothing.

The combination of raw physical strength and incredible gentleness was deeply compelling. Add in the clear respect he commanded from even the most hard-edged men and women in SnowDancer, and there was something about this brown-eyed wolf that had Desiree's leopard padding inside her skin, wanting a taste.

He looked up at a hail from a SnowDancer lieutenant right then.

A jeans-and-T-shirt-clad Indigo crouched down beside him a moment later, her long black hair pulled into a ponytail, and the two of them fell into an easy conversation. He even laughed in response to something the wolf lieutenant said. So, he wasn't worried about talking to dominant females. It was specifically *Desiree* that he didn't want to talk to. That left her in a quandary. Leopard or wolf, some rules were written in stone.

If a submissive said or even intimated no, a dominant backed off. Immediately.

Submissives simply didn't have the ability to fight against a dominant, especially not when it came to sexual aggression from someone they were meant to be able to trust—a packmate or an ally. The submissive would simply get more and more uncomfortable and distressed. Desiree scowled, hating the idea that she might hurt the beautiful man with the careful hands. She didn't want to; she just wanted to know him. One more try, she told herself, and if he made it clear he didn't want her, she'd clamp down on her need to touch him and no damn argument.

That thought was uppermost in her mind the next evening when she turned up before sunset to do a security shift. She liked the evening shifts up here—it was quiet, and thanks to the sizeable area they had to patrol, she rarely ran into the other soldiers. Desiree wasn't a loner by any means, but she was feline enough to enjoy a touch of peace and quiet at times, especially when the starlit night sky was as stunning as it got up in the Sierra Nevada.

Not that the sky was the focus of her attention tonight.

Felix, however, was nowhere to be seen. It hadn't taken her long to figure out his name—all she'd had to do was engage one of his packmates in conversation and it had popped out naturally enough, since Felix was in charge of this entire planting operation. Lips twisting in disappointment at not seeing him, she put down the gift she'd brought in the hope it would break the ice, and left to do a security sweep of her section.

After the way the packs had been attacked, no one was taking any chances. Desiree had fought in San Francisco itself, come up against Pure Psy attackers in hand-to-hand combat, but it had been the most brutal here. The reason for the denuded ground, however, was a violent power that had saved the lives of SnowDancer's soldiers and devastated the enemy.

Hawke's mate, Desiree thought, was one hell of a woman.

When she finished her sweep, it was to find her gift sitting exactly where she'd left it. Sighing, she leaned back against a tree . . .

and straightened almost immediately. There he was, on the very edge of the current planting area, using a shovel to turn some soil. She'd noticed that about him—even though he was technically the boss here, he liked to get his hands dirty.

About to head over to him with her gift, she glanced around to make sure no one else was nearby. It wasn't that she didn't want people to know she was courting him—hell, she was as possessive as any dominant and she *wanted* him. But it might make him uncomfortable. Only when she was certain the coast was clear did she walk forward, keeping her stride easy so as not to make him feel hunted.

FELIX had just bent down to plant a seedling in the new hole he'd created when the hairs rose on his arms, the scent on the air lemon spice and something wilder, more feline. Skin heating, he busied himself using his hands to scoop out a bit more soil and put it to the side.

She crouched across from him the same as she'd done before, but instead of speaking, she placed a small pot between them. It was boat shaped with a pale blue glaze and planted in it was a tiny, beautifully shaped maple tree. He couldn't help it; he reached out to touch the leaves of the masterful bonsai. He had nothing this stunning in his collection, having only begun to teach himself the art in the past year.

"I'm sorry." It was a quiet feminine murmur.

Jerking up his head, he met the startling green of her gaze for a split second before breaking the eye contact. Dominant-to-submissive eye contact was difficult to hold at the best of times for a submissive; even more so when there was sexual desire involved.

"For coming on so aggressively yesterday," she added in that voice with its slight husky edge that made his skin prickle. "I didn't mean to make you uncomfortable. My only excuse is that I wanted to get to know the man who's coaxing this entire area back to life."

His wolf stirred, the human part of him intrigued that she'd mentioned his horticultural skill rather than his looks. He knew he was good-looking—it wasn't something to be proud of, wasn't something he'd achieved. It was genetic luck. But this, the plants, the earth? He'd *earned* this through sheer hard work.

"If you want me to back off, I will." It was a solemn statement. "I hope you like the plant—one of the other soldiers mentioned you had miniature trees and I figured they must be bonsai. My dad's into them." She waited for a second before rising to her feet, and he knew she'd taken his silence as a response.

Desiree wouldn't bother him again.

"Did you get it from him?" he said before he could stop himself.

It would've been far more sensible to let her go, but he couldn't bear the thought that she'd believe he didn't find her attractive. He'd heard that, beneath their tough skins, dominant leopard females were touchy about things like that. No matter how much he wanted to protect himself, it didn't mean he had to hurt her.

A smile he could hear in her voice as she came back down on her haunches, the jeans she wore today taut over her thighs. "Yeah. He actually gave it to me for my birthday. I've been terrified I'd kill it the entire month it sat on the table in my aerie—I swear the thing chases me in my nightmares."

His lips curved. "Won't your father miss it when he visits?"

"Actually, I'm fairly certain he's sorry he gave it to me." Unhidden love in her tone when she spoke of her father. "It's one of his babies, you know."

Felix nodded, as attached to his own plants.

"I think he'd be much happier to know it's with you." Her braids brushed her thighs as she shifted a little. "He was talking the other day about how he approves of the plan you've come up with to reforest this region."

Felix frowned. The alphas of both packs were aware of his plans, of course, but pretty much the only other person who had detailed knowledge of those plans was the DarkRiver ranger in overall charge of the flora in the leopard pack's territory. Heavily built, with tightly curled black hair threaded with a bare few strands of gray, Harry was a gentle giant of a man. "Is Harry your father?"

"Yes."

That meant Meenakshi, the petite former classical dancer who was Harry's mate, and who'd dropped by with Harry a week earlier, was Desiree's mother. He wondered what her parents thought of their dominant daughter, but that was a very personal question and he wasn't going down that road with Desiree.

"So . . ." Desiree held out a hand. "Friends?"

Felix had soil on his hands, having not worn gloves because he loved the feel of the earth. He used the excuse not to touch her. Skin privileges were important and he didn't want to initiate them with Desiree . . . because he was afraid that once he started, he wouldn't be able to stop. And the line had to be drawn here, now. "Friends," he said, flicking her a quick look before he glanced down.

She stayed with him for another few minutes, asking about the planting and the trees, questions which didn't stress his wolf and that he could answer in as much depth as interested her. Once again, he watched her leave, a strong, intelligent, and sensual woman who'd only ever see him as a pretty diversion. When it came time to choose a mate, she'd go for someone stronger, someone dominant, someone who was the total opposite of Felix.

Chapter 2

THE PLANTING AREA was quite a way down from the SnowDancer den, but Felix had decided to run home today, his wolf needing to stretch. Stripping in the garden shed, he set his clothes aside and shifted. Agony and ecstasy, piercing pleasure spliced with pain, his wolf skin forming out of the millions of particles of light that had once been his human form. Then he was shaking that skin into place, the white-streaked light brown of his fur settling.

His packmates teased him that his fur was as pretty in wolf form as his hair was in his human form. A few of them had even threatened to comb and braid him. He knew the teases, had grown up with them, and he ragged his friends as wickedly in turn. Drew, one of the worst, had cheerfully taken Felix's teasing during the time when the other man had been flamboyantly and—at first— unsuccessfully courting Indigo.

As Felix stepped out into the cool night air, he considered what Drew would've done if Desiree had approached him while he'd been single. Not talked about plants, that was for sure. Felix's wolf growled, and the human part of him winced at the harsh reminder. Just because he wasn't dominant didn't mean he didn't have value. *Every* member of SnowDancer had value. That was why it was such a strong, stable pack.

He couldn't allow his unwilling response to a leopard soldier to mess him up again after he'd spent years putting himself back together after the last time he'd played with a dominant. Sinking deep into the wolf's mind, he let the animal take over and they padded carefully out of the planted area . . . to pick up a trail scented with lemon spice that held a wilder undertone.

Desiree had passed this way during her watch and he was tempted, just for a second, to follow, to discover if she found him as intriguing in this form as she did while he was human. Then he came to his senses and headed homeward, the little bonsai she'd given him safely ensconced in the garden shed for the night. He'd take it home in the truck tomorrow.

Tonight, he ran under a darkening sky still swirled with faint glimmers of vivid orange and red. The colors faded during his run and the stars were starting to appear by the time he neared the den. Slowing to take a seat on the edge of a waterfall, he looked up and watched the stars glitter to life like frozen diamonds, and when the wildness of his nature wanted to sing to those stars, he lifted his head in a howl that was answered from other parts of the territory.

Their ensuing song was pure, primal music.

Home. Family. Friends.

Wolf content and the man in a better place, Felix turned and covered the final distance to the den. He padded to his quarters in wolf form, would've gone in using the special pressure switch built low into the door, but his sixteen-year-old sister was in the corridor and came running over to kneel beside him. "Felix!" Throwing her arms around him, she rubbed her face against his fur as if she hadn't seen him for years.

He returned the affection, Madison a beloved member of their small family pack that existed within the larger SnowDancer pack. At so many years younger than him, Maddy had always been a pup in Felix's mind, a pup of whom he was deeply protective. But even as she drew back, her bright eyes the same color as his, and started to tell him all about a new project, he saw the strength in her, felt the dominance of her.

His slender baby sister was growing into a soldier, but he knew without question that she'd never attempt to use her dominance against him. That would break the bonds of trust and of family. Those bonds had taken a lifetime to form . . . and such trust wasn't a gift easily handed to a stranger.

"I *hate* history homework." Maddy rolled her eyes, then leaned close to whisper, "Can I hide out in your quarters so Dad doesn't make me do it?"

Felix gently nipped the tip of her nose in answer, their familial hierarchy set in stone. She'd be his baby sister always. And he was her big brother. Making a face at him, she rubbed her nose, her lower lip quivering. He growled, used to her tricks.

She stuck out her tongue at him. "Okay, okay. I'm going home to read about history so ancient it should be in cobwebs." Another wildly affectionate hug before she rose to her feet. "If I go missing, it's probably because I turned into a skeleton myself. I'll tell Mom and Dad you said hi and that you turfed me out without a thought to my wounded heart."

Wolf huffing in laughter at her dramatics, he watched her make her way down the corridor, a graceful brunette girl in a short skirt, well-worn boots, and a slouchy sweater, a girl who hadn't yet reached her full adult height—that pink denim skirt hadn't been so short on her when she'd asked for it for her birthday. The same genes that had given him his six feet, three inches of height would, he was betting, take Maddy to at least five foot nine.

Smiling at the thought of how annoyed she'd be at once *again* growing out of her favorite clothes, he pressed his paw against the pressure switch to open his door. Once inside, he nudged the door closed and shifted back into his human form in a fracture of light and painful ecstasy. He stretched as he walked to the bathroom, more than ready for a shower.

As he washed off the sweat and grit from his body, he started thinking about scents. He wondered what he smelled like to a cat—probably of dirt and plants. Not sexy, but he was who he was . . . and Desiree seemed to see him, at least. The bonsai had been a thoughtful gift. Not only had she gone to the trouble of finding out that he loved—

"Stop it," he told himself in the mirror after he'd dried off. "You are *not* getting into anything with her." Dark-eyed Carisma had been a smart, sexy dominant, too, had courted him with gifts and affection.

The gauche eighteen-year-old he'd been had fallen for it hook, line, and sinker.

"Fool me once," he muttered under his breath and, scowling, dressed in fresh jeans and a white T-shirt before heading to one of the common rooms to grab dinner.

"Felix! Felix!"

A deep smile creasing his face, he grabbed the little boy running toward him. Ben didn't hesitate to hitch a companionable arm around Felix's shoulders as Felix settled him on his hip and continued to walk. "You smell like soap," the boy announced. "Did your mom make you take a bath?" It was a commiserating question.

Felix's shoulders shook. "I was dirty from planting trees," he said through the wolf's laughter.

"I got dirty from falling in a mud pool two days ago!" Ben announced gleefully, his silky dark brown hair shining under the den lights that had segued automatically from simulated sunlight to a softer glow that told those within that night had fallen.

"Yeah?" he said in response to Ben's story. "I bet you had to have a bath."

"No! Hawke threw me in the pond to clean me off!" Ben's excitement was infectious. "That was much better than a bath."

Felix kissed the top of Ben's head, his wolf already conscious the boy would grow up to be strong, fiercely so. It was easy to know with some of the little ones, even before they knew it themselves. Right now, however, Ben was still a very small boy, and like all the children in the den, he trusted Felix without question. Submissives had that effect on the most vulnerable members of their pack, the reason why they were tasked with evacuating the pups should it ever become necessary.

"Do your mom and dad know you're out here playing?" he asked, aware Ben had a curious streak a mile wide.

"Uh-huh. Mama's with Lara over there." He waved in the direction of the common room where Felix was headed. "She made cake! And I got to eat the first piece. It was really big and it even spoiled my dinner, but Mama said it was okay this one time."

Having reached the doorway, Felix saw that the cake was in the process of being demolished by those in the room. "Hey," he said when Drew went for a second slice, having wolfed down one while Felix watched.

The other male looked at him with narrowed blue eyes, the brighter light in this room picking up fine glints of copper in the thick brown of his hair. "I'll fight you for it." He held out a fisted hand for a game of rock, paper, scissors.

Snorting, Lara swept away the last slice and handed it to Felix, the soft black of her corkscrew curls bouncing around her fine-boned face, her eyes a clear tawny brown and her skin a natural dark tan. "Eat it before he decides to pounce."

"Please." Drew tugged at one of her curls, the golden skin of his arm marked by thin scratches that meant he'd probably been playing rough-and-tumble games with the pups. "I have manners."

"Of a leopard," another soldier said with a sly grin, the crumbs on his T-shirt telling Felix he'd successfully navigated the cake free-for-all.

"Leopards are nice!" Ben said loyally, having two very good—and equally mischievous—friends in DarkRiver.

Sighing, Drew shook his head. "So young and already corrupted."

"I'm going to mention you said that to Mercy," Felix threatened and took a seat at the table with Ben in his lap.

"Mercy doesn't count. She's an honorary wolf." Drew sprawled in the chair across from him, smiling his thanks when Ben's mom, Ava, brought them some coffee, having gone across to top up her own and Lara's cups.

"Spence have baby duty?" Felix asked the maternal female, whose dark eyes and hair were identical to that of her son.

Ava's smile held love, affection, and pride in equal measures. "He's showing her off to a couple of his photographer friends who're visiting from the other side of the territory."

"Mercy's not a wolf!" Ben said suddenly, his frown deep and his small face scrunched up in thought. "She's a leopard. I saw her. She's all golden with spots."

Felix suddenly wondered what Desiree looked like in her leopard form. She was so sleek and dangerously sensual in her human form that she'd no doubt be gorgeous as a cat. "Here," he whispered to Ben, sneaking him a bite of cake.

Giggling, the little boy totally gave himself away to his mom, but Ava just smiled and reached over to pluck him into her lap. "What are you doing, my little cake fiend?" A snuggle, a kiss, Ben's laughter filling the air.

Felix grinned, his wolf watching through his eyes. This was what he wanted. A mate, cubs to protect and love, a woman who'd see value in him, not simply a body she wanted to fuck. Losing his taste for cake at that harsh reminder, he nudged the remainder of the slice over to Drew. The other man gave him a frowning look but didn't say anything. Not then.

It was twenty minutes later, the two of them now alone in the common room, that Drew leaned forward. "What's up?"

Felix chewed the bite of lasagna he'd taken. It was divine, deserved his full concentration. Pity then that his taste buds had gone into rebellion and everything suddenly tasted like dust. "I'm an idiot."

"About anything in particular?"

It was hard to remember that Drew was a dominant at times like this—not only a dominant, but the pack's tracker, tasked with hunting down and executing rogue SnowDancers. It was one of the most dangerous positions in the pack.

"Women," Felix muttered, hoping that'd be the end of it.

Drew's smile was smug. "Ah."

"Oh, shut up." The other male was so happily mated that Felix wanted to throw something at him at times.

Grinning, his eyes wolf, Drew jerked up his head. "Desiree, huh?"

Felix's mouth fell open. "How did you . . . ?"

"Oh, please, Felix. It's a pack; we're nosy."

Obviously, one of the SnowDancer soldiers on security patrol had seen Desiree approach him last night. "She's a dominant."

"So?"

Yeah, Drew would say that. He'd gone hell-for-leather for a lieutenant older and more dominant than him. There was one critical difference, however. Drew wasn't, and never would be, a submissive. When Indigo snarled at him, he snarled back. In the same situation, Felix's wolf instincts would urge him to bare his neck, submit to the lethal predator in the room.

His hand tightened on the fork and he took another big bite to shut himself up before he said something stupid. Drew didn't take the hint. "Look," he said, "if you're worried she's with someone, she's not. Far as I know, Dezi hasn't been dating anyone for the past few months."

Dezi.

For some reason, it irritated Felix that Drew knew her nickname when he hadn't. "I'm not looking for a short-term lover, Drew," he said bluntly. "I'm ready for more." He'd been ready most of his adult life, his drive toward building a home and a family a powerful one.

Eyes meeting his for a long minute, longer than Felix's wolf was usually comfortable with when it came to a dominant, the other male nodded. "I get that. Dezi won't push where she isn't wanted—you tell her no?"

Felix ducked his head, ate another bite of lasagna . . . then admitted his muck-up. "I accepted her friendship."

Drew groaned, leaning his elbows on the table to drop his head into his hands. "Damn it, Felix, you know better. She's interested in you—and you *know* how she'll take that."

Yes, he knew. Dominants didn't really understand subtle when they were sexually interested in someone. Blunt was always the best response. "I'll tell her tomorrow. I just . . . didn't want to hurt her feelings." His hand fisted under the table at the lie; the cold, hard truth was that he'd wanted to talk to her again, wanted to hear that husky voice rasp over his skin as she asked him questions about his work that seemed to hold a genuine interest.

He reminded himself that Carisma, too, had asked him questions like that at the start. Humoring him, he'd realized afterward. He'd poured out his dreams into her hands, and all she'd given him in return was a pat on the cheek and a kiss good-bye before she'd gone on to mate with a fellow soldier. Yeah, no way in hell was he ever going through that again.

Chapter 3

DESIREE WAS EXCITED about a man for the first time in what seemed like forever. She'd gone through her young and wild phase like most leopard females, but that had been years ago. Though touch was as important to her as to any changeling, she'd been abstaining from intimate skin privileges for long, lonely months. There was just no one she wanted to be with, and though friends had offered to help her ease her touch hunger, she'd turned them down.

There was nothing wrong in being with a friend, in finding comfort in each other's arms, skin to skin as her soul craved, but she wanted more. Felix . . . There was something there, something that had her smiling as she arrived on watch to find him putting her bonsai in the passenger seat of his beat-up old truck. It had hurt her the previous day when he hadn't taken it home, though she'd told herself he could hardly carry it in his mouth.

But, oh, he was a beautiful wolf. It had taken all her self-control to keep her distance when she'd returned to this area in the evening just in time to see him exit the shed in his lupine form; she'd wanted to run her fingers through his luxuriant fur as badly as she wanted to pet that gorgeous hair of his. "Hi."

A quick glimpse from below a fan of long lashes, his skin stretched taut over the dramatic bones of his face. Not a blush this time. No, this was harsh tension. Her smile faded. Stopping a couple of feet away, she leaned against the side of the truck. "Is something the matter?"

He blew out a breath, his shoulders rigid under the battered gray T-shirt he wore, the fabric skimming down the hard planes of his upper body. "I can't do this." Quiet, intense words.

A punch to the stomach couldn't have taken her more by surprise. The spark between them, she'd been certain he'd felt it, too. "You don't like me?" She wasn't the giving-up type, had to know if there was something she could do to stop him from walking away before she'd even gotten to know him.

When his cheekbones flushed, his fingers tense on the edge of the open door, she realized she'd come perilously close to using her dominance against him. Shit, shit, shit. That wasn't how it worked, how she wanted this to work. The cold truth was that a dominant could *compel* a pack submissive to obey her on the sexual level. Felix wasn't pack but as a blood ally, he was close enough—his wolf might just obey her.

Even the idea of it made her skin crawl.

Turning away, she braced her hands on her knees, nausea twisting her gut into knots and shame flooding her mouth with bile.

"Dezi?" A careful touch on her shoulder. "Are you okay?"

Gentle hands even now, she thought. He'd never be violent, Felix, would never tear and claw. It was always what she'd sought from lovers before—primal fury, her leopard wanting to tangle with a man who was her match. But today, she began to get an inkling of why none of those lovers had ever truly satisfied her.

"I'm sorry," she said again, staring at the ground so she wouldn't inadvertently lock her eyes with his, make him back down. "I didn't mean to use my strength against you."

"What?" Confusion in his voice, his big hand stroking her back, petting her. "You didn't do that."

"I was pushing you."

He actually laughed, the rich, masculine sound stroking through the fur of the leopard inside her skin. "News flash, Dezi. Dominants do that. A lot." He shifted to crouch down beside her, his hand still big and warm on her back. "The rest of us have learned to handle it."

This time, it was Desiree who looked at him through her lashes, their eyes catching for a fleeting instant before he broke the contact. "Please look at me," she said softly. "I need to know for sure that I didn't hurt you."

His Adam's apple moving as he swallowed, he nonetheless held her gaze for a long second. A deep, luscious brown, his irises were almost swallowed up by his pupils. When he broke contact again, she read the flush on his cheekbones, the tension in his muscles in a different light. "You do want me," she whispered, her fingers trembling. "Then why . . ."

His hand fisted on her back. "I can't be your toy, Dezi."

She sucked in a breath.

"Shit," he muttered. "That came out wrong. I just . . . I'm ready to settle down, find a long-term lover or a mate. I want pups and a home and a family I can spoil and adore." He lifted his head, their eyes meeting for another split second. "You know that can't happen between us."

Dezi wanted to argue with him, but she knew he was right. Her leopard was drawn to strength, to power. She couldn't change that, as he couldn't change the fact that he needed a partner who wouldn't discomfort or inadvertently scare his wolf. "Damn." It was a soft whisper. "I really like you."

She saw his lips curve, the lower one fuller than the upper, and wished she could see the gorgeous entirety of his smile. "I like you, too." Petting her back again, he said, "Friends? For real."

"Yeah . . . friends." The most fascinating man she'd ever met and there was no way she could have him, not without hurting him.

DESIREE kicked at the fallen pine needles outside her parents' Yosemite home, trying to walk off her temper before she went in for a late lunch with her mother. She hadn't had a restful sleep after her shift, her body torn up with primal sexual desire focused on a man she simply could not touch.

"You'll kick a hole in the earth all the way back to your *nana* and *nani* in Kashmir if you keep doing that."

Desiree groaned at the sound of that clear voice with its lilting accent. "Hi, Mom." Shoving her hands into the pockets of her jeans, she met green eyes the same shade as her own and answered in one of the Kashmiri languages her mother had taught her as a toddler. "At least that way, they could visit us more easily." Her maternal grandparents lived in a remote area of the mountainous region.

"Don't be silly, cublet. You know your *nani* would never stand for tramping through a dirty tunnel. She likes to fly in the jets." Petite and in dancer shape, her silky brown skin unlined, Meenakshi slipped her arm into Desiree's. "Now, come inside. Tell your ma what's wrong."

"Nothing's wrong," she muttered, feeling sulky and frustrated.

That earned her a pat on the arm and a crook of a finger. Surrendering, Desiree leaned down and was kissed on the cheek, Meenakshi's hand warm on Desiree's other cheek as the scents of fire and water mingled with growing green things enveloped her. The fire and water was her mother—an elemental, artistic creature. The growing green things, that came from her dad, Harry's and Meenakshi's scents permanently entwined after so many years as a mated pair.

Bad mood easing as the scent of home and of family sank into her bones, Desiree followed her mom through the trees and into the house where she'd grown up. Meenakshi waved her into a seat at the kitchen table and pulled out a skillet. She wasn't the best cook on the planet, but she did a spiced omelet that Desiree loved, complete with sliced chilies, onions, a sprig of coriander . . . and lashings of love.

It was exactly that favorite that she made for Desiree today.

Putting it in front of Desiree along with a small bowl of steaming rice, her mother said, "You need carbs as well as protein. Eat." She placed a platter of cut fruit on the table for afterward.

Sitting down with a toasted bagel that she spread with cream cheese for her own lunch, Meenakshi sighed. "Twenty-seven years and six months since I discovered this and it remains my delicious nemesis." She took a big bite, made a blissful sound in her throat.

Desiree laughed. "I know. My fault." Meenakshi had apparently started craving bagels with cream cheese during her first pregnancy, hadn't been able to eat them during her second, then started again right afterward. "At least I didn't make you eat pickles and strawberry ice cream. Together."

Her mother's eyes widened. "Who's eating that?"

"Ria," Desiree said, knowing Meenakshi hated missing out on any interpack gossip. "Annie told me Ria sent Emmett out in the middle of the night to find pickles. He bought a jumbo jar and she ate them inside of a day." She shook her head. "Apparently, she dips the pickles in the ice cream."

Meenakshi's smile was affectionate. "I can't wait for their cub to be born. And I bet you the baby grows up and either hates pickles or adores them. No middle ground. Just like you can't stand cream cheese and your sister loves bananas more than is good for her."

"Sonu call yesterday or today?" Her sister, Sonal, might be roaming the world, but she made sure to touch base regularly, aware Meenakshi worried about her "cublets."

Her mother's face lit up even as she groaned. "Look at this!" She thrust her phone at Desiree. "Your sister is jumping off perfectly good bridges, just like you did!"

Desiree laughed at the image of her younger sibling's gleeful grin as she bungee jumped off a mist-shrouded bridge somewhere in South America. She decided not to tell her mom that Sonal had already jumped out of a plane. Twice. Those messages had come directly to Desiree. For a cat, her sister had an unusually strong taste for the air. No surprise then that Sonal intended to become a pilot once she'd satisfied her need to roam.

They spoke about Sonal and about other family things until Desiree was halfway through her meal. At which point, she told her mother everything, because that was what she'd always done—Meenakshi's love was a fierce force of nature. It centered and comforted Desiree as much as her father's calm, solid presence.

"Hmm," Meenakshi said afterward. "He's right, your Felix."

"He's not my Felix." That was the problem.

"Stop sulking, cublet. It doesn't suit you."

"I only do it with you."

Laughing softly, Meenakshi reached out to tweak one of Desiree's braids. "My pretty, brilliant baby, you know what you're like. Your cat fights chains tooth and nail. It'll take a very strong man indeed to tie you down."

"He's strong," Desiree said with a scowl. "Submissive doesn't mean weak, you know that." That was a mistake only outsiders ever made. Every changeling raised in a balanced pack knew that all submissives would fight to the death to protect the vulnerable under their care, their courage unflinching even under attack from dominants they could have no hope of defeating.

Meenakshi raised a perfectly shaped eyebrow. "*I* know that. But does your leopard know that?"

Desiree worried her lower lip with her teeth, the leopard prowling frustrated and confused inside her skin. "I want him more than I've ever wanted a man in my life," she whispered. "And I can't bear to hurt him."

She met her mother's intent gaze. "He's so talented, Mom, so gifted. I swear he literally coaxes the trees to settle into the soil, to grow." Rubbing a fisted hand against her heart, she swallowed. "I feel this hunger to *know* him, to find out all the pieces of him and hold those pieces close so nothing can ever harm him."

Meenakshi set her cup on the table. "That's more than want, sweetheart."

"I know." She folded her arms around her middle, hugging herself tight. "I just don't know if it's enough for Felix."

A week after she'd agreed to be his friend and nothing more, Felix watched Desiree joke with a fellow DarkRiver soldier as all the adults who'd been helping with the planting that day gathered for an impromptu party. The soldiers had worked out a watch rotation that meant everyone could join in, and Felix had done a run up to the den in the truck to sneak out food and drinks.

Now they sat among the trees to the left of the denuded section, the dark gold of sunset turning the entire area into an oil painting. Felix, seated with his back against a pine, a beer in his left hand, should've been relaxed, content. He was ahead of schedule, the mood of the pack lifting with each new square of greenery. The seedlings were taking well, and he had every hope that by this time next year, the denuded area would be covered thickly enough that the pack no longer saw it as a vulnerability.

Instead of being happy, however, he was irritable and aggravated, and it wasn't difficult to figure out why. His body hadn't let him get much sleep since the day Desiree stepped out of the trees and sauntered over to him on those stunning legs currently encased in sleek black jeans. He dreamed about the lemon spice and wild cat scent of her, woke up aroused and hungry. Meanwhile, she was leaning against the big male leopard, shoulder to shoulder, the two of them so easy with skin privileges they'd probably end up in bed tonight.

Squeezing his beer bottle tight to the point that he was in danger of fracturing it, he got up and decided to walk off his mood. He left the bottle on a crate the others were using as a table and, hands in the pockets of his jeans, began to stride toward a stream about a ten-minute walk away—hopefully, his head would be in the right space by the time he made the round-trip.

Lemon spice in the air.

"Felix."

Freezing at the sound of that husky voice, he hesitated only a split second before carrying on.

She came after him, her long legs matching his stride, though he was a solid five inches taller. "You're mad at me."

He gritted his jaw. "No."

"You've been scowling at me since the party started. What did I do?"

"Nothing." No, she'd been . . . friendly. No more dazzling smile, no more flirting, no more sense of invitation in her voice. It was exactly what he'd asked for, and it infuriated him.

Not leaving, she kept walking with him until they were far enough away from the party that Felix could no longer hear the others. Then she cut in front of him. Bringing himself to a halt, he stared past her gray-T-shirt-clad shoulder, though having her this close to his neck deeply discomforted his wolf. A single move and she could rip out his jugular, sever his carotid.

"I'm stubborn, Felix." Her voice held the edge of a growl. "Tell me what I did to offend you."

He knew he was tangling with a stronger predator, his wolf clawing at him to back off, but he couldn't. Not today. "I want to go for a walk. Do I need to ask your permission?"

Flinching, she unfolded her arms. "Fine." She stalked past him, back toward the party. "Do what you want."

Fuck. He stared after her, knowing he should let her go. "Dezi." If she didn't stop, he couldn't make her. That was the thing. He couldn't ever make her do anything she didn't want to do, would always have to trust that she'd never break his faith if they . . .

She stopped, turned on her heel. "Yes?"

Shoulders tight at the edgy response, he looked at the ground, back at her. "You can come with, if you want."

A glare, but she fell in beside him again, and they walked in silence all the way to the stream. Sunset was fading into evening by the time they arrived to take a seat on a fallen log beside the water; Felix's vision had adapted automatically to the fading light and he knew hers would've done the same.

Hand fisting and unfisting by his side, he finally blurted it out. "Are you going home with him?"

"Who?" She angled her body slightly toward him. "Barker?" It was an incredulous question.

Felix stared out at the trees on the other side of the stream, his skin flushing from the force of her gaze. "Why do you sound like that? He's a strong dominant. The females in my pack find him very attractive."

"We trained together," Desiree said dryly. "I've put him flat on his back in a fight multiple times—that doesn't make me want to jump his bones."

He was the one who flinched this time. Because should it ever come to a physical fight between the two of them, Desiree would eviscerate him. He didn't have the killer instinct of a dominant, didn't want it.

Groaning, she leaned her head against his shoulder. "Why do I always say the wrong things around you?"

It startled him, the uncertainty in her tone. Chancing a glance at her, the weight of her head against his shoulder something that gave him pleasure, he said, "I don't know what to say to you, either."

"That's not true." Her braids moved against him as she shook her head. "We have perfectly great conversations when other people are around."

She was right. He now knew that she loved climbing, that her mom was overprotective and made her check in after a night shift even though she'd moved out years ago, and that, same as him, she had a younger sister she adored. "I like talking to you," he admitted.

It was worth the admission of vulnerability to see her lips curve in *that* smile, the dazzling one she hadn't given him for a week. "Ditto." A frown and she shifted to straddle the fallen trunk so she was facing his profile. "What if we're wrong, Felix?"

He hated losing her touch, even if it had only been through his shirt. "What?"

"Us." The single word fell between them, bringing silence in its wake. "We're both just assuming we can't make it—what if we could?"

Felix forced himself to breathe. "Your cat—"

"Wants to bite you, lick you, claw you a little." Her voice dropped. "Just enough for it to feel good."

His body pounded, his blood hot. Digging his nails into the palm of his hand, he made himself say it. "Skin privileges aren't enough."

"They're a start." Shifting closer, she still didn't touch him. "Don't you think if you're getting grumpy about me being near another man, you should reassess your friends-only rule?"

He swallowed, considered how he'd feel if she did go home with another man. His wolf raged, clawing and slashing inside his mind. And he knew he was about to make what could well be the biggest mistake of his life. "Okay," he said, even as another part of him screamed that he was being a stupid goddamned idiot a second time around.

Only this time, it was worse. He'd been a pup when Carisma tore him up. He was a full-grown man now, his emotions mature. If he did this with Desiree and it all went wrong, then he wasn't sure he'd have it in him to ever again take a risk on a woman.

Chapter 4

DESIREE FROZE, NOT sure she'd heard Felix right. "Okay?" She shifted another inch closer to him. "Baby, you have to be crystal clear. I won't touch you otherwise." She couldn't—*wouldn't*—risk even the whisper of coercion. "You hold the reins here."

His breath hitched, one of his hands locked around the wrist of the other where he sat with his arms braced on his knees. "Not just friends," he said, quiet but resolute. "I want skin privileges."

"Intimate?" She pushed because she had to be sure.

A nod.

Shuddering, she shifted close enough that the front of her body pressed against the side of his. "You have no idea how hard it's been to keep my distance this past week," she whispered, wrenching back her instinct to take, to brand; first she had to coax him to her. "I dream of you." She raised one hand to gently trace the line of his jaw, felt heat burn under his skin.

Not all submissives were shy, but her submissive was. Desiree had never thought she'd find that hot, but oh, she did. She wanted to seduce him until he smiled that gorgeous smile at her, the one that melted her knees and stole her breath, wanted to coax him until he stopped being so stiff and wary and turned to her in total trust.

That, however, would take time. She was asking his wolf to trust a predator with far bigger teeth, asking him to fight his primal instinct to get the hell away. Forcing her leopard into patience, she continued to stroke the line of his jaw, loving being able to touch him. His skin was rough with stubble, the abrasive texture delicious.

Caress by gentle caress, she coaxed him, her body a wall around his own but one that didn't trap. When he did finally relax, turning his face a fraction into her caresses, she felt like purring. Instead, she petted him some more, saw his hand ease its grip on his other wrist, saw the blood rush back into his abused skin. Unable to totally resist temptation, she leaned forward and pressed her lips to his jaw.

The masculine heat of him burned into her, his physical strength gloriously apparent in the flex of his body as he turned enough that it was an invitation. Heart slamming against her ribs, she cupped the side of his face and drew him into a slow, sweet kiss. He tasted so good, felt good, smelled good. She wanted to devour her gorgeous Felix piece by piece.

Coax, be gentle, seduce, she reminded herself. *Slow, slow, slow.*

His arm came around her at last and she was startled to feel his hand close gently over her nape. It was a possessive hold she'd have expected from a dominant, but then again, she'd never dated a submissive.

Leopard unworried by it because it knew it could escape the tie at any time, it brushed against the inside of Desiree's skin, intent on sinning blissfully with her wolf. He tasted of a lick of beer, but underneath the bitterness of hops was a taste that was pure, healthy male. Pure Felix. She tried to shift closer, was stopped by the way they were seated, his upper body twisted to meet her kiss.

Placing her hand on his throat, she—

He wasn't there any longer, having jerked away to the other side of the trunk. Reeling, she tried to think what she'd done, but her mind was too scrambled, her breasts swollen and aching. She shifted off the trunk to go to the stream, kneel down, and throw some cold water on her face. The shock of it made her cat bristle, snapped her mind awake. "I touched your throat."

Felix, his own breathing not exactly even, said, "It's a sensitive area."

Desiree wanted to slap herself. That was a sensitive area in leopard culture, too, but doubly so in wolf. She went to apologize, found her leopard against it. Closing her mouth, she tried to unravel the animal's thinking. "Want to try again?" she asked, facing Felix.

His eyes widened before a slow smile dawned on his lips. "Not turned off yet?"

Desiree realized she truly wasn't. It was fun seducing him—her leopard really, really liked playing with Felix. "Not even close." Prowling closer in slow movements that didn't threaten, she knelt in front of him, her hands on his knees. "You'll have to bend closer." He was several inches taller than her, and seated on the trunk as he was, it put him even higher.

Lips still holding the edge of a smile, he dipped his head toward her. This time, she kept her hands on his knees as she seduced him with her mouth. His own was firm, mobile, delicious. When she bit down a little to test how he'd react, he shuddered.

Okay, then, she thought with an inward grin, her wolf wasn't against biting.

Pricking him gently with her claws through his jeans, she licked over the sensual hurt . . . and he put a careful hand on the back of her neck again, sliding beneath her braids. It was asking for permission but it was also possessive. She liked it. Purring in her throat, she let him know she didn't take it as a threat and his hand curved firmly around her nape, skin to skin.

His breath ragged, he said, "I can feel your purr."

"Imagine what it'll be like when we're both naked."

Red on his cheeks. It made her want to pounce on him. God, he was *adorable*. In a hotly sexy way, all big shoulders and gentle hands. She couldn't resist kissing him some more, the feel of his muscles going taut under her lightly stroking fingers seducing her in turn. She'd always thought she liked it hard and fast and a little rough, with a partner who fought her for control, but there was *definitely* nothing wrong with coaxing a wolf to play with her. Not at all.

Breasts aching, she shifted a little farther between his legs . . . and immediately felt his thrumming awareness. Careful, she warned herself, careful, careful. Staying otherwise motionless, she used her mouth to pet him until some of the renewed tension leached out of his body. Then, and much as she wanted to take this all the way, claim full sexual skin privileges, she eased back.

Those skin privileges would take time and intense trust on Felix's part.

In bed, he'd be more vulnerable than he'd ever before been, reliant on her word that she wouldn't use her dominance to force compliance. It was something she'd never before considered, and it made her realize just how much courage it took to be a submissive in a predatory changeling pack, how much heart.

Nuzzling the side of his face as he stroked his hand over her nape, she said, "Want to shift and go running together?"

FELIX'S wolf adored running with Desiree. He was bigger than her as a wolf, but she was so sleek and fast that when they raced, it was an even competition. He even beat her a few times, and she pretended to sulk. It made his wolf bare its canines in a laugh, but only when she wasn't looking—the animal wasn't yet sure she wouldn't take the sight as a challenge. A physical fight between them could have only one ending.

He might be bigger, might even be stronger, but he wasn't a predator. Not in that way. Desiree was built to protect those she called her own, built to fight claw and tooth, built with the ruthless ability to take down anyone in her path. Without her ferocity and that of the other dominants, her pack would be easy prey for their enemies.

The two of them ran across the mountains of the Sierra Nevada and he showed her places she hadn't known existed, for this was wolf land, Felix's backyard. When the moon came up, they sat on an outlook and watched it spotlight the world. He was sorry when they had to return because it was time for Desiree to do her security rotation, but as they shifted back into human form and dressed with their backs to one another in an unspoken courtesy, he was happy. And terrified.

Whatever he'd felt as a naive eighteen-year-old, it had been a pale shadow of the emotion now growing inside him. He'd been a boy then. Young and fragile hearted and eager as a puppy. With maturity had come knowledge about himself, as well as an increasing depth of feeling. He no longer bounded like a puppy, had learned to shield himself against hurt, but the way Desiree touched him, the way she treated him . . . it made the puppy want to come out of hiding. Made him want to rub his cheek against her, let her nuzzle at his throat, trust her.

Shivering at the idea of her lush, persuasive mouth on his throat, he'd buttoned his buff-colored shirt halfway when she prowled around to face him, her walk lazily feline. "Let me," she said and took over the task. "You are so built."

He blushed, as he seemed to be doing permanently around her. "What I do, the work, it's physical."

She petted her hands over his chest after finishing with the buttons. "Oh, I know. I watch your butt when you bend over to haul those big seedling pots around."

Skin heating even further, Felix dared narrow his eyes, though he could only hold hers for a split second. "Stop teasing me."

A husky chuckle. "But it's so much fun." Petting hands on his chest again. "I love how you blush. Makes me want to bite you."

His cock grew hard between his legs once more. "I think you need to get bitten," he muttered, his wolf peeking out from between its paws to see if he'd offended her.

Desiree threw back her head and laughed, the sound wildfire around his senses. "Dare you," she said afterward, green eyes sparkling.

Felix almost did it, almost trusted her to purr rather than strike out at him, but it was too soon. His wolf froze and so did the man. Sliding her hand into his, Desiree squeezed. "Offer's open. Anytime you want."

FELIX couldn't stop thinking of Desiree's words, her voice, her scent as he got to work the next morning. She'd kept his hand in hers as they walked back to the others, making her claim on him clear. As a result, he'd been on the receiving end of more than a few winks and wolf whistles since then. It was all good-natured and he managed to hold his own, shooting back a few one-liners himself. That is, until Hawke appeared and angled his head toward the trees in a silent order.

Rising at once, Felix walked to join his alpha in the privacy of the forest. "Is something wrong?"

Hair of silver-gold glittering in the sunlight lancing through the canopy, Hawke said, "I heard Desiree made a move on you."

Pulse thumping, Felix nodded.

"Are you fine with that?" It was a blunt question. "I know the more dominant leopard females can come on strong—with interpack dating still new, they don't always read our cues well. If you found it difficult to say no to her, tell me now."

Felix flushed. "No, it was . . . I wanted it, want her."

Hawke reached out to grip the side of his face and jaw. "Look at me."

Unable to refuse a direct order, Felix obeyed his alpha, his wolf sitting stock-still inside him as it stared into the pale blue eyes of the most dangerous predator in the entire region. Hawke could move like lightning in either form, his body a muscled and dangerous machine.

"You really okay?"

"Yes."

Hawke released his grip. "In that case," he said as Felix broke the eye contact in shuddering relief, "have fun and try not to get scratched too hard." Amused words.

Felix felt his lips curve at the memory of the claws that had pricked him through his jeans. He'd liked it, liked that even though he was submissive to her dominant, she didn't see him as too weak to play with the way she wanted to play with a male. "You're a good alpha, Hawke," he said as they walked back, conscious the other man had made specific time in his day to check up on a packmate he'd worried might be in over his head.

Hawke paused, then wrapped an arm around his neck in an affectionate contact between two wolves. "Come on, you might as well put me to work for a half hour while I'm down here."

That was another thing that made Hawke such a great alpha—he didn't ever denigrate the work of others in his pack. Felix was nowhere near the power structure, but he was the horticultural expert and, in this arena, Hawke always gave his ideas weight. He'd asked Felix to sit in on the strategy meeting for this section of their territory, had requested he arrive with a plan for replanting. That plan had been discussed in detail, with the alpha and his lieutenants questioning Felix's decisions and giving him the go-ahead only once he'd satisfied them he knew exactly what he was doing.

Same as they'd do with any other operation that involved the safety of the pack.

No special treatment. No condescension.

Giving Hawke a shovel, he said, "You might want to dig near the juveniles. They turned up to do extra shifts voluntarily. I suspect it's because they want to flirt away from the maternal females, but still."

Surprisingly, Hawke scowled when Felix had expected an amused and affectionate grin. "I don't blame them." The alpha's scowl deepened. "Would you believe Nell told me off for kissing Sienna in the corridor?"

Felix couldn't fight his own grin. "Way I heard it, you were doing more than kissing. Wasn't there a half-unbuttoned shirt involved?"

Hawke's bad-tempered growl reverberated through Felix's bones. "I can't wait to have ammunition against you. I hope Dezi pounces on you in public."

The idea made Felix's entire body go hot. The idea that Dezi might one day pounce on him for more than sex, that she might claim him not only for a night but for forever, it threatened to stagger, to bring him to his knees.

Too soon, warned his wolf, too soon. *Pull back.*

Felix tried, but he knew it was a losing battle. This was why he hadn't wanted to get involved with her in the first place—she drew him too strongly, made him want too much. If her leopard decided he wasn't enough, if she walked away . . . it would hurt. Bad.

"YOU and the cute gardener, huh?"

Desiree grinned at Mercy's sly words as the sentinel climbed up to sit on the little porch off Desiree's aerie, where Desiree was having a late lunch. The evening before had been her final night shift on this rotation, which meant she now had her nights free to seduce her *very* cute horticultural expert. "Word travels fast."

Mercy shrugged, her long red ponytail sliding over the deep green of the scoop-necked tee she'd paired with her jeans. "You know the pack—the information highway has nothing on us." She glanced at the savory muffin Desiree was devouring. "Is that one of Tammy's?"

"Yeah. Want one? There're two more on the table inside." She'd dropped by the healer's house on her way home from her shift, hoping to grab a cup of coffee before she crashed for a few hours. It never kept her up, not after a late shift.

As it was, Tamsyn had not only given her coffee but made her scrambled eggs and bacon, then packed the muffins for her to take home. All while cheerfully managing the chaos that came with having to get her twin cubs ready for preschool on her own, since her mate hadn't yet made it home from a night shift of his own. And that was before another DarkRiver soldier dropped by, a hopeful look on his face.

"Healers are flat-out amazing," Desiree said to Mercy when the sentinel, who'd popped inside to grab a muffin, returned with one in hand. "She doesn't blink an eye when we turn up for breakfast without warning, no matter if it's two people or ten."

"Healers love looking after and being surrounded by family." Mercy took a bite, chewed, swallowed. "Remember that time when Nate took the boys out fishing and the pack thought we'd give Tammy a break and not bother her, give her the day to herself?"

"Man, she was *mad*." Desiree had never seen Tamsyn so fired up. "I heard her ask Lucas if the pack would like to kick her heart some more." Wincing, she shook her head. "I never want to make her mad again."

They ate in companionable silence for several minutes.

"Don't get me wrong," Mercy said when Desiree had almost finished her muffin. "I think Felix is gorgeous and sweet, but you thought this through?"

Desiree put aside her near-empty plate, a sudden knot in her stomach. "My leopard likes him. The human half of me likes him just as much."

"You know that might not be enough. Unless . . . is this a fling for you both? I didn't get that vibe from Felix, but—"

"No." Desiree curled her hands tightly over the edge of the porch. "No, he's not the fling type." He was too solid, too stable. "This is the start of a relationship."

Mercy nodded, face solemn. "I'm not going to interfere. I know what it's like to fall hard for a wolf." A grin that made her eyes glow golden. "I just wanted you to know I'm here if you need to unload, or if you need to talk about the possible repercussions or road bumps."

"Thanks." Desiree appreciated the offer, aware Mercy understood the instincts of the leopard within her better than most. "The pack stuff—"

"Not an issue," Mercy interrupted. "After me and Riley, Hawke and Lucas both agreed that the packmates in question can choose their allegiance, and that there's no reason for either one to change packs if he or she doesn't want to."

That took one major worry off Desiree's mind. She couldn't imagine not being part of DarkRiver, and Felix was as attached to SnowDancer. "I just . . . I have no desire to hurt him. It would crush me if I did. I'm going into this with my heart wide open."

Mercy didn't say anything, but they both knew that wasn't enough. Because they weren't human, were changeling, their leopards an integral aspect of their nature. And while Desiree's leopard liked Felix, enjoyed playing with him, for a dominant leopard female to mate, the leopard had to consider the male its match.

It infuriated Desiree that anyone might ever consider Felix "less" in any way, but she knew her leopard might end up being the worst offender. Because sometimes, the human heart didn't win. Sometimes the untamed animal within made the choice and that choice could be a ruthless one that tore Felix and Desiree apart.

Chapter 5

FELIX DIDN'T LINGER at the work site for the first time since the replanting had begun. Driving his trusty old truck to the den, one of the lieutenants in the passenger seat, and the flatbed filled with tired but raucous packmates arguing about the plays in a recent football game, he felt cautiously happy, excited.

Desiree had messaged him earlier that day to ask him out to dinner. It was stupid how happy that made him. Part of him had been prepared to hear from her only at night, in the context of intimate skin privileges. It would've been a kick to the gut and he'd have ended things then and there, regardless of how much he wanted her, but it would have also been a painfully expected thing.

A dinner invitation wasn't.

Leopard females of Desiree's dominance liked to be chased, or that was what Felix had always believed. He'd been trying to figure out if that meant he could ask her out without stepping on her toes, but she'd beaten him to it and he felt like that damn, vulnerable puppy again. All excited and nervous and—

"Felix, slow down before this old jalopy falls apart."

Checking the speedometer at Indigo's drawl, he eased his foot off the accelerator and twisted to glance guiltily through the back window. "Are they okay?" he said, returning his attention to the forest track.

Indigo snorted. "Hard cases, each and every one." She stretched out her long legs. "Never seen you so eager to leave your babies."

Felix smiled at the gentle teasing. The seedlings *were* babies—of the forest, of the land that succored them. "The soldiers on security detail have promised to babysit. Drew said he'd sing them a lullaby."

Indigo laughed at the reference to her playful mate, her love for Drew an echo in the air. "Tell me. I won't blab."

"Do I look like I was born yesterday?"

"I'll guess, then. It has something to do with the gorgeous Desiree, doesn't it?" A pause. "You're blushing, so I declare myself right."

Felix cursed his inability to keep his cool where Desiree was concerned. "We're going on a date."

"Anyplace I know?"

He shrugged, trying not to betray the depth of his excitement. "It's a surprise."

"You know what they say about cats and surprises," Indigo said darkly.

Felix shot her a startled look, conscious she was good friends with Mercy, and realized he'd been had. "Very funny."

A wicked grin that lit up the vivid purple-blue of her eyes. "Hey, I had to do it."

He parked in the den garage a few minutes later and though everyone else took off with shouted thanks or quick slaps on the back, Indigo fell in beside him. "Want some advice?"

"No."

Of course, packmates being packmates, that didn't stop her. "Dominant or submissive, a woman likes feeling wanted."

Felix thought of the way Drew had courted Indigo so outrageously, until the entire den had been on tenterhooks waiting to see what the other man would do next. "You liked all the things Drew did?"

"He did drive me a little mad," Indigo admitted with a slow smile, "but I never wondered if he found me attractive. Something to be said about that."

Her words circled in Felix's brain as he showered. It wasn't that he didn't know how to make a woman feel good—he did. Only, most of the women he'd dated after returning to the den had been submissives like him. There was no question of hierarchy between them, of who should lead the dance. But that, he thought, didn't make Indigo any less right.

He dressed carefully in clean jeans and a chocolate-colored shirt that brought out his eyes, according to the young designer who'd gifted it to him after Felix did a show for him gratis. It had horrified Felix's booker, but Felix had already known he was about to leave the modeling world for good, having been accepted into a horticultural apprenticeship.

Why not go out doing a show for a designer he liked who needed a hand up?

Ready and with several minutes to spare, he ducked out to one of the pack's two massive greenhouses. Both were concealed from aerial view courtesy of some very clever positioning and creative camouflage that nonetheless didn't block the sunlight needed by the plants—and Felix was the one in charge of how the greenhouses were utilized. The pack had asked him to take up a position with them after he'd qualified, and he couldn't have been more delighted to accept. He loved working in SnowDancer territory, loved that everyone came to him for anything to do with plants.

Four years on and he'd been promoted to the head of the horticultural team when his boss retired. Today, at thirty-one, he managed a staff of five, their primary task to make sure SnowDancer had an independent source of fresh fruits and vegetables notwithstanding the season. That self-sufficiency became especially important in winter, when heavy snow could bog down the roads out of the Sierra Nevada and make supply runs difficult.

As for the flowers he and his staff nurtured—they weren't for the stomach but the heart.

Smiling at the thought of some of the floral requests his team had fulfilled for packmates, he worked quickly to make a special bouquet. This wasn't usually his job—he had a teenager on his team who was training as a florist—but he wanted this to come from his own hands . . . his own heart. It took him longer than he'd anticipated and he was a little breathless when he met Dezi just outside the White Zone, where she'd parked her vehicle.

Dressed in black jeans that hugged her legs, paired with black ankle boots and a V-neck red T-shirt made of a silky-looking fabric, she took his breath away. And that was before she shot him a smile that dazzled. "Are those for me?"

He located a few of his brain cells, worked out how to speak. "Yes." Wanting to kiss that smile into his own mouth, he passed across the bouquet of sweet pea blooms and Chinese hellebore and blackberry lilies. The blackberry lilies glowed with the colors of sunset, the petals dotted with dark spots like those of a leopard.

Touching a petal, he said, "I was late because I was hunting for this one. I wanted the bouquet to be unique and beautiful . . . like you."

Desiree's eyes grew wide, her hand pressing to his jaw as she rose on tiptoe to touch her lips to his in a sweetly tender caress. "No one's ever given me flowers before."

Man and wolf both stared. "But you should get flowers every day."

DESIREE found herself lost for words. Men found her exciting, a little wild, strong . . . but no one had ever looked at her as Felix was doing. As if, along with the strength, she was also the pretty, feminine type of woman due flowers as a matter of course. It wasn't something she'd ever really thought about before, but she had the feeling she could become addicted to getting flowers from this brown-eyed wolf, and most of all to the way he looked at her when he gave them to her.

As if she was the most wonderful thing he'd ever laid eyes on.

Wanting to kiss him senseless, she brushed her fingertips over the velvet and color of the flowers he'd put together just for her, then satisfied her need by taking his hand. "Come on or we'll miss our reservations."

Felix laughed when she brought the car to a stop halfway down the mountain. "Reservations?"

She grinned and went to grab the picnic basket in back, but he'd already seen it, lifting it out with an easy strength that made her want to shape her hands over every taut, muscled inch of his body. Damn, but the man was hot. And sweet and smart and good with his hands to go with it. Was it any wonder she wanted to sigh and pounce on him at the same time?

Touching her fingers to one of the blooms in the bouquet she was leaving safely in the car, she picked up the picnic blanket with a racing heart, tucked her arm into his, and led him to a stunning glade she'd discovered a month before while on a solo run late one night.

Situated beside a small, clear spring that burbled water out over smooth rocks, it was private and lit with the last faint glow of the setting sun as they walked to it, but she'd snuck up here earlier and added solar-powered fairy lights. Those lights flicked on three seconds after they reached the spot, pretty dots of color in the dark.

Felix froze.

Desiree's skin burned. Shit, who was she to try to be all romantic—but it was too late to take down the lights. Ready to fire back a flippant response if Felix teased her or if he laughed, she heard: "You did this?" It was a rough whisper. "For *me*?"

His unhidden pleasure was like sunshine in her blood.

"First time ever," she admitted. "I'm not very good at romantic gestures." Being one of the boys had always come much easier.

Felix wrapped a careful arm around her waist. "I think you're really good at it."

Drawing in his scent, she felt her cat stretch out in a pleasured arch, a purr caught in her throat. "Let's set up the blanket." She forced herself to separate from him and flicked out the tartan blanket; her reward was to see him set the basket to the left and lie down on the blanket, his eyes on the fairy lights above.

A shy glance before he raised his hand toward her. Her blood warm and heavy, she came down onto the blanket and—careful to watch for his responses—placed her head on his chest, her fingers spread over the warm strength of him. He didn't jerk, his arm coming around her, and they lay together in contented silence for long minutes.

When Felix began to play with her braided hair, his fingers brushing her nape now and then, she couldn't restrain her purr. He halted . . . but only for a second. Boneless after several minutes of the lazy petting, she luxuriated in the rumble of his chest when he spoke to ask, "Who does these braids?"

"I do." It took some calisthenics, but she was pretty good at it now.

"I've never seen your hair out of them."

She ran her hand down his side. "It's much neater and easier to handle like this while I'm working." Her hair was all exuberant waves otherwise.

"Would you . . ." A pause, his chest rising. "Would you wear it unbraided for me one day?"

A thousand butterflies fluttered in her stomach. "Anytime you ask."

When wolf song rose on the air minutes later, she almost felt Felix's wolf prick its ears in interest, but he didn't join in. "They'll figure out where we are," he said to her when she asked why. "Nosey parkers."

Laughing, Desiree rose up on her elbow to look down at him. His gaze connected with hers for a powerful instant, skated away long before she'd had a chance to drink in his gorgeous eyes. Patience, she counseled herself not for the first time. In being with her, she was asking Felix to go against his most deeply rooted instincts. If her leopard was confused by what was happening between them, so was his wolf.

"So wolves are the same as cats in that respect at least," she said lightly. "Pack gossip runs fast and hot."

He spread his hand on her lower back, a delicious, heavy weight. "I lived in private apartments and hotel rooms while I was working as a model," he told her. "No Drew poking his head in to tease me, no Madison knocking to ask if I wanted to treat her to takeout, no one hassling me about my life or bending my ear about their own life." A deep breath, his next words quiet and potent with emotion. "I *hated* it."

Desiree stroked her fingers through his mink-dark hair, the strands cool, heavy silk. "Why did you travel so far? Everything I know about you says you're a man who prefers home and family."

He folded one arm behind his head. "You might have noticed I'm a little shy." Color on his cheekbones.

Desiree couldn't help it. She reached down and kissed each blade-sharp cheekbone in turn. His lips tugged up at the corners. "I used to be much worse," he told her. "It frustrated me until I couldn't breathe sometimes. I'm happy being submissive—I have no desire to become a dominant—but I *hated* being so shy. It was crippling."

"So you decided to take up one of the most aggressive and brutal jobs in the world as far as self-esteem is concerned?"

He shrugged at her dry comment. "I had to figure out some way to make myself get over the shyness or I knew I was going to end up imprisoned in the den." Shaking his head, he said, "It would've made me resent the place and the people I loved and I couldn't bear that."

His decision displayed a deep internal strength that had her leopard paying careful attention; this man, the animal realized, was far more complex than simply being a sweet, smart playmate. "How long were you away from the den?"

He didn't immediately answer, his gaze connecting with hers again for a fleeting instant. "Your eyes have gone leopard."

"My cat likes you, wolf."

Hand flexing against her lower back, he made eye contact again, holding it for long, beautiful seconds this time.

"I was gone five years," he said after breaking the intimacy of the connection. "Even though I couldn't return home often, I stayed tightly connected with my family and the pack. After that, I spent two years apprenticed to a horticultural expert in another state—but that was close enough that I could visit the den regularly."

Desiree petted his hair again, loving the feel of it, loving even more how his eyes closed in unspoken trust and his breathing evened out. "Do you ever miss it? That jet-setting life?"

"No." Simple. Absolute. No room for doubt. "What about you? Do you like to travel?"

She wanted to kiss each one of his lashes where they lay in a dark fan against his skin. Man, she was so sunk. "I roamed for a couple of years when I was younger," she said, her voice huskier than usual. "Most leopards do." It was part of their nature. "But while I liked seeing the world, visiting other packs, it was fun only because I knew I could come home anytime I liked."

Felix's eyes opened to reveal pupils dilated in pleasure from her petting. "You wouldn't mind being with someone who's a homebody?" His heart thudded under her hand as he asked that question, as he let her see that he was thinking beyond this moment, beyond skin privileges.

"I'd love it," Desiree whispered, her own heart thudding as hard. "I'm a homebody, too." She could feel her smile deepening as all the hopeful joy inside her fought to escape. "I'm also a really good cook. Bet you didn't expect that."

FELIX was forced to admit he hadn't; she was so much the soldier that he'd never linked her to anything domestic. "Did you make the picnic?"

"Yes." Sitting up, she reached for the basket. "I even made dessert."

Rising to a seated position beside her, Felix tried to hold on to his heart when it wanted to burst out of his chest and lay itself at her feet. It was all happening too fast, too hard, but she was destroying him. More than one woman had tried to seduce him over the course of his lifetime. In the modeling world, would-be lovers had attempted to do it with fancy dinners and dressed in sexy clothes. Within the pack, it was flirtation and sensual play.

No one, however, had ever done something so painfully romantic, spent so much time and effort to create a night that would make him feel special, with no expectation of a return. Desiree knew full well his wolf wouldn't permit total skin privileges tonight, that they might *never* get to that point, and she'd *still* given him romance.

How was he supposed to hold on, keep himself from falling?

Swallowing the raw emotion in his throat, he said, "What's that?" as she set out pieces of French bread, then spread them with something fresh and herb-scented she had in a small jar. She topped the bread with chopped onions, tomatoes, and green peppers.

"My take on bruschetta." She lifted a piece to his lips.

Taking a bite, he groaned. "More."

Smile bright, she fed him the rest. He picked up the second slice before she could and held it out to her. She bit at it, threatened to nibble on his fingers. He decided he wouldn't mind, his wolf charmed into lowering its guard by this dangerous, beautiful cat who treated him as a man. Not a submissive, not a pretty plaything. A man.

It only got better from there.

The night was intimate and magical.

Picnic eaten, they lay on the blanket again, talking and occasionally kissing. Felix's heart slammed against his ribs each time his lips touched Desiree's, her long and limber body rubbing against his. She was so small in comparison to him, her weight far less. It made him feel intensely protective though he knew it was a foolish thought, given her lethal nature and skills.

That didn't change how he felt. When they pressed up against each other for a kiss, he turned and took her with him, ensuring she was on top so her back wouldn't be against the hard ground. Afterward, their breaths short, he dared stroke her throat with his hand.

She shivered, some of her braids falling over one shoulder to kiss his chest. "Why does that feel so good?"

Felix's wolf nudged at him, guilt twisting in his abdomen. "I shouldn't be doing this," he admitted, unable to steal the gift.

"Why not?" Desiree closed her fingers over his wrist but her grip was light, more caressing than caging.

"It's intimate," he admitted. "Between wolves. To touch the throat, it means a lot."

Desiree's eyelids lowered, leopard-green eyes glinting at him from between her lashes. "Sneaky."

He drew in a deep breath, released it. "Yes."

"I'm a cat," she said, leaning forward to flick the tip of her tongue across the seam of his lips in a quick, playful caress. "I *like* sneaky." Then she took the hand he'd dropped off to the side and brought it back to her throat. "Pet me."

The husky demand made his already hard cock throb.

Chapter 6

AROUSAL A FIST around his throat, his respiration shallow, and his wolf astonished at her trust, Felix stroked lightly with his fingertips. They were rough because of his work but Desiree purred at the sensation, her eyes fully closed as she arched her neck. The move pressed her pelvis against his and it took every ounce of control he had not to grind against her.

She hadn't given him the go-ahead for such intimate skin privileges and, in spite of his need, Felix wasn't sure either one of them was ready to push that hard and that fast. His wolf found her incredibly sexy, but it remained painfully aware that she could rip out his throat before he realized she'd moved.

When her claws pricked him, he froze in his stroking.

Her eyes opened a little. "Don't stop." Flexing her claws against him again, she suddenly dropped her head to meet his gaze. "Oh, sorry."

Felix was the one who grabbed her wrist this time, doing it without thinking. "No," he said. "I don't mind." He was a wolf; being a little rough in bed was all part of the fun as far as he was concerned. "I just wasn't sure if you were telling me to stop."

Lips curving, she did that flexing thing with her claws again. "I'm kneading at you. It's a very bad kitty habit."

His cock pulsed at her purring tone. "I like it," he said in an echo of what she'd said to him earlier and, breath tight, tugged on her wrist.

She came toward him with a lazy, feline smile, her hair sliding around him as they kissed. The taste of her was dark, intense, luscious. Growling low in his throat, he moved his hands to her lower back, his fingers on the taut curve of her ass. He really wanted to pet that ass, was just about to do it when Desiree kissed her way across his jaw to nip at his throat.

His wolf took over.

DESIREE knew she'd messed up the instant Felix went motionless around her. He'd been all sexy, delicious male an instant before, his mouth and his hands doing hot, beautiful things to her. "Damn," she whispered, raising her head from his throat at once. "And right after you told me how important the throat is to a wolf."

Felix didn't immediately answer, his eyes the rich, dark amber of his wolf. "Fuck," he said when he did speak, the single word harsh and low.

A second after that, his cheekbones flushed a deep red. It wasn't shyness this time, she realized. His jaw was set with brutal hardness, his beautifully shaped lips pressed into a thin white line. Desiree frowned, about to ask him what was wrong, when he shifted slightly beneath her and she realized the answer. Her act in nipping at his throat had seriously shifted the balance of power, and in so doing, had put paid to his erection.

His very nice erection.

Not sure how to handle this—dominant or submissive, he was a guy, and guys tended to conflate masculinity with sexual prowess—she rolled off him to lie on the blanket on her back, her face turned toward his. "I'm really sorry I forgot." She didn't mind taking the blame for what had been her mistake. "Forgive me?"

His hand was fisted bone white against his thigh, and it sounded like his jawbones were grinding against one another. When he spoke, the words were gritted out. "That's not the problem and you know it."

Scowling, she rose up on her elbow to look down at him. "So we hit a hiccup." It wasn't the first time, probably wouldn't be the last. "Don't tell me you weren't enjoying it till then."

Felix braced one arm below his head again, that hand fisted as tightly as the one by his thigh. "When I'm in bed with a woman, I want to feel like a goddamn man, not like I've had my balls cut off."

Desiree flinched at the soul-deep stab. Sitting up fully, her arms around her raised knees, she sucked in deep drafts of the cold night air, but it did nothing to stop the burning in her gut, in her eyes. The second she heard Felix move behind her, she got to her feet and, striding to the nearest tree, climbed easily up into the branches.

"I should get these lights down," she said, though she didn't really have to; the lights were solar powered and gave off so little illumination that they weren't a threat to either pack's security. She'd intended to leave them here, figuring someone else would eventually stumble across the glade. It had delighted her cat to think of that person's surprised wonder.

Now all she felt when she saw them was pain and humiliation.

"Dezi." Felix's deep voice ruffled her fur the wrong way, made her want to snarl. And because she was hurting and close to crying, she gave in to the urge, saw him jerk where he stood below the tree.

That didn't make her feel good.

Ashamed of herself, she returned to tugging on the string of lights, not doing much of anything to actually unravel them.

"*Desiree.*"

Surprised he hadn't backed off after her harsh response, she glared down at him. "What?" It came out another snarl.

Again, he didn't back off. Hands on his hips, he looked up. "Come down here. You know I can't climb like you."

She made a face at him, not feeling particularly charitable right now. "I didn't ask you to stay."

A growl rippled on the air.

It made her claws release. With a dominant, she'd have jumped to the ground and gone claw to claw with him. Doing that with Felix wouldn't release the anger and tension. It would just make it worse.

"I didn't mean you!" he yelled up at her. "I was talking about *me*! I'm the one who couldn't fucking keep it up!"

"Because of me!" Desiree yelled back, jumping to the ground. "It's the truth so stop dancing around it."

"You know I didn't mean it that way." Felix held her gaze for a single, powerful second, his eyes blazing. "You're the sexiest woman I've ever met. The problem is with me."

Desiree's anger spilled out and away from her, leaving her empty, her emotions a bleak gray. "No," she whispered. "You aren't a problem."

Felix was a man at home in his skin, part of the reason she'd been attracted to him from the start. The idea that she'd made him see himself as damaged or not enough? It hurt worse than any words he'd spoken in the heat of the moment. "I'm not the problem, either." Sadness clenched its fingers around her heart, squeezed so hard the pain was blinding. "We're exactly who we're meant to be."

"And maybe," he finished, his voice echoing her bleak realization, "we're just not meant to be who we are together."

FELIX buried himself in work the next day, but even as he dug his hands into the earth, he couldn't help looking out for his cat with the green eyes, though he knew that seeing her would only twist the knife deeper. After their disaster of a date, it was impossible to avoid the harsh reality that he and Desiree weren't compatible on the level of the hierarchy.

Felix had never thought he was a proud man, but it turned out he had a mile-wide streak when it came to Desiree. Every time he remembered his body's icy and demoralizing response to her little nip, he felt his gut twist. That wasn't how it was meant to be. He might be a submissive, but he was built to care for those who were his own. Yet he couldn't even give Desiree the skin-to-skin contact she needed without—

"Hey, Felix."

Hunkered down next to a seedling in the final row, beside the tall firs still standing, he shifted his center of gravity to absorb Drew's slap on the shoulder. The other man came down beside him. "It's getting dark, man. You intending to plant at night?"

Felix patted down the soil and, stripping off his gloves, shifted to rest his back against one of the nearby firs without meeting Drew's gaze. When he looked around, he saw that he and the SnowDancer tracker were the only ones here. "Where are the rest of the security people?"

"If you could see them, they wouldn't be doing their job." Drew sounded like he was grinning. "Here. I grabbed you this."

Accepting the bottle of water with a nod of thanks, Felix twisted off the lid and took a drink. Still not looking at Drew, he said, "How do you do it with Indigo?"

"That's a very personal question, Felix."

Felix frowned, then realized what he'd said. Lips twitching as an unexpected laugh built in him, he shook his head. "I didn't mean that."

Drew's blue eyes were laughing when Felix glanced at where the other man was still hunkered down, their gazes catching for an instant. "Good, because otherwise, I'd have to beat you up."

Finishing off the water, he ran a hand through his sweat-dampened hair. "I meant the fact that she's more dominant." Drew was very, very strong, but Indigo was a lieutenant.

"I love her." A simple, powerful statement. "I don't need to go all caveman to do that, to give my mate what she needs."

"No," Felix said quietly. "Because you're a dominant, too." The power balance between Indigo and Drew was far different to that between Felix and Desiree. The dominant default was to fight, even against a stronger predator.

Coming to sit beside him, Drew bumped Felix's shoulder with his own. "I bet Riley fifty bucks that you and Dezi had a fight."

Well aware Drew's older brother was far too mature to take the bet, Felix didn't rise to the bait. But he did need to talk, and this dangerous, playful tracker was a friend he trusted deeply. "It was worse than a fight, Drew." Blowing out a breath, he thought about how much to admit, his pride having taken a severe beating. "I—" He shook his head, banging the back of it against the tree trunk in a staccato rhythm. "She touched my throat with her teeth."

"Well," Drew said quietly, "that can be extremely hot, or extremely bad if the trust isn't there first."

"I should've been able to handle it."

"Bullshit." Drew snorted. "If Hawke went for my throat, I'd freeze the fucking hell where I was and start thinking of ways to convince him that whatever he thought I did, I didn't do it."

Felix knew Drew, knew how the other man used humor to get through to people, but he couldn't laugh this time. "Hawke isn't your lover."

"That's true. He's not really my type. I mean, with that hair and everything." Tapping his own empty water bottle against his thigh,

Drew said, "Look, Felix, you two tried to rush things and it looks like you got burned. You have to figure out if you want it enough to risk the burn again, or if it's time to move on."

Felix couldn't stop thinking about Desiree, but she hadn't turned up tonight. So maybe she'd already made that decision for both of them. "When you were going after Indigo, doing all that stuff to court her"—some of it pretty outrageous—"where'd you get the confidence?"

"Desperation." Drew's lips tugged up in a lopsided smile. "I was crazy for her and not about to give up just because she wanted to treat me like a teenager."

A feminine growl sounded from behind them. "I treated you like the menace you are," Indigo said, striding over to look down at Drew.

Unabashed, the other male grinned and curved one hand around his mate's calf. "I scented you, Lieutenant."

"Smart-ass." Indigo held out a hand, and when Drew took it, tugged her mate up to his feet.

Felix watched the easy movement, watched as Drew stole a kiss then whispered something in Indigo's ear, and he felt the hunger inside him spread and grow. Deep and rooted and directed very much toward a certain cat.

"You on watch with me, Indy?"

Drew's voice as he spoke to Indigo broke into Felix's thoughts, reminded him he needed to get up and moving. By the time he put away his gloves and other tools, then checked the seedlings one last time, Indigo and Drew had continued on to their watch positions—having made sure to say good-bye before they left.

Drew had mouthed, *Worth the burn?* to him before disappearing into the trees.

Dezi was definitely worth the burn, Felix thought, suddenly angry that she'd so easily walk away. Scowling, he pulled open the door to the truck, then slammed it shut without getting in. He was in no mood to get into a vehicle. Stripping, he threw his clothes in the open back, and shifted. His wolf flowed out of him in a shower of light, the shift an exquisite agony and a piercing pleasure. When it was over, he shook himself to settle the white-streaked light brown of his fur. And then he went tracking.

DESIREE wasn't used to walking away. From anything. She was the kind of person who got the bit between her teeth and didn't let go. It was part of what made her such a good senior soldier for the pack. So keeping her distance from Felix was taking one hell of an effort. Smashing fist after fist into the punching bag that hung in one of the trees not far from her aerie—thanks to the area's use as a training ground—she tried to punch out her fury and her need.

It had all seemed so simple the previous night. She was bad for Felix's self-confidence and he was bad for hers; they'd be better off apart. "It was just a bloody erection," she muttered now, pummeling the bag in a rapid-fire burst, the ponytail in which she'd scraped back her braids hitting her back with each movement. "And I might've overreacted to his comment, but I'm over it."

A good night's sleep had helped her shrug off her hurt. He truly hadn't meant for his words to wound her—he'd been talking from his dick. And guys and their dicks were a whole other ball of wax. Scowling, she punched some more. If she could get over it, why couldn't he? This wasn't a dominant/submissive thing. This was the two of them reacting too quickly without stopping to think ab—

She swiveled on her heel at the scent on the breeze, rich earth and autumn warmth.

Felix.

Stripping off the boxing gloves, she left them in the little hollow in the tree trunk where she'd found them and headed toward the scent. She found him under her aerie, a stunning wolf whose fur rippled with gradations of color and whose eyes were an intense amber. Standing proud and strong, his ears pricked, it was clear he'd heard her coming.

Desiree wanted desperately to stroke him, to tumble with him to the earth, to just nuzzle her face to his throat. Folding her arms, and tensing her abdomen in an effort to still the butterflies, she tapped her foot. "You took your time."

Light fractured. The wolf dissolved as she watched, turning into a gorgeous, sexy man who was bare to his smooth, pettable skin. Nakedness after a shift was nothing unusual among changelings, but this wasn't Desiree's usual packmate. This was Felix, who scrambled her brain cells and made her thighs clench as her inner muscles spasmed on emptiness, her body instantly wet and ready.

Breath catching in her throat, she closed her eyes. "Put on some damn clothes!"

"Um, where do you expect me to get clothes?"

"Grr." Making her way to her aerie tree by memory, she opened her eyes only when she was past him. Then she climbed up and, once inside her home, found a pair of sweatpants Jamie had left behind one day when her fellow soldier decided to run home in leopard form. She'd thrown it in the wash with her own stuff, so it was clean. Chucking it down to the gorgeous naked wolf below her aerie, she jumped back to the ground.

Felix froze in the act of pulling on the sweatpants. "Wow," he whispered, his eyes wide. "That was incredible."

Her cat wanted to purr. Ordering it to behave, she rose up from her landing crouch. "Not that I don't want to bite your butt, but maybe you should finish dressing."

Hot red color on his cheeks, he finished pulling on the sweatpants over that very bitable butt. Then, to her surprise, he turned to face her, his arms folded across his chest. And though his eyes didn't meet hers, his posture held a stubbornness that told her he wasn't going to back down. "You didn't come to the planting area today."

"You said you didn't want to see me anymore."

"No, I didn't. You decided it would be better for the both of us."

Desiree opened her mouth to argue . . . and realized he was right. They hadn't really discussed the future, just the fact that perhaps they were bad for one another. "Damn it." She went to shove her hands through her hair, remembered it was tied back, and curled her fingers into tight fists. "Did I pull rank?" She was infuriated and frustrated both.

"No," Felix said. "I think thinking you know best is just a natural character flaw."

"*Grr.*" Claws slicing out, she glared at him. "Did you come here to pick a fight?"

He paused for a second before nodding slowly. "Yes."

Chapter 7

"YES?" DESIREE STARED at him. "Submissives do not pick fights with dominants."

"Is that what we are? Dominant and submissive?" Shoulders tightening, his skin smooth and healthy over rippling muscle. "I thought we could be more."

Courage, she thought again, he had so *much* courage. It shattered her defenses. "I'd like that, too," she said, her voice husky. "But I'm afraid of hurting you."

His skin grew taut over his jawline. "A relationship will never work if you're constantly pulling back. Either I can handle you full throttle or I can't. End of story."

She went to open her mouth to argue, closed it. He was right. A true relationship needed to be in balance. Blowing out a breath, she flexed her fingers. "We've been rushing things." Her claws slid back into her skin. "I know part of that is my fault, but part of the fault is with you—for being so damn irresistible."

A hint of a smile on his lips, that slightly full lower one tempting her to indulge. "I agree we've been rushing, but I can't slow it down when I'm with you. Any ideas?"

"No hanky-panky for the next week," Desiree said, though her leopard was in rampant disagreement. It wanted Felix. Wanted to bite and lick and mark. "We date like we're fourteen-year-olds on our first dates."

Lines marred Felix's forehead. "No."

"No?" She put her hands on her hips. "I'm trying to figure out a solution." Attempting to give the trust between them time to build to the point where they could try sexy things again without worry. Because she wanted to try all kinds of sexy things with Felix. *All* kinds.

"Sixteen-year-olds," he said. "Who aren't ready to go all the way. Nothing below the waist and the throat's out for now."

A smile built inside her. "Done." Entire body relaxing, she allowed herself to caress him with her eyes, saw his breathing alter, sensed his scent change as he became aware of her petting gaze. "I want to lick you," she said on a purr. "But there shall be no licking tonight. Sixteen-year-olds do not lick at the start of a date."

"Want to watch a movie together?" Felix asked, his rich brown eyes meeting her own for a single, glorious second as, around them, the trees rustled in a cool night wind.

"Yeah," she said and turned to the tree. Claws out, she clambered up and was on her porch before she remembered her date wasn't a cat.

She peered over.

Standing at the foot of the tree, the large trunk bare of any handholds, Felix scowled and sliced out his claws. As she watched, he copied her ascent *exactly*, using the same grips, the same foot brace positions. He wasn't anywhere near as agile as even a young leopard, but he made it to the porch without slipping.

"I knew you were smart," she murmured, "but that was phenomenal." She knew the speed at which she climbed—that he'd been able to separate out the movements and remember the precise order . . . wow.

A flush on his cheekbones, but his smile told her it wasn't embarrassment. "I like watching you," he said, and her heart melted into goo.

This was ridiculous. She was a tough-shit soldier. Acting like a teenager. And it felt really good. Slipping her hand into his, she tugged him into her home. It was simple—a two-level aerie, though the second level was only a large, shallow step up from the first. The first level was a living room slash dining area slash kitchenette, with the bedroom on the second level.

Instead of a wall, she'd opted for curtains to block out her bedroom. Most of the time, the curtains stayed open—those who visited were her friends and family. Today, however, she walked over and let them down. It was too distracting to have the bed in her line of sight while a half-naked Felix was prowling around her living area, his eyes wolf-amber with interest.

He stopped in front of the wall she'd covered with framed snapshots of family and packmates. "Is this your sister?" he asked with unerring accuracy, zeroing in on an image of a laughing young woman with wild curls she wore in a short, bouncy cut. "Same green eyes."

"Yes—her name's Sonal; Sonu to pretty much everyone." Desiree felt a deep tug of love inside her for the sister who'd been her chatty little shadow throughout childhood, and with whom she still had a fierce bond. "She's off roaming now, seeing the world, meeting other packs, and, to our mother's despair, bungee jumping off bridges."

Felix turned his head. "Did you do that, too, when you roamed?"

Laughing, she admitted the truth. "Yes. That's where Sonu got the idea!"

Desiree's roaming days had been a time of play, but they had also seasoned her, given her leopard room to grow. And as she'd told Felix, it had only been fun because she'd known she could return to Dark-

River at any time. Pack was home . . . and this man—beyond the sexual heat between them—aroused the same feelings of belonging and comfort and peace in her.

Because she couldn't be near him and not touch, she put her hand on his lower back.

He stiffened.

Dropping her hand at once, she said, "What?" She hadn't thought that was a sensitive zone, but she'd never dated a wolf before.

Felix's muscles remained tense as he said, "I had an ex who used to touch me there, just like that. She hurt me."

The simple statement said far more than any florid words. Claws pricking the insides of her skin, Desiree tried to keep her growl from her voice. "Shall I go hunt her down?"

A startled smile before Felix tangled his fingers with her own. "No, but thanks for the offer."

Leopard happy that he'd accepted it, though it was still snarling at the idea of him being hurt, Desiree told him about the other photographs before ducking into the bathroom for a quick shower to wash off the sweat from her punching session.

Felix asked to use the shower after her.

"I came straight from planting," he said. "I'll pull on these sweatpants again after, but it'd be good to wash off the day."

"Here's a fresh towel."

Smile deep as he accepted it, he said, "I won't be long."

The water began to run seconds later.

Trying not to think about him naked and wet so close, she busied herself throwing together some food. It wasn't much, just sandwiches and fruit, but Felix's eyes gleamed in appreciation when he came out with damp hair and beads of water still on his shoulders from where he'd missed them with the towel.

She bit her tongue to stop herself from offering to dry him, not sure she could control herself once she started. "Dig in," she said. "You must be starving."

They talked throughout the meal, no awkward silences . . . though the sexual tension beneath the surface was a killer, a thread stretched increasingly taut.

Afterward, they sat together in the small love seat she had in her living area in lieu of the flat cushions most of her packmates preferred, and argued about which movie to watch. "I am not watching that," she said with a scowl. "It's a weird art house flick that'll probably have sepulchral music and no plotline."

"Snob."

"You want to watch something with subtitles and *I'm* the snob?" She bared her teeth at him before she thought about it.

He bared his teeth back. "I speak French. Learned it while I was working there."

"We're still not watching the gloomy movie." Seated in the crook of his arm, and having kept her hands very firmly to herself, she picked something else. "How about this?"

"You want to watch gory horror on a romantic date?"

Desiree hesitated, then laid it out. Might as well be honest so he knew who and what he was getting. "Told you I'm not good at the romance deal. I'm not very girly."

"I think you're very girly." Felix's voice stroked over her, made her shiver.

WATCHING Desiree's breasts rise as her lashes lowered, Felix had an epiphany. She was a dominant, yes, and pushy with it at times, but that didn't mean she had endless self-confidence. She had doubts and worries just like him, needed reassurance. Part of him had always understood that, but he hadn't really internalized it. The dominants always appeared so confident and strong that they seemed not to need anyone.

But Desiree . . .

Running one of her now free braids through his fingers, he tugged off the colored bead that anchored it and placed it on the table where she'd put a bowl of popcorn. She didn't protest, curling up against him as he slowly, methodically unraveled first one, then all of her painstakingly done braids. Her hair was crackling wild silk over his hands, sticking possessively to his hands and chest.

Desiree, meanwhile, was all loose and limber, a quiet purr under her skin. Not speaking, he continued to pet her until her eyes closed, her pulse languid. "What did you do today?" he asked quietly.

"Ran a patrol," she murmured. "Babysat five rambunctious cubs for a few hours, punched a bag hanging from a tree, agreed not to pounce on a certain wolf."

The wolf inside him padded to the surface of his skin, seduced out of its instinctive wariness. "Why were you babysitting?" It wasn't that dominants didn't babysit—they pulled their weight when it came to raising the pack's children. He was simply curious about her.

"Umm." Rubbing her cheek against his chest, she said, "Can I stretch out over your lap?"

Body hardening, he said, "Yeah."

Her movements quintessentially feline, she lay down with her head on his thighs, her feet up on the arm of the love seat and her eyes lazy. Colored a yellow-green at that moment, they made it clear her leopard was close to her skin. "Pet me some more."

He smiled at the demand and, heart thudding, used one hand to continue to play with her hair while he put his other one on the smooth skin of her abdomen after pushing up her tank top. She arched slightly under his touch, eyes closing again, but didn't protest. Rubbing his thumb over her skin, he felt his nerves fade even as a different kind of tension rose to fever pitch inside him.

"I was babysitting because these cubs are at the age where they need the occasional hard run and I was free. It was fun." Her purr rose in volume. "You have the best hands."

Unable to resist the verbal petting, he bent his head and initiated a kiss. Her hand rose to fist in his hair, but she remained lazily quiescent below him. His heart was a roar in his ears as he bit down lightly on her lower lip. A deeper purr, her clawed hand moving to his shoulder to knead gently at him. "Bad kitty," he murmured.

She nipped at his lips. "Bad girls are more fun."

He continued to kiss her, taste her, his cock growing harder with each second that passed. When she ran her hand down his chest to scrape her claws lightly over one of his nipples, he hissed out a breath. His wolf wasn't quite sure whether to worry or wallow in the lightning bolt of pleasure, and he stilled for a second.

"No?" Desiree asked, licking her tongue across his lower lip.

She was such a cat, he thought, wondering if she'd lick him everywhere. "I like it," he said. "Wolf's just thinking about the claws."

"Okay. While you're thinking, I'll just enjoy myself." She shaped his pecs, ran her hand down his side. "Do sixteen-year-olds do this?"

"I was too shy at sixteen." He'd barely made eye contact with girls. "But I say yes." He loved her hands on him.

Desiree's smile grew deeper. "Me, too."

Kissing her again, he enjoyed petting a cat who was enjoying him in turn. It was slow and sexy and for the first time since they'd come together, neither one of them made a misstep that caused things to end prematurely. When it did end, it was because they drew apart, conscious of not making the same mistake and rushing things again.

His erection was at breaking point by then, but it was a good pain, a pain that told him they were getting this unexpected relationship right.

A week later and things were still going well. Felix and Desiree hadn't had a lot of time together because of conflicting work schedules, but the time that they had, they spent with one another. Still, Felix wanted more.

Which was why he was outside Riley's office right now.

SnowDancer's senior lieutenant and Drew's brother was standing by his desk looking at a holo-map projected onto the right wall, but glanced at Felix the instant he entered the doorway. Dark haired with deep brown eyes and a solid build, Riley exuded a sense of innate stability and calm. That didn't mean he wasn't deadly—he was probably one of the few wolves in the pack who could go up against their alpha in a real fight.

"Felix," he said in greeting, his body clad in an olive green T-shirt and black cargo pants. "You need some more bodies for the replanting?"

"No." Felix leaned his back up against the wall by the door. "I was hoping to talk about the schedules."

"You've earned whatever time you want off," the senior lieutenant said over one of those wide shoulders. "Consider it done."

"That's not it." Running a hand through his hair, Felix said, "Is it possible to coordinate with DarkRiver?"

Riley turned, giving Felix his full attention. "Explain."

Felix felt the push of Riley's quiet but intense dominance against his skin, but it didn't intimidate; his wolf was nearly as comfortable with the lieutenant as it was with Riley's far more playful younger brother. "It's tough for me and Dezi to see each other," he said. "She's been on night shift the past three days, and I have to work days."

Nodding, Riley rubbed his jaw. "I guess Mercy and I didn't really notice it because I could set my own schedule," he said, referring to his own feline mate. "Leave it with me. I'll need to discuss it with Hawke." A slow smile. "I bet neither Lucas nor Hawke thought of all the flow-on effects of interpack dating."

"I'm glad we're doing it, though," Felix said with a smile of his own, his heart doing damn backflips inside his chest at the thought of his cat.

Riley laughed. "You won't hear me arguing."

Thanking the lieutenant, Felix left to take care of his duties, and the next time he saw Desiree, it was that night. Raising an eyebrow, she said, "You got me hauled in front of my alpha."

Having glimpsed the teasing glint in her eye, he shrugged. "Our conflicting schedules weren't good for romance."

Desiree's laugh wrapped around him. "Well, thanks to you, Mr. Smarty-Pants, we both have the night off and free. Want to go dancing?"

"Sure." He'd take any excuse to hold her close. "Did Lucas say anything about us?" The DarkRiver alpha was just as attuned to his pack as Hawke was to SnowDancer.

"Just that if I planned to seduce you into DarkRiver, I had his full support." A deep grin. "Your horticultural skills are in hot demand."

Felix felt his skin heat, both at the compliment and at the idea of being seduced by this wild, beautiful cat. "Shall I change? For dancing?" He was wearing jeans, boots, and a white T-shirt, all clean, since he'd showered before meeting her, but well loved. Desiree, on the other hand, was wearing tight black jeans and a beautiful rust-colored top that skimmed her curves, her hair out of its braids and straightened to a slick shine. It was pretty but he liked the crackling wildness better.

"Are you kidding?" She nipped him on the jaw, a caress he'd not only become used to from her, but that he adored. "Those jeans cup your butt just right."

He didn't blush this time; he grinned. "You can bite it later." When she laughed and kissed him again, he knew he was starting to learn how to deal with his cat.

Wrapping an arm around her shoulders, he led her to the SUV he'd signed out of the pack's fleet. "You want to drive?" Dominants were weird about being driven sometimes and Felix didn't mind making this small accommodation.

"No," Desiree said with a smile. "I feel like being chauffeured today."

The drive was fun, easy.

"Look at the line outside Wild," Desiree said, motioning at the club popular with younger packmates.

"It's good to see them having fun again." Both SnowDancer and DarkRiver packmates had stayed close to home in the weeks directly after the battle, everyone stunned at the violence and needing to be around pack.

"But," he added, "I'm glad we're not going in there." He and Desiree were headed to a place that was more dinner and dancing, the music good but the volume low enough that conversation didn't mean having to shout; he'd used the SUV's built-in comm to call ahead and book them a table.

"Did you do the club thing when you were younger?"

He shrugged. "Now and then—I don't really like being crushed in with too many people."

"I know." He could hear the smile in her voice. "You like the outdoors, open spaces." Reaching over, she put her hand on his thigh, the possessive touch making his wolf's fur rub against the inside of his skin. "I can't believe you did modeling for as long as you did."

"I missed home until it hurt," he admitted, pulling into a parking space and closing his hand over hers. "Sometimes it felt as if I couldn't breathe." Squeezing her hand, he grinned. "I once turned wolf and ran through the Champ de Mars."

Desiree hooted at the mention of the famous park in Paris. "You didn't! What happened?"

"I nearly got arrested." A grin. "But the cops couldn't catch me." Wolf huffing with laughter inside him, he said, "Hardest part was sneaking back into my apartment building. The next time I did something like that, I made sure to cache my clothes in a place I could access but that other people wouldn't notice."

"Wait." Desiree turned in her seat, eyes yellow-green and glowing. "You did it *again*?"

"I spent time in a lot of cities," he said in his defense. "Milan, New York, Sydney, Paris again. But I usually tried to find a park at least." He laughed at the memories. "My favorite time was when a bunch of kids ran into me while I was a wolf and we played football until their moms noticed and freaked out, even though I was very well behaved and obviously changeling."

"Well, city people probably aren't used to seeing a great big wolf casually playing football." Desiree was utterly delighted by his stories, asked him to tell her more as they walked to Amore, the restaurant where they planned to eat dinner, dance a little, just enjoy being with one another.

The more he shared, the deeper she fell.

He was telling her about another model he'd known, when they arrived at the restaurant, to be told their table wouldn't be ready for another twenty minutes. In no hurry, they decided to hang out at the bar. They'd just grabbed their drinks and Desiree was cuddled up to Felix, telling him about her trainee soldier days, when some asshole patted her butt and said, "Hey, babe."

Chapter 8

ROLLING HER EYES, she turned to the big, muscle-bound idiot. "Touch me again and I'll rip off your hand."

All tanned skin and white teeth, he leaned against the bar. She was dead certain he was a nonpredatory changeling, but, from his behavior, it seemed likely he was one of the bulls from the local deer herd. They could be as cocky as predators.

"Want to dance?"

She couldn't believe the nerve of the moron. Deciding to ignore him, she turned back to Felix, to see that his jaw was clenched, his eyes wolf. "Hey." She put a hand on his chest. "Don't let some random dickhead ruin our night."

Felix's muscles remained bunched, but he looked back down at her. She smiled . . . and felt the asshole touch her again. Growling low in her throat as her claws sliced out, she spun around and clawed bloody lines across the back of his hand.

He hissed as blood welled, but didn't back off.

"Get out of her face." It was Felix's voice from behind her, his body pressed up against her back.

The other male smirked. "Or what?"

"Or I'll kick your fucking ass." Desiree slammed her drink down on the bar, aware of the entire place going dead quiet as the others around them picked up on the violence simmering in the air.

The asshole glanced at his friends, then back not at Desiree but at Felix. "What about you, pretty boy? You gonna stand there and let your girlfriend do all the work?"

Desiree's leopard went stock-still inside her skin. *This*, this was what had been holding her back. Not that Felix was less dominant, but whether he could accept—truly accept—a woman who was *more* dominant. And not only that, a woman who was a trained soldier, designed and built to fight.

So when he said, "What? Watch my seriously hot woman put you on your fat ass and look sexy while she's doing it? Oh, yeah, I'm definitely game for that," every single cell in her body exploded in violent pleasure.

She went to shoot him a grin, but the goddamn fuckwit who'd interrupted their date tried to touch her *again*. Snarling, she slammed out, and suddenly the bull wasn't so happy messing with her on his own. As his friends yelled and came at them, she was aware of Felix falling in beside her. They shared a grin before wading in to the melee together—and it was a melee. It seemed like everyone was ready for a good fight tonight in this very nice, very respectable establishment.

He fought side by side with her throughout and it was at that moment that she understood the true depth of his courage. He didn't have the aggressive instincts of a dominant, but like all SnowDancer submissives, he'd been trained in combat, so that he wouldn't be help-less if he was ever the only line of defense for their most vulnerable.

Tonight, she saw what it meant when a submissive fought for someone he cared about.

He was all teeth and claws and fury and an unflinching refusal to surrender, even against bigger, more violent opponents. And he never, *never* got in her way. Instead, he was there to back her up, give her anything she needed; he made sure her flank was protected, that she never had to worry about sneak attacks.

His kicks found their mark time and again, and he smashed more than one jaw.

She saw him take a brutal punch to the gut as the instigator of the fight got in under his guard, but Felix ignored the injury to ensure she remained covered. Desiree, on the other hand, was enraged. This time, she got the offending asshole bull deliberately in the face.

"If you want to play for real," she snarled as he stumbled back, bleeding, "then let me show you my fucking claws."

FELIX had seen dominants fight before. You couldn't be part of SnowDancer and not have witnessed that, even if it was only in a combat simulation. As it was, with the recent violence, he'd seen it in truth. But he'd never seen anyone fight like Desiree. Her moves were silken, sinuous, and could turn deadly with a whisper-light change in pressure or force.

He didn't think the idiots who'd initiated this had any idea she was pulling her punches. "Damn, you're beautiful," he said when they came face-to-face for a split second, their eyes colliding. He wanted to kiss her so badly at that instant.

But then he heard another angry battle yell and it was on again.

Four minutes later, an unbruised and unbloodied Desiree buffed her nails on the silken fabric of her top as she stood with her boot on the chest of the man who'd been stupid enough to touch her without permission. "Now, I'm going to go have my dinner," she said to her very bruised and battered and clawed-up opponent. "Unless you'd like me to further kick your mangy ass?"

The bull groaned, spreading his hands in surrender.

"Yeah, that's what I thought." Turning, she hauled Felix down to her mouth with her hand around his nape, claws pricking his skin. He went, his wolf perfectly happy to be in the control of this very dangerous woman—because that dangerous woman had just laid out ten other people while treating him as a partner.

There'd been no condescension, no ignoring him. She'd worked with him, left her back open—trusting him to watch it. At one stage, they'd been fighting back-to-back. And now she didn't protest when he wrapped his own hand around her nape and held her tight as they kissed. It was hot, it was wet, and it was perfect.

"A-*hem*."

Breaking apart at the pointed sound, they turned to find the owner of the restaurant glaring at them out of eyes of uptilted jet. "Really?" the petite woman said, tapping her stiletto-clad foot. "You had to put a dent in my brand-new bar *and* bend three stools?"

Desiree grinned. "Hey, at least we didn't break anything."

"Oh, shut up." The woman went over and using the pointed tip of her shoe, prodded sharply at the bull who'd started it all. "Get up, you whiny baby, and call your herd leader. You're about to get one hell of a bill."

Felix tugged Desiree away from the irritated owner—who happened to be a human member of SnowDancer. Walking over to the restaurant section, where they received a round of clapping and grinning woohoos, they took the table pointed out by a smiling waiter. "So," Felix said, picking up the menu, "that was nice. What shall we do for our next date?"

Desiree's eyes sparkled at him from over the top of her own menu . . . and that was the instant he realized he was holding her gaze, had been doing so since their kiss. His wolf paused, considered whether to lower its eyes, but could find no reason to do so. She was no longer an unknown dominant whose actions and reactions he couldn't predict. She was Desiree and she didn't see eye contact from him as a challenge; she saw it as natural, as what should be.

Suddenly, he didn't want to be here, with all these other people.

Her pupils dilated in front of him, her scent sharpening and softening at the same time. "My place is closer from here," she whispered.

"Done." Leaving a tip for the befuddled waiter, who'd just brought them a complimentary starter, he got up and, taking Desiree's hand, headed out the door.

Her place might've been closer, but it wasn't *close*, and by the time he brought the SUV to a stop at the only viable parking spot—which was still about a twenty-minute run from her aerie, his body was at fever pitch.

"We could just—" Desiree began, her chest rising and falling as if she'd run a marathon.

"No. I want all night. I don't want to have to stop later so we can run to your place."

Desiree groaned, pulled him close for a kiss that scrambled his brain cells, then took off. He raced after her. She was *fast*, far faster than he was, but that was all right, because he had the endurance to track her, no matter how fast she went. And she never went out of sight—because she wasn't running away. She was flirting with him in the way only a cat could do.

When she lunged up to her aerie, he just stood there and watched the beauty of her. Until she began to strip, dropping her clothes off the porch. He started to climb. His first sight of her naked body made everything in him ignite. He was on her in a heartbeat, his hands on her waist, his arm muscles bunching as he lifted.

She wrapped her legs around him, her own arms around his neck and her mouth locked to his. Stumbling, weaving, drunk from her kiss, her taste, he somehow managed to get them into the aerie and to her bed. When he came down on top of her, she pricked at him with her claws but he knew that pricking now, knew she wasn't telling him to stop. Nipping and kissing at her mouth, her jaw, her throat, he rubbed himself against her and knew he was going to go off like a rocket if he got naked.

"Felix." A purr of sound, her own mouth kissing down his jaw to his throat.

He shuddered, the intimacy of the caress making his wolf want to throw back its head in an ecstatic howl. But he needed her mouth on his, too, and tugged up her head to initiate another kiss. She growled low in her throat at being stopped in her self-appointed task.

Breaking the kiss, he pressed his forehead to hers, their breaths mingling. "I know you're not mad." His smile felt as if it filled his entire body.

Eyes going cat, she ran her clawed hands lightly down his back. "Why are you still wearing clothes?" An instant later, those claws got busy and his T-shirt was in shreds that he tugged off to leave his upper half bare.

Her heels digging into his ass, Desiree flipped their positions so that he ended up on the bottom. "All mine," she purred, leaning down to flick her tongue over his lower lip.

Blood hot and cock like stone, he reached up to close his hands over the luscious mounds of her breasts, tug at her nipples. She threw back her head, her unhidden pleasure in his touch making him feel like a god. Shifting his hands to run them up her back, he tilted her forward until he could suck and lick and bite at her.

A sharp nip of his ear when he got a little too rough, her nails digging into his nape. Licking over the inadvertent hurt, he reached down between her legs. She was liquid under his fingertips. Shudders rocking him at the evidence of just how much she wanted him, her scent lush and erotic, he found her clit, tugged gently.

Exhaling in a jagged rhythm, she kissed him. "I'll go over," she warned, her body undulating on his fingers as if she couldn't stop herself.

"Go," he said, the single word a harsh whisper. "I want to watch." Pressing the pad of his thumb to her clit as he slid a single finger inside her, he caressed her in a short, hard rhythm.

Her nails dug into his chest so hard that he scented blood, but that was fine. Better than fine. They were changeling. Wolf and leopard. Getting wild between the sheets was part of their nature and he fucking loved that Desiree was getting wild with him. He petted her through her orgasm even as sweat broke out over his own body, his control razor thin.

Purring in the aftermath, she melted across his body, coming down to claim a lazy, possessive kiss. With one hand, she nudged his aside, as if she was too sensitive, the fingers of her other hand playing with the flat disks of his nipples. He groaned and rubbed his denim-clad cock up against her.

She grazed his jaw with her teeth and, smile slow and very female, said, "I'm going to be a lazy cat and make you do all the work." A shift up his body, her damp heat coming into contact with his abdomen.

Fuck!

Rolling over so she was pinned under him, he took a hard, slamming kiss before rising and somehow shoving off his jeans and underwear. His shoes and socks he'd kicked off earlier, so he was naked in a matter of seconds.

"My beautiful man," Desiree said, her gaze leopard.

Covering her body with his own once more, he gripped the headboard of her bed with one hand, her thigh with the other. "You're the beautiful one." The words were rough, growled, but he meant every one. She was strong and sexy and just flat-out perfect.

Then his brain quit working, the erotic scent of her desire mingling with the scalding heat of her on the tip of his cock to make him a creature of pure raw need. Thrusting deep, he was aware of her body arching, her cry shattering the air.

"Dezi?" he ground out, afraid he'd hurt her.

Her answer was to wrap her legs around his hips and rise toward him in wordless demand.

It was all he needed.

Surrendering his mouth to her own when she sought it, he pulled out and thrust deep again and again. His rhythm was ragged, his heart thunder . . . and then Desiree's teeth closed over the pulse in his neck hard enough to leave a mark. The orgasm tore through him so hot and so hard that he felt his claws slice out.

The last thing he remembered was making sure he didn't cut her. After that there was only pleasure, only Desiree in his arms.

FELIX came back to his senses to find that he'd managed to flip them over at the last second so he didn't crush Desiree's smaller body. His breathing was harsh as he tried to recover from the hardest orgasm of his life, his body still locked with Desiree's, and his hand still very firmly on her nape.

He didn't remember putting it there, but since she was lying purring on his chest, she clearly didn't mind the hold. Trying to find words in his fried brain, he came up with, "Damn."

A husky laugh, Desiree rising up enough to look down at him. Her eyes were night-glow, her skin bearing the marks of his possession. "You have some moves, Felix Grady." It was an admiring statement.

His wolf preened. Releasing her nape, he ran his hand down the curve of her spine to lie on her butt. "That was nothing," he said, feeling just a little smug. "Wait till I really get started."

She squeezed his semi-hard cock with her internal muscles, making him groan. "Ditto." A nuzzle. "I forgot about your bruises."

"What bruises?" He'd felt nothing but pleasure, was still drunk on it.

Sitting up fully on him, she checked his abdomen and side regardless. "This one's going to turn a lovely shade of purple soon," she muttered, petting the spot with a tenderness that made something deep inside him ache.

"I'm good," he managed to get out. "It was worth it."

"Wasn't it?" A bright grin before she touched his jaw to nudge his head to the side. "I marked you," she said, her tone deeply satisfied. "Now everyone will know you're mine."

He grew harder inside her, his skin stretching tight over his body and his heart hurting with emotion. That wasn't just sexual possessiveness in her voice, in her expression; it was the kind of bone-deep possessiveness he'd seen in Indigo's eyes when she looked at Drew. It said, *Mine,* and told everyone else to back the hell off. It also held a deep, deep vein of affection . . . maybe even of . . . love.

"I love you," he said, taking a risk that could destroy him.

Desiree's face lit up. "I love you, too," she said without hesitation.

It threatened to make his heart explode. But even with emotion crashing over him, never had he felt more content in his skin—he was a predatory changeling submissive and his lover's every word, every action, every smile told him he was perfect exactly as he was. Desiree, he knew with absolute confidence, didn't want him to change, would never see him as not enough.

"Mine," she said aloud with another possessive smile. "Gorgeous mind, huge heart, a body built for sin, and deliciously talented hands." A kiss punctuated each word. "And all of you is mine." She pricked his chest with her claws.

He hissed out a breath. "What was that for?"

"Just staking my claim." A narrow-eyed look but he saw the playful cat behind it.

Felix's lips curved in a smile that surely cracked his face. "All yours," he said, his wolf daring to imagine what she'd do if he made the same blatant claim in turn.

When she leaned down to suck on the bite mark she'd made over his pulse point, he groaned at the raw pleasure of being touched by this woman who was his lover in every way . . . but his wolf was suddenly distracted by something even more powerful, even more primal.

Maybe it was a subtle change in Desiree's scent, maybe it was the way she looked at him with those feline eyes that were so affectionate and so delighted with him, maybe it was just visceral instinct, but his bones sang with a knowledge so beautiful that it gripped his heart and squeezed, *squeezed*.

Chapter 9

"FELIX?" DESIREE RAISED her head, her eyebrows drawn together over eyes glowing yellow-green. "What's the matter, baby?"

It was only then that he realized he'd gone motionless as his wolf tried desperately to calculate his next move. But he couldn't calculate. He was too fucking happy. "Now I *know* your cat likes me," he whispered through a throat scraped raw with emotion.

Tilting her head slightly to the side, Desiree rolled her eyes. "Of course my cat likes you. Who do you think bit you?"

He smiled, feeling just a bit wicked. "Come here, cat. I want to pet you."

Smile playful, she stretched out her upper body over him as they kissed. He couldn't stop grinning and when she raised her head, suspicion painted her expression. Nipping at his lips and jaw, she growled in the back of her throat. "You look like you have a secret."

Grin even wider, he tried to flip them, was stopped by the senior soldier now scowling at him. He laughed. "You really hate not knowing, don't you?"

"*Grr.*"

"God, I *love* you."

Her eyes shifted from cat to human. Nuzzling him affectionately, she allowed him to flip them this time, their ensuing loving slow and deep and full of soft whispers. "Dezi?" he murmured when she was once more boneless in his arms.

"Hmm?"

Holding her gaze, he smiled again. "We're in the mating dance." It was a changeling truth that the male always knew before the female so he could figure out ways to hold on to his wild mate, but until the dance had kicked in, Felix hadn't known if that would hold true for a submissive male paired with a dominant female. "Your cat *really* likes me," he said as Desiree's mouth fell open.

"You sneak!" She threatened to claw furrows down his back. "That's why you had that smug happy look on your face."

"Yes," he admitted, smug and happy.

Wrapping his arms tight around her, his wolf in his eyes, he growled at her. "I'm going to catch you, cat."

"Do your worst, wolf." Slitted green eyes. "This cat doesn't plan on being easy prey."

That was a serious challenge from a dominant female, but Felix was playing for keeps. "I never expect easy with you," he said, dipping his head and biting her exactly where she'd bitten him, his wolf as possessive of her as she was of him.

And that wolf knew she'd permit the aggressive caress.

She did, her purr vibrating against him.

Now we dance.

FELIX was still dazzled and overwhelmed the next morning, his wolf ecstatic. But he also knew he had to push himself even more than he'd already done. Dezi wanted to be with him, but he had to win her, had to convince her cat their lifelong dance would be worth it.

He thought of what he'd seen his packmates do to court their mates. Drew with his tricks that had annoyed Indigo, then made her laugh; Hawke throwing Sienna over his shoulder and carrying her out of a bar—though, admittedly, Felix wasn't sure Sienna considered that part of their courtship; Cooper with his messages and song requests on the packwide radio frequency.

All those acts had fit the man in question and the woman he wanted to claim.

The thing that would fit Felix and Desiree . . . it would take a little planning.

"Hi," he said to Desiree that night, after meeting her at the end of her watch. "Want to go for a run?"

She narrowed her eyes at him. "You want to go for a run? After *ignoring* me the entire day?"

"Sorry. Busy day." She had no idea. "We could run to your place."

"Yeah, why don't we do that?"

Then she took off. This time, she wasn't playing—and she was *fast*. That was fine with Felix. He enjoyed tracking her . . . and thinking about the look on her face when she reached home.

DESIREE was steamed. There were *rules* to the mating dance. Well, okay, maybe there weren't actual rules. It was different for every couple. But if written rules had existed, the one thing the rule book would say in bright flashing neon letters was that *you weren't supposed to just ignore it*!

Her leopard snarled. It adored Felix, but right now, it could've cheerfully clawed him bloody. She wasn't expecting high romance, she thought with a stabbing pain in her heart. Felix knew she wasn't good with the girly thing, maybe figured she didn't really need any of the trappings of the dance. Her eyes burned. Stupid. He was amazing. Just because he didn't want to dance with her didn't mean that she should be angry.

Only she was. Really, really angry. And sad. Mad and sad . . . and home.

Breath coming in hard pants, she looked over her shoulder and realized she'd left Felix behind long ago. Great. Now he'd probably be angry about that. He'd never given any indication that he had a problem with the fact she was stronger and faster, but men could be idiotic about such things.

She thought about going back for him, but if he was mad, her return would just rub salt in the wound. *And*, she was still mad at *him*.

How could he just ignore the mating dance? He'd said he wanted her. He'd said they were going to play, that he was going to win her. Didn't he realize that he had to convince the leopard to be his? The human heart's love wasn't enough to bring the bond into being. The cat had to agree and right now, that cat was feeling as feral as the human woman.

Confused under the mad, she climbed up to her aerie, her nostrils flaring at the autumn and earth of Felix's scent. It was on her skin now, in her blood, in her home. But . . .

She frowned.

There were far too many scents emanating from her home, sweet and wild and unexpected, but she sensed no danger, heard nothing to say anyone else was nearby. Opening her door with care, she stepped inside . . . and yelped as something fell on her. It was soft and smelled pretty and it was red and pink and yellow and white and a hundred other colors.

Laughing, her leopard batting at the petals that were all over her, she waded her way through the thousands, *millions* of flower petals that filled the aerie. How had he even done this?! Utterly delighted, she fell back into the petals. There were so many that the scented carpet cushioned her fall, the velvety petals touching every inch of exposed skin. She wanted to be naked in them.

Heart giddy with wild joy, she shifted. The beautiful pain of the change rippled through her, her body turning into a million sparks of light before re-forming into the leopard who was her other half. That leopard pounced and played in the petals and, when it caught the scent of its mate, hid itself in the delicate forest.

"Desiree?"

The leopard pounced, taking Felix's big, muscled body down into the mass of petals. Laughing, he wrestled with her, his hands in her fur and yellow and peach-colored petals stuck to the mink-dark of his hair. "My wolf wants out," he said a heartbeat before he shifted.

She watched him shift, didn't interrupt, and once the wolf shook its skin into place, they played again, tussling in the petals. The crushed softness released sweet, sweet scents into the air as the wolf growled and bit playfully at her throat. She growled back, pretending to claw him. He huffed in his throat.

They both shifted back at almost the same instant and Desiree found herself pinning down a gorgeous naked man with eyes of wolf-amber. "You liked it," he said, his cheeks deeply creased.

Desiree nuzzled him in answer. She'd heard she was supposed to play it cool with some of the mating dance stuff, but she didn't want to play it cool. She wanted to lick him up like ice cream. So she flicked out her tongue, tasted him. "How did you get all these petals in here?" she asked, licking her way up his throat and along his jaw until she reached the firm but sensual curves of his mouth. She nipped his lips, met his gaze. "Tell me."

"Nope." Hands moving over her back to cup her ass, he squeezed. "I'm not done, either."

Feeling all happy and bubbly inside, she growled at him again. "I can make you talk."

"I'm tough." He reached down between her legs, stroked.

A purr formed in her chest. Nuzzling Felix again, she sat up to straddle him, this man who gave her romance, who danced with her. Claws out, she raked them lightly down his chest. He groaned, his hands once more on her ass. "Come here."

"No. I'm going to torture you, make you tell me the details of how you did this." Shifting lower down on his thighs, she wrapped her hands around his cock, stroked up then down.

Felix shuddered, muscles rippling. When his claws pricked her skin, her leopard prowled to the surface, her vision altering as her eyes semishifted. "So you think you can convince me to mate with you?" She caressed him with her hands again.

His breath caught, his hips pumping up into her grip. "Yeah," he said, before doing something sneaky and unexpected that managed to flip her.

She fell into the petals, not having anticipated the maneuver from her submissive lover. Brushing the petals from her face, she said, "Where did you learn that?"

Coming down over her, his body braced on one arm, he kissed her and the kiss was long and soft and delicious. "I asked Drew to teach me a few things," he said afterward, his hand firmly on her breast. "I figured I needed to get myself some tricks to deal with my mate."

She ran her claws down his back, hard enough to bite. "I'm not your mate yet."

"Just a matter of time." That gorgeous smile back in full force, he bent down to scrape his teeth over her jaw.

Growling, she tussled with him, tumbling him to his back. He managed to get her under him again, their bodies rubbing against each other. The scent of arousal grew hotter, deeper, until the tussling was slower, her claws kneading his shoulders as she welcomed him into her body. His cock was thick and hard; the stretching sensation made her moan and wrap herself around him.

She held him close as they moved together, his breath mingling with hers and his skin sliding hot and a little damp over hers. She loved how he smelled, how he felt, everything about him. Her leopard was in full agreement, but she was a cat, wanted to play some more, wanted to see what else he had up his sleeve.

FELIX received more than a bit of gentle ribbing after people glimpsed his smile the next day—and especially when he stripped to go for a run and word got out about the claw marks on his back. Whistles sounded from his packmates, but he could handle it. As long as Desiree wanted to be his, he could handle everything.

Including a mating dance with a cat.

He thought of her smile the previous night, of the way she'd pounced so playfully on him, and knew he'd got it right. He'd surprised and delighted her. But the game wasn't over yet, wouldn't be over until he'd won her. So he found out her watch route and left her cake pops, sparkly bracelets made of faceted crystal, tiny chocolate sculptures, and other silly, fun things in secret places, then messaged her clues.

Her DarkRiver packmates accidentally found a few of the treats and, after figuring out what was going on, started turning up along her watch route to see what she'd discover next. Word spread to the wolves, and suddenly Felix had to avoid not one but *two* groups of nosy packmates when he went to hide the treats.

Then there was his mom, who beamed at him whenever she saw him, then tried to get him to confess his plans, and his dad, who slapped him on the back and said, "That's my boy! Showing these cats how to court a woman."

His sister, meanwhile, teamed up with Drew and Sienna to distract packmates so Felix could slip away quietly to hide his surprises for Desiree.

As for Desiree's parents—Harry had taken his measure during a work shift, while Meenakshi had invited him down for a "little chat" that turned out to be more of an interrogation. Felix had liked Harry since their first meeting and, during the interrogation, he fell a little in love with fierce, protective Meenakshi. Apparently, he passed muster, because they'd smiled and wished him luck—then told him he'd need it with their independent and strong soldier daughter.

His courtship of Desiree had become far more public than he'd intended, but Felix found himself dealing with it without worry.

Because he had Desiree.

And he was going to keep his cat.

DESIREE bit into a cake pop with a goofy grin on her face. Felix had hidden this one high up in a tree. The climb had to have taken him forever, which made it matter all the more. Sitting on the tree limb, legs swinging, she suddenly caught his scent when the breeze shifted. She froze and, finishing the cake, walked very carefully through the canopy until she was almost right on top of him.

He was hiding something else, this time in the roots of a tree. She saw the hint of a sparkle before his body blocked it.

Her leopard grinned at having caught him.

Muscles bunched, she pounced. They went rolling to the forest floor, Felix's startled eyes looking up into hers as she stretched out on top of him. "You were meant to be in the other sector," he said with a scowl.

"I know." She'd swapped sectors with another soldier after deciding to see if she could find some of his hidden treats before he sent her the clues. "What did you hide for me?"

He gripped her hips. "Bad kitties don't get presents."

Pretending to growl at him, she wiggled out of his hold and went to the tree roots. His gift was hidden in a small hole among the roots. It wasn't a necklace or a bracelet. No, it was a string of tiny sparkling beads meant to tie off braids. Her eyes burned at the beauty and perfection of the gift. "Where did you get this?"

Nuzzling at her from behind, he said, "Special order from New York."

He was so damn wonderful. And she wanted the whole wide world to know he was hers, for no one to ever again question their relationship. Placing the beads on the ground with care, she turned into his arms and kissed him. He groaned, hitching her onto his thighs as he knelt on the ground. "Say yes," he whispered. "Say yes, Dezi."

Her heart overflowing with love, Desiree wrapped her arms around him, put her lips right to his ear, and said, "Yes."

The mating bond ignited, stealing her breath and making the air rush out of his lungs. His arms locked around her, hers around him as the power of it gripped them both by the throat and demanded everything they had. Trembling in the aftermath, Felix in a similar condition, she realized she could feel the earth and the warmth of him inside her now.

Her leopard stretched out in pure, happy delight as Felix fell back, taking both of them to the forest floor. Lying flat on his back, his hands on her hips, he watched her push the hair off her face . . . and he smiled. A gorgeous, deep smile that creased his cheeks and that was so infectious she was grinning madly when she kissed him. "You taste smug."

"I am smug," he said, shifting his hands to her ass. "I just convinced my impossibly beautiful, dangerously sexy dominant leopard changeling to mate with me." Amber eyes glowed with the wolf's delight. "This smug isn't going to wear off for a while." He groaned as she rubbed her body over his hard one. "Especially if you keep doing things like that."

Desiree decided she liked him smug. She particularly liked how he held her eyes as they just lay there looking at one another with matching grins. "I feel slightly drunk."

"Yeah, the mating bond packs a punch." He ran a hand over her back. "Thanks for hitting on me right back at the start."

"Thanks for taking the risk and playing with me." Running her fingers through his hair, she rubbed her nose against his. "So, where are we going to live?"

Epilogue

THEY ENDED UP building an aerie near the SnowDancer den. As a wolf and for his work, Felix needed to be physically closer to his pack, and Desiree was plenty fast enough to run down to DarkRiver land whenever she wanted. Settling in the den was out, however—she loved the sense of family and stability that was Pack, but she'd go nuts living that close to so many packmates.

The aerie was a happy medium, ensuring her leopard had its own small territory while giving Felix quick access to the den. Desiree didn't stick to the aerie, of course, coming in and out of the den as needed. And Felix came down with her to see her parents and pack-mates regularly. The distance could've been problematic with her own responsibilities as a DarkRiver senior soldier, but Riley and Mercy had figured things out so she now worked with both the SnowDancer and DarkRiver teams.

Her alpha had cupped her face at the news of her mating and, panther-green eyes holding her own, said, "You may have mated with a wolf but you're DarkRiver—no way in hell am I allowing Hawke to steal you." A snarl. "You're on the road to becoming a sentinel and I expect the same things from you that I expect from my other sentinels."

"Yes, sir," Desiree said, Lucas's approval the icing on her joy.

"It'll mean a lot of hard work and long hours for you," Lucas warned. "Your mate going to be able to handle it?"

"Absolutely." Desiree had not a doubt in her mind about that, not after Felix had offered to leave his beloved greenhouses and find a position at a lower elevation, should she need to remain in Dark-River territory.

It had taken her over a month to convince him that she'd be more than fine with an aerie near the SnowDancer den. Leopards were far more independent than wolves in terms of their living arrangements, and it wasn't as if she didn't see packmates on a regular basis—especially given the increased cooperation between DarkRiver and SnowDancer.

Plus, her sister was grown and currently roaming the world, while Felix's sister was a teenager who looked to him often for advice.

When Desiree did need to be in DarkRiver territory for a longer period, she and Felix bunked in her old aerie, Felix adjusting his own schedule so he could come down with her. He'd already started talking to her father about setting up a greenhouse on Dark-River land, and he was never not busy when in leopard territory. Once, she'd returned from a sentinel and senior soldier meeting to find three small leopard cubs asleep on the sofa beside him as he drew up plans for the proposed greenhouse.

"Emergency babysitting," he'd said with a smile.

People trusted him not just because he was Desiree's mate but because he was Felix: strong and honorable and with a quiet courage that meant he'd fight to the death to protect the innocents in his care.

"We're making it work," she said to him six months later, as they sat on the balcony of their SnowDancer aerie, spring a crisp green scent in the air around them. "We're really making it work."

"Of course we are." Picking up her hand, he kissed her knuckles. "We belong to each other. Whatever it takes to stay together, that's what we'll do."

Yes, Desiree thought as the setting sun's rays hit them both. It gilded his hair, stroked his skin with gold. "I really love that our folks get along." The four were having dinner together that night, having clicked at their very first meeting.

Desiree loved Felix's mom and dad, could see where he'd gotten his heart and warmth. "When's Maddy back from her camping trip?" That trip, run by Riley, was meant to teach the pack's young dominants advanced survival skills.

"Two days." Felix's smile was affectionate. "She wanted me to ask if she could go on patrol with you sometimes after she comes back, to get some experience."

"Sure. But why didn't she just ask me?"

"You know she idolizes you." Another kiss on her knuckles. "I'm her hero for mating with you."

Her lips quirked. "You're her hero anyway." The way Felix treated his sibling, and all the other young cubs and pups who were drawn to him, it was simply another indication of the huge heart that beat in his chest.

And the way he treated her . . .

Her eyes stung, her throat closing up.

He gave her flowers *every day.*

"Hey." His arm coming around her, tucking her into the protective warmth of him. "What's wrong?"

"Nothing," she said, her voice husky as she looked up into the eyes that never hesitated to meet hers now, the trust between them an unbreakable thread. "I'm really happy, Felix." Sometimes she just had to say it aloud, release all the happiness building inside her lest it explode.

Her mate's startled half laugh, half smile was her reward. "Me, too," he whispered. "I'm so glad we didn't give up."

"Want to go exploring together?" she asked some time later, after the sun had set and the stars had started to sparkle. "Indigo told me about a hidden waterfall about a mile from here."

"I'd go anywhere with you, Dezi."

Her heart, it was all achy and full of puppies and rainbows and all kinds of other things that weren't the least tough-shit and Desiree didn't care. Not here, not with Felix. Nipping affectionately at his throat, she said, "Come on, mate. My cat wants to race your wolf."

"Only after we're on the ground." A scowl. "If I try to jump off the aerie like a certain cat, I'll break both legs."

Desiree laughed . . . and her sneaky wolf mate pounced on her.

FLIRTATION
OF FATE

Promises

KENJI SAW GARNET take off into the trees.

The party to celebrate their alpha's mating was going full blast and he could tell from the way Garnet had danced and laughed that she was more than enjoying herself, but he'd predicted she'd sneak out to the lake sooner or later. Garnet was as much a pack animal as the rest of the SnowDancer wolves around her, but she loved the lake deep in central den territory, always visited when she was up in the Sierra Nevada mountains.

He followed her even though he knew he shouldn't. He'd made himself a promise a long time ago when it came to Garnet and a whole lot of that promise depended on keeping his distance. But tonight the stars were out and he'd had a couple of beers and he'd been watching her dance with everyone but him except for that one time when he'd broken in for half a song; his defenses were at an all-time low.

He just wanted to spend a few minutes alone with her.

Yeah? And what if she isn't looking for alone time by the lake? What if she's heading off to exchange skin privileges with another packmate?

Kenji's gut lurched, his claws pricking the insides of his skin.

If he saw Garnet with another man, he'd force himself to walk away as he'd been doing since the day of her twenty-first birthday, seven years earlier. No matter if he wanted to tear that other man to shreds. He'd had a long time to learn to control his primal instincts where Garnet was concerned.

He refused to think about the fact that it was getting harder rather than easier to rein in his possessiveness. As if as he matured, so did his need for her. He'd probably go to his grave loving Garnet Sheridan.

Tonight, however, he didn't have to call on his dwindling reserves of strength. It soon became clear that Garnet wasn't meeting a lover. A smile on her face and her eyes looking up at the stars, she was walking barefoot and unhurried through the forest in a direction that would eventually spit her out at the lake. He stayed upwind, content to see her so simply *happy*.

Not at all stalkerlike and creepy, Tanaka.

Shut the fuck up. It's only one moment.

The rest of the time, she ran the Los Angeles den—which wasn't in L.A. proper at all, but in the Santa Ana Mountains, and he ran the den at the southern end of the San Gabriel Mountains, his remit including the San Fernando Valley. Garnet's geographic region was smaller but it had more people packed in, with the attendant higher incidents of trouble, so they had around the same level of responsibility.

Busy as they were in their own regions, their paths only crossed via comm conferences, or the occasional pack event. They worked together to keep pack lands safe and they flirted in a way that was all sarcasm and razor-sharp wit, but that was where it stopped. He couldn't—*wouldn't*—cross that line. Even if he slipped up and betrayed his need for her, it wouldn't be a total disaster—after all these years, he was pretty sure Garnet didn't take anything personal he said seriously.

As he watched, she took a deep breath of the cool mountain air and did a little swirl. Her soft blonde hair was up in a fancy knot and her midthigh-length dress was the color of a blood orange and fitted, but at that instant, she moved as if she were a pixie with flowers in her hair, one who wore a frothy summer dress.

The image made him smile. Garnet had never been the frothy-skirt type—she'd always been so small that she'd had to fight to be taken seriously, even as a powerful dominant. Now only the stupid didn't realize that she was as lethal as any of her fellow lieutenants. However, there were no hard edges on Garnet. Not only was she petite, one of the smallest adults in the pack, her face was delicate, her hair fine, the tiny tendrils around her face kissing skin of sun gold.

His fingers curled into his palms as he fought the urge to reach out and thrust his hands into her hair, bunching the softness in his grip as he brought his mouth down on the lush temptation of her own.

GARNET was enjoying the brilliantly clear mountain night and trying *not* to think about a certain man and how damn good he'd felt against her during their dance, when she caught the scent of oak and fire and something intensely masculine. A scent that had surrounded her a half hour before, when Kenji broke into her dance with another SnowDancer lieutenant. She'd caught it on her skin afterward, a silent, aggravating taunt.

Her wolf rising to the surface of her skin on the memory, she growled low in her throat. "Go away, Kenji." There was no need to raise her voice—his hearing was as good as her own, and he was close. He must've stayed upwind to sneak up on her.

"Why do you have to be like that?" he said, prowling out of the trees to fall into step beside her, tall and graceful and with the handsome features of a Japanese pop star. All clean angles and dramatic bones. That his slightly overlong hair was dyed a rich purple and sprayed with tiny golden stars only added to the effect.

She'd have thought it an affectation, except that he'd been doing things like that since he was a kid too young to think about being cool. As a seven-year-old, he'd once drawn "tattoos" on himself with permanent marker.

Then there was the time he'd painted his hair with house paint. She could still remember his shaved head afterward—it had been the only way his parents could strip off the toxic paint, as shifting might've redistributed the paint all through his wolf fur. They'd been more distressed than Kenji. He'd asked the barber to cut zigzag patterns into the resulting stubble.

She liked the way he wore it now, how it was just long enough to hint at rebellion, the strands thick and silky.

"Going to the lake?" he asked, green eyes locked on her.

Putting a half meter of distance between them because she knew it wasn't a good idea to be alone with gorgeous, teasing Kenji Tanaka when she'd had a drink or three and her inhibitions were lowered, she said, "Going to the lake—*to be alone.*"

He closed the distance that separated them. His boots touched her bare toes, he was so close—and neither part of her changeling nature would allow her to give way now that he'd pushed. Not moving her feet an inch, she tipped back her head to look him in the eyes.

He frowned, stepped back. "Sorry. I keep forgetting you're shorter than me."

She couldn't figure out if that was a compliment or an insult. "I'm leaving now. Don't follow me."

"You sure can hold on to a mad, Garnet," he said when she would've turned away. "Like an elephant holds on to its memories." His voice was playful, light, as they'd been with each other for so long now.

"Go away," she said again, a staggering sense of loss echoing inside her. *No,* she ordered herself, *you* do not *go there.* Kenji's and her time had come and gone. No second chances, not when Kenji had shown her exactly how badly he could hurt her if she opened her heart to him.

And not when the man he'd become was nothing like the smart, laughing boy with whom she'd once fallen in love. Kenji was a great lieutenant, a packmate she could rely on in a crunch and one who made her roll her eyes with his outrageous flirting, but he didn't know the meaning of commitment when it came to women.

"Shoo," she said when he stuck stubbornly close. "I want to be alone."

"One of those times, huh?" Sliding his hands into the pockets of his jeans, his black shirt sitting easily on wide shoulders, he continued to walk beside her. "You never minded me going with you before."

"I was twelve." And thought he hung the moon.

Reaching out, he tugged on a tendril of her hair. "We used to be friends."

She stopped, faced him. "It was a long time ago." More precisely, seven years and two months ago—otherwise known as the night of her twenty-first birthday. But she wasn't about to bring up that night, a night that had devastated her tender and hopeful heart.

What she had to remember was that it had also saved her.

It would've been far worse had she ended up with Kenji only for him to walk away a short time later when another woman caught his eye. Because, unlike him, she'd been weaving dreams of a permanent relationship, perhaps even a mating if they were lucky. "How's Britney?" she said instead of dwelling on the lost dreams of the girl she'd been.

"Britney?" Dull confusion in the green eyes that were a throwback to his paternal great-grandmother. Then a light sparked. "Britney Matthews?"

Claws pricking at her palms, she smiled sweetly. "You know any other Britneys you banged like a drum?"

A hot red burn on the high planes of his cheekbones. "That was a lifetime ago. I was eighteen! You're mad about that?" He shook his head, eyebrows drawing together. "I thought you—"

Garnet cut him off before he could mention the night they'd never spoken about, never would speak about; there wasn't anything to say. Kenji had led her on, stolen her heart, then kicked her to the curb, the end. But they did have other things to discuss, because now that she'd brought up Britney, she *was* mad. Maybe it was the alcohol talking, but she had things to say to Kenji "Casanova" Tanaka about his taste in women.

"You knew how awful she was to me, how she made my life a living hell, and you not only took her to prom, you dated her for a *year*!"

A befuddled expression on his face. "I know you two didn't like each other, but I thought it was, you know, girl stuff."

"*Girl stuff?*" Was he really that clueless? "She tried to make my nickname Runt." The only reason it hadn't caught on was that pretty much all her friends and packmates already called her Jem, and she had enough dominance even at sixteen to scare most people into shutting the hell up before they used anything else.

Kenji had always called her Garnet. He'd just liked it.

As she'd liked hearing her given name on his lips.

"I thought she was just messing with you when she said that." He scowled. "You never minded when I called you Short Stuff."

That was because he'd been her friend, who she knew didn't mean anything by it. The same way she'd affectionately called him Beanpole when he first got his height. By eighteen, the muscle had caught up with the height and he'd been gorgeous. "Jesus, Kenji, Britney was a first-class bitch." Garnet wasn't about to pull her punches. "She got her kicks from picking on younger girls."

"It's not like you couldn't handle her."

She'd still been a teenage girl with the attendant fragile ego . . .

and she'd been carrying around a truck-sized crush on her older brother's best friend. The same friend who was standing in front of her right now. "Whatever. I lost all respect for you the day you hooked up with her."

His mouth fell open. "I was a teenage boy!" he reiterated. "She had boobs out to here and legs up to there and she thought I was the best thing since sliced bread!"

Garnet had apple-sized breasts, if she was being generous, and, given her height, her legs were never going to be a supermodel's. Baring her teeth and folding her arms across her chest, she smirked. "All. Respect. Lost." She leaned toward him. "Poof."

"Yeah?" Suddenly belligerent, he got in her face. "What about you? Dating No-Brains Bacon?"

Seeing red, she pushed at his chest. "His name was Barton, and he was a nice guy!"

"Who had a lot of space inside his skull. Must've been all the knocks he took on the football field."

Garnet refused to admit that sweet Barton had, in fact, been a little intellectually challenged. "At least he knew how to handle a real woman."

Kenji's growl made her own chest rumble in challenge. "You were fucking fifteen when he moved on you," he gritted out. "I should've done more than punch out his lights."

Garnet's eyes went wolf. "That was *you*?" Barton had broken things off with her without warning, after turning up with a black eye he'd shrugged off as a training injury.

Kenji's muscles bunched. "He was a fucking senior and you were—"

Garnet plowed her fist into Kenji's face, slamming his head sideways.

He jerked, one hand going to his jaw. "What the fuck, Garnet?"

"That was for Barton," she said, her breath ragged. "And for me. Thanks to you, I had to go stag to the junior dance."

His eye already looking like it might blacken, causing a twinge of remorse in her gut, Kenji said, "Better than you being taken advantage of by a guy who should've known better."

Furious heat flooded her face, wiping out all traces of remorse. "I knew what I was doing."

"Fifteen!" Kenji said again, his voice more growl than sound. "And you still looked like a kid. He was a fucking deviant."

"I had boobs!" She shoved her hands under those boobs. "Just because you go for balloon-sized tits doesn't mean anyone who dates me is a deviant!"

Eyes flicking up from her breasts, Kenji growled low in his throat. "That's not what I said."

"Yeah? Sure sounded like it."

"God damn it, Garnet, I—" No warning, just his strong, beautiful hands thrusting into her hair and his mouth slamming down on hers.

Pleasure, raw and violent and vicious, punched through her with the force of a freight train. *Finally,* her body sighed. *Finally.*

Hard on the heels of that pleasure came fury. Jerking up her knee, she would've got Kenji right in the family jewels if he hadn't twisted out of the way, breaking the contact between them. "Good move," she said with a glare, even as her wolf lunged against her skin, wanting more, wanting *him.* "What did you think you were doing?"

"What I should've done when you were twenty-one." Chest heaving and hair falling over his face, he stared at her with eyes gone the pale, husky amber of his wolf.

Feeling her own wolf in her eyes, Garnet was the one who growled this time. "You missed that chance," she said. "And I dodged a bullet."

He flinched, but she wasn't done. "Keep your hands to yourself or next time I'll rip them off. I'm not interested in being a notch on Kenji Tanaka's bedpost."

She strode past him, refusing to acknowledge the horrible sense of loss that pulsed beneath her anger like a deep, dark bruise. The same way she'd refused to cry when Kenji stood her up on her twenty-first birthday. She'd dressed up for him, even had a friend do her makeup and hair. Everyone had thought she'd made such an effort because of the party her year-mates had thrown her . . . but she'd done it for Kenji. Her friend and the boy she'd always gone to with her problems and hopes and dreams.

Even when he'd been a hormonal idiot dating Britney, he'd never let her down.

At twenty, heading into twenty-one, she'd finally been old enough that he'd allowed himself to look at her as a woman, not a girl. She'd been *so* happy, because that crush of hers? It had never truly disappeared. He'd courted her, *specifically* asked to be her date the night of the party. Then he hadn't come. She'd been worried about him, had called around frantically . . . only to discover that he'd gone out dancing with not one but *two* female packmates.

Kenji Tanaka could go drown himself in the goddamn lake for all she cared.

Chapter 1

IT WAS THREE months after Garnet had punched him, and Kenji's black eye had long faded. Just as well. Maybe soon, he'd forget the taste of her, the feel of her, the scent of her so close, the magnificent anger that had turned her blue eyes a molten wolf-gold. *What the fuck* had he been thinking? It had been hard enough to stay away from her when he'd never indulged his bone-deep hunger for her.

Now?

It was proving impossible.

And to top it all off, he'd just arrived at her den, was scheduled to spend the next four days here. *Four days.* The only thing that might stop him from going mad was that Riaz and Indigo would also be present, the other two lieutenants unknowingly providing a buffer. The four of them planned to discuss the security protocols around this part of SnowDancer's territory, which basically meant Kenji's and Garnet's sectors.

Cooper had charge of the den at the other end of the San Gabriel range, but since he had to keep an eye on a border as well, Indigo and Riaz would go to him after finishing up here. It'd allow the three to physically test security ideas, give further depth to the report they'd make to their alpha.

All of this was possible because the Psy were currently mostly focused inward, and it was a review that was sorely needed. Snow-Dancer had been so busy coming up with strategy after strategy to deal with everything that had been happening back-to-back over the past year that there'd been no time for a more in-depth assessment.

Indigo and Riaz's task was to ensure all the pieces fit together seamlessly, and that the entire SnowDancer command structure knew exactly what was happening security-wise across the territory. Snow-Dancer was so strong as a pack despite their geographic spread because they never lost sight of the fact that they were *one*.

Garnet might punch him out in a personal fight, but she'd be there in a heartbeat if Kenji needed backup in any other situation.

Running his hands through his hair as he shoved down his need, he grinned. He'd had the naturally black strands dyed just for Garnet. His hair was currently dark pink with streaks of cobalt and dark sapphire. Really, it was sedate for him, but he doubted Garnet would agree. She tended to curl her lip every time he joined a comm conference with a different look.

His packmate Louisa, a hairdresser and colorist, loved him. Called him a walking billboard for her services even though, these days, he never allowed her to do the permanent DNA bonding that meant the color would "stick" even once he shifted. Mostly, nothing showed up when he was in wolf form, his molecules rearranging themselves into another pattern, the pattern that created the timber wolf who was also him, but there had been that one time when he'd ended up with a sparkly gold ear.

Never again.

Despite the limitation that meant each look rarely lasted past a day—more often only hours—he didn't even have to go to Louisa. If she thought he'd gone too long without a change, she'd hunt him down. Once, when he'd been too busy, she'd done it right at his desk as he continued to handle pack business, including their new alliance with the BlackSea changelings. He'd ended up with tiny silver stars all over his hair.

The pups in his den had adored it.

Garnet had asked him if he'd fallen into a play vat at the day-care center.

He grinned again; maybe he'd have Louisa redo that look. Or maybe not. Grin fading, he looked at his hair again. Needling Garnet had always been a way to stay connected to her while keeping physically away—but if he was serious about letting her go, he had to stop the needling, stop the flirting, cut that final fragile tie between them. He'd already given up her friendship, given up her laughter and the way she'd once looked at him. Only this remained.

Not yet, whispered the desperation inside his soul. *She hasn't chosen a mate, isn't with anyone. We don't have to give up every part of her.*

Blowing out a breath at the words that only reiterated his craving to call Garnet his own, he walked out of the guest room to which he'd been shown. He'd arrived at Garnet's den fifteen minutes earlier, had taken the time to stow his gear and try to get his head on straight, but it was time to touch base with her, begin work.

The first person he ran into was a hugely gravid Ruby.

Garnet's older sister ran—or tried to run—toward him. "Kenny!" Her legs were covered by colorful leggings, her top half by a stretchy black top.

Wrapping her gently in his arms, he pretended to bite her ear. "Stop that, or I'll start calling you Crumpet." An infamous nickname arising from an incident when Ruby had been a juvenile.

She elbowed him, all frown and big blue eyes under a short and tumbled cap of shiny blonde hair. "Shuddup about that. I'm a highly respected maternal now."

"And I'm a lieutenant." He bent down to kiss her on the cheek.

"A gorgeous one at that." Patting his jaw with a slender hand, her nails painted hot red, she smiled in open affection. "Thanks for the foot spa voucher. How did you know my ankles are currently cankles?"

"I bet your ankles are as sexy as always." Except for the belly and a slight, rosy fullness to her cheeks, Ruby looked exactly the same as always: petite and ready to take on the world.

Just like her younger sister.

"You're too smooth for your own good, Kenji Tanaka, but as one of your year group, I'm immune. Remember those mud fights? Man, you had a wicked left arm." Laughter in blue eyes that were so like Garnet's. "Now, spill. Did Steele say something?" she asked, referring to her twin and Kenji's best friend.

"He wouldn't dare lest the wrath of Ruby fall on him."

Said bundle of wrath tried to cuff Kenji around the ear.

"I got the idea from Louisa," he admitted with a grin. "Wanted to send you a gift and she said she would've killed for a foot spa when she was pregnant." The hairdresser had been spraying gold sparkles on his hair at the time, while he signed off on den expenditures.

He'd wanted to be ready for an upcoming comm meeting with Garnet.

"Well, you hit a home run." Ruby crooked a finger and, when he bent closer, kissed him on the cheek. "Talking of pups . . . I always thought you and Garnet would . . . you know."

Knives stabbed straight into his gut couldn't have hurt more than that simple, playful statement. "Yeah?" He gave her a teasing smile and said the expected thing, the one that wouldn't expose the raw wound that was his heart. "She'll fall to my charms one of these days, never fear."

Fresh lines formed between Ruby's eyes. "Um." She glanced around before waving him closer. "You don't know about Revel, do you?"

"Revel?" Kenji's skin began to chill. "Of course I know Rev. He was promoted a few months back, shifted dens to take up a higher-level position." The other male was a slender but dangerously fast-in-combat packmate Kenji had always liked.

"Uh-huh. He's become Garnet's right-hand man since his transfer here."

"Are you telling me Rev and Garnet are an item?" They hadn't been at the mating ceremony; Kenji would've known.

Ruby lifted her left hand into the horizontal position, waved it from side to side. "Two dates and a third on the way." Dropping her hand to her belly, she rubbed. "I like you and I like Revel, so I'm not going to play favorites—but, Kenji, if you're planning to make a move, it better be now. Garnet's taking him more seriously than any other guy she's ever dated."

"Come on, Ruby, you know you like me best," Kenji said, playing along even though he felt as if he'd been drop-kicked. Ruby and Garnet were close—if Ruby thought this relationship had the potential to be serious, then she had to have picked up that impression directly from Garnet.

In front of him, Garnet's older sister rolled her eyes but her lips tilted up at the corners, a tiny dimple appearing on one edge. Garnet had the same hidden dimple. Kenji had imagined kissing it countless times, imagined her laughing and nuzzling at him after the caress.

"I like you, but you've been a bit of a horn dog."

Ruby's words poured ice-cold water on his fantasies. "So I had a man-slut period." He flashed a smile that worked at keeping people from looking too deep, from actually thinking back on that period and realizing that hey, maybe Kenji Tanaka's reputation was far more scandalous than the reality.

His rep was another line of defense, another way to push Garnet away. "Not the first wolf to lose it the first few years after the hormones hit," he added, and that much was true. Newly mature wolves had been known to indulge in skin privileges like it was going out of business.

Just the past week, Kenji had walked into the weight room in his den to discover torn clothes scattered over the machines. The scents in the air had made it clear it hadn't been because of a fight, and since the training rooms were all considered communal spaces, it had been a clear violation of den policy.

He'd pinned a still-almost-in-one-piece shirt on the door to the room, written: *Lost & Found—see Kenji.*

The red-faced miscreants had skulked in an hour later, after word ran through the den. Well aware how hard it could be to control a body driven by the most primal urges, and knowing that the ribbing they were no doubt already taking from their denmates was punishment enough, Kenji had simply reminded them to stay in private spaces and to clean up after themselves.

"Kenji," Ruby said now, "you went way beyond losing it." She poked him gently in the chest. "It's like you were determined to bang every bangable woman within banging distance."

"Stop saying 'bang.'" Kenji put a careful hand on her belly after making eye contact and getting the okay. "Your pup's going to get the wrong idea about his future uncle Kenji." It hurt to play this way while knowing there was no chance in hell he'd ever have Garnet for his own; it just fucking *hurt.*

And he was the one who'd made certain of that through his own conscious actions.

The only reason he could bear it was because seeing the ache of quiet loss in Garnet's eyes would be even worse. Years ago, before he'd done his best to cut the bond that tied him to Garnet, his wolf had urged him to tell her the truth, let her decide if she wanted to be with him. But he couldn't—because he knew her heart. She was far too generous for her own good. She'd have decided for him regardless of what it would mean for her.

Kenji couldn't have lived with that decision then and he couldn't live with it now: he never wanted to steal her dreams. And the one dream being with him would destroy, she'd had since childhood. He could give her everything . . . except the *one thing* she'd never wavered on wanting over the years.

In front of him, Ruby stretched, placing one hand on her lower back. "This pup is going to give me a herniated disk if he doesn't pop out soon." She smiled and stroked her belly. "Mommy loves you, baby boy. She wants to hold you."

Kenji tucked a strand of her hair behind her ear and the question, it just came out. "So it's really serious between Garnet and Rev?" He had no right to ask that, but he could no more stop himself than he could stop loving Garnet.

"Revel's not your competition." Ruby's expression softened. "That's what I'm trying to tell you: Garnet might think you're cute, but she also thinks you're a player." She drew out the last word. "My smart, sexy sister has no need to date players—she's looking for a long-term thing, not a quick you-know-what."

Yeah, he knew. He'd always known. Had intended to be her long-term guy since the day he'd first realized his best friend's younger sister was no longer the pigtailed kid he'd chased in countless games of tag. "Garnet's special, Ruby," he said, unable to bear that she might believe he didn't know that truth.

"Yeah, well, you might've missed the boat, Kenny." Patting him on the cheek again, Ruby started to walk past. "My bladder is the size of a peanut."

Turning, Kenji watched her to make sure her balance was okay. She was tiny and the belly was huge. Garnet would be the same way when she became pregnant.

Kenji rubbed a fist over his heart. "Shut it down," he ordered himself. "You let her be happy. If you love her, you goddamn *let her be happy.*"

With that quiet, raw order to himself, he turned on his heel and jogged the rest of the way to the meeting, figuring he must be the last to arrive. He'd had to leave later than expected because of a situation in his den, and then the heavy rain had slowed him down even further. However, when he entered the small break room he'd been told was the location of the meeting, he found only Garnet within.

Dressed in faded blue jeans that hugged her legs before disappearing into knee-high boots of dark brown, topped with a simple white sweater with a wide but high neck, her hair up in a rough knot at the back of her head and held in place by a hair stick, she looked young and beautiful. But the power in her, it hummed against his skin, made his wolf's fur stir.

This woman, the wolf knew, was its match in every way.

"Riaz and Indigo?" he asked, bracing his hands on either side of the doorway to keep from lunging at her.

"Delayed by a major accident that's caused gridlock." Garnet poured herself a coffee from the carafe set on a warmer on the counter, then scowled and poured him one, too.

It did something to him when she automatically added one sugar to his.

"A car's automatic nav system shorted out, owner didn't react in time," she said as she stirred the sugar in. "He went into the back of a truck. No fatalities, thankfully, but the truck was carrying hazardous material that the authorities are scrambling to contain."

"Damn, the rain can't be helping," he said and, having somehow wrenched his body under control, walked inside to take his coffee from her. "We have anyone in the cleanup team?" Given Snow-Dancer's power in the California region, they also took a lot of responsibility for it—including helping with incidents that could affect the ecosystem.

Garnet nodded. "One of our people is leading the containment effort, with backup from a mixed team, all trained to SnowDancer specifications." She took a sip of coffee. "Weather forecast is also saying the rain might turn into a storm. If that happens, Indigo and Riaz will have to stay put until it's safe to drive up here."

"Yeah, the winds were picking up the final half hour of my drive up." Kenji drew in the scent of the coffee in a vain attempt to drown out the far more delicious scent that was Garnet. "I was in one of our gruntiest all-wheel drives and, with the mud and wind, it was having trouble gripping the road."

The sheer amount of precipitation hitting the mountains meant the land was struggling to handle it. It didn't matter how far civilization advanced, Mother Nature still packed a punch—and that was exactly how changelings liked it. Wolf or leopard, deer or swan, it was about living in harmony with the world rather than beating it into submission.

So, once you left the cities, the roads up to their dens were less roads and more tracks. It meant occasional delays such as this, but it also meant they left no permanent scars through their surroundings. Should a pack disappear, nature would reclaim those tracks within mere months.

"I told them we can always reschedule if the weather goes on this way," Garnet added.

"Sure." Sitting his ass down on one of the two battered sofas, he grabbed a sandwich off the tray of lunch goodies on the coffee table in between. "You want to start without them?" he said after taking and swallowing a bite.

"Yes." Her eyes flicked to his hair. "I didn't know we were meant to be in fancy dress."

His wolf bared its teeth at the deadpan sarcasm, delighted by what it stubbornly took as play. "Simple daywear," he said with a nonchalant shrug. "I thought about pairing it with something black and blue, ran out of time."

She scowled again at his reference to her punch, but he caught the shadow of that hidden dimple. "So," he said, warmth rushing through him, "the routes into the city."

They'd been talking things over for only about twenty minutes when Revel ran in, tall and with warm-toned skin of golden brown against a black tee he wore with black jeans and boots. The expression on the senior soldier's face had them both jerking to their feet. Though Kenji and Garnet occupied an equal position in the pack hierarchy, Garnet was the one who spoke. This was her den and Kenji's wolf understood the rules of behavior on an instinctive level.

Here, he was her backup.

"What is it?"

"Russ Carmichael is dead," Revel said shortly, his skin flushed and his breathing fast enough that it was clear he'd run here full tilt. His next words made the reason for his urgency clear. "And it looks like Shane did it."

Chapter 2

"HAS ANYONE TOUCHED the body?" Garnet asked as she and Kenji followed Revel to the scene.

"Eloise found them in Russ's quarters and she stayed in the doorway while she called me, but I had to go in to check for signs of life. Shane's alive and needed medical help, so I sent for Lorenzo." He glanced at her, dark eyes holding a question. "You weren't picking up your phone."

Garnet reached into her back pocket, came up empty. "Damn, I must've left it in my quarters." Dropping her hand, she said, "Doesn't matter—I'll grab it later. For now, can you get me a forensic kit from stores?" They had a couple of trained forensic techs in the den, but since the two were rarely needed for pack matters, both worked at external jobs and were currently away at an out-of-state conference.

That wasn't, however, a major handicap. All SnowDancer lieutenants and their most senior packmates underwent a rigorous training course to ensure they could handle such situations. Revel was still completing his training after his promotion, but Garnet had recently done a refresher course alongside Kenji and the other lieutenants.

"You have the updated codes?" she said to Revel before he broke off to grab the kit.

"Yep." His gaze shifted to over her head. "Hey, Kenji," he said, no hint of annoyance or tension in his tone at the sight of a lieutenant notorious for flirting with Garnet.

That Kenji outranked Revel had nothing to do with it. Neither did the current situation. Wolves had been known to growl and snarl at romantic rivals while working together to deal with an emergency.

No, it was Revel.

Garnet had always liked that about the senior soldier—that he was so confident, so centered, and so reliable. Part of her winced at that description even as it rolled through her mind. It hardly sounded exciting, and Revel *was* exciting. He was beautiful, for one, all quiet, intense eyes and fluid muscle; he was also a dominant and dangerous with it.

All the women, and yes, a few appreciative men, too, watched when Revel moved.

She had to remember that, not get caught up in the wild sexiness and wit and wickedness that was Kenji Tanaka, only to come out alone and hurt on the other side. She'd been there, done that, had the bruised knuckles to prove it.

"Good to see you, Rev," Kenji replied, his own tone friendly, with no apparent undertone. "Despite the circumstances."

"We'll catch up later."

The two men bumped fists, and then Revel was gone.

Two minutes later, she and Kenji arrived in front of a room sternly guarded by a tall young packmate with a blunt fringe of mahogany hair against skin of dark cinnamon brown. "Lorenzo got here sixty seconds ago," Eloise said before Garnet could speak, and though the junior soldier's voice was calm, her mouth was pinched, her eyes a stark wolf-yellow. "He's in there working on Shane." The gleaming strands of her shoulder-length braid became apparent when she angled her head toward the door, her profile strong.

Garnet didn't immediately step inside the doorway. Instead, she turned a flinty gaze on the packmates buzzing about at the end of the corridor, and suddenly everyone had someplace else to be. Only when the corridor was clear did she move forward. "Lorenzo," she said, looking into the room without entering, "what's the damage?"

Kenji put his back against the wall on the opposite side of the door from Eloise, close enough to listen without butting into Garnet's space. It caused a flicker of pleased surprise in her wolf. She and Kenji had worked together on pack business for the past three years, ever since she made lieutenant—at the same age at which he'd originally been promoted. However, given their different specialties, they'd never had reason to work side by side this closely.

Cocky as he was, part of her had been waiting for him to attempt to take charge.

"Shane's unconscious." Lorenzo's familiar accented voice broke into her thoughts, the healer having lived in El Salvador until two years earlier. His birth pack was small and the only wolf one in the entire country—but, oddly, it had been gifted with the births of *two* highly talented healers of a similar age.

The situation had left neither one truly fulfilled: healers as strong as Lorenzo and his packmate needed their own group of people to nurture. The El Salvador pack was tight-knit and the two healers were best friends, but there was simply too much drive and energy between them and nowhere for it to go.

Meanwhile, before Lorenzo's SnowDancer mate snagged him, Garnet's den had been making do with three junior healers supervised remotely by SnowDancer's head healer, Lara. These days, a deeply contented Lorenzo acted as Lara's deputy in a number of matters, including training the younger crop of healers.

Garnet trusted him without question.

"He has a pretty big bump on the back of his head," Lorenzo

continued. "He'll have to be carried out. Some facial bruising. Possible broken ribs, too." A compact man with silvered black hair against skin of a honeyed brown, the den healer got up from his crouch beside Shane's sprawled form. "Stretcher's on its way, but you can have a quick look at the scene as it is. I'm going to take a few readings from Russ's body."

Garnet glanced at Kenji. "Can you take some photos?" If she didn't have to worry about him attempting to pit his dominance against hers, she could use his support.

"No problem." He slid out his phone as he entered the room with her, his shoulders fluidly muscled under the white of his shirt, the sleeves of which he'd rolled back to the elbows.

He wore the shirt untucked over jeans of dark blue denim, his only ornamentation—aside from his hair—a handcrafted pendant carved from black hardwood and polished until it gleamed like stone, which he wore at his throat on a rawhide tie. She was used to seeing that circular pendant with its simple spiral pattern. His maternal grandfather had made it for him, and Kenji wore it in remembrance after losing the other man to an unexpected lung ailment three years earlier.

Now he began to snap photos from beside her while she took in the scene; neither one of them would move any farther into the room at this point.

Death was a sticky, iron-rich scent in the air, but it wasn't old death. No, the iron was too bright, tasted "wet" to her senses, while Shane's breath was a living warmth. Russ, by contrast, was bleak white in death. The fifty-four-year-old lay on his side on the floor; he was facing Shane's feet, an improbably small red stain on the front of his white shirt, and his head resting against the oat-colored carpet that showed every drop of blood. There was no pool of dark red, just droplets. Russ's skin appeared plastic with lack of life even from a distance, his head covered by sandy brown hair cut with military precision.

A delicate handkerchief lay half-crumpled and streaked with blood on the carpet beside his curled-up left hand, as if it had fallen from his fist. The dried blood Garnet could just glimpse on his palm seemed to support that theory.

Shane, meanwhile, lay on his front on the carpet not far from a display cabinet. He was facing the door, his hands flung out as if he'd tried to break a fall and his head turned to the side. Dark blond hair stuck to his tanned skin, and though he, too, was motionless, his skin held an undertone of pink.

Unlike Russ's starched shirt of crisp white and formal black pants, Shane was dressed in clean jeans and a simple button-down shirt in pale blue, the sleeves long. "That look like blood to you?" She pointed to a spot on the back of Shane's right forearm, the brownish red distinct against the blue of the shirt.

"Possible." Kenji began to record the scene with snapshots and video both. "Can't see any on his hands from this angle."

Neither could Garnet, but what struck her as an assassin's blade—the blade long and thin—lay below Shane's right hand. While the blade was bloody, the carved hilt was clean, so even if he had zero blood on his hands, the lack might not be significant. It would depend on the wound or wounds the blade had inflicted. To her untrained eye, it seemed as if Russ had only a single slice in his shirt.

"This couldn't have happened long ago." Kenji slid away his phone just as Revel arrived with the forensics kit.

"Thanks." Garnet frowned. "Athena," she said, referring to Russ's ex and Shane's current lover.

"I'll take care of telling her," Revel said, his eyes taking in the scene once more. "And I'll handle any other pack business that comes up in the interim."

"After you speak to Athena, call Hawke, give him the heads-up." The SnowDancer alpha needed to know about this situation. "Tell him I'll make a full report once I have anything new to share."

"Consider it done."

Giving him a small smile of thanks, this dark-eyed wolf who was so much better for her than the wild one who'd broken her heart, she returned to her conversation with Kenji. "I know Shane was working night shift this month on scheduled den maintenance." Things it was easier to do while most packmates were asleep and the corridors clear. "He would've gone off shift around seven, seven thirty."

She glanced at her watch. "It's only just past twelve thirty now, so, given his clean shirt and jeans, the aftershave I can smell under the blood, if we allow an hour for him to get to his quarters, shower, dress, maybe grab some breakfast, the earliest it could've happened was eight, eight thirty, give or take." They'd have to verify all of that, of course, but it was a good place to start.

Moving into the corridor when Lorenzo's assistant arrived with a hover-stretcher, onto which Kenji helped them load Shane, Garnet noted the lack of blood on the front of Shane's shirt as well as the bruising on his face. His palms, fully visible now, also proved devoid of any traces of blood.

Kenji followed her gaze, took several more photographs with his phone.

"Once you stabilize Shane," she said to Lorenzo, "take swabs for evidence, bag his clothes, do everything possible to preserve any evidence." Inside a pack's territory, pack law *was* the law. And as the most senior member of SnowDancer in the region, Garnet was the final judge, the one who held Shane's life in her hands—because predatory changelings believed in merciless and deadly justice when it came to the crime of murder.

Garnet had to be damn sure of any decision she made.

"I'll take care to preserve everything I can," Lorenzo assured her.

Having told his assistant to return to the infirmary to keep an eye on an elderly packmate in there for observation, Lorenzo then moved the stretcher into the corridor using the controls on one end. Eyes of an unusual, striking hazel-gray held Garnet's, tiny lines flaring out at the corners. "I'll call if I discover anything immediately important."

Looking into the room again once Lorenzo left, Garnet forced herself to concentrate on Russ's lifeless body. She was so focused on the grim task that she jerked when Kenji ran the back of his hand, warm and a little rough, over her cheek. It sparked little lightning strikes through her unwary flesh, made her forget the cold engendered by this room, this death, to remember only a man with sinful green eyes.

Damn it.

Glancing up, she went to tell Kenji to cut it out, but his solemn expression stopped her. He got it, understood the crushing weight on her shoulders, foresaw the pitiless sentence she might have to mete out—Russ's family would be given the final say, as was only right, but it was near certain that the family would expect her to act on their behalf.

"Ready to rock and roll?" Kenji asked, that pretty hair of his sliding forward as he shifted his attention to the body.

"Yes." The contact with a packmate she respected regardless of the painful history between them, the skin privileges given and accepted in friendship, without any expectation of deeper intimacy, steadied her wolf. "My forensics people are in Dallas, so we're it."

Opening the kit, they gloved up together, pulled on paper-thin and transparent plas coveralls, sealed their shoes in plas booties as fine, and tugged up transparent masks to reduce the risk of any further DNA contamination. Only then did they move into the room.

Kenji went to Russ's fallen form, but Garnet walked around to the back of the door. One thing was clear at first glance. "This dead bolt is still in a locked position." It had been torn violently away from the wooden frame around the doorway but remained in one piece on the door itself.

KENJI had crouched down by the handkerchief crumpled on the carpet, intending to examine it more closely, but Garnet's words had him rising to join her. He caught her scent as she moved back a step, the steel and strength of it an unmissable song even through all the ugliness in this room. "Like it's been forced." Frowning, he said, "Eloise." He didn't raise his voice, didn't have to, given the acute nature of changeling hearing.

The girl appeared in the doorway, her focus determinedly on Garnet and Kenji rather than the gruesome scene. "Yes, sir?"

"Did you force the door?"

Eloise's face crumpled. "I had to."

"You didn't do anything wrong," Garnet said at once, her tone calm but demanding the younger wolf's attention. "We just need to know the sequence of events."

Swallowing, the junior soldier squared her shoulders and put her hands behind her back. "I smelled blood and when no one answered, I thought maybe Russ and Shane had hurt each other." She bit down on her lower lip. "I could scent them around the door, like they'd both touched it not long ago. I swear I didn't touch anything after I saw them inside."

Realizing he was missing something, Kenji decided to wait to ask Garnet, but she filled him in then and there. "Russ was in a long-term relationship with Athena. We're talking going on ten years. Five months ago, she broke it off with him. A month ago, she moved in with Shane."

"Ah." A love triangle could explain the entire thing.

Pack was family, and loyalty was branded into a SnowDancer's bones, but they were also wolves. And wolves in love could be hot tempered, especially when in competition for a lover. Shit happened. Usually not this deadly, however. No question that things might escalate to a bloody fight now and then, but Kenji could think of no other incidence of the cold and apparently premeditated murder of a rival.

"You okay to keep standing guard?" Garnet held Eloise's eyes. "No shame if you want some time out. I don't like being around this kind of violence, either."

The girl gave her lieutenant a grateful but steady look. "I'll be all right. It was just the shock, you know?" Taking a deep breath, she turned to go back outside. "I won't let anyone in without permission."

Garnet shut the door behind Eloise, ensuring privacy. "This dead bolt can only be set from the inside."

Kenji nodded; the dead bolt was an old-fashioned one where the thick metal bolt had to be manually slid across. "No mechanism on the other side." A separate thumb-scan lock had been added to the door, likely during a denwide upgrade, and it was probably what Russ had used day to day.

"I don't suppose you scent a Psy?" she asked. "A teleporter would make a convenient villain right now."

Kenji wished he could answer yes to that bleak joke of a question. "No unexpected scents. Aside from me and you, Rev, Lorenzo, and Eloise, the only other scents in this room are of Russ and Shane." He paused, took another deep breath to confirm his initial reading. "No hint of anyone else—unless I'm missing it? I don't know

Athena." Even five months away couldn't erase a scent imprint that had been laid down over years.

Garnet rubbed the back of her forearm across her forehead, her gloved hand curled into a fist. "Russ hired a chemical steam cleaner from somewhere and did the whole apartment the week after she moved out. I could smell the disinfectant for a month afterward." Dropping her arm, she turned her attention to the body. "And that was just when I passed by in the corridor. I don't know how he stood the reek in the apartment itself."

Kenji stared at the dead man, trying to bring up a memory of this packmate and failing. That wasn't unusual, not with SnowDancer numbering over ten thousand across the territory, with new people mating in and out on a regular basis. Hawke alone knew each and every SnowDancer, though they could all recognize one another by a layer of scent impossible to explain to an outsider except to say that it came from Hawke, an acknowledgment by their alpha that this person was pack.

Accepting that he and Russ had apparently never crossed paths, Kenji walked carefully around the body. "I guess he was hurt, wanted to wipe away all traces of his lover." Kenji, meanwhile, still had the gift he'd meant to give Garnet seven years earlier, on the night Fate kicked him in the guts, left him bleeding.

His eyes lingered on her as she crouched by the body. The hood of the coveralls hid her hair, but he knew the fine strands would've glinted like spun gold in the artificial sunlight that illuminated the room. "Russ didn't have a new lover?" he asked before the silence could grow too long, betray too much.

A shake of her head. "Not as far as I know."

He hunkered down on the other side of the body. "This handkerchief. It's feminine." Carefully tugging at the bunched edges to open it, he found what he was looking for: a delicately embroidered *A*.

Garnet blew out a breath, sorrow darkening the sky blue of her eyes. "Russ," she murmured softly, "you've finally managed to surprise me." Her gaze skimmed to where Shane's body had lain, paused. "No, it definitely can't have been Shane's unless they fought over it. Looks like Russ was clutching it in his hand, pressed it to his wound, and it fell from his hand when he collapsed."

It seemed very high drama to Kenji, but again, this was a wolf they were talking about. Pressed white shirt and razor-creased pants or not, Russ had still been born with the same primal drives as any SnowDancer. He might've erased Athena from his home, but he'd clearly failed at erasing her from his heart.

Sound familiar, Tanaka?

No, he answered the mocking voice in his head. *I never tried to erase my love for Garnet. I'll be buried with her name on my heart.*

"Lorenzo will have to check," he said, a surge of aged emotion turning his voice husky, "but far as I can tell, Russ was stabbed once in the heart and bled out where he lay."

"Blood follows gravity." Garnet pointed out the dark, dark spots of blood on the carpet below Russ's chest, as well as the thin trail of red down his side that indicated he hadn't moved after collapsing. "Unless it was a lucky fatal stab, it seems he had plenty of time to go for help. Might be he hit his head when he fell."

Kenji looked around, saw no evidence Russ had tried to crawl to the door. "You want me to check the part of his head that's against the carpet?"

Garnet frowned in thought, finally said, "No, leave it. I want Lorenzo to have first go at the body. He should be back soon, unless there's more wrong with Shane than a concussion."

Getting to his feet with a nod, Kenji walked over to look at the knife. "Fancy hilt." Scrolling patterns on the metal, a green jewel at the tip.

"Shit." Garnet gritted her teeth as she came to join him, her dominance a pulse under her skin and her worry tension across her shoulders. "Shane collects knives. He's done it for years."

Wolf and man, both parts of Kenji wanted desperately to comfort Garnet, to take some of the weight, but he knew she'd push him away the instant he made the offer. This was her den, her responsibility. "Wolves aren't immune to stupidity or jealousy," he reminded her, his own jealousy a snarling monster held barely in check. "You can't keep them safe from their own choices."

A flinty glance, the blue of her eyes unimpressed. "You'd feel responsible, too, if this was your territory."

"Yeah, well, being a lieutenant doesn't save a wolf from idiocy, either." He made himself break the eye contact before she saw too much. "It's not looking good for Shane, is it?"

"Seems a slam dunk. Door locked from the inside. A man who died where he fell. Another man found unconscious nearby with the murder weapon."

Kenji's skin prickled. "Then why don't you sound convinced?"

Chapter 3

GARNET FORCIBLY RELAXED her jaw when a tension ache alerted her to how tightly she'd clenched it. "Shane is a sweet, kind man," she told Kenji. "If this had been the other way around, I'd have believed it, but Shane stabbing Russ?" She felt her hair stick rubbing against the hood of the coveralls as she shook her head.

"Russ was a hothead?"

"No, he was just . . . rigid. That's the word." Garnet didn't want to speak ill of the dead, but she needed to fill Kenji in on the context around this entire inexplicable scene. "He taught high-level math. University stuff. I often got the feeling he would've liked to arrange people like he did his math equations—all neat and tidy and contained."

"Born that way?"

"No, not like what you're thinking." Garnet would've understood a mind that simply functioned differently, accepted it. "Russ *chose* to look down on others and to consider himself above most of his packmates. And, after Athena left him, he chose to be bitter and to stew in his anger rather than accepting the comfort offered by friends and family." None of that meant he'd deserved to be murdered.

No one deserved to have his or her life stolen.

She lifted her hand to pinch her nose between two fingers,

dropped it when she remembered she was wearing gloves. "Damn it, Kenji. Shane is a good man, and he's really good for Athena."

"Nothing's set in stone yet." Kenji's voice was tempered and his vision obviously clear for being unclouded by personal connections. "No use worrying about it until you know for sure."

It was exactly the advice she needed at that moment.

Nodding, she said, "Let's walk through the rest of the apartment, take the samples we need. We'll check DNA everywhere, in case we're wrong and someone else was here."

They'd just finished the detail-oriented task when the door opened to reveal Lorenzo. "Am I okay to come in, examine the body?" the healer asked, his gaze lingering first on Garnet then on Kenji.

She knew what he was doing: checking on their emotional and mental well-being. That was part of his role in SnowDancer because, as had become apparent during the Territorial Wars of the eighteenth century, a messed-up dominant at the helm could wreck the equilibrium of hundreds, possibly thousands. Lara played the same role in the Sierra Nevada den, had the authority to overrule even Hawke when it came to their alpha's physical, mental, or emotional health.

"Yes." Garnet pulled down her mask, pushed off the hood. "We've recorded and sampled everything." Waiting until Lorenzo was inside, she asked him to check if Russ had a head wound.

"Let me see." Gently lifting their fallen packmate's head, the healer said, "No blood below." He ran his gloved fingers over Russ's scalp, taking his time and covering every inch of the skull. "No obvious contusions, though I can't absolutely confirm until I have him on the autopsy table."

Frustration gnawed at Garnet. If Russ hadn't been knocked out, why hadn't he tried to get help? All he'd have had to do was crawl a few feet to the door, bang on it. "Shane?" He was the only one who might have the answers.

"Unconscious."

"Would Russ's wound have been immediately fatal?" Kenji asked, his thoughts no doubt mirroring hers.

Lorenzo bent over the chest wound, the silver in his hair a genetic trait that had little to do with his age. "I'll do a full examination once I get him out of here," he said after a minute, "but, given the type of blade, I have a suspicion the knife might've hit the thoracic aorta. That could've had an instant effect, depending on the severity of the transection."

Lorenzo indicated the wound. "There's too little blood for a fatal stabbing, *unless* the blood has collected in the chest cavity." He leaned in closer, seeming to be paying particular attention to Russ's neck. "The position of the body makes that hard to confirm with a hundred percent certainty on a surface examination, but I'll know as soon as I open him up on the autopsy table."

Kenji, his own hood pushed back, mask down, folded his arms. "Cut to the aorta sounds like a precision hit." His green eyes were like chips of clear jade. "That would require seriously cold blood."

"Anyone can get lucky—or unlucky. And remember," Lorenzo warned, "it's speculation at this point." Face gentling as he turned back to Russ, he reached out to touch his fingers to the other man's closed eyelids. "No life should end this way."

No, Garnet thought, her resolve ironclad: regardless of how much she liked Shane, if he'd done this, then he'd pay in blood. That was pack law and it existed for a reason—because they weren't human, they were changeling; they were wolf.

Her eyes met Kenji's . . . and the wolf that was her other self, it lunged against her skin, its most primal instincts unleashed by the events of the morning. It wanted to claw him bloody, to take payment in kind for the hurt he'd caused, the bond he'd rejected . . . and it wanted to pin him down, bite him in an aggression that had nothing to do with vengeance.

Garnet hauled back the wildest part of herself with gritted teeth, managed to regain control. Waiting until after Lorenzo had left with Russ's body, she turned to the man she should've forgotten long ago. Puppy love, nothing more. Only it had never been so simple between her and Kenji and he'd damn well known it. When he'd rejected her, he'd rejected a promise so precious, she'd never truly forgive him for it.

"You have any luck scanning the knife for prints?" she asked, her voice calm through a rigid effort of will. Because if there was one thing she wouldn't do, it was let Kenji Tanaka see the depth of the injury he'd inflicted.

"Yes. One set," he said, holding up the slim scanner from the forensics kit. "A little smeared, but clear enough for comparison."

"I'll have Revel check if we have Shane's on file. If not, it'll be easy enough to get a set." That was when she suddenly remembered an incident that had her spine going stiff and her wolf baring its teeth.

Kenji's entire body went predator-still, as if she'd spoken her dark thoughts aloud. "What?"

"Russ and Shane got into it two weeks ago." Garnet hadn't witnessed the exchange, but she'd received a detailed report from one of her senior people who'd broken it up. "Russ tracked Shane down on the job one day, confronted him about 'stealing' Athena away. No blows exchanged but only because cooler heads prevailed."

Putting the evidence bag that held the knife to one side and powering down the print scanner, Kenji raised an eyebrow. "Did Shane steal Athena?" The slight sardonic edge in his tone made his opinion of Russ's accusations clear: dominant or submissive, wolf females made up their own minds.

As had Athena.

"Athena should've left Russ long ago." Garnet and Lorenzo had both been concerned enough about the relationship to keep a close eye on the former couple.

Kenji's jaw was suddenly a brutally hard line. "We talking abuse?"

"No. I would've put a stop to that at once." Being in a pack meant living by pack rules. One of those rules was no abuse of any kind against another.

"Then?" The silken strands of Kenji's hair slid against one another as he turned toward her.

The familiar angles and contours of his face came as a small shock each time—he was so gorgeous with his high cheekbones and pretty green eyes and she couldn't keep from noticing, no matter how hard she tried. But of course, it had never been about Kenji's looks.

"Athena's this artistic, slightly flighty, but very sweet woman," she said instead of lingering on the strong line of Kenji's neck, because that way lay dangerous temptation. "She's gifted, no question about it. Her pencil drawings are incredible." Garnet had one hanging in her quarters. "But Russ, he controlled her. Wouldn't even 'allow' her to have a little show for packmates."

Muscles taut, she shook her head. "I took her aside any number of times to ask her if she wanted out, but she always patted my hand and said she understood how Russ thought and that they were happy."

Garnet blew out a breath, dropped her hands to her sides. "I had to accept that, since she's an adult wolf and there was nothing actionable in Russ's behavior." The truth was that the heart wasn't always sensible or logical or rational. If it had been, Garnet would've forgotten her personal green-eyed weakness long ago.

"It wasn't even a hierarchy thing," she said, intuiting Kenji's next question. "They had about the same level of dominance." Russ hadn't been controlling Athena through her wolf. "Just a case of bad taste, I guess." Her gaze met Kenji's. "Woman like Athena, once she makes a choice about a man, she's stubborn enough to stick to it no matter how bad the situation is for her."

Those beautiful shoulders tensed, Kenji's response holding the edge of a growl. "Seems to me she made a choice to stay. And when the situation became toxic, she walked away."

Garnet had never walked away—Kenji hadn't given her that chance. And even now, she wanted to ask him why. The question had dug into her brain for years. They'd been friends. If he'd had cold feet about a possible relationship, why hadn't he just told her? Why hurt her? Why create a distance between them that had remained unbridged until they both became lieutenants and had to find a way to deal with one another?

They'd settled on biting wit, sarcasm, and razor-edged flirtation.

"So," Kenji said when she stayed silent, his voice still rough. "We've done everything we can here. You want to have another look around before we leave?"

"Yes." Suiting action to words, she began to cover the room, but there wasn't much in the living area aside from the furniture she'd already noted, including the small glass-fronted display cabinet that held honors Russ had won in his field. He'd stripped the cabinet of all traces of his life with Athena, including the photos that had once fought for space atop it, while Athena had taken the sampler she'd made for the wall above.

Garnet had seen the room's pre-breakup state the times she'd spoken to Athena while Russ was away at work. She'd talked to Russ, too, made it clear she was unimpressed by his controlling attitude toward his lover.

His response echoed in her memory.

"I would never hurt Athena." Face stiff and shoulders squared, he'd ground out the words. "Just because our relationship isn't what you think it should be doesn't give you the right to interfere."

Garnet had been forced to concede that Russ did love Athena. It hadn't been a warm, generous love. No, it had been small and jealous and suffocating, but it had been a kind of love nonetheless. That understanding was why Garnet had made certain an older packmate checked in on Russ after the breakup—she'd known he wouldn't talk to her, but she'd hoped he'd confide in a peer who was a friend.

He hadn't, had shut down all efforts to offer comfort or friendly companionship.

Chest aching because Russ would now never have the chance to make another choice, she walked out of the living area and down the hallway to his bedroom.

She saw nothing she hadn't seen earlier.

The bed was messed up, but there was no smell of sex. Just two masculine scents—Russ's and Shane's. Given their relationship, the only thing they were likely to have been doing in here was fighting. Sheets were tangled and half pulled off the bed and there were holes in the internal walls.

Like the main SnowDancer den, Garnet's den was hewn out of stone, but the internal rooms were created much the same as rooms anywhere. Russ's apartment was near the center of the den, which meant only the floor was stone; Russ had placed carpet over that. The same pale shade as in the living room, the carpet nonetheless clearly showed the flecks of white paint and fragmented shards from the damaged walls.

Rubbing a fleck between her fingers, Garnet had a thought. "Kenji," she said without raising her voice, "did you notice if either Russ or Shane had broken skin on his knuckles?"

He answered from Russ's study. "Russ, yeah. Not sure about Shane."

Making a note to check that, she continued to examine the room. She even forced herself to go through the cupboards and drawers again. It was in the lowest drawer that she found a photo of Athena; Russ had hidden it facedown under a stack of math papers . . . but he'd kept it. "Ah, hell."

People were so damn complicated.

KENJI exited the study and went to stand in the doorway to the bedroom. He could've gone elsewhere, but he wanted to watch Garnet work, wanted to drink her in. As it was, her scent sank into his cells between one breath and the next. Or that was what it felt like. As if she was already branded into his skin, a place only a lover or a mate had the right to be.

His gut twisted.

He'd sell his soul to have the right to call her either one of those two words.

"I still can't make heads or tails of his study," he said, going to shove his hair back only to realize he was still gloved. That hand, when he paused it midmove, held the finest tremor. Yeah, it wasn't getting any easier to ignore the violent pull inside him when it came to Garnet. "It's all math stuff. I don't think it was disturbed—he was so neat, any search would be obvious."

"Russ's been tutoring a couple of grad students." Closing the drawer she'd been examining, Garnet got to her feet with a grace that seemed more akin to the cats than to a wolf. She'd always been like that, lithe and fluid and beautiful in motion.

"Once we've confirmed the sequence of events," she said, "I'll have the students help Athena go through the study."

Folding his arms, Kenji leaned against the doorjamb. "You think she'll want to?"

"Love's a hard beast to slay," Garnet murmured, her eyes on the holes in the walls. "Athena came to me a month ago, wanted to make sure Russ was all right." A faint, sad smile. "Two people can't live together for a decade and forget each other in a heartbeat."

Kenji wondered if he'd have been strong enough to walk away from Garnet had they already been a couple. The answer was a visceral *hell, no.* He'd have been selfish, held on to her with bleeding and broken fingers if need be . . . and he'd have watched her slowly realize what it meant to be with him.

It would've killed him.

"Kitchen's the only place left," Garnet said on the heels of the silent sucker punch of his thoughts.

Not trusting himself to speak, he followed her to the small kitchen in back of the apartment. It was spic-and-span. Neatly set out on the counter was the lonely tableau they'd noted in their first sweep: one cup, one plate, a pair of utensils.

"Sad," Kenji murmured.

Garnet's mouth was bracketed by white lines on either side as she shook her head. "He could've chosen to eat with packmates at any time."

Kenji wanted to rub those lines away with his thumb, tell her this wasn't her fault. "Yeah." The only time Kenji ate on his own was when he was so exhausted he just wanted to bolt down a meal and crash—or during the rare times when he felt like being alone. Otherwise, he ate in one of the communal break rooms. That was every packmate's right, paid for by SnowDancer's various business profits and investments.

The pack had made that decision in the aftermath of the Territorial Wars, at a time when the wild game had long since migrated to areas without war. SnowDancer had survived the wars with enough members to remain a pack, but it had also absorbed members from other more devastated groups. Those people had become pack under a searing mountain sky, and together, they'd created a charter that held to this day.

Part of that charter was that no pack member would ever go hungry in pack lands.

Too many of the survivors had known hunger.

However, ask any wolf and that wolf would tell you it wasn't only about the food, but about togetherness, about being a pack. Kenji's bonds with his packmates had been sealed into stone over years of meals taken together, hundreds of times when he'd casually taken charge of making sure a small pup ate properly or the occasional time when he'd laughingly participated in a food fight.

Couples and families usually had more meals on their own than single wolves, but even then, the balance was weighted toward being with pack, using the time to catch up and connect. As a child, Kenji had eaten with Garnet's family more than once and he hadn't been the only nonfamily member at the table.

"I guess Russ either liked eating alone," Kenji said, "or wanted to wallow in self-pity." He shrugged, feeling more than a twinge of sympathy for his dead packmate. "He'd been dumped, then seen his ex hook up with a younger man—big hit for anyone." The male ego could be a fragile thing. "And from what you've said, I don't think he'd have seen it coming."

"You're right." Garnet walked around the kitchen, checking cabinets and drawers once again. "He'd probably have made it out given enough time."

Kenji saw the tension bunch across her shoulders, but he wasn't prepared for her to turn around and slam her hands down on the counter as her claws sliced out, perforating her gloves. "No one had to die!"

His wolf rose up into an alert position inside him, hackles raised.

Not because of her growled statement. Because of the distress hidden beneath her anger—and because she was still growling low and deep, her eyes having gone pure wolf. Placing his hand on one deceptively delicate-appearing shoulder, he made his tone hard. "Throttle it." It was an order. "Your denmates need you calm and in control."

Baring her teeth at him, she said, "Get your hand off me," in a voice that was more wolf than woman.

He heard the unspoken coda: *Don't you dare give me orders in my own den.*

Kenji decided to dice with his life.

Because what most people didn't realize was that Garnet was actually more feral than Kenji. She ran her den with aplomb, gave off the image of being totally civilized . . . but she wasn't. Piss her off enough and the wolf was right there, ready to rip off your head. Or punch you in the face. Of course, that wolf only appeared with those she considered equals.

Raising an eyebrow, he leaned in close enough that he could count every one of her golden eyelashes. "Make me."

He didn't even try to avoid it when she shoved off his hold with a clawed hand, leaving four thin scrapes on the skin of his wrist. "Feel better?" His heart pounded at the scent of blood, at the wild physical contact, at the feeling of being marked by the one woman whose brand he'd always wanted to wear.

"Or," he added with a deliberately wicked smile, "would you like to beat up on me some more?"

"Bite me," she muttered, but her eyes were less gold and more blue now . . . though the wolf, it was still very much present.

So present that he could almost see her fur bristling.

Chapter 4

KENJI WOULDN'T HAVE been surprised had Garnet drawn more blood, but she narrowed her eyes at him and said, "Let's go talk to Athena. If anyone knows what led to this, she will."

After they both stripped off and disposed of the forensic gear they'd been wearing, Kenji stayed back with Eloise while Garnet first took the samples to Lorenzo; the healer was authorized to run most of the necessary biological tests. Anything he couldn't process, he'd keep in a special locked and temperature-controlled storage cabinet.

"She's amazing," Eloise said softly as Garnet strode away, the younger woman's voice full of shimmering hero worship.

"Yeah." Leaning against the wall, Kenji held his grazed arm by his side and fought not to go after Garnet, beg for more contact. He'd take another clawing if that was all she'd give him.

And it wasn't because he was a player.

Contrary to general pack opinion, Kenji hadn't exchanged intimate skin privileges with anyone for over a year.

Changelings needed touch to stay stable, but the affectionate cuddles he received from pups, the hugs from friends, had helped paper over, if not fill, the void. His body hurt with a deep sexual ache and his wolf was desperately lonely, but it had started to hurt being with anyone, too. Because no one else was Garnet. No one else would ever be Garnet.

Neither wolf nor man wanted anyone but her.

Rubbing his fist over his heart again, he tried not to think about how things could've been different, how he could've had the right to call her his own as they grew into their skin and strength side by side, but his brain, it was a runaway train. And it wanted to go straight back to the most painful moment of his life.

For so long, Garnet had just been his friend Steele's tiny kid sister. Smart and funny even when she was butting in and being annoying. She'd also been painfully kind. He'd never forget how she'd hugged him fiercely tight when she'd found him crying as a ten-year-old after his parents had another massive fight—and she'd never told anyone, keeping his hurt to herself.

Then the night of her high school graduation, she'd laughed and hugged him after he gave her a journal for her upcoming trip to France, and his wolf had quivered in shocked understanding inside him: after all that time, he'd finally *seen* her. Seen the strong, highly intelligent, and beautiful woman she'd become. But she'd still been Steele's kid sister, still only eighteen to his twenty.

So he'd gripped his need in a merciless fist and given her the room and the time to spread her wings, find her feet, all the while knowing she was his, the key to his lock. Too fucking bad for him that Fate didn't agree.

Hearing Eloise scuff her shoe on the stone of the den floor, he focused on the young soldier, all determination and ruler-straight spine and lines of strain around the eyes. "Garnet must respect your skills a hell of a lot."

A wide-eyed look that turned shyly hopeful. "Really?"

Kenji gave a small nod. "Most juniors would've been relieved the instant the alarm went up." He didn't know this pup well enough to offer her a touch or a hug, but he could give her the same in words. "Remember that when you are relieved. It's not because she has any concerns about your ability to do the task, but because it's not your time right now."

Eloise swallowed, blinked. "I just . . . I was freaked, you know?" she admitted in a whisper. "I didn't maintain." A jagged breath. "I screamed for a second before I stopped myself."

"That just means you're flesh and blood, with a heart. It's what you did afterward that matters—you summoned help and held the scene. No senior could've done better."

Eloise's shoulders straightened, a smile lighting up her eyes.

Garnet's boot-clad footsteps sounded at that instant. She appeared around the corner seconds later, her expression grim once more. With her were a male and a female Kenji knew, both dominants far more experienced than Eloise.

"Eloise," Garnet said, and walked a short distance away with the younger woman, her hand on Eloise's back.

Whatever she said had Eloise nodding before she returned Garnet's hug and left.

Since Kenji and the new guards had exchanged hellos by the time Garnet returned to them, there was no further delay. He fell in beside her, ready to back her up whatever came next.

"You still speak French?" he asked, his mind yet filled with snapshots of how she'd looked when she'd returned from France—so bright and confident and bursting with life. Like Eloise, she'd been hopeful and wide-eyed, but unlike Eloise, she'd already had a core of steel that marked her as a dominant with the strength to become lieutenant.

Only she hadn't been hard. Hot tempered, yes, but never hard, not even when she'd been a teenage girl bloodying the noses of boys who thought they could dominate her in the hierarchy simply because she was petite. She'd brought Kenji back a braided leather bracelet he still wore, but only when there was no chance she'd see it.

"And that's a relevant question, how?"

"I figure I get a random free question after you mauled me."

Eyes flicking to his arm, she scowled. "Let me see that."

It was nothing but a scratch, but he lifted his wrist toward her anyway, let her put her hands on him. "Faker," she muttered, dropping his arm . . . after a gentle pat over the scratches. "You should know better than to challenge another lieutenant, especially in her territory."

His skin burned where she'd touched him, licks of fire that warmed the cold places within. "Danger's my middle name, don't you know."

Garnet's response was a stream of fluent French.

"*Hell*, that's sexy." He pressed a hand over his heart, his wolf so delighted she was playing with him that it ran around excited as a pup. "You probably said something about spinach, right? Or told me to eat a sock."

Her lips quirked, that adorable, unlieutenant-like dimple peeking out. "You'll just have to live in suspense, Kenji Danger Tanaka."

Undone, he said, "Where are we going?" Not that he cared, so long as he was with her.

Her expression turned solemn. "Athena and Shane's place is down this way."

It took a brisk five-minute walk to reach the apartment.

Kenji frowned. "Did they request these rooms?"

"Yes." Garnet's shoulder brushed his arm as she paused. "You're thinking they were trying to avoid conflict."

"Yeah." Heart pounding at the physical sign that maybe she wasn't so generally pissed at him any longer, he dared tug on a curling tendril that had escaped the hair stick, giving her the skin privileges she needed to find her center. "Doesn't fit with Shane going after Russ."

"Nothing fits in this goddamn mess," Garnet muttered before closing the final distance to the apartment door and raising her hand to knock—but not until she'd glanced over at him, said, "Thanks for putting your body in the line of fire."

"Anytime, Garnet." Whatever she needed, he'd do, he'd *be*.

IT was Athena's friend Julie, black haired and with skin the shade of dark autumn leaves, her features lovely and elegant, who opened the door.

Garnet stepped through with her head clear and her wolf's frustrated anger focused into lieutenant composure. All thanks to a sexy, playful wolf she'd done her best to ignore for seven years. Kenji had always been good at that, at making other people feel better. She hadn't missed the light in Eloise's eyes, had figured out the cause pretty damn quick.

Kenji Tanaka had always had *such* a generous heart.

That appeared unchanged, and it didn't fit at all with how he'd destroyed their friendship with a harsh coldness that bewildered her to this day. He'd *hurt* her and he hadn't seemed to care. He hadn't said sorry for standing her up, hadn't even wished her a belated happy birthday. Instead, he'd ignored her, as if they'd never been friends.

Back then, she'd been so angry that she'd taken his actions at face value, especially given his increasingly wild behavior in the months and years immediately following. Kenji had come very close to going totally off the rails with his partying and dangerous stunts, had been placed on probation when it came to his status in the pack.

It was one hell of a serious disciplinary measure for a wolf everyone had thought would make lieutenant.

Not seeming to care about that, either, he'd carried on with his recklessness—until the day he'd jumped off the top of the highest accessible waterfall in den territory.

Garnet had seen the jump by sheer chance, had felt her scream lock in her throat, her entire body going ice-cold. *No,* she'd thought, *no!* She'd frantically searched the churned-up water for his body, but he hadn't broken his neck that day, just a few ribs.

Garnet had intended to tear him a new one for that stupid stunt, but Hawke had hauled him off into the trees while he was still wet and injured, their alpha's grip on Kenji's nape unforgiving. They hadn't reappeared for hours; and whatever had happened that day, Kenji had stopped the flat-out crazy behavior. But he hadn't picked up the violin he'd abandoned—and he hadn't halted his odyssey through the female population of SnowDancer.

Garnet's wolf flexed its claws inside her, but even that wolf, primal and proud, was wondering if maybe in her anger and hurt, she'd missed something vital all those years ago. But that mystery would have to wait, no matter how it tore at her. Today, she had to focus on Russ and Shane.

"Jem! Oh, Jem, tell me it's not true!" Athena rushed into her arms as soon as Garnet entered the living area. Her perfume was as delicate and floral as her sundress, her hair a mass of wild mahogany curls around a striking Botticelli face.

Beside Garnet, Kenji held Julie close, lending his strength to a packmate who needed it.

It took several minutes for Athena to be in any condition to talk. Sitting down with her while Kenji wandered into the kitchenette to talk to Julie as she made some coffee, Garnet took the older woman's hand. It trembled. "Why did Shane go over to Russ's, Athena?"

Athena's normally creamy skin was blotchy and devoid of its usual glow when she answered, her hazel-green eyes huge in a face that seemed all jagged bone. "Russ, he called." A hiccuping breath, her voice as soft as always. "He said he wanted to clear the air, have a quiet drink with Shane."

"That doesn't sound like Russ." He'd held on to his grudges like pups hang on to their favorite toys.

"Actually, I could see him making that call." A smile curved Athena's lips but it was a terrible mockery formed of sadness. "Russ likes . . . liked, things in neat boxes. Me and Shane, we were a loose end." She looked down at the carpet, but Garnet had the feeling she was seeing the man who'd been an integral part of her life for a decade. "So he'd shake hands with Shane and that would be it. The box would be closed and he could carry on."

Smile fading, Athena looked up to meet Garnet's gaze. "I was happy for him, thought he was finally moving on from our relationship." Her voice broke on the last word. "I d-didn't h-hate him. I wanted g-good things for him."

Garnet allowed her packmate to regain her composure before saying, "He called this morning?"

"No, last night. He wanted Shane to go over then." The blood vessels in her swollen eyes spidery red lines against the white, Athena accepted the mug of coffee Julie handed over, giving her friend a shaky smile of thanks as the shorter woman sat down on her other side.

Taking her own coffee from Kenji as he leaned against the side of the sofa, Garnet waited.

"But Shane was just leaving for a night shift," Athena continued. "So Russ suggested that maybe Shane could drop by in the morning for a few minutes instead." She gave a tight smile. "Russ always hated having to redo his schedule—he liked things as he liked them."

Taking a deep breath of the coffee aroma, she swallowed, her nose stuffy when she spoke again. "Shane didn't want to go, but I said he should, that it'd make things so much easier if we didn't have to avoid Russ in the den." Another breath, this one jerky. "I *sent* him." Her hands tightened on the coffee mug, her voice rising in pitch.

Athena's pain made Garnet's heart hurt, but she had to be a lieutenant today, not just a sympathetic packmate. "How was Shane this morning before he left?" she asked before Athena could give in to hysteria.

Athena jerked almost to attention at Garnet's blade of a tone, instinct trumping the dark spiral of her thoughts. "I didn't see him," she whispered. "I was giving an art class in the nursery and I left early to set up. But I know he wouldn't have had a knife." Her big, guileless eyes pleaded with Garnet. "He's not that kind of a man."

Kenji stirred, his scent brushing over Garnet in a caress that felt disconcertingly intimate. "Do you know if there's a blade missing from his collection?"

"I haven't looked." Athena set down her coffee mug before her trembling spilled the hot liquid over the sides. "I didn't want to look. I *know* Shane didn't go there with the intention of hurting Russ."

"May we look?" Garnet put her own mug on the same low table.

Rubbing away her tears with her knuckles, Athena hesitated, suddenly appearing far smaller than her five feet, nine inches of height. "I don't want to do anything to hurt Shane."

The truth was that as head of the den, Garnet could go ahead without Athena's permission, but the other woman was already fragile, didn't need to be forced into a choice that made her feel as if she was betraying the man she loved. Better if Athena understood that she was helping her lover as much as she could.

Cupping her packmate's face in her hands, Garnet spoke to woman and wolf both. "You know I'll be fair," she said. "To do that, I have to know all the facts."

Face crumpling even as her eyes turned the yellow of her wolf, Athena gave a staccato nod. "Julie c-can show you the k-key . . ."

Garnet glanced at Kenji. Putting his own coffee beside hers, he left with Julie while Garnet tugged Athena close and held her tight.

"I n-n-never meant for this to happen," Athena said, her voice muffled against Garnet's neck. "I just . . . couldn't live inside a box anymore." She drew back, raised her hand to her mouth. "I n-never th-thought—"

"Hey." Garnet took Athena's hand away from her mouth, tipped up her chin. "No wolf in my den is *ever* going to be made to feel guilty for the actions of another." Even as she spoke, she was telling herself to take her own damn advice. "You just remember that this entire scenario involves adults. Part of being an adult is making our own decisions. You didn't make either Shane or Russ do anything. Understood?"

Athena nodded jerkily just as Julie returned. Leaving the generally more pragmatic and steady woman to sit with Athena, Garnet went to join Kenji in the small room that functioned as a combined art studio and hobby area. Seeing her, Kenji opened a closet at the back to reveal a tall set of drawers with a glass display case on top. The knives within the case were obviously much older and far more ornate than the one that had been used on Russ.

"You go through the drawers?" she asked him.

"No, I figured you'd want to be here for that." He pulled open the first slender drawer.

The two of them examined the contents in silence, moved on to the next.

"Damn." Garnet's breath got stuck in her chest, each inhalation as sharp as the blades in front of them—because there was a gap. Arranged smallest to largest, each knife in this set had a green jewel in the hilt, as well as distinctive scrollwork.

Kenji took out his phone, pulled up a photograph of the murder weapon. "Perfect match."

Folding her arms, Garnet stared at the accusatory gap in the blue velvet of the drawer lining, but it had no more secrets to tell. "Let's go see if Revel's matched the fingerprints—I asked him to take care of it on my way back from the infirmary."

Locking the case, Kenji pocketed the key. "I think we should lock up the whole studio. Just in case."

"Good idea." It turned out the door to the studio had a never-used thumb-scan lock that Garnet programmed to respond to only her or Kenji.

The living room was empty when the two of them returned to it. She followed Athena's scent to the bedroom, where she found the artistic woman lying down while Julie patted her back. Catching Julie's eye, Garnet motioned that they were leaving.

Before she could step away from the doorway, however, Athena sat up. Shoving her curls out of her face, she said, "Can I see Shane?" It was a plea.

"No, I'm sorry, Athena. No one can speak to Shane until I've had a chance to interview him." She'd swung by her quarters and picked up her phone earlier, aware Lorenzo would alert her the instant Shane began to show signs of consciousness. "I'll tell you as soon as I'm done; you have my word."

Athena's face threatened to crumple again. She was a sweet and talented wolf with a gentle heart but she wasn't the strongest of them. So when she squared her shoulders and set her jaw, Garnet's own wolf looked at her with new eyes.

Love, it seemed, could make warriors out of even the most fragile.

"I don't believe it." Athena's voice was fierce. "I don't think Shane would hurt Russ. He's just not built that way." Yellow wolf eyes locked with Garnet's in a show of truly unexpected strength. "You do this right, Jem. You find the truth."

Chapter 5

KENJI SAW THE renewed lines of strain around Garnet's mouth as they left Athena and Shane's quarters, and though his wolf snarled, wanting to take care of things, he knew there was nothing he could do but back her. Even had she been his, it was all he could've done—Garnet would allow nothing else.

The thought had just passed through his head when a pack of pups in wolf form ran down the corridor, clearly racing. He knew without asking that they were breaking the rules, but with it being so wet outside, all the den kids were probably going stir-crazy.

He'd certainly broken this particular rule more than once as a pup.

Garnet didn't stop or censure them. Laughing in open delight, she stood in place as they streamed around and through her spread legs. Looking at the pack of brown-furred bodies, Kenji noted the tiny one at the back who was determined to keep up but falling behind. The runt of the group.

Garnet had been like that. Tiny and fierce and refusing to be left behind.

Not stopping to question his instincts, he tugged off his necklace and dropped it on the floor. It was unlikely the shift would cause any damage to something as solid as the pendant, but he wasn't about to take the chance.

A second later, he shifted and raced to grab the huffing and trailing pup in his mouth, taking a firm grip halfway along the pup's small body. Then he loped after the other little ones, racing past them to the far end of the corridor, where he put down his tiny burden. Turning, the pup bounced and yipped at Kenji excitedly, and when his friends skated to a stop in front of him, their tiny claws scratchy on the stone, Kenji's pup made a noise that in human form would've been a smug raspberry.

Chuckling inside at having given the pup one victory at least, Kenji left them to their boisterous play and padded back to Garnet. Who had her hands on her hips and was trying to look stern. "All the parents are trying to teach this lot not to shift while in their clothes, and there you go, setting a bad example."

He pretended to bite her leg.

She laughed . . . and then her hand, it was in his fur, gripping lightly as she crouched down in front of him. "Your room's on the way to my office." Affection in her words, in her touch as she ran her free hand through his fur. "You can get fresh clothes."

Looking into eyes gone a wolfish gold, his own wolf's heart beat huge and hard inside its chest. That wolf, too, loved her. And that wolf, too, knew they had to let her go. But the animal was closer to its primal self, possessiveness in its veins.

Tugging out of her hold before that primal heart could give in, he nipped at her jaw.

"Kenji!" She laughed again, and the sound, it was like warm rain over his senses.

When she growled playfully and threatened to nip at his nose in vengeance, he danced out of reach and would've loped off toward his room. Except the pups had seen them tussling and ran excitedly back to join in the play. So of course he tumbled with them while

Garnet let tiny pups climb all over her, her eyes bright and her hands gentle on their squirmy little bodies.

He finally slipped away—his grandfather's pendant gripped carefully in his teeth—when the now happily exhausted pups started curling up to nap right there in the corridor, piling on top of one another to snuggle in. He knew they'd be fine—during rainy days in particular, he'd often had to avoid more than one furry bundle in the corridors of his own den. Their caretakers would eventually track them down and carry them back to the nursery.

Once in his room, he decided to leave off the pendant since he'd broken the rawhide tie when he took it off. Shifting, he ran the smoothness of it between his finger and thumb for a second, his heart clenching as he remembered the bighearted, loving man who'd given it to him. He was glad his grandfather had never known the long-term repercussions of the joyous trip on which he'd taken Kenji when Kenji was a boy. It would've killed the older man.

Breathing past the ache of a grief that still caught him unawares sometimes when he thought of his grandfather, he was in a fresh pair of jeans and a white T-shirt by the time Garnet made it to outside his room. Reaching out to ruffle his hair, she said, "You lost the colors."

He'd bent instinctively so she could reach, had to force himself to straighten. "I feel naked. Like my butt's showing."

Dimple appearing, she pulled out a glitter pen from her pocket. "Want me to go wild?"

His shoulders shook at the gleam in her eye. "Where did you get that?"

"FOUND it in the break room before our meeting, meant to drop it off with the school supplies." Slipping the pen back into her pocket,

Garnet curled her fingers into her hands, the sensation of Kenji's hair against her palm a living memory. Warm silk, heavy and glossy. "You're still good with kids." She'd always thought he'd make an incredible father if he'd only stop his crash-and-burn approach to relationships.

"My mom says it's because I'm half-pup myself." The dangerous, heartbreaker smile that creased his cheeks made it clear he didn't consider that an insult. "You still intending to have as many as you can?"

She blinked at the realization that he'd remembered her dreams, but then, Kenji had a habit of remembering things she'd said to him . . . and vice versa. As a teen, he'd once found her an out-of-print comic book for her collection after she mentioned it exactly once. Not long afterward, she'd tracked down a particular candy bar he wanted to eat.

They'd always taken care of one another in small ways, right up to the night Kenji had broken them in two. Hurting and angering her so much that she'd been blinded by it.

"Yep," she said, her resolve to figure out the mystery of that night set in stone—she'd know the truth before Kenji left the den. And if that truth was a painful one, if Kenji had simply changed his mind and no longer cared about her, so be it. But given his behavior today, she didn't think the answer was so simple.

"You always used to say ten was a good number." His smile deepened and yes, there was no one more gorgeous than Kenji Tanaka when he smiled that way.

"I might've been a little off base there." Her dry response made him chuckle; the sound, it sank into her bones, made them ache. "But three or four, absolutely."

Kenji rocked back on his heels, his thumbs hooked into the back pockets of his jeans. The action pulled his T-shirt across his chest, defined the ridged planes of his body. "With your family's track record of fertility, I figure you're gonna hit a home run soon as you find your man"—was there a hitch there, a subtle tightening of his facial muscles?—"and start making the attempt."

Continuing to watch him with a care she'd avoided for years, Garnet said, "I'm hoping." Ruby and Steele weren't Garnet's only siblings—she had six others, a near-impossible number in changeling terms. Four sets of twins, plus Garnet.

"Ruby's definitely carrying one, right?" Kenji's tone had an odd undertone she couldn't quite decipher. "I didn't miss another set of Sheridan twins?" he added as they began to walk side by side, Kenji automatically shortening his stride to accommodate hers.

"Definitely one this time." Fur ruffled by what she'd sensed in his voice, Garnet turned to look at him, came up against a wall of good humor.

Her eyes narrowed.

Kenji had been good at hiding things as a child, too, had learned to do so in the midst of the war zone that had been his parents' relationship. Why hadn't she remembered that at twenty-one? Because, she admitted, she'd been young and inexperienced, a dominant predatory changeling swimming in hormones, her pride a touchy thing. She'd also been more than a little in love with Kenji Tanaka.

She'd wanted to claw Kenji bloody. Pride alone had stopped her.

Kenji had been a couple of years older. Old enough to have predicted her response . . . to have counted on it?

"My brother Jasper," she said, her brain gnawing at the issue like a wolf with a bone, "you remember him?"

"Sure. He's in Alexei's sector."

"His mate is carrying twins. They're ecstatic."

Kenji's grin sliced through her heart. "I hadn't heard. I'll have to give him a call. What's a good gift for twin pups?"

There he went again, being the amazing, generous boy she'd

grown up with instead of the daredevil lothario he'd become in his early twenties. "Nothing matchy-matchy," she warned him. "According to Jas, he's still scarred from his matchy-matchy childhood."

Kenji's chuckle went straight through her, making the tiny hairs on her arms prickle. "I remember how your brothers would constantly want to swap clothes with me and their other friends. We got the best of the bargain, though."

Shoving down her primal response to him once more, Garnet nodded. "Mom's an amazing tailor." One who was secretly working on three adorable baby tuxedos—one for Ruby's pup, two for Jasper's pups. "This is my office."

Revel was at the computer behind the dark wood of her desk when they entered. "Fingerprints on the knife are a match to Shane's," he said as soon as they shut the door behind themselves, his face set in harsh lines. "I ran the program twice to be sure there was no mistake."

Garnet's gut tensed—but dealing with the tough and the hard was part of a lieutenant's job. Folding her arms, she set her feet apart. "Show me the location of the prints." Something about them had been niggling at her ever since she took a quick look at the scan of the murder weapon before assigning Revel the task of identifying the prints.

Revel put up the images on the large screen on the back wall of her office. Then, coming around to the front of the desk, he pointed out the four slightly smeared but readable prints on the handle of the blade. "Perfect." He paused, his hands on his hips. "Honestly, it's a little too perfect. If the room hadn't been locked from the inside, I'd be tempted to say planted."

Kenji moved closer to the screen, the artificial sunlight making his hair gleam blue-black. "This knife is pristine except for those four prints. The others we saw in the set all had smudges, signs of repeated handling."

"Shane did handle them." Garnet had visited with him over his collection about three months back, curious to see an ancient knife another packmate had described to her. "He enjoyed sharing his hobby with others, talking about the history of the knives." She could still remember how his square-jawed face had glowed as he spoke about the workmanship, the hands through which each blade had passed.

To Shane, it was about the art rather than the utility of the blades as weapons.

She took a few steps forward, until she stood with Rev on one side, Kenji on the other. Both strong. Both intelligent. Both blood loyal to SnowDancer. Both beautiful. But only one made her heart thunder and her blood grow hot and her temper fire as violently as her passion.

Damn it.

Gritting her teeth, she focused on the blade that had taken a man's life. "None of that means he didn't clean this knife," she said slowly, "but even if he did wipe it down, he'd have had to have picked it up from his collection, hidden it on himself somewhere."

She glanced at Revel. "Did Lorenzo mention spotting gloves in Shane's pockets?" The healer would've removed the clothing to ensure he didn't miss an injury, but it had the side effect of preserving evidence.

"Give me a sec." Revel made the call to the infirmary, shook his head after a short delay. "Lorenzo just went and checked. No gloves."

Kenji, who'd been staring at the prints the entire time, picked up a thick black marker from Garnet's desk and closed his fingers over it.

"Yes." Revel's rich brown eyes were intent on Kenji's grip. "If we put aside the oddness of the weapon not having any other prints, Shane's are *precisely* where they'd be if he closed his hand over the hilt to use it."

Garnet's gut churned; they were missing something, of that she was certain. "Kenji, you mind lying on the floor in the same position as Shane?"

Eyes dark and lips set in an unsmiling line, an expression she'd rarely seen on his face, Kenji arranged himself on the colorful woven rug she'd placed over the stone. Garnet knelt beside him once he stopped moving, put the marker in his hand, and closed his fingers over it.

Revel, having hunkered down on the other side, whistled. "Flawless match to the type of prints on the knife. You think Shane was set up?"

"I think things aren't adding up." Anger licked through her veins at the idea of being played for a fool, with a man's life as the stakes. "We need to talk to Athena again, find out who else might have had access to that particular knife."

KENJI pushed up to his feet. Garnet and Revel rose with him.

"Check in with Lorenzo," Garnet said to her right-hand man. "See if he's learned anything new from Russ's body."

"Will do." Flicking her a quick, playful salute, Revel left.

Kenji knew he should shut it, but his brain couldn't control whatever stupid part of his anatomy was driving his mouth. "I thought you two were dating."

A flicker in the glorious blue of Garnet's eyes. "I see you keep up with pack gossip."

"I'm a faithful listener of *Deja's Delici-News*."

Snorting at his mention of the packmate who had a wickedly funny nighttime show on the packwide radio station, she said, "Whether we're dating or not, I'm still the lieutenant in charge of this den."

"Yeah, but there are times for the hierarchy, and there are times

to haul your lover close and kiss the life out of her." Wolf changelings, especially the dominants, weren't exactly known to be shy or
concerned about public displays of affection, *especially* when in the
presence of another changeling who might be a threat to their claim
on a lover.

Revel hadn't even blinked at Kenji's presence. That made no sense,
not when the other man and Garnet had only been on two dates so
far. Kenji's reputation and tendency to flirt with Garnet alone should've
made Rev bristle. Garnet deserved bristling, deserved a man who
knew her worth and was ready to fight to keep her by his side.

Kenji wanted to snarl at the idea that anyone would take her for
granted.

"The man who avoids relationships like the plague knows so
much about how to treat a lover?" A laser-sharp question, Garnet's
gaze so direct it was unsettling.

Standing his ground, he said, "If I had a chance at a lover like
you, then yeah, I'd push my claim. Hierarchy be damned." The
words came out a near growl, his claws pricking at the insides of
his skin as his wolf, forgetting all the reasons it shouldn't, readied
itself to do exactly that.

"Careful, Kenji." Garnet ran a clawed hand over his cheek and
down his throat, her voice soft, a warning and a dangerous invitation both. "I might start to take you seriously."

Kenji shuddered, unable to control his visceral response to Garnet's challenge. Her eyes gleamed. "You and I are overdue for a
conversation," she said slowly. "We'll be having it after we put this
situation to bed."

His blood was still pumping when they left the office to walk back
to Athena's quarters, his wolf an inch from his skin. He'd betrayed
himself and Garnet had caught him. *Shit.* All these years, he'd been
right to keep his distance—put him close to Garnet for a few hours

and he lost it, became that lovesick boy again. Only now, his emotions were impossibly stronger.

Because Garnet? She was no longer the girl he'd worshipped; she'd become a tough-as-nails lieutenant who was respected and loved by her packmates. And she'd done it without changing herself or losing the ability to play with their most innocent. Was it any wonder that the more he saw of the woman she'd become, the deeper he fell?

He was fucking screwed.

"Door's open," Garnet said when they reached Athena's apartment. "Athena," she called out.

The other woman's voice was barely audible but it appeared to come from the direction of the bedroom. "Come in, Jem."

Kenji went with Garnet to the bedroom door but stayed outside while she went in to talk to the older woman—who'd struck him as delicate in spite of her earlier spirited defense of her lover. Kenji had delicate packmates in his den, too, ensured they were safe and protected and happy, same as the rest of his denmates, but he'd never been attracted to delicate.

He wanted to pat those men and women on the head and say, "There, there."

Garnet would tear off his arm and snap it in half if he tried that with her. She'd probably use his finger bones for toothpicks for good measure. He grinned. How messed up was it that he found it hot that she was so fucking dangerous? And even though that was a singularly inappropriate thought to be having right this instant, it steadied him in a way nothing else could've done.

He listened as, inside the room, Athena told Garnet that Julie had popped out, would be back in ten minutes. Allowing the other woman to talk until she was settled, Garnet asked her who else might've had access to the knives.

"You know Shane," Athena said in her soft and breathy tone, a tremor beneath the surface. "He's always showing them off."

"Would he notice if one was missing?"

"Not right away, but he tidies and cleans them every Sunday." Her tone changed, warmed, as if she was smiling. "It's his hobby, you know? I do my art and he sits with me and we talk and he babies his knives. To him, they're works of art, too."

"It's Thursday today, so who's had access to the knives since Shane's last cleaning session?" Garnet's voice was gentle but firm, compassion and strength entwined.

"Well, aside from me," Athena said, "there was Taneese and her mate, Cameron. Cameron has an interest in Chinese weaponry from a particular era and Shane had a special blade to show him." Her voice steadied as she went through her memories. "The men went into the studio, but I'm pretty sure Shane just took out that one blade to show Cameron."

"You didn't see?"

"No, I was chatting to Taneese, but Shane and Cameron went in and came back out together." A pause. "I'm sure Cameron was never alone with the knives."

"Okay. Who else?"

"Two younger packmates who're working part-time with Shane. Mitchell and Eloise."

Kenji straightened at the name of the young soldier who'd discovered the murder. Coincidence? If so, it was a damn convenient one.

"That's it?" Garnet's response betrayed neither surprise nor shock.

Athena took time to answer. "Yes." The tremor returned. "It's been a quiet week. We w-were planning to hold a dinner party on

Saturday. It's not really Shane's kind of thing, but he indulges me."
A shaky sniff. "Russ never let me do things like that—he just didn't
like people all that much."

The sadness and pain in her words made Kenji wonder why she'd
stayed with Russ for so long, but while SnowDancers had a primal
wolf heart, they also had a human one. The animal's clarity and
simplicity was at times overwhelmed by the complexities and inexplicable yearnings of their human side.

"Do you lock your door when you go out?"

"No. Who does?" A wet laugh. "But Shane padlocks the studio to
make sure pups don't hurt themselves if they come in while we're out.
They can get into the unlikeliest places, can't they?" Another pause,
her next words soaked with a poignant sense of loss. "I always wanted
a pup of my own, but Russ . . . I loved him once, but he was so much
work. And now I'm too old."

Kenji's heart ached.

"There are always children in the world who need love," Garnet
said gently. "After this is all over, we can talk about your options."

"You believe Shane is innocent?" Athena's voice rose into a higher
pitch.

Garnet's reply was tempered. "I'm keeping an open mind."

Chapter 6

DESPITE HER CALM while with Athena, Garnet's heart was racing, her skin tight and her wolf's body at quivering attention. She forced herself to keep her silence until she and Kenji had left the apartment. "Did you hear?"

"Eloise."

"Exactly." She stopped in the corridor, hands on her hips. "Before we talk to her, I want to find out if she was connected to Russ in any way." The idea of the girl as a criminal mastermind didn't fit with what Garnet knew about her, but everyone had secrets.

"Want me to do the same for this Mitchell guy?" asked the green-eyed man in front of her, a man who was very good at keeping secrets of his own.

"No," she said after a moment's thought. "Rev will have better luck since he's based in this den." Mentally reviewing the schedule for senior members of the den, she found a gap. "Can you do a security shift, cover for me?"

It was raining outside, the environment no picnic, but Kenji didn't even hesitate. "Consider it done. Who do I get the route from?"

Garnet told him, then asked, "You have business at your own den you have to look in on?" His responsibilities were as heavy as her own and as critical to the health of the pack.

"Emi and I have messaged." He held up his phone. "She's got everything at the den under control and I made sure the international stuff would keep for a couple of days at least." Sliding away his phone, he said, "I'd better go grab the route." A pause, his expression intent and his focus so absolute that she felt as if she was the center of his universe. "You'll figure this out, don't ever doubt that."

Breath tight in her lungs, Garnet watched him walk away, his stride long and his body gorgeously powerful under the simulated late-afternoon sunlight of the corridor. He was being *her* Kenji again, no dominance games, no making things hard for her, and definitely no chasing after women.

And the fact that those jeans hugged his butt oh-so-nicely . . . Well, she had a pulse. She noticed. Especially when it was Kenji. She'd tried damn hard not to notice for a lot of years, but trying not to notice Kenji Tanaka was like trying not to notice a golden-maned lion sitting smack bang in the middle of your bed.

It was impossible.

Connecting with Revel on the phone once Kenji was out of sight, she went to meet the man she should've been thinking about. As Revel walked toward her, tall, dark, and sensually beautiful, Kenji's words rang in her mind.

Yeah, but there are times for the hierarchy, and there are times to haul your lover close and kiss the life out of her.

Garnet knew that despite his more sophisticated exterior, Revel was no more civilized than Kenji. If he'd decided on her, he'd have acted all growly and possessive, regardless of her anger or the rules of the hierarchy. Wolf males couldn't always help themselves with their courtship behavior. Neither could wolf females.

If Revel hadn't been acting as he should, then neither had she.

Garnet blew out a breath; in truth, she'd known hours ago that she had to break things off with Revel. It was the only right course of action until she'd got to the heart of this thing between her and Kenji; an attraction that she'd finally accepted had simply gone into hibernation seven years ago. It was awake now, and awake with a vengeance.

She thought of how he'd shuddered when she'd scraped her claws over his throat, how he hadn't slapped away her hand or done anything else aggressive—both perfectly acceptable responses from a dominant touched unexpectedly in a highly vulnerable spot—and felt her blood heat. Kenji had no more gotten over her than she'd gotten over him.

So they'd figure this out. One way or another.

"Lorenzo?" she asked once Revel was close enough.

A shake of his head. "He hasn't got to Russ yet—had a couple of small injuries come in. Juveniles getting a little too enthusiastic with indoor soccer."

Garnet made a mental note to look in on the kids later. "Let's hope the weather clears soon." Wolves, young or old, didn't do well cooped up. "I need you to follow up on something Athena told me." She recapped the information on Mitchell's possible access to the knives. "Connections, motives, anything relevant."

Nodding, he glanced at the heavy black watch he wore, similar to the one Kenji favored. "I'm meant to be taking a combat class in ten. I can switch with Felicia, do her session tomorrow."

"Sounds good."

When the silky dark of Revel's gaze met hers again, it wasn't senior soldier to lieutenant, but man to woman. "Can you take a couple of minutes for a personal discussion?"

"Yes," she said, knowing there was no point delaying this. "Let's go into my office." She'd seen juveniles padding around in wolf form farther down the corridor—they wouldn't intentionally listen in, but all pups had big ears.

Revel spoke the instant they had privacy, his deep voice quiet but potent. "You've never once looked at me the way you look at Kenji."

Not ready for such a blunt assault, Garnet sucked in her stomach, clenched one fist. "You've only seen us together for a few minutes at most." The idea that she was wearing her heart on her sleeve, it aggravated her wolf.

She might do that *after*, but right now, a big part of her was still pissed at Kenji.

Revel smiled that slow, beautiful smile that had always drawn her . . . but not the way Kenji's green eyes and wicked grin drew her. It didn't make her insides flip, didn't make her brain go kind of fuzzy. "I really thought we'd be good together," she said before he could speak. "I wasn't jerking you around."

"I know." Revel cupped her jaw with one hand. "As for you and Kenji, I saw the two of you dancing together at Hawke's mating celebration, too."

Leaning in without warning, he kissed her, an unexpectedly hot and wet and tangled thing, his hand gripping her jaw and his body heat buffeting her senses. "Sorry." A grin that was utterly unrepentant. "Had to try and make you breathless at least once."

"Goal achieved," she gasped, but even then, deep within, she was steady, watchful.

Pretty and intelligent and dangerous though he was, Revel wasn't for her.

"When you asked me out," he said after releasing her, "I figured whatever you and Kenji had, it must've burned out, but it's obvious to anyone with a single functioning brain cell that your flame's going strong." He rubbed his thumb over her cheekbone. "What I don't get is why you two aren't already together."

She scowled. "Reasons."

"If it's because Kenji was a bit of a horn dog for a while, you should know he's been a monk for the past year."

Garnet stared at him. "How could you *possibly* know that?"

"Emi's a senior soldier in Kenji's den," he reminded her, naming a year-mate. "We gossip."

All wolves gossiped. It was part of being in a pack. "Do you gossip about me?" It came out a growl.

"Of course we do." His eyes turned wolf-amber swirled with green. "But only among the three of us—me and Emi and Pia." The latter SnowDancer was his twin and had transferred with him to Garnet's den, the two having always worked well as a unit.

Pia had also recently been promoted, but where Revel was good when it came to dealing with the management of a den, Pia did better with more practical matters like taking charge of the training and security schedules. Regardless, the two were as thick as thieves—and best friends with Emi Lucenko. As Revel now proved.

"We act as one another's vaults and release valves," he said. "It's good for Pia and me to have a non-twin in the mix and the contact's good for Emi, too. You know how quiet she can be, how she holds everything inside."

"Hmm." Arms folded, Garnet leaned against the door.

She told herself not to ask, but she couldn't stop herself—Kenji's indiscriminate behavior when it came to skin privileges was something she needed to understand. And if her response was fueled by a jealousy she'd never before consciously acknowledged, well, it was time to stop lying to herself. "How does Emi know Kenji's been a monk?"

"Not one but two women suddenly asked her if he was sick. It took a little careful questioning but she finally figured out it was because he was turning everyone down, even friends with whom he'd previously exchanged skin privileges." Revel's expression turned solemn. "So she started keeping an eye on him and it looks like Kenji's been sleeping alone for a long time."

Worry woke in Garnet, a sharp, biting beast. Changelings needed skin contact, needed physical connection. It fed their souls, soothed the animal that was part of their being. Without it, they could go into a deep depression, turn violently aggressive, or just start to lose emotional and mental cohesion. "Why didn't Emi do anything?" The senior soldier had to know Kenji's physical isolation was dangerous.

"She talked to him, said he seemed fine. No edge, no sudden temper or mood swings, same Kenji he's always been."

Garnet had to admit Kenji looked fine, but as she'd already remembered, Kenji Tanaka was great at putting on a front. He'd done it all the time as a child while his parents were yelling down the den and snarling at one another. Satoshi and Miko Tanaka were a rare changeling couple who'd been together and stable long enough to produce a child, but who now couldn't stand one another.

They'd separated for good when Kenji was twelve, but their relationship had been a battlefield long before then. Kenji had never seemed affected by the loudness of their fights or how passionately they made up. He'd always been the fun kid, the one who could make everyone laugh—and who could play the violin with so much wild emotion that it made adults weep and children dance.

Garnet had seen below that talented, laughing surface only because she'd caught him out when he was ten and she was eight.

She'd found him curled up all alone behind a tree by the lake, crying so hard his body shook. It had hurt her to see her friend so sad. Going up to hug him hadn't even been a question, and Kenji had let her. He'd always let her hug him, no matter how annoyed they might be with each other. She'd take advantage of that.

"All right," she said in a meticulously even tone. "Go find out about Mitchell."

Revel nodded.

She touched his forearm as he went to open the door, his skin lightly dusted with dark hair. "When you do meet her, she'll be a lucky woman."

A cocky smile she might've expected from Kenji but never from Revel—which showed exactly how deeply she knew one man and not the other. Because if her normally serious right-hand man had such cockiness in him, he needed a mate who could bring out that playful side . . . just as Kenji needed a mate who saw beneath the carefree face he presented to the world, a woman he could trust with his hurts as well as his joy.

"I know," Revel said, grazing his fingers over her cheek.

Leaving the office, the two of them headed in different directions. Garnet decided to go to the packmate who was in charge of the junior soldiers, see what he had to say about Eloise.

"Good kid," was Yejun's summation. "A little too straitlaced, but she's loosening up." His grin made it clear the experienced trainer liked Eloise, regardless of her straitlaced nature. "You think she had something to do with what happened to Russ?"

Garnet kept her answer simple, uninflammatory. She had no intention of causing Eloise any trouble if her young packmate had simply been in the wrong place at the wrong time. "She found him—I have to clear her."

"Right." Yejun's nod made the simulated sunlight of the den gleam on his cleanly shaved head. "Well"—the grizzled old wolf scratched his stubbled jaw, his brown skin lined with life—"I can't see her getting heated up over Russ." A dubious expression. "That girl has the pups trailing after her with their tongues hanging out."

He shook his head. "Boys these days, they have no pride when it comes to a strong woman with dangerous curves."

Garnet wasn't about to fall for his morose tone. "Did you at that age?"

A big laugh, eyes glinting mischievously. "Hell no. Pride gets you a lonely bed." His expression turned smug. "*My* bed is filled with a gorgeous armful of strong woman with highly dangerous curves—you think I lassoed my mate by being a shrinking violet? Hah!"

Garnet's lips twitched. Since Yejun's mate, Sabrina, was a powerful wolf who'd held Revel's position until she decided to semi-retire—emphasis on the *semi*, Garnet had a good idea of what their courtship must've involved. "Anything else I should know about Eloise as it applies to this situation?"

Tinkering with a small device he was apparently fixing, Yejun took a moment to think. "I know Eloise is studying as well as doing her soldier training. I'm fairly certain it involves math, so she could've been a student of Russ's." Lines formed between his eyebrows. "And yeah, she picked up a few hours of work with the den maintenance team to save up for a special trip."

"Thanks, Yejun. I'll check it all out." She touched his shoulder as she left—just because he was a mature packmate in a stable relationship didn't mean he didn't need the occasional physical sign of affection from the most dominant wolf in the den.

Every wolf needed to know he or she was valued.

Popping in to see the pack's overall chief of education afterward, Garnet affected a mock-stern expression. "Putting up your feet on the job? Tut-tut."

Ruby poked out her tongue in Garnet's direction. "I think my baby is going to be a twenty-pound sumo wrestler."

Chuckling, Garnet walked over to where her sister was stretched out on the sofa placed against one wall of her office. "I thought I authorized your maternity leave."

"I'd go mad if I wasn't looking out for my kids." Ruby moaned as Garnet sat down and began to massage her feet. "Did I ever tell you you're my favorite sister?"

"You can never tell me enough." Kissing her older sister's belly with the easy skin privileges that existed between siblings, Garnet said, "Talk to me about Eloise. Any connection to Russ?"

It turned out that Russ had been Eloise's senior adviser—the man who was meant to guide her through her studies. It also meant he'd held a certain power over her.

Deciding she now had enough to go to Eloise, Garnet left her tardy nephew with a pat on his mother's straining belly and tracked down the young woman to her room in the section reserved for junior soldiers. "Russ was your adviser," she said bluntly when Eloise opened the door.

Face paling under the warm tone of her skin, Eloise nodded jerkily. "That's why I was by his room," she said without prompting. "I was going to see him about—"

"About what?" Garnet prompted when a look of pure panic flashed across Eloise's features, her hand tightening to bone whiteness on the edge of the door.

"I swear I didn't hurt him," the younger woman said in a pleading tone, her wolf rising to turn her eyes a tawny golden brown. "I wouldn't."

Going with gut instinct, Garnet leaned in to cup Eloise's cheeks. "Talk to me, sweetheart." As lieutenant, she had to be tough, but she also had to be flexible. SnowDancer wasn't a pack that ran on fear—it ran on respect and affection and loyalty.

Shuffling closer when Garnet lowered her hands, like a pup seeking contact, Eloise all but whispered her next words. "He was blocking me from progressing to a graduate degree, even though I'd met all the requirements." She bit down hard on her lower lip. "He said I needed to do another year of undergraduate papers."

Garnet wrapped an arm around the girl. "I see." Technically, Russ couldn't have stopped Eloise, but his words would've held weight with the SnowDancer education board.

All SnowDancer pups had an automatic right to education up to and including an undergraduate degree—or comparable courses outside the tertiary system. Anyone who wanted a graduate education or further training could also get it on the pack so long as they then worked for the pack for a certain number of years, ranging from three to five. However, to access the graduate fund, students had to keep up their grades throughout and report regularly to their advisers, which advisers then in turn apprised the board.

"He only did it out of spite," Eloise rasped, her eyelashes wet and clumped together. "I solved an equation he couldn't. I didn't mean to show him up. I just thought that was what I was supposed to do, so I did it." She hiccuped and sniffed, rubbing at her tears with the sleeves of her sweater—which she'd pulled over her hands like a child. "I could tell he was mad, but I never thought he'd be vindictive. He was meant to be my teacher, my support."

Garnet felt sick, her wolf standing at tense attention inside her. Wrapping Eloise in both arms and rubbing her cheek against the younger woman's, she said, "Why didn't you come to me?" If her packmates didn't feel like they could talk to her about such situations, then she had a serious problem on her hands. Protecting the vulnerable was her job and her responsibility.

The idea that she might've failed rocked her very sense of self.

Eloise cuddled into her, tall and strong and suddenly as needy as a hurt pup. "I put myself in your diary for next week," she said. "But

I wanted to talk to Russ one more time, try to figure things out on my own. I'm old enough." That last was said with a mutinous edge that made Garnet's stomach stop twisting.

A young wolf flexing her claws was normal. It said good things about Garnet's leadership that Eloise had the confidence to stand up against a much older packmate. "Good," she said. "You *are* old enough to start to fight your own battles—but I'm glad to see you're also sensible enough to go to a senior packmate when the situation is beyond your ability to handle."

Straightening, Eloise scowled, the fierce SnowDancer soldier in her rising back to the surface now that she'd been reassured her dominant wasn't angry with her. "I was planning to tell Russ that I was going to you—I thought he'd back off then because we both knew he was wrong. All my grades prove it."

The younger woman's scowl faded as quickly as it had formed, her throat moving as she swallowed. "And even though he was being nasty, I didn't want to get him in trouble. He never showed it, but I could tell he was hurting from losing Athena."

Proud of this child of the pack and dead certain she'd had nothing to do with Russ's death, Garnet cut to the heart of the matter. "Where were you between seven and ten this morning?" Lorenzo hadn't yet confirmed time of death, but Garnet was certain that whatever had happened had occurred soon after Shane's arrival in Russ's quarters.

No way the two men had sat around chatting for hours.

Eloise's eyes widened before she began to pink up until even the dark cinnamon brown of her skin couldn't hide it. "Don't tell anyone," she whispered after glancing around to make sure no one else was close enough to listen in, "but I was with Chase. We slept in."

"Ah." At eighteen, Chase was younger than Eloise by three years.

He was also a strong wolf unlikely to be intimidated by Eloise's own strength. "I won't breathe a word."

"I'm not embarrassed or anything." Eloise's continuing blush was adorable, the way she was twisting her hands together even more so. "He's younger but he's . . . wow!" A sound that reminded Garnet of how, at the same age, she'd sighed over a certain green-eyed wolf. "I just want it to be private and secret between the two of us for a while."

"I understand, sweetheart." Packmates were wonderful and Garnet would never want to live away from a busy, active den, but it was also nice to have a little private time to become a couple before several hundred curious wolves started poking their noses in. "Stay right here."

Walking a short distance away, she made a couple of calls. Thanks to the weather, Chase hadn't driven out to the technical college he attended five days a week, instead choosing to study in the den. SnowDancer had an excellent remote-access system they'd set up in conjunction with multiple schools for exactly such circumstances.

Coming on the line when she located him, he confirmed that Eloise had been with him at the time of the murder. To his credit, he also immediately asked after his girlfriend. "Is she okay? I wanted to stay with her, but she kicked me out." Raw frustration and worry in every word. "Said she was fine, but I could tell she wasn't."

So young, Garnet thought affectionately. "Here's a tip, Chase. Sometimes you have to fight to look after a woman as strong as Eloise."

"I'm on my way. I can catch up on this lesson tonight."

Hanging up, Garnet asked Eloise about her part-time job.

The young soldier answered without hesitation. "The den maintenance team needed a few bodies for manual labor. Cleaning out ducts, that kind of thing. It's low-stress, plus"—her eyes grew brighter—"I get to watch the engineers work on the behind-the-scenes systems."

"Did you work often with Shane?"

Shaking her head, Eloise said, "Only a couple of times." Her face turned solemn. "He was so nice. I dropped one of his special tools and it went to pieces, but he didn't get angry, just showed me how to fix it."

That was Garnet's impression of Shane, too: calm and patient, no violent temper. "And his knife collection? Did he invite you to look at it?"

"No, I asked. I was just curious." Eloise lifted up both shoulders. "One of my friends had seen it, said it was interesting."

Garnet caught no hint of subterfuge in any of Eloise's answers; she let the young woman go with the admonition that she wasn't to share any details of what she'd seen at the scene.

"I won't," Eloise promised. "Not even with Chase."

Ten minutes later, Revel told Garnet that Mitchell had no connection to either Russ or Shane; he'd just tagged along to see the knives because he'd had some free time to kill. "I'd bet my place in the pack that he wasn't lying," Revel said. "I got the impression he was more interested in Athena's art than in the knives."

Garnet continued to investigate, managed to unearth a couple of packmates who'd seen Eloise and Chase sneak into his room—she'd known the two couldn't have fooled everyone. Sometimes, though, even wolves could be circumspect. Not often, but now and then.

Walking to the main den entrance after confirming the young couple's whereabouts, Garnet poked out her head. Her den had been dug out of the side of a mountain, similarly to the main SnowDancer den; it was solid stone and quite safe. It was also naturally soundproof, so it wasn't until she opened the door a crack and looked outside that she saw the night darkness beyond, mature trees bent over like saplings by a merciless wind.

The rain that hit her face felt like a thousand needles digging into her flesh.

Ice chilled her blood.

Everyone should've come in the instant the weather turned from irritating but bearable to deadly—her people weren't stupid and neither was Kenji. But according to the roster on the opposite wall, no one had made it back. No one.

Chapter 7

ABOUT TO HIT the emergency callback alarm that would blast out a high-pitched noise that was uncomfortable for wolf ears but highly effective in making them pay attention, she spied a couple of wet wolf bodies. Pulling the heavy door fully open, she let in the rain and the wind so her packmates could whip through the opening.

When the two sentries looked back at her, their gray pelts plastered to their bodies, she said, "Did you see Kenji or Pia?" The roster confirmed they were the only ones still out there; she'd have been alerted if anyone unauthorized had headed out, or if someone hadn't made it home.

Both wolves shook their heads, one of them sneezing midway. Lifting a paw to his muzzle, he rubbed.

"Go," she said to the bedraggled pair. "Get dry. They must be on their way back in."

The two went to the door instead and poked out their noses. She tapped them both firmly on those noses, to their yelps and offended looks. "Don't even think about going back out to look for them. Then I'll have four people to worry about instead of two. Go get dry. *Now.*"

Giving in, they padded off down the corridor, their paws leaving muddy prints on the stone and their bodies dripping. It'd be gone soon enough. One of the maternal females' favorite punishments was to make miscreant kids and juveniles clean anything that could be cleaned. Since this was a wolf den with plenty of mischievous pups, dirt was rarely allowed to linger more than ten or fifteen minutes.

She looked back out into the rain, her pulse in her mouth. Kenji was familiar with this area and he was one hell of a tough wolf, but it wasn't his own region. It was possible he'd become turned around in the vicious weather. As for Pia, she was a smart, experienced senior soldier. If she wasn't back, there was a problem.

"Jem, I just saw Josephine and Roan. They only now come in?" Revel stepped up beside her, his eyes on the storm and his slender body humming with barely contained tension. "Something's wrong with Pia," he said without waiting for a response from her. "I've had this growing bad feeling over the past half hour. Couldn't stand it anymore, came to check she'd returned."

Garnet had serious respect for the twin bond—she'd seen it in action with the twins among her own siblings. Steele would probably know the instant Ruby went into labor despite the fact that they were in different dens at the moment.

Not that she'd needed Revel's statement; her own instincts were screaming at her. "I think we'd better go out, look for her and Kenji." Unlike the exhausted Roan and Josephine, Garnet and Revel were fresh, would be better able to weather the storm.

Her blood roared in her ears, her mouth dry as she began to tug up her sweater, then thought to hell with it and decided to go straight into the shift. She could always get more clothes; she didn't want to delay a second. And much as she liked Revel's fiery twin, it was Kenji at the forefront of her mind. He *had* to be okay.

He was so dominant in her thoughts that when she caught a flash of white the split second before she would've gone into the shift, she thought she was imagining things. But no, it was Kenji's T-shirt that had caught her eye. He had a limp wolf in his arms, and he looked like he was about a second away from collapse. Garnet and Revel took off into the rain at the same instant, heading straight for him.

Revel gathered his sister's wolf form into his arms, while Garnet wrapped an arm around Kenji's waist, pulled one of his own arms over her shoulders, and all but dragged him to the den. "Close the door!" she yelled to a couple of juveniles who'd come over with mops, clearly on cleanup patrol.

"Yes, sir!" They hurried to shut out the driving rain.

Garnet, meanwhile, was struggling to keep Kenji going. "Where are you hurt?"

"Just exhausted," he said, his voice a little slurred. "Carried Pia all the way."

And he'd done it in what had felt like a gale-force wind. No wonder his body was searching for a place to collapse and rest. "You sure you're not hurt?" She'd never seen him this wiped out.

"Cut on face, but that's it." It came out mumbled.

Since her quarters were closer than the infirmary, she dragged him there and propped him up against the nearest wall. And saw that the "cut" on his face was more like a gash; it was bleeding all down his cheek. The wound on his stomach, on the other hand, had stained his torn T-shirt a pinkish red in the time it had taken her to get him to her room. "Kenji!"

Following her gaze, he looked down, blinked. "Huh. Can't feel that." Then he slid down the wall to collapse into a sitting position on the floor.

Garnet bit back her fear, quickly checked his pulse while trying to put pressure on his stomach wound. Blood continued to pulse out, slow but steady. Skin chilled and water dripping into her eyes,

she managed to dig out her phone with one hand, called the infirmary. "Kenji's got bleeding wounds," she told Lorenzo's assistant,
Gavin. "I need medical help."

To her surprise, it was Lorenzo who entered her quarters only
minutes later.

"Pia?" she asked as the healer put down his medical kit and knelt
in front of Kenji.

"Heavy bruising, broken leg." The front of Lorenzo's shirt was
damp, no doubt from his examination of Pia. "The break's a clean
one—Gavin can easily set it. I've made sure she has no internal
injuries."

Pushing up Kenji's T-shirt to expose the muscled and bloody
plane of his abdomen, he asked Garnet to hold up the sodden material while he shone a light on the wound, then scanned it with a
handheld device. "This isn't as bad as it looks," he murmured in his
native Spanish before switching back to English. "A deep gouge,
no impact on his internal organs."

Garnet felt no relief at Lorenzo's words, not with Kenji slumped
bleeding in front of her. Tangling her hand with Kenji's to reassure
her wolf of the steady beat of his life, she faced Lorenzo's profile. "Then
why is he out?" Kenji was a lieutenant, with the attendant strength.
If it was a simple scratch, he'd have shrugged it off, kept going.

Ignoring the snarl in her tone with the ease of long experience
dealing with scared and worried wolves, the healer checked the
back of Kenji's head. "Knot, just as I suspected."

Ice cracked through Garnet's veins. "You knew he hit his head?"

"Pia regained consciousness just as Rev got her to the infirmary."
Lorenzo continued to work, using his healing abilities on Kenji's head
wound. "She shifted, said Kenji saw her fall into a gully, came down
to bring her up—he asked her to shift so she'd be easier to carry."

Garnet hated seeing Kenji so still. Kenji was never still. Kenji was wicked smiles and color and infuriating flirtation. "Did he fall in the gully while going down to get her?"

Lorenzo shook his head, the silver in his hair glinting under the light. "He slid down part of the way after skidding on the mud. There were rocks on the slope, according to Pia." Frowning, he shifted position slightly so he could better access Kenji's head wound. "I'm guessing he whacked his head on one. Stomach injury probably happened when he pushed through the damaged trees at the bottom of the gully—Pia crashed straight into them. The sharp end of a broken branch could've raked Kenji's stomach while he was trying to get to her."

Unfettered respect on his face, in his voice, as he added, "Kenji might look like a pretty rock star but he's pure wolf. That gully is some distance away, never mind how steep it is, and the storm's brutal."

Kenji's eyes flickered on those words.

Fingers tightening around his, Garnet blew out a breath. "I'm going to strangle all four of them." Her voice threatened to shake. "They should've been back well before the weather got this bad." At a certain point, there was no need for security; nature provided its own deterrent.

"Don't blame them." Lorenzo removed his hand from the back of Kenji's head. "I was watching the satellite feed—it turned vicious with very little warning. They came in as fast as they could."

"Yeah, Garnet," Kenji mumbled, his long, talented fingers curling around hers. "Don't be mad."

Relief a crushing weight on her, she lifted their linked hands to press a kiss to his knuckles. His smile was faint, shaky, before his eyes closed again. "Lorenzo?"

"He's fine, in a natural sleep. Let me deal with these cuts." Lorenzo did so using his abilities as well as medical equipment, until both the gouge on Kenji's stomach and the cut on his cheek were covered by delicate new skin. "A little rest and he'll be up and running."

Garnet's brain started functioning properly again now that she knew Kenji was safe. Frowning, she said, "Why is Shane still out?" It had only taken Lorenzo ten minutes to stabilize Kenji.

"He got a real whack on the head—Kenji's was just a glancing blow by comparison."

Hand yet linked with Kenji's, Garnet considered Lorenzo's words. "Hit with something heavy?"

"I'd say so. You find anything?"

"No, but there was a coffee table there with a solid edge." A little distant for Shane to have hit it as he went down, but that was the only possible source of a head injury that Garnet could think of in Russ's living area.

Lorenzo twisted his mouth, shook his head. "I can't rule out the coffee table, but my gut says it was a blow from above." Picking up one of his medical instruments, he raised it over his own head, brought it down as if on the back of another skull. "Like that."

"Can you model it to confirm your hunch?" She knew the healer had the software.

"I'm no expert at it, but I'm fairly certain my compatriot in Kenji's sector is. I'll send her the details, have her put it together." He touched Garnet's hair with the gentle hand of a healer, but his tone was that of a packmate who had the authority to overrule her in certain circumstances. "Russ is dead, Shane is unconscious, and it's too dangerous outside for anyone to even think about sneaking up on the den. You can take a breath."

"Athena," she began.

"I gave her a sedative—she's high-strung at the best of times, so sleep will do her good." His eyes turned to steel. "As it'll do you. An emotionally exhausted lieutenant is no good for the den."

Woman and wolf, both parts of her knew he was right. She could all but feel the strain pounding in her temples. "Thanks, Lorenzo."

A tug of a loose tendril of her hair before the healer left. It wasn't until a minute later that she realized she should've asked him to help her shift Kenji.

"Kenji!" she snapped, putting every ounce of her considerable dominance in her voice.

Of course it didn't have the same effect on him as it would've had on someone more submissive. Kenji Tanaka had always gone his own way.

Lines formed on his forehead, though his eyes remained closed. "What?" It was a growly rumble.

Shivering from the auditory caress, she said, "Shift." He'd be much easier to dry off—plus she wouldn't have to worry about stripping him of his drenched clothes.

And thinking of Kenji naked was not good for her blood pressure. "I'll rub you dry," she cajoled when he stayed stubbornly in human form. *"Kenji."*

He growled at her, the bad-tempered growl of a wolf who just wanted to sleep.

"Fine," she said, though she wanted to hold him close and never let him go. "Stay in your wet clothes. Look like a drowned rat."

The world fractured into a shower of astonishing light and then there was a handsome black timber wolf lying in front of her. A very wet wolf who sneezed before putting his head down on his paws. Getting up, Garnet found a large, absorbent towel. Rubbing Kenji down with one hand, she called Revel with the other. "Pia doing okay? Why was she unconscious?"

"Just the broken leg—pain put her out," Revel answered. "She's pretty pissed about the entire situation, says she knew that gully was there but got messed up in the rain." A short pause, his tone holding a deep vein of affection when he came back on the line. "Sorry, Pia says she isn't pissed. She's fucking pissed."

Garnet's wolf huffed in laughter inside her. "That's definitely Pia."

"Yeah." He sounded distracted. "Damn it, Pia, stop fidgeting and let Gavin do his job." A growl rolled down the line. "Shit, sorry, Jem. My sister's being a pa— Pia, *for the love of God*, behave or I'll get Grace on the comm."

The threat to bring in their deeply submissive younger sister wouldn't have made sense to anyone who hadn't grown up in a Snow-Dancer den—and thus didn't know that submissives could become ferally protective when one of their people was hurt. And since Grace knew full well her sister would never harm a hair on her head, she'd take shameless advantage and force Pia to rest and to heal.

"I'm calling Grace right now unless you start acting like a woman with a fucking broken leg," Revel threatened.

Garnet raised an eyebrow at the feminine response she picked up through the receiver. "Is my Spanish rusty or did she just call you a—"

"Your Spanish isn't rusty." Revel's tone was still more wolf than man. "Our mother has threatened to wash out Pia's mouth with soap more than once." Another small pause before he said, "How's Kenji? Pain-in-the-ass here is worried about him."

"Clean bill of health." Thank God. "Just needs some sleep."

"It's been a long day. We should all get some rest," Revel replied. "We can pick up the investigation in the morning—Shane might be awake by then."

"Agreed." Hanging up with a quick good night, she began to rub Kenji down in earnest. He protested grumpily when she rubbed too hard on his ears. "Sorry, princess."

A growl, a clawed paw swiping at her—only he wasn't really swiping. He was just pretending. Smiling, she finished with the towel. "You need a blow-dry."

The growl was louder this time and held a distinct thread of insult.

"I thought you'd be used to it with all the hair colors," she teased, combing her fingers through his damp fur. "Do you want to sleep here or in the nice comfortable bed over there?"

His ears pricked up.

"I'm not letting you on the bed if you're going to make it damp." She rose, went to the cupboard, grabbed another towel.

And returned to discover a gorgeous naked man on her bedroom floor, half-asleep, his skin a flawless, luscious shade between lightest brown and dark gold. All over.

Closing her eyes because damn it, this was *Kenji*, the one man her body seemed unable to resist, she threw him the towel. "Wake up."

His eyes opened a little and he began to dry off with sluggish motions when she made it clear she wasn't going to help. A woman had limits! Since watching him run the towel over the honed ridges and valleys of his body was driving her crazy with the urge to pounce and lick him up, she ducked out to grab some food. By the time she returned, he was asleep. On the floor. At least he'd left the towel over his hips.

God, Kenji Tanaka was beautiful.

All graceful lines and hard muscle and tattoos inked through a special process that meant the ink "stuck" through the shift. Her favorite was the large kanji for "love" that he'd had inked on the back of his upper left shoulder. Now she saw that there was a line of more angular, smaller letters going down parallel to the kanji. It was highly stylized and difficult to read but she was sure the lettering was in katakana.

Kenji had studied Japanese writing as a child, not only because his parents wanted him fluent in both spoken and written Japanese, but because he loved his maternal grandfather, who had very little English. Kenji had taught her a few things back then, but after not using it all these years, she'd forgotten the meaning behind the symbols. She'd have to ask him. As she'd have to ask about the other new pieces she'd spotted on his body.

Like the ink peeking out from under the towel high on his thigh.

Garnet's fingers itched to tug away the towel and feast her senses on the wildly sexy man in front of her, but she wasn't that far gone. Yet. No matter how good he smelled. Oak and fire, sin and wickedness.

Picking up the plate holding the steak she'd grabbed for him, she waved it under his nose. If that didn't wake him up, he was truly out for the count and she'd have to do what she could to make him comfortable. But his eyes flicked open. Drawing away the steak before he could lunge at it, she said, "Get into bed." She wouldn't usually eat in bed, but she didn't think anything would entice Kenji to move once he was no longer hungry.

Might as well make sure he was comfortable first.

As it was, she had to tug him up and shove him to the bed—all the while trying not to ogle his body. It was hard. She wanted to bite him. And pet him. And kick him for breaking her twenty-one-year-old heart. He sure as hell had better have a good explanation for his behavior, or she *would* take her long overdue revenge.

Pushing him into bed, she helped him sit up, hauled a comforter to his waist, then gave him the steak. He stared at the plate for a minute before stabbing the steak with his fork and lifting it up to eat.

Leaving him to it, she grabbed a change of clothes—sweatpants and a tank as well as a fresh pair of panties—and went to the bathroom to get out of her own damp clothes. By the time she came out, Kenji had almost finished his steak. She gave him more food and ate some herself while sitting cross-legged on the bed facing him.

They drank water, since anything else would be a bad idea with Kenji having had a bump on the head. "Feeling better?" she asked after he'd demolished an enormous meal that'd fuel his body's healing process.

Jaw cracking in a huge yawn, he nodded. "Muscles feel like noodles, though—that fucking wind." He froze in the midst of sliding down into the bed and, though he was clearly struggling to keep his eyes open, said, "Should I go to my own room?"

"You can stay," she said, her heart huge inside her chest at the idea of Kenji's scent on her sheets, on her. "Just don't try any funny business."

A sinful, sleepy smile that reminded her of the playful boy he'd been. "No promises."

Garnet didn't reply because he was already asleep, his lashes throwing shadows on his cheeks and his damp hair a sleek black.

Oddly pleased at this glimpse of him without any of his usual shields, she leaned over and tugged the comforter to partway up his chest. When she moved to clear away their plates, he frowned in his sleep. "I'll be back," she murmured before rising to put the plates on the small table she used as a workspace when she didn't feel like staying at her office.

Going into the bathroom, she cleaned her teeth, washed her face . . . and admitted she was stalling. Because as soon as she walked into the bedroom, she'd be sleeping cuddled up next to Kenji. Gorgeous, infuriating, strong, and the only man who had ever made her heart go boom.

"He needs you tonight." She took a deep breath on those words and undid the loose ponytail into which she'd scraped up her hair after rubbing it close to dry with a towel.

Irrespective of what lay between them, what history, what secrets, what pain, tonight Kenji was a packmate who needed comfort. That was all. He'd probably be fine on his own but if he'd been isolating himself sexually for over a year, then the last thing he needed was more aloneness. Scowling at the idea of Kenji hurting himself that way, she went back into the bedroom and crawled under the comforter.

He moved in his sleep, curving his body around hers until he was spooning her, one arm around her waist, the other thrown above his head. He burned but it wasn't a fever. It was just Kenji. Sliding her hand over his muscled forearm, she closed her own eyes and snuggled in.

It should've been awkward, sleeping with a naked Kenji when they'd never done anything like this, but she fell into a deep, sweet sleep, her wolf curled up next to Kenji's heat. It felt like coming home.

Chapter 8

KENJI WOKE FEELING better than he had in forever. Nothing hurt inside him, nothing ached. Nuzzling against the warm skin of the packmate curled up with her back to his chest, he nudged his thigh a little higher. He'd slid it between hers and now it pressed up against the hot center of her—

His eyes blinked open.

He already knew who he held, her scent intimately familiar to him. Garnet's golden hair was soft against his arm and shoulder, her body small and lithely feminine, her breathing even in sleep.

Kenji's own heart, however, was slamming against his rib cage, every muscle in his body tense and his cock rock hard. He knew he had to pull away before she woke, but he *couldn't*. His wolf didn't want to go back to being cold and alone and without her. Something broke in him at even the idea of losing her when he was finally, *finally* holding her as he'd always hungered to do.

Moving with utmost care, he curled himself even tighter around her, breathed her in . . . and felt her shift. He slid away his thigh before she could ask him to, but instead of pulling away, she turned and cuddled into his chest, her own arm sliding over his ribs to curl against his back.

Not awake, he realized, just changing position.

Heart still hammering so hard it hurt, he nudged at her head with his arm. She lifted it without waking and he slid his arm under before curving it around her. His thigh, he pushed back between hers. It wasn't sexual, despite his aching cock. He just wanted to be close to her, their limbs interlocked.

She didn't stop any of it, didn't even stir.

That wrecked him, betraying as it did a level of trust that wasn't instinctive for a dominant predatory changeling of Garnet's strength. He would never hurt her, of course he wouldn't, but it meant everything that despite all the years and anger between them, she knew that truth so deeply that she could sleep without concern in his arms.

Nuzzling his chin on her hair, he closed his eyes and just sank into her scent, into the feel of her skin against his, her curves and her softness, and below that, a steely strength that called to the predator within him. His wolf knew bone deep who Garnet was to him, who she was meant to be . . . and it was because she meant so much that he'd let her go.

When she finally stirred, he didn't move, not wanting to end this before he had to. Stroking her hand down his back, she yawned lazily before rubbing her cheek against his chest. "How's your head?"

His heart, it filled his entire body, this huge, needy, painful thing. "Good. Did Lorenzo do me?"

A smile he saw because he'd brushed away the strands of hair stuck to her cheek. "Yeah, Lorenzo did you. All night."

Grinning at the sheer rightness of playing with her, he rubbed his chin on her hair again. "I feel good."

She continued to pet his back with a small, capable hand that unknowingly held his heart. "What's up with not sharing skin privileges with anyone for a year?"

He went to ask her how she knew, shut his mouth before the

words escaped. They were part of a pack. Secrets were hard to keep. "I just wanted to know if I could do it."

Lines forming on her brow, Garnet drew back but didn't pull away from him. Instead, she wriggled up until she could look him in the eye. "You're lying to me."

Yes, he was, but hell if he'd tell her the truth. That the reason he'd stopped sharing intimate skin privileges was because no one was her. No one would ever be his Garnet. "You know my family history," he said instead. "Tanaka men have a constitutional inability to keep it in our pants."

Garnet's response was a growl of sound, her eyes molten gold. "Kenji, you're a lieutenant. You know how to commit."

"Before he retired, my dad's father was a lieutenant, too," he reminded her, telling himself to break this dangerous physical contact.

He couldn't.

Having Garnet skin to skin against him was filling the dried-up well inside him, making him whole; he needed a little more. Just a little more. "His relationship with my grandmother lasted five years, just long enough to produce my dad. I love him but I've lost track of his lady friends at this point—though I do know he's currently beating out my father for the sheer speed with which he goes through women."

Garnet kept petting him and even if it was out of pity because of his touch-starved status, he'd take it. "Are you trying to tell me you became a player because you thought it was inevitable?"

Kenji shrugged. The truth was, he hadn't played around any more than anyone else in his year group—he'd probably done *less* because he'd known he wanted the right to call Garnet his own since the day of her high school graduation. But his few exploits had gotten blown out of all proportion because wild behavior was expected from a Tanaka. That had irritated him when he was younger; he'd worried Garnet would believe the rumors.

Later, he'd used it as a shield.

No one would wonder why Kenji was relentlessly single if he built a reputation as a man who simply couldn't decide on a woman. Only Garnet's brother Steele had never fallen for it. To this day, Kenji's best friend couldn't understand why Kenji and Garnet weren't together. Kenji had never told Steele the truth. Not even Hawke knew all of it, though Kenji had a feeling his alpha suspected. Only the senior SnowDancer healer and the healer in his den had the details, and neither would ever break his confidence.

"That's a load of b.s." Garnet's tone was flat. "Something's going on with you, has been for a while, hasn't it?"

He knew he was walking a risky road—his defenses were down and Garnet had a razor-sharp intelligence. *Tell her,* snarled the part of him that had fallen for her a lifetime ago. Strangling that voice, he luxuriated in the sensation of her against him . . . and stayed. "Me?" A deliberately teasing smile. "I'm an open book."

"Uh-huh. Why did you stop playing the violin?"

His gut clenched, his body going stiff before he could control the response. "What?"

"Yeah, what?" Her nose touched his, her expression that of a hunting wolf. "You loved making music."

The last time he'd played, he'd played for Garnet. The idea of putting bow to string when she wasn't there to listen, it had made him want to break the instrument into a thousand pieces. "I grew out of it." In the end, he hadn't broken his violin, had instead locked it in its case and hidden it away at the back of the closet.

"Liar."

The words, the challenge, shoved past his defenses. "Prove it."

Narrowed eyes before Garnet began to play dirty, running her hand over his chest and her foot up his calf. He grabbed her wrist even as his breath caught. "I don't want you to be with me because you think I need skin privileges." It wasn't what he'd intended to say, instinct trumping reason and turning his words into a growl of sound.

Letting her claws release after tugging away her hand, Garnet pricked his shoulders with them. Her eyes held a determined and distinctly wolfish light. "Baby, we've been flirting for years." She pressed up against him, small and curved in all the right places and his sweet, private addiction. "I've just decided it's time to do something about it."

He scowled in an effort to hide his raging need. "I'm getting out of bed." Gripping her wrists, he tugged off her hands. "I might've managed to keep it in my pants for a year, but I'm not good for you." Let her think he was worried about his ability to be loyal, when staying loyal to her was branded into his bones.

He'd walk on fire for Garnet. She was *it* for him, had always been it.

"There it is again, a lie." Teeth showing, she gripped his jaw when he would've looked away, her hold that of a pissed-off dominant female. "What the hell are you hiding from me, Tanaka?"

Fuck. "Nothing."

Growling low in her throat, she pressed up so close that their breath mingled. "Tell me." It was an order.

His own claws released, his wolf rising to the surface. Baring his teeth at her, he said, "Careful you don't forget who you're challenging."

Her lips curved, pure delight in her expression and that tiny dimple taunting him. "As if you'd hurt me, you big, bad, gorgeous wolf." A nuzzle of her nose against his, her hand gentling to pet his cheek, his jaw.

Fuck again. "We should go see if Shane is awake," he said, desperate to escape before he surrendered and took the one thing he wanted—*needed*—more than he needed to breathe.

Garnet nipped at his jaw. When he jerked, hands falling to grip at her hips, she smiled again, and this time, it was the smile of a SnowDancer with a highly specific goal in mind. "Agreed. But we'll be picking this up later." Rolling out of bed on that promise, she shot him a smile that was pure sin. "You have no clothes."

He growled at her before shifting. Shaking his fur into place, he went to her door and used the footpad to open it before slipping out. Her scent followed him out, his fur branded with her touch, his jaw feeling the lingering echo of her bite. A man would get away with nothing with Garnet. And a man who wanted to keep a secret had better as hell keep his distance, as Kenji had done for so long.

The only other choice was to tell her everything. Tell her why he wasn't man enough, wolf enough, for her. The therapist the healer had forced him to go see had told him to stop thinking that way, and on a conscious level at least, Kenji knew the therapist was right. But deep in his gut, in the most primal part of himself, in the wolf's heart itself, there was a hole he was afraid nothing would ever fill.

He didn't want Garnet to have to live with that sense of loss, too.

GARNET was on her way to grab a quick breakfast when she ran into Ruby. "What are you doing waddling about?" she teased her sister before bending to speak to the belly that had taken over Ruby's tiny frame. "Hey, little man."

"Lorenzo says I should waddle. Might hurry my pup up." Tucking her arm into Garnet's when Garnet rose to her full height, Ruby leaned into her, the familiar scent of her making Garnet's wolf brush affectionately against her skin. "Be my breakfast date?"

"Where's your beloved?" Ruby and her mate were joined at the hip with Ruby so close to her due date.

"Emergency with Grandma Maisey. Her computronics went down and you know she only trusts Tex to fix it."

"Grandma Maisey" was actually a friend of their maternal grandmother. They'd grown up calling her Grandma, while their maternal grandmother was Grammy and their paternal grandmother was Nanna. "Hmm." Garnet tapped her lower lip with a finger. "*Convenient* how Grandma Maisey's systems always break down or have a glitch right when Tex is driving you up the wall with his hovering."

Ruby giggled, eyes dancing. "Wolves are the *worst* hoverers," she said. "It's adorable really, how protective he is, but every so often, I want to waddle about without him nearby ready to catch me."

Well aware her older sister was nuts for the tall drink of water who was her mate, Garnet wrapped an arm around Ruby's shoulders. Ruby was one of the few members of the Sheridan family with whom Garnet could do that—everyone but one other sister had ended up on their father's side of the genetic height lottery. Ruby's twin, Steele, was six foot four. Needless to say, taking family photos required some judicious management—and clever use of hidden boxes.

Kenji's pups would be tall, she thought suddenly. His entire family was tall. Even if certain short genes mingled with his, she didn't think they'd hold sway.

Smiling at the thought of wild and beautiful Kenji with a newborn in his arms, she looked down when Ruby squeezed her arm. "I told Kenji I liked both him and Revel equally, and I do, but for *you*, it's only ever been Kenji."

Garnet wasn't surprised at Ruby's out-of-the-blue statement— her sister knew her. "Rev and I aren't an item anymore," she told her sister. "As for Kenji, he's holding something back."

"I figured. Otherwise, that man would have hunted you down long ago." Ruby's tone was definitive. "Kenji Tanaka is not one to sit back when he wants something."

That was exactly why it had hurt so much that he'd let her go. "I'll get it out of him," Garnet murmured. "First I have to put this situation with Russ and Shane to bed." Only after that could she focus on her personal needs and desires—and on one stubborn wolf lieutenant.

SHE'D just finished breakfast, while Ruby was nibbling at hers, when Lorenzo alerted her that Shane was awake. Kenji, who'd come into the communal dining area a couple of minutes after her and Ruby, saw her get up, said, "You want me to cover something for you?"

"I was meant to take a training session for the junior soldiers."

"On it."

Garnet couldn't understand how she'd thought, even for a minute, that Kenji would be an unreliable lover. She'd have to watch his habit of hiding things under a laughing, playful facade—because he was going to be hers. She'd made up her mind. They were through with this game of hide-and-seek and obfuscation.

And after this morning, after the panic she'd sensed in him at her teasing, she knew damn well he was in no way immune to her. In fact, she was starting to suspect Kenji had a mile-wide vulnerable streak when it came to her. That both confused and delighted her. Confused because why the heck would a man who felt that way walk away from her, and delighted because she damn well had a vulnerable streak when it came to him.

Crossing over to him, she very deliberately ran the back of her hand over his cheek. Males weren't the only ones who had a possessive streak and Kenji Tanaka needed to learn that Garnet Sheridan could play as dirty as any dominant. "Thank you, baby."

His eyes glittered, and then he actually flushed—with temper. Grinning as the other packmates in the room, including an overjoyed Ruby, whistled and hooted, she left him simmering and began to walk down the corridor.

Her mood grew darker the closer she got to the infirmary. She entered to find Shane sitting up in bed, a lost expression on his face. "Jem!" He clung to her hand when she took a seat on the bed; the bruises on his face had turned black overnight but Lorenzo had managed to keep the swelling to a minimum.

"What's happening?" Shane's voice rose, his breathing ragged. "Why isn't Athena here?"

"She'll be here soon." Garnet had no intention of keeping Shane isolated now that he was conscious; that wasn't good for any wolf, much less one who'd been hurt. "I need to talk to you first."

Shane's deep blue eyes locked on her face. "Why?" he pleaded. "Why am I here? I don't—"

Garnet interrupted before the usually steady-tempered man could spiral into panic. "I want you to tell me what you did yesterday morning after you got off your shift," she said, careful not to suggest anything with her words. "Go through it step-by-step."

"Yesterday morning?" Frowning, he let go of her hand to rub at his temple. "I was tired," he said slowly. "I'd started my shift early, pulled extra hours to help out after one of the other maintenance techs got sick. Wanted to go straight home and crash but I promised Russ I'd meet him after work."

"Why did you agree to meet him?"

A twisted smile. "I really love Athena and, for some reason, she has a soft spot for that cold bastard. Feels sorry for him."

Garnet noted his natural use of the present tense when speaking about Russ. "Go on."

"I thought if I could make peace with Russ, it'd make her happy, you know?"

Garnet sensed no deception in him but it was possible that, horrified by what he'd done, Shane had blocked it out. "Did you take anything with you?"

"No, I left my tools at work as usual, but I did pop home to have a quick shower. Didn't want to meet Russ all dusty and sweaty—he always looks down his damn nose at me." Shane shrugged. "I'm just as qualified as him, just as educated, but he was always insinuating I was stupid. Asshole."

Garnet focused on the first part of Shane's statement. He said he'd returned to the apartment, but Athena had specifically denied seeing him the morning of the murder. "What did Athena say when you told her you were keeping your appointment with Russ?"

"She was out so I never saw her." No hesitation, no tension in his response. "I think she might've been teaching a class. But," he continued, "it wasn't a big deal. I'd already discussed the whole Russ situation with her before I left for work the night before." A smile that made creases form in his cheeks. "She was proud of me for being willing to let bygones be bygones, especially after Russ was such a prick and hassled me in front of my workmates."

A more suspicious mind might say that Athena had been setting Shane up to be the perfect fall guy, but Garnet couldn't quite see it. For flighty, artistic Athena to have used affable Shane in that way, she'd have to be cold-blooded and pragmatic to the extreme under her delicate appearance. Then again, Athena had lived with Russ for years. Maybe she'd absorbed some of his skills at making plans.

But what possible motive could the older woman have to kill her ex?

Long-buried anger? Money? Garnet would check Russ's will, find out if he'd changed it after the separation. Though, given the way he'd hauled in that chemical carpet cleaner so quickly, she'd bet on Russ having long ago drafted a new will. That left Athena with only the flimsy motive of revenge for past wrongs.

"Did you take Russ a peacemaking gift?"

Shane shook his head, his dark blond hair soft and tumbled. "I knew he wouldn't take it."

"So after your shower . . ."

"I went over to Russ's—didn't want to waste too much time on it, to be honest. Needed to catch some shut-eye." Eyes scrunched up, he rubbed his temple again. "And then . . ."

"Yes?"

"I . . ." His breath was suddenly fast and shallow. "I can't remember." Sweat broke out over his brow. "I can't remember anything after that. Why can't I remember?"

Garnet gripped his face between her hands. "Slow it down. *Breathe.*" It took three more clipped orders, her wolf rising to roughen her voice, but she stopped Shane from hyperventilating. Then, once he was calm, she took him back through the entire morning of the murder.

He still couldn't recall anything beyond walking out of his apartment to go to Russ's.

Leaving him with an order to do a simple calming exercise that would keep his mind occupied, she stepped out to talk to Lorenzo.

"I've known Shane since I moved into the den," the healer said after hearing her report. "He's a piss-poor liar. Can't even bluff at poker."

Garnet tended to agree. "What are the options? That he's too traumatized by his actions to go back to that point in time, or the knock on the head scrambled his wiring?"

"Exactly." Lorenzo rubbed his jaw, his heavy gaze going to the door of Shane's infirmary room. "Either way, it's not good for Shane, is it? If he can't defend himself?"

Garnet had a bad feeling in her gut, a nauseating sense of being made the fool. "Maybe there's a third possibility," she murmured. "Maybe he didn't see anything. His morning ended soon after he stepped inside Russ's quarters." She stared at the images on the back-lit screen on one wall of Lorenzo's office. "Were you able to confirm he was hit from behind?"

"Yes, the digital model just came through." Lorenzo's gaze was suddenly a dark wolf-amber. "You think someone else was in that room." The healer shook his head. "But that dead bolt . . ."

Yes, that was the problem.

Chapter 9

LORENZO FOLDED HIS arms, his shirt straining across heavily muscled shoulders. "I want Shane to be innocent, but I didn't catch any unknown scents in the room, so even the wild card of a rogue teleporter is out of the question. And trust me, I seriously tried to figure out how to make that a viable scenario." A vein pulsed at his temple. "Once you strike that from the possibilities . . ."

That *damn* door locked from the inside. "I'm going to bring Shane up to speed." He deserved to know, and—"His reaction might tell us something."

"I'll get in touch with Athena, tell her she can visit." Lorenzo's eyes went to the door of Shane's room again. "He shouldn't be alone."

"No." Even the toughest wolf had his breaking point.

Leaving Lorenzo, Garnet reentered Shane's room and told him about the murder. His face froze, his eyes staring at her in blank disbelief before his big body began to shake. "Did I do that?" he whispered, begging her for an answer with his gaze. "Is that why I don't remember?"

"I can't answer that question, not yet." Garnet brushed back his hair, offering the comfort of pack even as she kept her tone hard, unyielding. Shane's wolf needed to know his dominant was in charge. "*Nothing* is going to happen until I'm satisfied I know everything there is to know about this situation."

"Athena." Shane's eyes welled up and it was the first time she'd ever seen the big, friendly male in such a raw emotional state. "That's why she's not here."

"Athena's been desperate to see you." Garnet glanced over her shoulder. "In fact, I think I can scent—"

"Shane!" Running into the room on a wave of lush, feminine scent and whirling multihued skirts, Athena fell sobbing into Shane's arms.

Instead of collapsing himself, Shane's shoulders squared, his tears retreating. As if in looking after her, he'd found his strength. "Shh," he murmured, running a work-roughened hand over the silken mahogany of Athena's curls. "Jem will figure this out. You know she will."

Dark blue eyes met hers, entreaty and a fragile hope in their depths.

Yes, Garnet promised without words before leaving the room and closing the door to give the couple privacy. Her next step was to return to Lorenzo. "Autopsy on Russ?" she asked.

"Done." Getting to his feet, he turned on the backlit medical screen and pulled up a scan of Russ's heart, pointed out a particular area using the index finger of his left hand. "Knife just nicked the aorta."

Garnet put her hands on her hips, frowned. "Would that have made Russ collapse where he stood?"

A shake of Lorenzo's head. "A total transection of the aorta and it's game over. He would've exsanguinated before help could arrive. This"—he tapped the image—"was a slow bleed."

Garnet chewed that over. "Could Russ have had a heart attack from the stress?" *Something* had stopped him from seeking help.

But Lorenzo gave another negative shake of his head. "I checked. Injury-wise, he has the stab wound, scraped knuckles, a few light bruises on his face, but no signs of any other medical or physical event."

Folding her arms, Garnet thought back to when Shane had grabbed her hand. "The skin on Shane's knuckles looked unbroken to me."

"No damage that I detected," Lorenzo agreed. "Aside from the bump on the head—there was a hairline fracture there, by the way"—he pointed out the evidence on another scan—"Shane has those bruises on his face and significant bruising to the ribs. I can't prove it but I don't think they were made by fists."

Lowering her arms, Garnet turned to look at Lorenzo. "Are you saying he was kicked?"

"He's a big man, strong, too, but he's got no defensive injuries on his hands or arms." Lorenzo brought up photos of Shane's upper limbs as they'd been when he was first brought in. "So whether it was kicks or blows from an unknown weapon, I'd bet my career that he was already down when it was done."

The hairs rose on the back of Garnet's neck, her skin tingling. "Leaving aside the lack of defensive injuries," she said, "if he'd hit Russ hard enough to cause Russ's bruises, we'd expect visible damage, right?"

"He could've got lucky." Lorenzo didn't sound convinced. "As for Russ . . . it's almost as if he lay down and died." Tiny lines flaring out from the corners of his eyes, the healer ran a hand through his hair. "Only one reason I can think of for Russ to just give up that way and it makes me sick to my stomach to even consider it."

"That Athena's the one who dealt the killing blow and Shane's covering for her." Garnet clenched her jaw so hard it hurt. "I can't see it, Lorenzo. Quite aside from the fact that she's about as dangerous as a cream puff, she has an alibi." Garnet had run into the head of the nursery at breakfast and confirmed that Athena had come in early to prep for her class, was in the nursery during the window of time when the murder had most likely taken place. "Unless," she said, facing Lorenzo's profile, "you think time of death was later in the morning?"

"No." A definitive shake of his head. "I've processed all the data. Time of death was between seven thirty and eight thirty. I lean toward the earlier end of the spectrum." Switching out the scans, he gave her a quick update on a juvenile with a broken wrist, before adding, "I know it makes your job harder, but thank God Athena has an alibi. It's taken Shane a long time to find someone with whom he's happy."

"Love can make people do stupid things." Just because Athena hadn't taken physical part in the murder didn't mean she wasn't involved. "Keep an eye on them. Call me immediately if you figure out anything else."

"I don't envy you this, Jem." Lorenzo's eyes were solemn.

Neither did Garnet, but this was her job, why she was a lieutenant.

Leaving his office on that thought, she went to look in on Pia—who was sulking at being growled at by Lorenzo for her terrible patient skills—then made her way to the indoor training arena. She needed to clear her head, figure out what it was she wasn't seeing. Because there was *something* niggling at her beyond the fact they still had to confirm the origin of the blow to Shane's skull.

A couple of pups in wolf form joined her halfway to her destination, and when she hunkered down to pet them, they didn't dart off. Normally, feeling their rapidly beating hearts beneath her palm, their fur soft as their curious noses sniffed at her, would've been enough to negate all the tension within. Not today. She was still wound up tight when she arrived at the training arena—after leaving the pups in their father's care. It turned out the siblings had run gleefully away while he was putting together their nursery bag for the day.

Leaning against the back wall of the arena, she watched Kenji take her second-year offensive/defensive class through a routine that was different from hers, but just as effective. He'd changed into plain gray sweatpants and a black T-shirt that hugged his pecs, his feet bare. She wanted to pounce on him. So when he asked for a volunteer to help display a set of moves, she raised her hand while jumping up and down.

His lips twitched before he fixed his features into a stern expression. "It seems we have an eager volunteer."

The students looked on with wide grins as Garnet sauntered over to join him.

"Be gentle," she said, loud enough to be overheard. "Don't forget I'm not as big as you."

Kenji snorted. "I haven't been taken in by that since you put me flat on my back when you were fifteen. I'm pretty sure you were wearing dangly earrings and a sparkly headband at the time."

Garnet's muscles stopped hurting, her stomach stopped churning.

She laughed, knew her eyes were dancing. Because Kenji was the one who'd taught her the move that had eventually put him flat on his back. He'd grinned while lying on the ground that day, after she'd successfully integrated the move into a sparring session; his green eyes had been wild with a pride that had made her feel ten feet tall.

Kenji Tanaka was one boy who'd never been threatened by her strength.

Wolf so happy to be sparring with him again that it was as eager as a pup, she fell into a relaxed stance. "Well, then, baby," she said to a round of excited gasps, "shall we play?"

Kenji's stern expression slipped into glittering frustration. Stern didn't really suit him anyway. He was meant for smiles and teasing and affection. Meant for stolen kisses and tumbling her to the floor with sneaky tricks.

Now, his slick black hair sliding forward a little, he showed her his teeth. "Let's play."

That was it. They went at it.

No slow motion to show the students how to do the same. This was about displaying what SnowDancer wolves *could* do if they worked hard and stayed in peak condition. The one thing she and Kenji did do was pull their kicks and punches so that nothing would leave a permanent bruise. At their speed, however, it wouldn't appear that way to their audience.

Garnet tapped Kenji with a roundhouse kick; he hit out with an open-handed jab to the side of her throat that was a featherlight kiss; she blocked a gut punch; he blocked one to the face.

If they hadn't pulled any one of those hits, the two of them would've been black-and-blue, with a few broken ribs into the bargain. As it was, by the end of the bout—ended by mutual agreement after a meeting of the eyes—they were breathing hard and sweating, but in otherwise much the same condition as when they'd started.

Putting her hands on her hips, she raised an eyebrow at Kenji as her pulse continued to race from the exercise—but mostly from tussling with the sexiest man she knew. "Glad to see old age hasn't slowed you down, Tanaka."

His lips curved without hesitation this time, wolf eyes full of the same joy that lit her blood. "I try, Sheridan." Turning to their grinning students, he said, "So, what did you learn?"

A hand went up. "That I never, *ever* want to meet either one of you in a dark alley."

Laughter ran through the ranks.

· · ·

SMILING at the smart-aleck remark that could've come from his own mouth when he'd been younger, Kenji caught the bottle of water Garnet threw over from the small cooler to one side of the training area. It felt so normal to do this, to play with her, to teach with her, that he was a little terrified. Not enough to regret a second of his time with her, however.

Never would he regret time spent with Garnet.

"Aside from that?" he prompted the kids after he'd taken a drink.

"That size doesn't matter if you know what you're doing," a smaller young male said slowly. "Jem was holding her own even though you're bigger and heavier than her."

Kenji thought of how he'd used to teach Garnet the things he was taught in his more advanced class, how quickly she'd always caught on. It hadn't been long before her trainers had realized that regardless of her age and size, she needed to be in the advanced class alongside him. "How did she hold her own?"

A pause before a girl answered. "She doesn't use quite the same moves—she's adapted them to make her size an advantage."

"Good. Keep talking."

The discussion was energetic and involved, and when Kenji separated the students out into unbalanced pairs to do self-run bouts, they went at it with frowns of concentration. He and Garnet watched over the group for ten minutes to make sure there were no major issues, before walking out together.

"Shane?" he asked once they were in the corridor.

Garnet narrowed her eyes. "We need to look at that room again," she said after filling him in on their main suspect's broken recollection of events as well as what she'd learned from Lorenzo. "My gut isn't settling."

Kenji felt he had a good handle on the players now and his instincts echoed Garnet's. "Ruby gave me deep background on Shane after you left the dining area today." Garnet's sister honestly knew everything about everyone. "If it had been him, I would've expected a heat-of-the-moment burst of anger and violence. The knife to the heart seems cold and showy at the same time."

"Exactly!" Reaching back to fix her ponytail, her white shirt stretching over the taut mounds of her breasts and drawing his eye like a laser, Garnet bit down on her lower lip. "Do you need to shower?" A teasing gleam in the blue of her eyes, her dimple in full taunting mode. "Not that you don't smell delicious."

Running a hand through his sweat-dampened hair, Kenji glared at her. "Stop messing with me." He had no defenses where Garnet was concerned and she'd figured that out.

A sinful smile as she closed the distance between them until her boots touched his bare feet. "But I like messing with you, Kenji Tanaka." Gripping the sides of his T-shirt while he stood frozen in place, unable to break contact, she rose on her toes and nuzzled a kiss to his throat. Right where his pulse ricocheted against his skin in a rapid tattoo.

Then she bit. Hard. Leaving a mark. A possessive, unmistakable mark.

Breath harsh and cock primed, he wound her ponytail in his hand. *"Garnet."* His chest rumbled.

Drawing in his scent on a luxurious breath, as if she couldn't get enough of him, the dangerous wolf who'd marked him rubbed her thumb over his jaw before stepping back. "We have to be lieutenants first." Her scent wrapped around him, steel and Garnet and slick, wet welcome.

"Five minutes," he ground out and stalked off to his quarters before he could talk himself out of it and right into Garnet's arms.

He twisted the water to ice-cold.

When he reached the scene after dressing in blue jeans and a thin gray sweater, boots on his feet, it was to see Garnet just coming around the corner. She'd showered, too, was wearing a pair of chocolate-colored pants that skimmed her legs and cupped her butt, teamed with a V-necked blue sweater and what he'd already figured out were her favorite brown boots.

"How are your folks?" she asked as she reached him. "I just saw the textured mural your mom did down in that corridor and it reminded me to ask."

Kenji didn't answer until they were inside Russ's quarters with the door shut behind them. "Dad's in Alexei's den. He's taken over the communications hub there." Alexei was the youngest Snow-Dancer lieutenant and had the smallest den to look after, but that den lay along a border and, as such, was in no way unimportant.

"Your dad's one of the best."

"Yep." Kenji knew his dad would be *the* best if he wasn't more interested in ballroom dancing and Moroccan rug weaving and herb gardening—just three of Satoshi Tanaka's intense and short-lived interests. "He sent me a yoga book the other week. That's his new thing." Kenji would bet his left arm that Satoshi was already sleeping with his limber young yoga teacher.

"If your dad's in Alexei's region," Garnet said with the wry smile of someone who'd grown up with him, "then your mom is surely not."

Kenji grinned—his parents' fights had scared him as a pup, but he'd come to terms with their relationship long ago. "She's in Tomás's region," he told her. "According to him, she's driving him crazy while creating art so beautiful it makes other wolves weep." A standard state of affairs for Miko Tanaka. "She calls me each Friday without fail and goes through every piece of gossip she's heard about me. It's like having my own personal spy network."

Garnet's laughter was a caress that made his wolf want to throw back its head and howl.

TELLING herself she could trace the edges of Kenji's smile later, Garnet said, "I gave one of her pieces to my parents for their mating anniversary." It would've been financially beyond her reach if Miko didn't have special secret pricing for packmates. The outside world paid high six figures for one of her unique multimedia works—and that was at the low end. Packmates paid what Miko thought they could bear.

As a lieutenant, Garnet was paid an amount commensurate with her heavy responsibilities. The pack's business assets were myriad and strong and, as such, all SnowDancers who either worked for the pack or held necessary positions in it—like the lieutenants and healers—were compensated fairly. Garnet would've done it for nothing, rarely spent what she was given, so she'd had a good sum saved up to offer Miko.

Only Kenji's mom had insisted on giving the stunning piece to her for what she'd said was the "future daughter-in-law" price. It was so outrageously low that Garnet had felt like a thief, but no amount of arguing by Garnet had changed Miko's mind that Garnet and Kenji were meant to be. Garnet might've refused to take the artwork had Miko not made it clear that she'd be mortally offended at even the suggestion of any such thing.

Clearly, Kenji's mother would be having the last laugh. "My folks love it," she added, "have it up in their living room."

"Yeah?" Kenji's cheeks creased. "You should've asked me for one. She sends me a piece every time she decides I need more culture in my life."

"You're sitting on a fortune there."

"Except that if I ever sold one, she'd rip off my head." Kenji laughed. "Your folks still doing the lovebirds thing?"

Garnet groaned. "I walked in on them making out like juveniles last time I was in the main den. No wonder I have eight brothers and sisters." Turning to the door with Kenji's laugh rippling over her skin, she stared at the dead bolt. "Is there *any* way this could've been relocked from the outside?"

Chapter 10

HIS SWEATER SITTING easily over wide shoulders, Kenji examined the lock. "I can't see how. It's got no fancy computronics that might've been hacked. Just a solid iron bar snicking into place."

"I talked to Revel on my way to meet you." She'd run into him as he was heading off to get Pia a favorite snack. "I asked him about magnets or other tricks and he said the same. It'd be impossible given the depth of the door—and the dead bolt's too stiff for anyone to have gone low-tech with a pulley system." It took a bit of grunt to push the bolt into the lock; Garnet had tested it during their forensic sweep.

"Revel a locksmith?"

"Engineer." The majority of SnowDancer soldiers had a secondary specialty. Kenji's was in international law, Garnet's in finance. She worked with their fellow lieutenant, Cooper, to keep SnowDancer's investments strong. However, after the massive attack on the pack earlier that year, she'd also made it a point to learn and study weapons that could be used against SnowDancer and its allies. She was no expert yet, but she was getting there, and Hawke had put her in charge of evaluating possible counterweapons.

Kenji, by contrast, had a brilliant facility for languages on top of his legal training and natural strategic skills. As a result, he dealt with a number of SnowDancer's major offshore business contacts and was point man for their alliance with the BlackSea changelings. Now his face grew dark, skin tight over the clean angles of his features. "Last night—"

"Rev and I decided to call it quits yesterday." She bumped her shoulder against Kenji's arm. "I'm free to seduce you."

Kenji focused those pretty green eyes on the door. "I don't see any scratches or anything else that would indicate this lock's been jimmied."

Grinning at this dangerous, wicked wolf's attempt to simply ignore her flirting, she returned her attention to the matter at hand. "And we found no forensic evidence on it to indicate Eloise touched it. Only sign of damage is from when she forced the door—"

"—and that damage seems to exonerate her," Kenji completed. "No way the door frame would've splintered that way *unless* the dead bolt was thrown. The part on the frame literally came away still attached to a chunk of wood." He paused. "Girl's strong."

"Hmm." Garnet went over how Eloise had seemed the day before, added that to what she knew about young female pride. "Damn it." It was a growl. "Even if she didn't break anything, girl has to have bruises to hell and back."

Kenji pulled out his phone, made a call to Lorenzo asking him to check up on Eloise. "I seem to recall a certain pint-sized Sheridan refusing to go to the infirmary after fracturing her ribs falling from the climbing frame."

"Shuddup." Shooting him a glare that did nothing to dim the wattage of that troublemaker smile she adored, Garnet went back to staring at the lock. "What the fuck are we missing?"

Kenji walked backward until he was standing not far from the spot where they'd found Shane. "Let's run this through. You be Shane. I'll be Russ."

"Okay, I come in." Garnet considered the personalities involved. "We're polite at first, but then the wrong words get spoken and we fight."

The two of them pretend-grappled all the way to the bedroom and back.

"I pull out my knife from—" She paused. "He wasn't wearing a jacket and it wouldn't have fit in his jeans pocket, so it would've had to have been in his boot." At Kenji's nod of agreement, she continued their reenactment of the murder. "I pull out my knife from my boot and stab you." Garnet made a stabbing motion. "Right to the heart."

Kenji clutched at his chest, then frowned and stood up straight instead of falling down. "Wait. When did Shane take the hit to the back of his head?"

That was what had been bothering her. "Let's figure out the how, then maybe we can figure out the timing."

Kenji nodded. "Any ideas?"

"It has to be something heavy and portable," she murmured. "Lorenzo's pretty sure it wasn't the edge of the coffee table and we didn't find any blood or hair on it."

The two of them began to search. It was Kenji who finally found it—a heavy metal flashlight that had rolled under the display cabinet and ended up hidden in a deep pool of shadow. They stopped long enough for Garnet to get an evidence kit, then pulled it out. The blood and hair on the end erased all doubt about whether or not it had been the weapon used to incapacitate Shane.

"Okay, Russ hits Shane with the flashlight," Garnet said as she bagged the flashlight so they could confirm DNA and check for fingerprints. "That begs the question of why Russ would be holding a flashlight in the first place. We didn't have any power outages that morning."

"It could've been lying on top of the display cabinet," Kenji suggested. "He picks it up to defend himself when he sees the knife. Shane stabs him, turns away for some reason, and Russ still has enough strength to whack him over the head?"

"I guess." Garnet frowned. "He was just so fastidious. Nothing out of place."

Kenji glanced around. "You're right. But you saw how dark it was under that cabinet—he could've lost something down there, been looking for it when Shane arrived."

It made sense but the sick, wrong feeling in Garnet's gut wouldn't subside. "I want to take another look at Russ's body."

ONCE in the small, isolated morgue at the far end of the infirmary suite, she, Kenji, and Lorenzo examined Russ's body with care, found nothing other than the marks of the autopsy and the killing wound, along with the light bruises and scraped knuckles Lorenzo had already noted.

Shoulder muscles bunched after Lorenzo returned the body to the temporary storage unit, Garnet paced the room. "Can we see his clothes as well as Shane's?" They were the only things left that might offer some kind of an answer. Garnet *was not* going to condemn Shane when an ever-expanding sense of wrongness continued to chill her blood.

"Here." The healer pulled out the evidence bags in which he'd stored the clothing, one bag for each item.

Taking one set after pulling on surgical gloves, Kenji went to the steel autopsy table and—after Lorenzo disinfected it to prevent contamination—laid out the clothes as Russ would've been wearing them, while she did the same with Shane's clothing on a neighboring table. Then they stood side by side between the two, their bodies touching in a line of warmth as they stared at each set in turn.

"This blood drop," Kenji said, pointing to a perfect teardrop low on Russ's shirt, "it doesn't fit the gravitational direction of the rest of the blood."

Garnet leaned in to see what he had, nodded. That one droplet went vertically downward, while the rest of the blood had gone sideways across one side of Russ's chest.

"Could've been from the knife after he was first stabbed," Lorenzo said.

Plausible, Garnet thought. "I know Shane doesn't have any visible blood on the front of his shirt, but what about microdroplets?"

"No microdroplets." Lorenzo's striking eyes went to Shane's shirt. "I double-checked."

Garnet turned over the shirt to point at the droplet she'd noticed on the back of Shane's forearm. It looked like it had splashed downward onto Shane's shirt, its shape pristine and undisturbed—as if Shane hadn't moved so much as a flicker after the droplet fell onto his body.

Her heart slammed against her ribs. "This blood, is it from Russ?"

"Yes. DNA confirmed."

"Damn," Kenji murmured at the same instant the pieces clicked together in her head, the ensuing pattern so incomprehensible that she and Kenji just stared at one another.

Turning as one, they headed back to the scene.

Lorenzo accompanied them. "What've you two figured out?"

"Let's see if we're right first," Kenji murmured once they were inside Russ's living area. "Be Shane, Lorenzo."

"You want me to lie down?"

"No, run this from the start." Garnet nodded at Kenji to pick it up.

"Okay, you enter. I shake your hand." Kenji snapped his fingers. "Forgot something I had for you in the other room. Please come with me."

"Something of Athena's that she accidentally left behind?" Garnet offered.

Nodding, Kenji said, "That works."

Lorenzo took a moment to think about it. "Okay, I agree to go," he said. "Just keeping the peace so this meeting is over as fast as possible and I can grab much-needed shut-eye."

"Fits with Shane's personality," Garnet said, and the three of them walked to the bedroom. "And it explains Shane's scent in the bedroom."

"Yes, and then, damn, I realize I left this unknown thing in the front room after all." Kenji led Lorenzo out. "It's just over there." He pointed.

When Lorenzo turned instinctively in that direction, Kenji reached toward the display cabinet next to him, picked up an imaginary flashlight, then brought it down lightly against the back of Lorenzo's head. "Slam with the flashlight and you're down."

A scowling Lorenzo nonetheless went to the floor.

"You dead-bolt the front door then go to the bedroom," Garnet said, disbelief a living being inside her, "mess it up, punch a hole in the wall . . . get the knife."

"But before the final act . . ."

Kenji rolled Lorenzo over and pretended to punch the healer's face before punching himself a couple of times. As Lorenzo's eyes widened in shocked understanding, Kenji rolled Lorenzo back over and aimed several pretend kicks at his ribs. Only then did he rise to his feet and use his phone in place of the knife to mimic stabbing himself before leaning down to place the "weapon" by Lorenzo's outflung hand.

"This is when the blood drops onto Shane's sleeve. Vertical droplet on Russ probably happened when he pulled out the blade," Garnet said softly as Kenji placed a hand over his heart and went to the ground in the position in which Russ had been found. "Explains everything."

Lorenzo and Kenji both sat up.

The healer's blood had leached from his skin, leaving it unnaturally stark. "Russ wasn't wearing a glove." He wrapped his arms loosely around his raised knees. "Why didn't we find his fingerprints on the blade?"

And the final piece slotted into place for Garnet.

"The handkerchief," she whispered. "He deliberately got blood on it to hide any metallic scent from the knife hilt."

Kenji ran a hand through his hair. "Could be it was also a parting shot aimed at Athena. Screw with her emotions, foster guilt."

"Yes." Garnet slid down to sit with her back to the door, unable to believe that one of her packmates had been filled with enough rage to orchestrate his own "murder."

KENJI'S heart rebelled at seeing that shocked, pained look on Garnet's face. Rising, he went to sit by her side. It was primal instinct to wrap an arm around her. "Adults, remember?" he murmured to her, bending to nuzzle at the soft, warm skin of her cheek. "We aren't their keepers. We can't control our packmates."

One hand closing over his raised knee as she allowed him to

tuck her against his side, Garnet nodded. "You're right." No shakiness, her breath steady. "It's just the idea that Russ hated Shane so much he was willing to die to hurt him . . . And Athena, too. The woman he was meant to love."

"We're seriously saying Russ did this to himself?" Lorenzo gripped at one of his wrists. "How did he get the knife?" The healer answered his own question an instant later. "No one locks their doors and he's no child—could've circumvented the lock on the studio door and on Shane's knife case."

"Athena's teaching schedule is available to anyone." Garnet stayed tucked up against Kenji as she spoke, the pressure of her body a physical reassurance to his wolf that she was all right. "Shane's work schedule wouldn't have been hard to figure out, either."

Easy, Kenji thought, for Russ to walk into the apartment when no one was home; and if he'd left the door open on his way out, his scent would've dissipated long before Athena and Shane returned. "It fits, but to exonerate Shane, we need hard evidence."

"Russ had a mathematical mind." Lorenzo's words were quiet. "A liking for everything in its place."

"The kind of man who might've come up with the perfect murder."

Garnet nodded at Kenji's statement, fine strands of her hair catching on the gray of his sweater. "Could be he kept a diary." Pulling out her phone, she got in touch with Athena. "No diary," she said after hanging up. "Athena did confirm he was meticulous in his research and planning, even if it involved a short trip out of town, or the purchase of a new appliance."

Lorenzo rubbed at his jaw, his stubble rasping against his skin. "If he did this, he did a damn good job." The healer's difficulty in believing the ugly truth was a good indicator of the probable reaction of the pack should Garnet and Kenji not find any physical evidence. "Doesn't make sense he'd leave behind proof that could undo all his planning."

Kenji's eyes went to the display cabinet and to all those academic accolades so prominently displayed. He felt Garnet's head move in the same direction. Pulling on gloves from the forensic kit, they moved as one to it, began to remove items with care. They'd almost emptied the cabinet when they discovered a photo of Russ and Athena in a simple black frame. It was the only piece that didn't relate to one of Russ's achievements . . . unless he'd seen Athena that way, been proud of having her as his lover.

Beside him, Garnet examined the frame with care. "Russ's scent is strong on this."

"Recent handling," Kenji said, his wolf at rigid attention inside him. "Do it."

FLIPPING the frame to expose the back, Garnet undid the clasps on the sides.

The folded piece of paper that lay between the backing and the photograph made her breath turn jagged inside her lungs.

Touching only the very edges, she unfolded it . . . and all the air whooshed out of her.

"Fuck," Kenji muttered.

Because, while the diagrams were mathematically precise, the plan was clear even to Garnet's untrained eye. "He left proof," she said on a hot wave of anger, "because he couldn't bear to die knowing his brilliant plan would die with him."

Kenji's jaw was an unforgiving line when he spoke. "It didn't matter if it wasn't found for decades. He died knowing it *would* one day be found—but by then, Shane would've been long executed."

"Shit." Lorenzo, having joined them by the cabinet, stared at the diagrams. "If his fingerprints are on that piece of paper . . ."

"His scent's all over it. I'm sure his prints will be, too." Garnet slipped the plan into a transparent evidence bag, passed it over to Lorenzo so he could examine it more closely.

"Russ held his grudges close and he stewed," Kenji said. "He would've spent a lot of time on this piece of paper—in a sense, it's his masterwork."

Garnet sat back on the carpet. "Changelings aren't perfect." Even as she spoke, she made a conscious choice to *not* be like Russ, to not stoke the anger roaring in her gut. "We have our good and our bad. Living in a pack, though, it helps."

"Russ chose to be alone." Kenji's green eyes turned pale amber in front of her. "Pack can't help those who choose to reject everything for which we stand."

Community, Garnet thought, strength in the group, love that encompassed even those who stepped outside the lines and made mistakes. That was the SnowDancer way. Russ had taken another path in his hate and his rage and it had ended in blood. Not, however, in the execution of an innocent man. *That* was what mattered.

TESTING confirmed Russ's and only Russ's fingerprints on the piece of paper on which the plan had been diagrammed and written out. An hour after that, they printed Shane's knife case and discovered Russ's prints on an inside surface as well as on the outside. Put together, the two pieces of evidence erased any and all lingering doubts that Russ had been the mastermind behind his own death.

"Oh, Russ," Athena whispered when told, her eyes bruised and her skin pale. Crying into her hands, she allowed Shane to comfort her, and, in a humbling act of generosity and forgiveness, both attended Russ's memorial service that night. There was no reason to delay it any further—he was a changeling, needed to be with the earth, not stuck in a cold refrigerator.

Wrapping him in a shroud made of natural fibers that would ease his passage to becoming one with the earth, they laid him to rest under the rain, beneath the spreading branches of a tree that Athena told them Russ had liked. "He said it had a mathematical ratio that made him happy," she said before placing a bunch of white roses on Russ's gently wrapped body. "I hope you find perfection in whatever lies on the other side of the veil."

Letting Athena have the last word, since those words had been touched by the echo of a love that had faded while leaving an imprint, Garnet helped lower Russ into the grave she, Kenji, Revel, and two other packmates had dug.

They placed no marker after the burial was complete. Changelings rarely did. Those who'd known Russ and would want to visit would remember the site, and those who didn't know—namely, the pups—would play near it and their laughter and voices would carry on the cycle of life. That was the SnowDancer way, though if a packmate wanted a marker, that marker was placed without question. Everyone grieved differently.

Walking back through the rain after a potent, solemn silence once it was done, Garnet wanted to go straight to her room and have a hot shower, wash away the pain and the anger that had colored each and every one of Russ's actions. What stopped her was her driving need to ensure her packmates were all right, her wolf an inch from her skin.

Sometimes only the most senior person in the den could give needed reassurance. Kenji's presence helped, but in this den, their packmates looked to her first. And today, even the strongest among them was shaken. Many just wanted a hug; some needed to talk through their emotions; others, just to be close to her as she did what she'd been born to do.

Kenji, her semiretired right-hand woman, Sabrina, and Revel stayed with her throughout, as did Lorenzo.

Her hair and clothes were drying by the time she finally returned to her quarters. Kenji came with her.

Chapter 11

ENTERING GARNET'S QUARTERS with her, Kenji watched her kick off her boots and shrug off the jacket that had been no real protection against the rain. He hated seeing her so drawn, sorrow yet heavy on her features for a packmate who had chosen such a bitter end to his life. All he wanted to do was hold her.

But if he did that, he wasn't certain he'd ever let her go. He wasn't that fucking strong. "I'll head to my quarters, get—"

She froze in the act of tugging up her tee. "Don't go."

Kenji cupped her cheek. "I won't take advantage of you when you're emotionally bruised." Yes, she'd messed with him earlier, made it clear she wanted him, but right now, she was hurting.

Rising on her toes to nuzzle his throat, that vulnerable area he never allowed anyone else to touch, she spoke, and her breath, it was hot against his skin. "We're pack, Kenji. I need skin privileges." Her hands on his chest, her voice soft. "But if you don't feel like sharing them with me, that's okay." No judgment in her voice, no demand. "A hug will be enough."

"*Garnet.*" Enclosing her tightly in his arms, this strong woman who carried over a thousand lives, young and old, on her shoulders, he rubbed his jaw against her temple. "I'm sorry for being an ass. Come on, get out of those clothes."

She held on to him for a while longer and he could feel her wolf close to the surface of her skin. His own wolf responded, his hands petting at her as the warmth of her body burned through his damp clothing to brand his skin. When the two of them separated at last, they stripped quickly and walked into the bathroom.

This wasn't about seduction but affection, but when Kenji stepped into the shower behind her and put his hands on her hips, his soul shuddered. Eyes burning, he wrapped his arms around her, burying his face in the curve of her neck.

"Hey." Melting into him, Garnet closed her hands over his. "You're warmer than the water." It sounded as if she was smiling, her voice husky.

He swallowed the lump in his throat with effort, then lifted his head from her neck and tugged her impossibly closer. "And you're still tiny."

A soft laugh that eased him; his tough Garnet was coming out of the grief that had gripped her since the moment they understood what Russ had done. "Why is that a surprise?"

"You're so huge, Garnet." Taking the shampoo, he poured some into his hand, put down the bottle, and worked the fresh-smelling goop into her hair, touching her with the possessive tenderness he'd always felt for her and her alone. "Like this raw wave of strength. I forget you're not that big in actual size."

"Good."

He chuckled at her smugly pleased response, nudging her forward so she could wash off the suds. Obeying, she waited until her hair was clean before picking up the soap to quickly slick it over her upper half. Then she turned to Kenji, doing his chest and shoulders while he washed his hair.

Kenji had always understood that if Garnet didn't cooperate by keeping her distance, there was no way in hell he could fight his response to her—so, for the first time in an eternity, he didn't even try. As he didn't try to keep his eyes from drinking in her petite but perfectly formed body. Water ran down his face as he lowered his gaze to her breasts, sliding up a hand a heartbeat later to cup one taut mound.

"You are so beautiful," he said roughly, running the pad of his thumb over her nipple. "I can't keep this to pack skin privileges." What use was it trying to hide his need when she'd already figured it out? Figured out that he'd do anything for her. "I want to bite and suck and adore. Order me to go."

Goose bumps breaking out over her skin, Garnet rose on tiptoe to nip at his mouth. "I seem to recall asking you to stay." It was a husky reminder, her next nip of his mouth sharp and dangerous. "You going to tell me what's been hurting you for so long?"

His gut grew tight, pleasure crashing under a roaring wave of ice. Unable to look at her as he admitted the brokenness in him, he used the excuse of washing off his face to turn into the spray, then gave her his back. "Soap my back."

She kissed his spine instead, curious fingers tracing the brushstrokes that made up his tattoo. "What does this mean?" Her fingers dancing over the katakana he'd had inked years ago, the characters deliberately stylized to fool the casual eye into not seeing them as characters at all.

Perhaps in some hidden part of himself, he'd wanted a packmate to figure it out, betray his secret so Garnet would know what she was to him. But for the most part, he'd been careful when he shifted around others, made it so no one ever had enough time to truly focus on the design that wasn't a design at all. "I taught you this combination once."

"It's been so long . . ."

He imagined her frowning in concentration behind him as she

mapped the characters with a fingertip. Each brush made his body tighten, his claws pricking against his skin and his wolf's fur so close to the surface that it was almost as if she stroked her fingers through his pelt and not over his human skin.

"They're written oddly," she murmured. "If this was straight, and this wasn't so deep . . . it would be *ga*." Triumph in her tone as she decoded the first syllable. "Hmm, that looks like it makes the *ga* into a long sound. This one . . . hah! Got it. It's the *n* sound—"

Sudden silence.

And he knew she understood, saw that he'd written her name next to the kanji for *ai* . . . for love. He'd been wearing his heart on his skin for the entire world to see, a quiet fuck-you to Fate for stealing her from him. *"Aishiteru."*

"Kenji." Slipping her arms around him on the raw, wet sound of his name, she rose on tiptoe and kissed each one of those characters.

Emotion choking his throat until he could hardly breathe, he braced his palms against the tile of the shower wall . . . then finally told her the secret he'd kept for seven long years. "You know when I was eleven, I went on that trip?"

"Yes, to a whole bunch of tropical islands." Another kiss. "Your grandfather took you."

"It was the most exciting thing I'd ever done." He'd deeply loved his maternal grandfather, a human sailor who'd mated a Snow-Dancer but who had never lost his passion for the sea. "Exciting enough that even my wolf got over its aversion to floating around on water and began to enjoy it." He'd jumped into warm aquamarine seas in wolf form, paddled around like a pup.

"Sofu used to call me *Umiōkami no mago*—the closest translation is 'the Seawolf's grandson.'" So much pride in his grandfather's voice as he said that, such a sense of belonging in Kenji's heart.

"He was the Seawolf?"

Kenji nodded. "My grandmother gave him that nickname when they fell in love." She'd made up the word by putting together the word for "sea," *umi*, and the word for "wolf," *ōkami*. "She said he might be human, but he had the heart of the wolf, and that the sea was his beloved mistress."

"She didn't mind?"

"No. Because the sea might've been his mistress, but Sobo was my grandfather's heart and his soul." Their mating had been a fearless, absolute thing. "He'd look over the side of the boat and chuckle at seeing me swimming, then shuck off his own clothes and dive in to join me. My grandmother joined us a week into it. She preferred to stay on the boat, but she'd laugh and talk with us while we swam."

He'd lost them both too young, his grandmother slipping into a forever sleep a week after burying her mate. It still hurt, knowing they were gone from this world, but they had left him with a treasure trove of memories—and the knowledge that love between a man and a woman could and did last.

"I was so jealous of you." Garnet's smile was in her voice. "Even though I used to get the worst seasickness as a kid!"

He wanted to close one hand over hers, lift it to his mouth for a kiss, but he couldn't make himself move. It felt as if his secret was an anchor holding him in this moment, frozen and rigid. "I learned to eat fish," he told her, sharing the joys first, "to lope on sand, to steer a yacht. I played with human and changeling children who'd grown up in the tropics, never seen a wolf, and I drank coconut water straight out of a coconut that fell to my feet one day while I was running on a beach."

"You came back brown as a walnut," she said. "And you were full of stories . . . until you got sick." Her voice trembled. "You were sick for a long time—I was *so* scared."

His paralysis broke.

Shifting to take her in his arms because he could do nothing else when Garnet sounded that way, Kenji forced himself to continue. "I didn't really understand too much at the time, but later, the healers told me it was a tropical fever. An unusual one that nobody quite understood—every so often things like that apparently pop up out of nowhere. Nature reminding us who's boss."

Garnet pulled back to look at him, her eyes stark. "Are you dying? Kenji—"

He immediately raised his hands to cup her face. "No. Sweetheart, no." Hugging her trembling form, he kissed her temple, her cheek, rocked her against him. "Shit, I never meant to scare you like that."

Her heart continued to pound hard against her skin. "Then what?"

"The healers couldn't make the fever go away," he said, because he couldn't just state his diagnosis. It wounded too much even after all this time. "Eventually, after they'd exhausted their own knowledge, they asked their contacts for help.

"To cut a long story short, someone knew a scientist who was working with experimental drugs, including one that seemed perfect for me. Since I was so close to death, the people in charge cleared the healers to administer it to me, on the understanding that the side effects were unknown."

Leaning back again, Garnet stroked his sides as she watched him with wolf eyes that saw too much. Only then did he realize he was breathing as if he'd run a race, his heart thumping.

"Those side effects aren't unknown anymore, are they, baby? What happened?"

He fought to delay the moment when she understood. "I was the first child given the drug, so I was, still am, anonymous subject number one and have to have a full medical checkup every six months—part of the deal to get me the drug."

He shrugged. "According to the contract, I could've walked away at twenty-one but I figured, what the hell. The scientists don't care about me as an individual, only about the drug's effectiveness, and it saved my life. Having to hang out in the infirmary for half a day a couple of times a year is little enough payment, especially if it might help another child down the road."

Garnet went motionless. "You had a checkup the day of my twenty-first, didn't you?"

"No," he said, his entire chest cavity crushing in on itself. "I had it two weeks earlier. That day, I had a meeting with the healer to go over the results." He tried not to feel the devastating sense of loss that always accompanied his thoughts of that day, that moment. "It was a standard part of the routine, and usually it was all 'no change, blah, blah.'"

Switching off the shower, Garnet petted his back, kissed his chest. "I'm here. Always, Kenji. *Always*."

He staggered inside at her promise, knew he could never hold her to it. Not when she didn't know. Looking into clear blue eyes that saw him as whole and strong, he made himself say it. "I can't father pups, Garnet." Words so rough, they barely sounded human even to him. "The chance is one percent—it would take a miracle. I—"

"I love you." A fury of emotion in Garnet's tone, her eyes stormy blue-gold. "You are *mine* and if you try to argue with me over that, if you even *think* about pulling the same shit you did seven years ago, so help me, God, I will deck you." Claws dug into his chest. "I am pissed as hell with you, Kenji Tanaka."

He stood his ground, his hands white-knuckled fists by his sides. "I couldn't do that to you." Couldn't destroy her dreams as his had been destroyed. "You've wanted pups since you were little. When you played family games, you *always* had to be the mom." So much so that most people had thought she'd turn out to be a maternal dominant.

The only reason she hadn't was that as she'd grown, she'd developed an even more aggressive protective instinct. That didn't mean her maternal streak no longer existed. Kenji had seen enough evidence to know it damn well did.

"You deserve to know what it's like to carry a pup," he said, touching one hand to her flat belly. "You deserve to go through the entire happy journey like your sister. I can't—" He swallowed, forced himself to finish. "I can't give you that."

THIS wonderful, infuriating man, Garnet thought, he was breaking her heart. "You idiot!" She shoved at his chest. "I always made you play the papa, didn't I?" Even as a child, no one but Kenji would do for that role. As she grew and began to view him through new eyes, she'd realized he was the only one she could see in that position in real life as well.

"I only wanted pups if they were yours!" Shaking with anger at him for the choice he'd made, a choice that had separated them for seven years, she nonetheless wanted only to hold him.

The diagnosis must've savaged him, upending his entire world.

He'd been a cocky newly adult wolf settling into his masculinity, confident and wild and driven by a potent cocktail of hormones. This would've shot a bullet right into the heart of his sense of self, bloodying and brutalizing him. He should've come to her, should've trusted her, should've trusted *them*, but she had to remember that he'd been young, too. Young and hurt and trying to love her the best way he could figure out how.

Not only that, she had to remember that if she had a powerful maternal instinct, then Kenji had a paternal one just as wide and deep. He'd always wanted a huge family, been adamant his pup wouldn't be an only child like he'd been, no matter what he had to do to make that happen. Even though she'd had to force him to join in her games, he'd only ever complained when Steele was around. Otherwise, he'd play patiently with her, coming up with all kinds of activities her pretend family could do.

Hurting for the pain he'd suffered in silence, Garnet kissed him again, hard enough to draw blood. "Soon as I was old enough to really start to understand what it meant to have children," she said, wanting him to have zero doubts about this, "I wanted them with you. Why do you think I was so angry when you started dating Balloon-Tits Britney?"

A startled laugh burst out of him, but it faded too soon, his expression solemn. "It's a big decision. It'll change all your plans for the future."

"You were the only constant in my dreams, Kenji." She had to make him understand that, understand who he was to her. How could he *possibly* not know? How could he possibly think she'd rather have pups than live a life with him? He was her other half and she was dead certain the only reason they weren't already mated was because he was blocking the bond with his aggravating, protective, loving need to give her the life he thought she wanted.

"And you know changeling fertility isn't the best," she continued when he stayed stubbornly silent. "Yes, I had hopes of having a ton of pups, but I never counted on being able to fall pregnant."

"Can you give up those hopes?" It was a hard question, but there was something broken in it, in him.

"We don't have to." Withdrawing her claws, she petted his chest, coaxing this wolf who was her own. "And no, I'm not talking about the one percent chance," she added when he stiffened. "I'm talking about Sam and Kieran and Ju and Tanya."

He sucked in a breath as she listed the names of four of their human packmates. All adopted into the pack as children by couples who had love in their hearts and the desire to shower that love on a pup who needed it. "Does their humanity make any difference to you?" she asked Kenji as he unbent enough to lower his head so she could kiss and caress him more easily. "Do you see them as different?"

"Of course not. They're pack." His fingers dug into her skin, his beautiful eyes devoid of defenses and so deeply vulnerable that it hurt. "I just . . . Ruby, the way she is. You wanted that."

Sliding her arms around his neck, she held him to her. "Sure," she said, because she had to accept her dreams so he'd know and accept that some dreams were critical, others flexible. "But loving a child, bringing her or him up? *That* I want more, and that we can do."

There were always children in need of love in the world and, given the pack's established and healthy nature, as well as its track record with adoptions, SnowDancer couples rarely had trouble with the process. No SnowDancer had *ever* returned a child to social services. Once a child was brought into the pack, he or she stayed pack. The end.

Kieran had once joked to Garnet that it was like being in the mafia, but there had been nothing but joy in his expression. A troubled kid of six when he was adopted, his biological mother having died of a drug overdose after his father went the same way two years prior, he'd expected to be dumped as he'd been on three previous occasions. So he hadn't even tried to be good.

"I didn't know then how possessive my new family was," he'd told her. "Or how any stunt I pulled, the maternals had already seen it ten times previously."

Laughter had spilled out of him. "I'd scrawl all over the walls of our family quarters with a permanent marker and my dad would tell me my artistic technique needed work. Even after I threw down the cleaning supplies and kicked holes in the walls, I still got a kiss good night as they tucked me into bed. And the next day, once I was calm, the three of us would fix those walls together. It took a while, but I finally figured out they wanted me even if I wasn't perfect. They loved me."

Garnet knew she and Kenji could love other hurting and lost children just as much. "When we're ready, we'll adopt as many pups as we can handle," she told Kenji. "But, baby, is that something you want?" He was perfect to her, but he'd been unbearably hurt and she'd never do anything to exacerbate the wound.

Kenji wrapped her up in his arms, his voice rough when he spoke. "You're enough. Anything else would be a bonus—but yeah, I still want rug rats. Human or wolf, they'll be ours to love." A shuddering sigh. "It was never about fathering them myself. I just . . . I didn't want to steal your choice."

"You are my choice, Kenji. *You*." Gripping his hair, she made him look into her eyes. "I have missed you for seven goddamn long years." Tears, hot and wet, rolled down her cheeks. "I'll always miss you if you're not with me. So don't you dare walk away again."

"I won't." It was a rasp. "You live in my heart, Garnet. Multiple times a day, I'd see something and want to tell you, only to realize I'd given away that right. Then I'd want to kick my own ass."

She laughed wetly. "That ass is now mine, so I'll be the one doing any ass kicking. Got it?"

"Got it."

She heard the conviction in his tone, saw it in his eyes, in his smile, and it was as if that was all the mating bond had been waiting for. It just . . . opened on his side and was a hurricane slamming through her. Because her own heart had been open to Kenji Tanaka for one hell of a long time.

She clung to him, he held on to her, and when it was over, she laughed in giddy delight.

"Wow," Kenji said, that smile she loved lighting up his whole face. "You pack a punch." A ravenous, possessive kiss that melted her bones, her calves straining as she rose on tiptoe to follow his mouth. "I'm not giving you back."

Breathless, she said, "Ditto." She went down flat on her feet again. "You're far too tall. How are we ever going to make this work?"

She'd been making a silly, happy joke, but his responding look burned.

A heartbeat later, she was hard up against the back wall of the shower and Kenji was pressed up against her stomach, his cock a rigid brand. Forearms braced on either side of her head, he looked down at her with eyes gone wolf. "Garnet." His voice was all growly. "I'm on edge."

Nipples tight and skin hot, she reached down to caress him. "We'll go slow next time."

Shuddering, he dropped his head as he thrust into her hand. It made a moan ripple out of her throat, her body primed and ready for him. But he didn't do what they both wanted and plunge into her. Pulling out of her possessive hold before kissing her with a raw ferocity that had her claws slicing out to scrape his shoulder, he bit at her lower lip, squeezed her breast, sucked on a pouting nipple on his way down her body.

Then he was pulling her leg over his shoulder and oh—

Her blood turned to honey as he used his tongue, his lips, to do delicious, wicked, exquisite things to her. He ate at her as if she was his final meal and he was starving. Clenching one hand in his hair, she came with a scream. He bit her inner thigh on the heels of it; it just made sated pleasure curl hot and warm in her gut.

Sliding his hands up the backs of her thighs as he rose to his feet, he hitched her up with a bunching of his arm muscles that made her feminine core flutter. And then he was pushing the hot steel of his

cock into her. It stretched her almost beyond bearing, but the discomfort was a sweet, welcome one. *There he is,* her body sighed, *there
he is. At last.*

Trusting him to hold her up while her hands roamed his shoulders
and chest and her legs locked around him, she went for his throat.
He growled but didn't stop the intimate caress as he thrust deep into
her body over and over again, his rhythm ragged. Not really thinking
now, Garnet pulled his head down to her own, took his mouth.

Kenji Tanaka was hers, and he was delicious.

That was the last rational thought she remembered having.

Epilogue

LYING IN BED afterward, sated and loose limbed as Kenji spooned her—they fit so well that way—Garnet sighed. "How the mighty have fallen."

Nipping at her shoulder, her mate growled at her. "You don't have to be so smug about it."

She laughed and flipped over onto her back so she could look up at his slightly sulky face. "I was talking about me."

A raised eyebrow.

"Never will I be a notch on Kenji Tanaka's bedpost," she said, paraphrasing the words she'd flung at him the night of Hawke's mating celebration. "Yet here I am, butt naked and with your hand oh-so-close to doing sinfully bad things to me again."

That hand moved in slow circles low on her navel, wolf eyes watching her with unhidden satisfaction—and raw happiness. "So, how do we do this?" A kiss on her dimple.

The caress made her go all mushy inside. Especially when he did it a second time around.

"We can't amalgamate our two dens and Hawke needs us where we are," he added with another mushy-making dimple kiss.

She'd never stop smiling if he kept doing that. "Yes." Snow-Dancer couldn't afford to put the two of them in the same den, not with the widespread nature of their territory. "We can rotate—I spend two days in your den, then we each have three days on our own, after which you come to my den for two days. Our seniors are capable of handling anything for forty-eight hours at a time."

Kenji nodded slowly. "Yes, and that way, we'd each have five-day stretches in our dens."

"Yep." That continuity was important for the health of the pack and for those who looked to them for leadership. "A two-day break won't bother anyone, and we'll be able to spend four days a week together."

It'd be hard, she thought, but doable. Neither one of them would be comfortable away from their dens and responsibilities for long periods, but being separated from her mate for longer than a few days was not happening.

Kenji brushed her hair off her face. "You sure, Garnet?"

She knew he was no longer talking about the mechanics of their relationship. Cupping his gorgeous, beloved face, nuzzling at him, she said, "Yes. I'm sure." Her mind suddenly recalled something she'd learned back during their first go-around. *"Dai suki, Kenji."* In Japanese culture, the words "I love you" were rarely spoken, so the fact that Kenji had said them to her just broke her in two.

This, what she'd said, it was technically far less potent: I *really* like you. But technicalities weren't everything in a language. Her words were as much a declaration of love as his roughly spoken *aishiteru*. It was all in the tone and when Kenji's eyes lit up, she knew she'd got the tone exactly right.

Brain fuzzy from the kiss he laid on her, she didn't understand all of his response, but she didn't need to: the bond was wide open on his end, and she knew his heart, it beat only for her. To her, their bond tasted of the wickedness and wildness and laughter that had always been Kenji and that told her he'd be all right.

He'd been bruised but not damaged on a fundamental level.

"We're going to have an extraordinary life together"—she gripped his hair hard, pulled—"and if you *ever* try to hide anything from me again, I will claw you to shreds."

Kenji's grin held pure delight. "All these years, we had fun, though, right?" Laughter in the wild green. "We managed to grow up together despite my best efforts to keep my distance."

Garnet thought of the countless times she'd called him up for a comm conference when she could've as easily shot him a quick e-mail and realized they'd never been out of contact for much longer than a week. He'd never chided her for those calls, either, had made many a spurious call of his own.

Then there were the postcards he'd sent her each time he had to go to an international destination to deal with a business matter. Taunting and flirtatious and designed to make her see red, those postcards had compelled her to respond. She'd once had a weed bouquet delivered to him. Another time, she'd changed his accommodation reservation so that he ended up having to stay overnight in a nudist colony.

Never had they actually talked about any of those tricks or postcards, the game played under the surface of their ordinary lives.

"Hell of a lot of fun." Smiling on that agreement, she ran her fingers through the heavy dampness of his hair. "Want to know a secret?"

"Always."

"I like the things you do to your hair. I only acted like I didn't to mess with you."

His cheeks creased as he used a thumb to caress her hip bone. "Want to know one of my secrets?"

"Always."

Kissing her dimple, melting her bones, he said, "You have no idea how many times I had to, um, take care of business after flirting with you."

"LET'S just say a certain battery-operated boyfriend did a lot of heavy lifting thanks to you." Throwing her leg over his with that sinful confession, Garnet ran her nails down his chest. "I know it must still hurt you—don't hide that from me, either."

Kenji hadn't talked to anyone about his diagnosis, not after he'd completed the mandatory counseling sessions. Even then, he hadn't really opened up, had done just enough to get his medical clearance. But this was Garnet, the woman who lived in his heart. "Yeah," he said, and then, for the first time, he spoke without shields about what the news had done to the twenty-three-year-old man he'd been.

Garnet listened, she never broke skin contact, and she loved him, the pulse of it a ferocious wildfire inside him, a wildfire that tasted of steel and Garnet. "I'm going to buy you a violin."

Yes, this woman understood the beat of his heart. "I still have mine," he admitted. "Couldn't bear to get rid of it."

Smile deep, she pushed playfully at his chest. "When do I get a recital?"

"I'm going to be rusty as hell," he warned.

"I'll rate you on a scale going from 'my ears are bleeding' to 'the angels weep.'"

A kiss from his mate, the sensual slide of skin on skin. The sound of his brain cells popping in delirious pleasure.

"I bought you a ring before your twenty-first," he said a long time later, watched her eyes widen. "I wasn't going to give it to you then, but it was like my talisman for what I hoped we'd become."

Poking at his abdomen with a censorious finger, she said, "You'd better still have it." It was a growl.

He grinned, because damn, that was Garnet. Demanding and strong and his. "I keep it in that little wooden box you gave me for my eighteenth birthday."

Her smile was luminous. "I made that box in woodworking class!" She kissed him. "It's awful. I was terrible at woodwork!"

"I know. The lid doesn't close properly and it's lopsided." He laughed along with her. "But you gave it to me."

"Stop it," she muttered, lower lip quivering. "You can't make me cry. I'm a hard-ass lieutenant."

He kissed the tip of her nose. "You can cry with me."

Tucking up her arms between them, she made a face at him. "I threw all the stuff you ever gave me down a big crevasse," she told him. "I did it the night after my twenty-first." Narrowed eyes. "I'm still not sorry."

His shoulders began to shake. "Good thing I never gave you that ring. It cost me three-quarters of all the cents I had at the time."

"Three-quarters? What happened to the last quarter?"

"I spent that on your twenty-first present. A bracelet from that designer you used to like—with the cut stones." Bright and sparkly but not large. Delicate. To suit her bones.

"Is it in the box?"

"No." The memory of the stones cutting into his palm as he stood numb and angry in the corridor outside the infirmary, it was as vivid now as the day it had happened. "I broke it I was holding it so hard . . . and it just seemed like a sign."

She petted the side of his face. "I'll forgive you that one." A nuzzling kiss. "Especially since I took a baseball bat to the snow globe you got me for my sixteenth."

He burst out laughing. "Remind me to never make you angry," he said when he could speak again. "I fucking *love* you."

Growling playfully, Garnet tumbled him over onto his back. "I love you, too, but I'm still mad at you for forcing us to wait this long. Make it up to me."

He ran his hand all the way down her back, stroked up again. "Come here."

A luscious kiss, then more, and more. Things were getting hot and sweaty and interesting when Garnet's phone went off and kept going off.

"Grr." Grabbing it, she stared at the screen. "It's Tex." She answered the call, started scrambling out of bed in the next heartbeat.

Wolf lunging to the surface of his skin as his brain clicked, Kenji got out and hauled on his own clothing.

RUBY'S pup might have been laggard to this point, but he was now in a tearing hurry. Garnet and Kenji made it to the infirmary with only two minutes to spare before a thin, angry cry hit the air. Lorenzo exited not long afterward, joy pulsing from him. "Strong little guy. Good lungs on him."

Tumbling into the room after a delighted-sounding Tex invited them in once Ruby was ready, Garnet and Kenji took in the wrinkled and furious little peanut on Ruby's chest and grinned.

"Did Steele call already?" Garnet asked.

Tex was the one who replied, his tone holding a deep vein of affection. "Yeah. About a minute after the birth—said he'd restrained himself for sixty seconds, but that was his limit. He's already booking a flight across."

Garnet's grin morphed into soft laughter. "I think this den is going to see an influx of Sheridans over the next week." Tiptoeing closer, she kissed the top of her sister's head before gently touching the baby's back. "Good job, sis."

Ruby's tired face beamed. "You, too, baby sister." A thrilled glance that flicked from Garnet to Kenji.

Garnet's phone beeped right then; she'd had it in hand, having expected the call. Touching the screen, she turned it toward Ruby and Tex so the couple could see the face of the man on the other end. She and Kenji leaned in to be able to see the screen at the same time.

"Congratulations, Ruby, Tex," their alpha said, his presence a punch of raw power no matter that he wasn't physically present. "I see my newest packmate isn't happy with his current environment."

The baby stopped making grumpy noises at the sound of his alpha's voice, going very still on Ruby's skin, as if listening intently.

"Hello, pup. Welcome." Hawke made a rumbling sound in his chest that had the baby's tiny body going soft and easy again, zero tension in him now that his primal core knew he was in no danger from the apex predator in the region.

"How do you *always* know about a birth?" Ruby asked with a mystified smile. "Wait a minute. Did Lorenzo call you?"

"Nope." Hawke winked, the thick fan of his silver-gold lashes coming down over an eye of a blue so pale, it was immediately clear that Hawke was changeling, was wolf. "It's an alpha thing." His gaze encompassed both Ruby and Tex. "I'll be there to welcome him in person within the week."

That was why Hawke was such a damn good alpha. He made it clear that every SnowDancer life mattered. Dominant or submissive. Old or young. Weak or strong. All were pack. All were his.

"Garnet."

Turning the screen in her direction, Garnet raised an eyebrow. "Yes?" She had a good idea of what was coming.

Wolf-blue eyes gleamed. "Where's your mate?"

Kenji shifted so he could scowl at Hawke. "Now you're just show-ing off."

An unrepentant grin. Their alpha's white shirt pulled across the breadth of his shoulders as he folded his arms, his exposed forearms muscled and golden. "You lovebirds want a honeymoon? I'll second two of the others to cover your dens while you canoodle."

"We'll get back to you on that." Kenji nuzzled at her, his hand possessive on her hip even though Hawke was no threat to his claim.

He was the one showing off now, Garnet realized. Showing off his mate to a wolf he respected. Maybe she should've been annoyed by that, but what the hell. It felt good to have his skin rubbing against hers when he nuzzled her again, all warm and a little rough with stubble, while his hair was cool, damp silk in contrast. She was proud of him, too, would show him off to all her friends. Gor-geous, sexy, wickedly smart Kenji Tanaka was now all hers.

The mating bond pulsed on both sides, fire and steel and *them*. Garnet and Kenji. Mated pair.

That sounded so good. Sounded *right*.

"We also have ideas on how we can balance our lives and dens," she added as Kenji went behind her. Wrapping his arms around her waist, he held her firm against the length of his body.

She ran her hand over his forearm, her body aching for his again and her wolf wanting to simply lie side by side with his wolf. Feel-ing his heartbeat, maybe nipping at him now and then to remind him she remained annoyed. But mostly, just being with him.

"Let's talk when you're ready." Hawke's grin deepened. "In the meantime, get a room."

Garnet and Kenji both growled at him before Garnet turned the screen back toward Ruby and Tex and the pup so Hawke could say good-bye. Sliding away the phone afterward, Garnet said, "What do you need?" to her sister.

"For you two to go back to having fun while we three snuggle." A dreamy, besotted expression on her face as she looked from her baby to her mate. "Come back with a burger and onion rings in three hours."

"On it." Kenji, who'd released Garnet to gently pet the baby's fist with one finger, saluted.

"With fries," Garnet promised, dropping another kiss on Ruby's head.

Tex was too smitten with his pup and his mate to notice when they left.

"A death and a birth," Garnet mused as they walked through the corridor. "The birth makes things feel normal, natural again."

Twining his fingers through hers, Kenji said, "A death, a birth"— lifting up her hand, he kissed her knuckles—"and a mating."

Mush, she was all mush again, emotion a knot in her throat. "Shift with me?"

No hesitation, light shattering the air as the agony and ecstasy of the shift reshaped their cells. It was an exquisite, beautiful pain. When it was over, her wolf stood face-to-face with a proud timber wolf with eyes of husky amber.

Her mate.

He bumped muzzles with her.

She bumped back.

And then they were racing through the den as their laughing packmates jumped out of the way and their hearts beat in tune. As they'd do until time ended.

ACKNOWLEDGMENTS

Thank you to Mamta Swaroop, MD, FACS, for her invaluable and patient help in explaining the consequences of knife wounds to the thoracic aorta.

Arigatou gozaimasu to my friend Akbar Rahman, for checking my rusty Japanese and helping me make up the word *umiōkami*.

I would've never predicted I would one day be discussing stab wounds and blades with a trauma surgeon, or how to invent words in the Japanese language; I love the research journeys on which writing takes me—and the people I get to meet as a result. Mamta and Akbar are both awesome. Any mistakes are mine (and I freely admit I did take artistic license here and there).